FLING

FLING

JOSEPH MURRAY

MACMILLAN

First published 2023 by Macmillan
an imprint of Pan Macmillan
The Smithson, 6 Briset Street, London EC1M 5NR
EU representative: Macmillan Publishers Ireland Ltd, 1st Floor,
The Liffey Trust Centre, 117–126 Sheriff Street Upper,
Dublin 1, D01 YC43
Associated companies throughout the world
www.panmacmillan.com

ISBN 978-1-5290-9866-2

1 3 5 7 9 8 6 4 2

A CIP catalogue record for this book is available from the British Library.

Typeset in Sabon by Jouve (UK), Milton Keynes
Printed and bound by CPI Group (UK) Ltd, Croydon, CR0 4YY

Visit **www.panmacmillan.com** to read more about all our books
and to buy them. You will also find features, author interviews and
news of any author events, and you can sign up for e-newsletters
so that you're always first to hear about our new releases.

For my wonderful parents Kathleen and Finian,
who taught me everything happens for a reason.

Synchronicity

(noun)

1. the experience of two or more events that are apparently causally unrelated or unlikely to occur together by chance, yet are experienced as occurring together in a meaningful manner.

   (*Carl Jung*)

2. an inexplicable and profoundly meaningful coincidence that stirs the soul and offers a glimpse of one's destiny.

   (*Phil Cousineau*)

Chapter 1

'Let's go home,' said Tara, feeling as if her life had just ended.

To her right, her husband Colin sat rigidly, trying to process the devastating news. Behind his desk, Dr White was explaining that the embryo transfer had been unsuccessful and that their third attempt at IVF had failed.

Time seemed to stand still for Tara in that moment. All she could hear was a strange ringing in her ears, as if a bomb had just been detonated. She couldn't take in what Dr White was saying, just the piercing hum of defeat.

But Tara didn't need to listen to know what was being said. She knew the spiel off by heart at this stage. She had known as soon as she saw the same tired, apologetic expression on Dr White's face that her dream of motherhood would remain just that.

A dream.

'Go home?' Colin said, turning to her. 'We literally just got here.'

'I know you must be disappointed, Tara, but rest assured, there is still hope,' Dr White said unconvincingly, as if reading from a teleprompter.

'I'm sorry, doctor, but I can't do this any more,' Tara said, picking up her handbag. 'I don't mean to be rude but I just really want to go home.'

'Tara, we need to know what our options are,' Colin said, visibly frustrated by Tara's eagerness to leave.

'Colin, we know how this goes. This is the part where we start everything again from scratch. Back to square one.'

'Well, many couples don't have a successful IVF treatment until their fourth or sometimes fifth try. In fact, we had one couple who weren't successful until their eighth round,' Dr White explained.

Tara winced at the thought. She couldn't bear the idea of going through the entire ordeal once more, let alone multiple times. She had retained a glimmer of hope after their first and second attempts failed but there was only so much disappointment she could take. Colin had kept telling her that the third time would be the charm. He had almost convinced her of it. Yet here she was, reliving the worst experience of her life for the third time in a row.

'Doctor, I think it's time we accepted that I'm not meant to be a mother,' Tara said with a heavy heart.

'Tara, stop that kind of talk,' Colin said.

'Oh come on, Colin, I'm almost thirty-seven. My eggs are basically tumbleweeds at this point.'

Dr White almost laughed, but Colin shot him a look of disapproval.

'Tara, it's only our third attempt. Come on, the fourth time's the charm!'

'You say that about every attempt, Colin. In a few years, you'll be saying the fifteenth time lucky. We've spent thirty grand on this already. We need to stop throwing good money after bad,' Tara said, still eyeing the door to leave. She felt smothered.

'Well, maybe they have a loyalty card programme or something,' Colin said, giving Dr White a hopeful glance.

'Oh yeah, Colin, we'll just get a stamp on our way out and

our next one will be free. We're talking about my eggs, not a cup of coffee,' Tara said, rolling her eyes. 'They don't care about our loyalty anyway. They sold us all of those stupid add-ons that made absolutely no difference.'

'Well, you did opt for the Premium Package,' Dr White explained.

'Yeah, and what do we have to show for it? I mean, for ten grand a pop, you could have thrown in a feckin' tote bag. Or a top that says "I tried IVF and all I got was this lousy T-shirt",' Tara said, frustrated.

'Tara, this is serious,' Colin said, mortified.

Tara knew she was being ridiculous. But she also knew if she didn't laugh, she would cry. And Tara was done crying. She had been through this rigmarole enough times to see how farcical it all was. She had every right to make jokes because that's exactly what the whole ordeal felt like.

One big joke.

'I completely understand your frustration, Tara,' Dr White said. 'But you can't make an omelette without breaking a few eggs.'

'Well, I'm sorry, doctor, but I ordered my eggs fertilized, not scrambled,' Tara said, standing up. 'Now, I'm sorry but I really just want to go home.' Tara turned and walked out of the room, her mind fully made up. Colin sighed and sluggishly got up off his chair.

'I'm sure she'll come around eventually,' Dr White said to Colin.

'You clearly don't know my wife,' Colin said, as he followed Tara to the car.

On the drive back, Tara was trying to process the news in silence. She didn't want to talk about it, she just wanted to go home. As she leaned against the window, twirling her ash-blonde hair, she noticed the sky was endlessly blue, teeming with pastel perfection. It annoyed her. Of course the sky would be clear on the one day she wanted rain. She wanted the sky to weep because she had no tears left. At least if there was a cloud, she could tell herself something about silver linings.

After the first IVF treatment didn't take, Tara was an emotional wreck. Even though she had never actually got pregnant, Tara mourned the many million possibilities that would never come to be. The second failed attempt was similar, but those tears were from anger, not despair. This time felt different, however. She didn't feel sad or angry. In fact, she didn't feel anything. It was like there was a void in her chest, an overwhelming emptiness. She suddenly found herself questioning her entire belief system. Tara's world view was complex at times, but if there was one belief that anchored her entire philosophy, it was her belief in destiny.

Tara truly believed there was a path for everyone and that one's life was predetermined by fate. She refused to accept the scientific theory that life was just random chaos. In her opinion, such a world view made life completely meaningless. After all, the universe had begun with chaos yet somehow formed spontaneous order. That was all the proof she needed that there was some force out there greater than her. Her father Paddy Fitzsimons had been a devout Catholic up until he passed away, and her mother Shannon was a renowned psychic healer by trade. Tara was therefore an unusual mix of religious and spiritual. She believed in a higher power but she saw it more as energy flowing rather than a bearded man in the sky. She knew she didn't have all the answers but she believed in belief. Whether one chose to call it fate, God's plan, kismet, predestination or destiny, it all came back to what her mother always told her.

Everything happens for a reason.

But what was the reason for this? Why was the universe preventing her dream from coming true? There was only one reason Tara could think of. The universe was quite clearly telling her that being a mother was not her destiny and she had no choice but to listen. It was a difficult pill to swallow but Tara knew denying it wouldn't get her anywhere. Trying IVF a fourth time would only be swimming against the currents of fate. She couldn't put herself through the ordeal again. But even though she had told Colin from day one that she would only try three times, she knew he wouldn't accept her decision.

Her mind began to reach backwards, to the night she first met Colin. She was a student at Trinity College Dublin at the time, but she always returned home to Galway to work weekends at O'Malley's pub. One fateful November night, a young man walked into O'Malley's while she was working and ordered a pint of Guinness. She expected to see a much older man, but when she turned around, there he was.

The man of her dreams.

Stupidly handsome, short brown hair, and ocean eyes deep enough to drown in.

That was the first time Tara experienced what she considered to be synchronicity, a strange gut feeling, like a mix of déjà vu and women's intuition. She had butterflies in her stomach, goosebumps along her arms and a tingle on the back of her neck. She felt like she had tuned into the universe's hidden frequency and was suddenly connected to the deeper vibrations of life. It was her spiritual compass that let her know she was on destiny's right path. Like she was with the right person in the right place at the right time.

She fell for Colin there and then. By the time his Guinness had settled, she was already his. 'Of all the pubs in all the towns in all of Ireland, you had to walk into mine,' she had told him. Against all rationality, she had thrown caution to the wind and got on the back of his motorcycle to Nimmo's Pier. When he kissed her in the shimmering moonlight, she began to melt in his arms and lost herself in sweet consensual surrender. She had snuck him into her bedroom later that night. Even though they had just met, she was ready to give herself to him completely, the way she would for the rest of her life. Her feelings weren't logical at the time, but when Tara got her gut feeling, she knew it was fate whispering that she was on the right track.

But Tara had never once got her gut feeling during the entire IVF process. She knew in her soul it wasn't meant to be. And even though Tara's dream of being a mother was over, she knew she would pick herself back up and find a new dream. The entire experience of constant failure had sucked the life out of her. She needed a dream that brought her endless joy, not endless disappointment. It was time to turn the page on failure and begin a new chapter of infinite possibility.

❦

Colin turned on the radio, uncomfortable with the silence in the car. He tuned straight to Radio Nova, a vintage station that he listened to religiously. As if the radio was mocking him, Depeche Mode's 'Enjoy the Silence' began to come through the speaker.

'At least lighten the mood with some ABBA,' Tara said.

'Tara, can we please just discuss our options?' Colin asked, turning the radio back off.

'Here we go,' Tara sighed as she straightened up in her seat.

'It's only our third try. Success is built on failure. We just have to fail better each time!'

'Colin, I'm really not interested in sound bites from a self-help book.'

'Well, that's how things are achieved, Tara. Nobody ever got what they wanted by just giving up.'

'I know your heart's in the right place, Colin, but there's a limit to how much failure a person can take. If you failed an exam once, sure, you would study and retake it. But don't you think that failing it three times might be a sign from the universe that you weren't supposed to study that particular subject?' Tara said, trying to make him see her point of view.

'Oh please don't start with your signs from the universe mumbo jumbo, Tara.'

'It's not mumbo jumbo, Colin. If you have to struggle and suffer for something, it's obviously not meant to be. If something is for you, it won't pass you. Things are supposed to just fall into place.'

'No, Tara, life is about fighting for what you want,' Colin said, trying to inspire her. 'It's worth giving it one last shot.'

'But it's not one more shot, Colin. It's dozens of shots, needles, hormone injections. The only shot I need is a shot of tequila.'

'All that stuff will be worth it once it works.'

'But then there's the fertility pills that turn me into a madwoman. And swallowing twenty different vitamins every morning. It's easy for you to say let's try again when all you do is fill up a cup.'

'Wow, so that's my only contribution?' Colin asked, offended. 'Who's the one who gives you the injections? Who has to deal with your mood swings when you're on the hormones?'

'Choose your next words very wisely . . .' she said, giving him a chance to retreat.

'I'm just saying that we are in this together. I've been with you every step of the way,' he said, diffusing the situation.

'Colin, I know that. But it's different. It's my body. I just can't go through it all again. We've been slowly drifting apart ever since we started this journey. I want our life back. I want to go back to being *Us*,' Tara explained.

'Why can't you see that it'll all be worth it in the end? There's still a fifteen per cent chance of success.'

'Yeah, which is a seventy-five per cent chance of failure, Colin,' Tara sighed.

Maths was never Tara's strong suit but Colin knew correcting her would only strengthen the point she was trying to make against him. 'Whatever the odds are, I know we can beat them,' he said.

'My uterus isn't a slot machine, Colin. Every time we gamble ten grand on this pipe dream, we always lose and the house always wins,' Tara said, putting her foot down.

'There are still so many options of improving our chances. Like if you were open to finding an egg donor—' Colin said.

'I told you from day one that I wanted to be the biological mother of my child,' Tara interrupted.

'You'd be giving birth to the baby. That basically makes it yours. Who cares if it's not your egg?'

'Well, for the record, your swimmers aren't exactly winning any Olympic medals either. I'll agree to an egg donor if you agree to a sperm donor,' Tara said, knowing full well Colin would rule out the idea.

'You must be joking. Then I wouldn't be the father!' Colin snapped.

'OK then, we'll mix your sperm with two other donors. Then twenty years later, we'll invite the three of you to the child's wedding in Greece and figure out who the father is,' Tara explained.

'I'm not stupid, Tara. I know that's basically the plot of *Mamma Mia!* You've made me watch it enough feckin' times,' Colin said, annoyed. 'I don't know how you can talk about this in such a joking tone.'

'Because all my tears have been used up, Colin. I want to laugh again. I'm done with failure. We can't keep doing the same thing over and over expecting a different result. That's the literal definition of insanity. I'm almost thirty-seven for God's sake,' she sighed.

'Oh, don't give me that excuse. Your mother had you at thirty-eight.'

'That's because it was her destiny. But it's clearly not mine. The universe obviously has other plans for me. Maybe I'm supposed to get my master's degree or start my own business or travel the world or—'

'You're supposed to be a mother,' Colin said, interrupting her.

Tara saw red. It wasn't so much what he said, but rather the way he said it. She was trying to reassure herself that she had a million different options for what to do with her life and now Colin was implying that she had some kind of womanly duty to give him a child. Whenever Colin made a comment like that, even by mistake, a switch flipped within her.

'Oh, because that's all women are supposed to do, is it? My only possible destiny is to bear my husband a child, is it?' she said, with fury in her eyes.

'I didn't mean it like that. Jesus, there you go again, turning into a completely different person.'

11

'I'm a Gemini, Colin. You knew you were getting a two-for-one deal when you married me,' Tara said.

'You can't keep using star signs to justify everything, Tara,' Colin sighed.

'That's such a Taurus thing to say,' she said, rolling her eyes.

'Why can't we just discuss other—'

'Colin, I know you want to keep talking about this,' Tara interrupted. 'But I've made my decision and I won't be discussing it again,' Tara said without emotion.

It was in that precise moment that Tara felt an invisible rift opened up between herself and Colin. They had been slowly growing apart for a long time, but now, without the shared goal of starting a family, she feared something had changed within the deeper workings of their marriage.

Silence returned to the car.

ॐ

As Colin drove home, he found himself deeply troubled by Tara's point of view. He couldn't understand why she had decided so quickly on both their behalf to stop trying for a child. He felt as if his right to have an opinion on the matter had been stripped from him, and yet her decision affected the rest of his life. Most of his savings had gone into IVF, and if they gave up now, it would all have been a complete waste. But as expensive as it was, it was a small price to pay for their dream. He couldn't just stand idly by and let her give up on their shared goal based on some excuse about destiny.

Colin didn't share Tara's mysticism. He often joked that he was a 'born-again atheist', and that humans were just tiny specs of dust living on a rock floating through space. Many found his perspective quite cynical, but Colin actually found it quite inspiring. If life was meaningless, he figured the meaning of life was to give your life meaning. If there was any law that the universe followed, it was Murphy's Law. Anything that can go wrong, will go wrong. There would always be obstacles to overcome, but that made winning all the more rewarding. Achieving your dreams meant nothing without some adversity.

That was what life was all about.

But starting a family was a team effort and his teammate had seemingly walked off the pitch just because they missed three shots. Life wasn't about the goals you missed, it was about the ones you scored. And there was still plenty of time left in the match. Where was Tara's fighting spirit, the one that he had fallen in love with?

Colin and Tara had always fought like cat and dog, that was nothing new. In fact, the running joke in their marriage was that Tara believed in love at first sight but Colin believed in love at first fight. After she had poured him that Guinness in O'Malley's eighteen years ago, he immediately began arguing that the Guinness was much better in Dublin than it was in Galway. As she went on a long-winded rant about how much of a chancer he was, he was becoming enchanted by the fiery, emerald-eyed redhead. It was the first in a long history of fights over the stupidest things. But they were always tongue-in-cheek, always playful. For years, arguing was practically part of their foreplay. Colin sometimes found himself initiating a lovers' quarrel over something silly just for the mind-blowing sex to which it would eventually lead.

But that sense of playfulness had slowly evaporated over the years. Sex had become a chore, a purely functional means to an end. It lacked any kind of emotion or spontaneity. Tara had her ovulation dates marked in her calendar and it made lovemaking so mechanical. The entire sexual experience had somehow become desexualized. It felt more like two mammals mating than two people making love. It was like they forgot to have sex during sex.

But now that Tara was talking about giving up on starting a family, he knew sex wouldn't even serve a purpose any more. Her rash decision meant the light at the end of Colin's tunnel had suddenly vanished. He knew the birth of their child would usher in a rebirth of their love. But if Tara gave up, how would they ever reignite that illusive spark?

He wondered what the rest of his life would look like without his ambition of becoming a dad ever coming to fruition. It was inconceivable to him. The life he had mapped out with Tara, gone in an instant. She wanted to let fate take the wheel, but he feared they were heading towards a cliff. Colin felt a chill in the car as he thought about the life he had built and the uncertainty of its future.

When they arrived home, the day had already begun to fade. Tara sat back up straight as Colin pulled onto Hillcrest Grove, the picturesque cul-de-sac on Dublin's well-to-do Southside where they lived. Hillcrest was the perfect neighbourhood. Too perfect. The lawns were always freshly cut, the Range Rovers were recently washed and the teeth were brightly bleached. Having been raised in the Galway countryside, Tara always felt like an outsider in Hillcrest. She found it so strange that the idea of 'suburbia' had crept into everyday Irish life. It all felt like an empty reference, a copy of something that never even existed in the first place. She was used to stone walls, not white picket fences. It was an uncanny veneer of perfection, a hyperreal curtain behind which lay nothing. But nonetheless, the show had to go on.

As they approached their driveway, Tara could see their neighbour Celine Loftus out on her front lawn, taking a selfie while gardening. Celine had ten thousand followers on social media and therefore considered herself to be an 'influencer'. Tara knew a narcissist when she saw one and Celine was more full of herself than a Russian doll. She looked down on anyone who wasn't a pure-bred Southsider and Tara had privately christened her the Wicked Witch of the South as a result of her snobbery.

Unfortunately, Celine did not have the appearance of a witch. On the contrary, she was sickeningly perfect. Bouncy blonde hair, high cheekbones and a pair of double D breasts that practically deserved their own Eircode. The women of Hillcrest worshipped the ground Celine walked on due to her number of followers, and they all worked as brand ambassadors for her vitamin company called Yummy Mummy. Although Tara couldn't prove it, her gut told her that Celine's business strategy was simply a pyramid scheme in disguise. Sadly, the Yummy Mummies were in far too deep to question their charismatic cult leader and so the pyramid continued to grow. Celine had tried to recruit Tara years ago but she had seen right through her cult-like tactics. As a result, Celine and Tara became instant frenemies, killing each other with kindness whenever they crossed paths.

Celine spotted Tara and Colin driving past her house and began waving them down frantically as if she had urgent news.

'Oh God,' Tara said to Colin. 'Celine is calling us. I still can't believe you told her we were doing IVF. She loves having that over me.' Tara rolled down her window and put on a fake smile.

'Well hello, you two, I was just out sowing some seeds.

Tara, you look terrible, is everything OK?' Celine said, leaning in to examine her face.

'Oh yeah, I'm fine. We were just out shopping and I didn't bother putting any make-up on,' Tara lied. She didn't want Celine gossiping yet again.

'Well, good for you not caring what people think. I've always admired your confidence,' Celine said.

The only thing worse than Celine's insults were her compliments. Whenever she would say something flattering, it always had a malicious undertone. Her backhanded compliments were like a warm hug followed by a cold knife in the back.

'Can we help you with something, Celine?' Tara asked, cutting to the chase.

Celine leaned in closer to the car. 'I just wanted to let you know before I announce it on social media tonight . . . I'M PREGNANT!'

Tara felt a sharp pain in her heart. Destiny was just rubbing salt in the wound at this stage.

'Congrats, Celine,' Colin said, leaning over.

'Thank you both so much. Four months already if you can believe it! I really wanted to have a third child before I turned thirty-five. I could just hear my biological clock going tick-tock, tick-tock, every single night,' she laughed.

Tara knew that this was a dig at her. Celine's tactlessness was always intentional. She also knew exactly what the next question would be.

'What about the two of you? A little bird told me you haven't been having much luck with IVF,' Celine said, feigning concern. 'You know, the top fertility specialist in the country is a dear follower of mine.'

'I think the phrase is "dear friend",' Tara muttered.

'Well, he would do anything for me. He has a ninety per

cent IVF success rate. Say the word and I'll get you on his client list.'

Tara could see this coming a mile away. Like all cult leaders, Celine employed the rule of reciprocity. If she did something for you, she would one day come to collect. With Celine, there was always a price, and Tara wasn't interested in making a deal with the devil, no matter how angelic she appeared.

'That would be amazing, Celine,' Colin butted in. Tara gave him a discreet elbow in the side.

'No thank you, Celine,' Tara said. 'We'll be fine.'

'Of course, Tara. But please let me know if you change your mind. There's nothing I wouldn't do for a fellow Girl Boss. And don't listen to what people say. You are not past your prime,' Celine said, with bright teeth and a dark smile.

Tara put up her window, relieved the conversation was over.

'That IVF friend of hers sounds promising. She might be able to help us, Tara,' Colin said, pulling into their driveway.

'She doesn't want to help us. She wants to own us. It's all just a ploy to turn me into another Yummy Mummy, trapped in her pyramid scheme so she can feel like Cleopatra. Trust me, if you ask Celine for help, you'll end up regretting it.'

'She was trying to be nice, Tara,' he sighed.

It never ceased to amaze her how little men knew about women. Then again, Celine had everyone fooled. Only Tara knew she was too sweet to be wholesome.

When she got out of the car, Tara looked up at 3 Hillcrest Grove. The setting sun was casting warm shades of blood orange onto the front of their house, like something out of an impressionist painting. It reminded Tara of when she first saw the home. Just like the moment she first saw Colin, Tara had experienced a synchronicity and she intuitively knew the house would one day be her own.

The stone-clad exterior walls looked like jagged little puzzle pieces that amounted to the home of Tara's dreams. The farmhouse chic interior made it feel like the cottage she grew up in, albeit a lot bigger. It was a behemoth to behold but she knew she would fill it with life, laughter and love, although Colin had forbidden any décor that read 'Live, Laugh, Love'. He did allow her, however, to get a plaque for above the front door with the Irish proverb '*Is glas iad na cnoic i bhfad uainn*', which meant 'Faraway hills are always greener'. It was supposed to remind her to appreciate what she had.

But now, as she opened the front door, the warm shades that lit up the front of the house were replaced by an icy chill of stark, blue reality. The size of the house meant that it was always cold, as if no amount of heat could feed the insatiable beast. She always thought the warmth of children would one day defrost its frozen hearth.

It seemed she had been wrong.

When she got into bed that night, Tara felt an overwhelming emptiness in her chest. At thirty-six years of age, with her dreams of motherhood shattered, she felt as if somewhere along the line, she had made some mistake, some kind of wrong turn that brought her away from her destiny.

Meeting Colin, finding her dream home, all of these things had just happened effortlessly. It was almost as if the more she wanted a child, the more unlikely it became. She felt like she was at a crossroads with no signposts to tell her which road led where and no spiritual compass to help her chose the path intuitively.

She had always believed that manifesting her future would lead her along her path to the life of her dreams. She still believed in destiny but she no longer felt it was on her side. She always felt as if the universe was rooting for her. Now, it felt like destiny had deserted her. Perhaps her fate wasn't something she would relish but rather something she would simply have to accept. Eventually, she came to a stark realization.

Tara had lost faith in fate.

Fate, however, had not lost faith in Tara.

Chapter 2

SIX MONTHS LATER

On a mid-September morning, Tara awoke to a feeling of emptiness that had become all too familiar. She looked over at Colin who was still fast asleep and snoring with the subtlety of a chainsaw. Her 7 a.m. alarm was ringing in her ear and she considered hitting snooze. There were times recently where she considered jeopardizing her entire career for a few extra minutes in bed.

'Turn off the alarm,' Colin groaned, waking up.

Colin didn't start work until 9.30 a.m., which gave him a thirty-minute lie-in every morning. She would have killed for that. But there was no use in complaining. The day had begun whether she wanted it to or not. She got out of bed and headed for a quick piping-hot shower. She knew her hair was due a wash but she couldn't bear the thought of blow-drying it, so she opted for a spray of her trusty dry shampoo instead. Although she found herself using more and more of it each time she put off washing her hair. After that, Tara brushed her teeth, applied an invisible amount of make-up and got dressed into a white blouse and a grey pantsuit.

When she walked into the kitchen, she went to make herself a coffee but found there were no cups in the cupboard.

There were never any cups in the cupboard any more.

Tara had the household chore of loading the dirty dishes into the dishwasher every night while Colin had the role of emptying the clean dishes out every morning. The problem was that Colin hadn't emptied it for three mornings in a row now. And when the dishwasher was full, she couldn't load it up, resulting in an overflow of dirty dishes in the sink. She knew she could empty the dishwasher herself but she refused to do it on principle. This was her life now.

She sighed and took a clean cup out of the machine to brew herself a pick-me-up. Lord knew she needed one.

The previous six months had been draining. By now, she had made peace with the idea of not becoming a mother but Colin refused to let it go. He had tried to bring it up on several occasions but Tara knew there was nothing to discuss. She had made up her mind and she desperately needed him to accept that fact so they could go back to the way things used to be. She wanted the life she had before the IVF failed, striking the heart of her marriage and leaving an agonizing wound. Their relationship needed to heal but Colin kept trying to pick at the scab.

As the days faded into weeks and the weeks into months, the rift between them had become greater and greater until eventually an ocean divided them in bed each night. She understood his pain but she also resented the way he tried to make her feel guilty for something out of her control. It broke Tara's heart that she couldn't have a child – but what good was it to continue failing? She wanted to focus on all the things she could do, not the one thing she couldn't. But Colin saw this decision as selfish. Heaven forbid a woman have a destiny other than bearing a child.

Colin came down the stairs in his morning robe, an item of clothing she had slowly grown to loathe. Without saying anything to her, he began to root around the freezer for something.

'What are you looking for?' she asked.

'I think we have two rib-eye steaks in here somewhere,' he replied. 'I'm going to defrost them for dinner.'

'On the top right shelf.'

'Ah,' Colin said, grabbing the steaks and putting them down on the counter. 'We've been eating too many microwave dinners recently. Be nice to have a proper meal.'

Tara knew this was a dig at her. It was true, she had become rather reliant on microwaveable meals but when Colin refused to lift a finger, why should she go above and beyond?

'Are you going to unload the dishwasher today?' Tara asked.

'Sure, I'll unload it when you go to work,' Colin said.

'You can't just unload it now? It's been full since Friday.'

'Do you need a cup?'

'No, I got one myself.'

'Oh perfect. I'll unload it before I go to work then.'

Tara winced. Because she knew he wouldn't. But she didn't want to fight. She didn't have the energy.

'Grand,' Tara said, picking up her handbag to leave. 'See you this evening then.'

'See you then.'

❧

Tara sat in the usual bumper-to-bumper traffic on her drive to work. It had been a cruel summer filled with inaccurate forecasts of sunshine followed by downpours of rain. But September was unusually warm this year, she noticed. As if summer's heat had been delayed.

It was during her morning commute that Tara performed the daily ritual of thinking about her future. She had always been a daydreamer, and even though she hated her snail-paced drive to work in her blue Nissan Micra, she had mastered the art of forgetting her surroundings and getting lost in a daze of her own thoughts.

Her birthday had passed in June and she was officially thirty-seven years old, although she didn't do anything to mark the occasion. As the big 4-0 got closer and closer, she felt as if birthdays were something to hide, not celebrate. But despite the fact that the IVF failing felt like a tragic ending to her lifelong ambition, Tara was determined to prove her life was just beginning.

The problem was, she still had no idea what she was meant to do with the rest of it. So many different roads stretched before her, yet here she was, trapped in the inertia of rush hour. If only she knew which lane would fast track her towards her fate. She had spent so many years waiting for another synchronicity, a sign from the universe that she was on the right path.

But no such sign came.

What she would have given to go back in time, to before her marriage began to tear at the seams. Tara didn't mind that Colin hadn't highlighted her thirty-seventh birthday. But it killed her that he seemed indifferent to their seventh wedding anniversary. Every year, he would get her a card, a bottle of wine, chocolates and a bouquet of flowers. This year, however, he had only produced a card. And not even a thoughtful, poignant card. A last-minute petrol station anniversary card with a short vacant message. It told her all she needed to know.

He just didn't seem to care.

Tara's mother had always told her that every relationship

has a flower and a gardener. Colin had always tended to her, nourishing her needs without her even having to ask, but since her decision to give up IVF, the dynamics within their marriage had changed. Colin used to be sunshine in human form and she had always been drawn to his light. Now, it seemed as if life had dimmed his spark. She found herself wilting in the shadow of his love rather than basking in its glory. What should have been the summer of her life became a harsh winter of indifference. As he slowly accepted the reality that his flower would bear him no fruit, she felt his desire to garden fade over time.

Maybe she was unable to bear his fruit, but didn't she still deserve to bloom?

As much as Tara hated to admit it, she did need a man to complete her. She wasn't a desert wildflower that could survive in solitude. She was a delicate orchid that needed nourishment. She missed her husband, or at least the man he used to be. At times she wished he hated her. It was the indifference she couldn't bear. Their old fiery repartee had been replaced with cold passive-aggression. Colin now just let her win every argument. 'Fine, you're right, I'm wrong,' he would say submissively. But Tara didn't want to be right, she didn't want to win. She wanted him to grab her in his arms and shut her up with a kiss. She wanted him to take her like the wind, the way he had done that night on Nimmo's Pier.

God, she missed that.

They had always been opposites – that was what once attracted them to one another. Now it seemed like some force had inverted the magnetism that once drew them close. They began pushing each other apart more and more, to the point where they forgot what it was that made them the perfect couple in the first place. It hadn't happened over night of course, but in a way, that made it worse. It was like she was witnessing her marriage fall apart in slow motion. She feared what another six months would do to them.

Maybe Colin simply wasn't attracted to her any more. She didn't exactly exude sex appeal, that much she knew. She felt like her libido's battery had been on 1 per cent for years but Colin seemed to have zero interest in recharging it. He never went to any effort to make her feel desired and so her desire for him began to fade.

Her sexual drought wasn't just metaphorical either, it was quite physical as well. At times, she felt dryer than the Sahara down there. Nobody had even told her that could happen. She had searched her symptoms on WebMD and convinced herself she had some kind of terminal illness. Tara had always been a hypochondriac and could turn a headache into a haemorrhage in just a few clicks. Her doctor reassured her, however, that what she was experiencing was a natural part of aging, especially for women who are no longer sexually active. But Tara wanted to be sexually active. She was only thirty-seven, for God's sake. She didn't ask for this dry spell. Her clouds were heavy.

She still desired desire.

She longed to be swept off her feet. Sure, she mused, most women like the idea of monogamy, but no woman likes the idea of monotony. Variety was the spice of life. Nothing would turn Tara on more than Colin taking some initiative. He used to be so hungry for new experiences. Like when he surprised her with Interrail passes in college and they had travelled around Europe, making love in a different city every night. Or when he would hear good things about a new restaurant and book them a table without her even needing to ask.

But now, if Tara wanted to do something, she would have to drip the idea into his mind over several weeks. Where had his spontaneity gone? She wasn't a high-maintenance woman.

Even a short road trip would be enough to get her blood pumping. Sitting in the passenger seat, listening to ABBA as Colin had one hand on the wheel and the other gently resting on her inner thigh.

ABBA had always been her favourite band, although most of their music was technically before her time. She'd always had vintage taste. The past just seemed simpler. She didn't care much for the grunge of the 90s when she was growing up. The rhythm of the 70s spoke to her soul.

But her current life wasn't worthy of an *ABBA Gold* score. Her inner soundtrack was a sad cacophony of melancholic minor notes. She wanted music in her life again. The void in her chest was growing, a black hole developing its own gravitational pull. She needed an antidote for the death she was living.

She needed to feel alive.

Tara heard a loud BEEP from the car behind her that jolted her out of her daydream musings and back into reality. The light in front of her was green and she accelerated towards the next section of bumper-to-bumper traffic.

She realized she was running late and momentarily considered driving in the bus lane and zipping past the traffic. But she knew she wouldn't. Tara often flirted with the idea of doing something bad but she lacked the follow-through. At the end of the day, she always stayed in her lane. She relaxed and reminded herself that she was late every morning, so in a way, she was still on schedule.

With another forty minutes left on her journey, Tara leaned over and turned on the radio to prevent her mind from wandering again. She flicked through the stations until she heard a distraught woman on *The Line*, a morning chat show where people phoned in to discuss topical issues. The woman was mid-sentence when Tara began listening.

'. . . I'm honestly sick to my stomach, Joe,' she whined.

Tara was intrigued. Whatever had happened to this woman, it must have been bad.

'That's awful, Mary,' Joe, the radio show's host said. 'And for anyone just joining us on their commute, we're discussing the new cheating app called Fling, where married people can find discreet, anonymous affairs online.'

Tara's curiosity was piqued and she turned up the volume, eager to hear the full story.

'Joe, the fact that this app even exists is an absolute disgrace to the country. When I first heard about it, I nearly fell off my chair and broke my neck. I practically had whiplash from pure shock, Joe. And then to discover that my husband Jim was on it behind my back?' Mary ranted.

Tara couldn't help but laugh at Mary's tone. She wasn't trying to be funny but she was so distraught that it became unintentionally hilarious.

'Mary, I'm reading here that thousands of people have downloaded Fling since it was launched last Friday. Why do you think there is such a demand for an app like this?' Joe said.

'Well, Joe, that just shows that Ireland has gone to the dogs. In my day, we had a little thing called shame, but it seems people today are completely and utterly shameless! I may get down on my knees and do a nine-day novena for the soul of this country. To think my Jim would make a fool of me after forty years of marriage,' Mary continued, barely breathing between sentences.

'We have another caller on the phone who is eager to share his side of the story,' Joe interrupted. 'Jim, you're now on *The Line*.'

Tara turned up the radio even further, eager to hear the situation explode. She could even make out the show echoing

27

in adjacent cars stuck in traffic. It was clear that she wasn't the only person dying to hear what happened next.

'Mary Muldoon, this is your husband, Jim, hang up this phone right now!' Jim demanded.

'JIM!' Mary screamed, recognizing her husband's voice. 'You should be the one to hang up. Haven't you embarrassed me enough?'

'You're the one making a show of us by airing our dirty laundry on *The Line*! Half the country listens to this show!' Jim snapped.

Tara was in shock at what she was hearing. She always enjoyed the show, but this was spectacular entertainment.

'You should have thought of that *before* you downloaded Fling!' Mary screeched.

'Well, you never told me our wedding vows were also a vow of celibacy! I might as well be a priest! Maybe if we actually had sex, I wouldn't have wanted to download Fling!' Jim yelled back.

'I'd sooner take my grave than touch a snake like you ever again Jim Muldoon! Well, you reap what you sow because I'm going to *fling* you out of the house right this second!' Mary exclaimed, hanging up the phone.

On Jim's line, Tara could hear a yelp of pain followed by a door slamming. It seemed Jim had been kicked out of the house just before his line went dead.

'Mary? Jim? We seem to have lost Mary and Jim Muldoon there. Whose side are you on? Is cheating ever justified? Are people driven to cheat? Public opinion is very divided on this Fling app, so we now have the entrepreneur who created it on the line. Richard Mulligan, you're very welcome to the show,' Joe said.

'Thank you for having me, Joe,' Richard said. His voice

was strikingly deep and Tara wondered what he looked like in real life.

'So, Richard, everyone is talking about your app Fling, and I believe you've had a very successful launch, is that right?'

'You're very right, Joe. We actually just hit a quarter million downloads,' Richard said confidently.

'Two hundred and fifty thousand people? That is a remarkable chunk of married people in this country. But I'm sure you're well aware that public opinion is quite divided on the matter,' Joe said, playing devil's advocate.

'Yes, I heard Mary and Jim on before me. I know many will side with Mary and many will side with Jim, but when two people are unhappy, infidelity is inevitable,' he said, sounding sure of himself.

'But what would you say to people who claim that you're destroying the sanctity of marriage by enabling cheating and perhaps even profiting from ending relationships?' Joe asked.

'Well, Joe, we did an anonymous survey last year and asked married people if they had the means to have an affair without the risk of getting caught. Ninety-two per cent of people said they fantasized about having an affair and eighty-six per cent said they would have one if they knew they could get away with it. It all goes back to supply and demand, Joe. And with a quarter million downloads, the demand is certainly there,' Richard said, his voice portraying a calm, masculine certainty.

Tara was shocked by how high the percentages were, but she herself had occasionally wondered what it would be like to sleep with someone other than Colin. The statistic made her feel a little less guilty. Like she was normal.

'When people have needs and desires that aren't being met, you can't blame them for wanting something more,' Richard continued. 'So many people feel trapped in their own lives and want to escape, even just for a little while. Within every human being there is an impulse to do something bad. Just to see if we can get away with it. And those who don't bend . . . break.'

Richard certainly had Tara's attention. That was exactly how she felt. It was as if he was speaking to her directly.

'Fling has been described by some as Tinder for married people. Do you think that's a fair comparison?' Joe asked.

'Not necessarily, because the user experience is very different. Fling is completely anonymous so it's totally discreet. No face pictures, no real names, no personal emails, nothing that can be traced back to you. Our algorithm finds you suitable matches not based on looks but rather on what you're looking for,' Richard explained.

'But how safe is it to meet someone online when you don't know who they really are?' Joe said, concerned.

'A valid question, Joe. One of Fling's rules is to never meet in a private place for the first time. If things move from the app to in-person, meeting in a public place like a restaurant is essential.'

'And you set up two perfect strangers for the perfect affair?'

'Exactly.'

'So you're like an evil Cupid, in a way,' Joe said, joking.

'That's one way of putting it. But evil spelled backwards is live. Most people these days are content with just surviving. Fling is for the people who want to feel alive.'

Tara felt her heart rate start to increase. Richard Mulligan certainly knew how to strike a chord.

'I'm just going to read out some of the texts we're getting in here, Richard. Paul from Donegal says, "I'm #TeamJim. If someone is unhappy, they will cheat, don't blame the app" . Maureen from Meath says, "The government should take action and ban this app, it makes cheating too easy!

#TeamMary". And Cathy from Cork says, "Someone needs to give that Richard Mulligan fella the punch in the face he deserves". Any response, Richard?'

'I can see why people would want to blame me for their unhappy marriages. But blaming the app for an affair is a bit like blaming a balaclava for a bank robbery,' Richard said smugly.

'And are you worried at all about the backlash over the app?' Joe asked.

'Absolutely not. All publicity is good publicity. I haven't even spent a cent on marketing yet. But I guarantee the people condemning this app are the ones who are using it the most. Hypocrisy is the backbone of society,' Richard said.

'And Richard, would you feel any guilt at all if your app led to a rise in divorces?' Joe asked.

'There's only one single cause of divorce, Joe.'

'And that is?'

'Marriage.'

'Richard, thank you so much for your time,' Joe said politely.

'My pleasure,' Richard said before hanging up.

'So what do you, our listeners, think about this Fling app? Would you have a discreet, anonymous affair if you could get away with it? Is it wrong or is monogamy a thing of the past? Let us know your opinion by using either #TeamMary or #TeamJim on social media,' Joe said, wrapping up.

Tara was intrigued by what she had just heard. Poor Mary had certainly been made a fool of, but she did sound like an awful old prude. She felt bad for Jim being publicly humiliated on the radio, but he did try and cheat. Then again, Richard Mulligan had said a lot of things about marriage that really resonated with her. And with a quarter of a million downloads, he had obviously tapped into something deep within people. Not necessarily the desire to do the wrong thing, but rather the desire to get away with breaking the rules.

Tara poked her head out her window to see miles of backed-up traffic still ahead of her. In that moment, something came over Tara, or rather, she overcame something. She looked in her left wing-mirror to see that no buses were coming. She indicated and edged into the bus lane. She put her foot down on the accelerator and headed towards the city centre.

Chapter 3

Tara arrived to work on time for the first time in years.

Her palms were sweating, her heart was racing and, when she finally parked her car in the building's underground car park, she felt an overwhelming rush. She had got away with it. She locked her car and stepped into the lift with a cheeky smile, ready for the week ahead.

She worked as a senior marketing consultant at a firm called Insight on Dublin's Grand Canal Dock. It was one of those ultra-modern marketing agencies that were obsessed with phrases like 'disruption' and 'growth-hacking' and had job titles such as 'data ninja' and 'brand rock star'. Tara found the jargon silly at times but the firm did have a good reputation for being innovative and creating campaigns that tended to go viral.

For all its innovation, however, Tara still found Insight to be a boys' club. She had fought hard for her seat at the table and although her male colleagues never overtly disrespected her, she knew she wasn't truly one of them, no matter how hard she tried. There was a subtle, trickle-down sexism that stemmed from the all-male board of directors. The kind of sexism that was invisible to the naked eye, hidden in plain sight.

Tara only ever got to work with clients looking to market female products. If the product was in any way feminine, it was considered 'Tara's territory'. It all came down to the same silly old adage. Blue is for boys and pink is for girls. She wished she could market more masculine products, just to prove she could. She made the same base salary as her male colleagues but they always snagged the big sports and alcohol accounts where the biggest commissions were.

She had made a conscious effort to defeminize herself in the office to overcome this hurdle. The dresses, pencil skirts and blouses she used to love wearing were gradually replaced with trousers and blazers. Even now, the grey pantsuit she was wearing made her look frumpy. It did absolutely nothing for her, but she hoped appearing androgynous would mean she wouldn't be assigned clients and products solely based on her gender. But thus far, her strategy hadn't been very effective.

She had been something of a rising star at the firm after her work for True U Cosmetics went viral. The campaign for their new make-up pallet centred around the idea of enhancing your natural beauty rather than changing how you looked. The creative featured women of all shapes and skin tones trying the pallet for the first time and capturing their genuine first impressions on camera. This led to a user-generated viral campaign with regular women sharing their initial impressions on social media. She had neatly tied the whole campaign together with a simple yet effective slogan and hashtag: #BecomeYourself.

Although the campaign was widely praised for being an intersectional feminist achievement, it made Tara feel like a fraud. She had championed the idea of female expression while suppressing her own. She had quite literally helped thousands of women become themselves but she lacked the confidence to practice what she preached. She was so jealous of the women that she herself had helped empower. She told herself it was a man's world and she was merely playing the game to win. But after all these years, why did it feel like she was constantly losing?

Tara got out of the lift and strolled through the hustle and bustle of Monday morning at Insight. Admittedly, the office space was rather nicely decorated, but Tara never really bought into the whole quirky idea of having bean bags, video games and ping pong tables in the workplace. She was the oldest of the senior marketing consultants. Marketing was a young person's game and staying alive at Insight meant having your finger on the pulse of the zeitgeist at all times. Although she was only thirty-seven, Tara often felt much older. On paper, she was a Millennial, but she was embarrassingly behind the times when it came to technology and pop culture. She had developed terrible imposter syndrome as a result, terrified someone was going to call her out for being a dinosaur.

She didn't have a 'boss' in the traditional sense of the word, but when she reported to the board every quarter, they made it abundantly clear that she was long overdue to reel in another big fish. She was itching for an opportunity to prove she hadn't lost her edge.

When she arrived at her office, Tara noticed her intern Emily had yet to arrive. Because Tara was always late, this was the first time Emily wasn't there to greet her with her second morning coffee. Tara sat down at her desk and started up her computer. Her office was ultra-modern, perhaps theatrically so. She could never understand how it was somehow minimalist and flamboyant at the same time. It was like the glass and chrome design was screaming 'LOOK HOW UNDERSTATED I AM!', a bizarre oxymoron.

Still, she loved the office's stunning view of where the River Liffey met the sea. She envied the river. It never stopped to question where or why it was flowing. It relied purely on natural instinct, its path fixed from beginning to end. Tara used to feel her life obeyed the same laws of nature. Now, her life felt like an ocean. She could swim in any direction but she didn't know which way would lead to shore.

At exactly 9.05 a.m., Emily arrived with Tara's coffee.

'You're early,' Emily said, surprised to see her.

'And you're late,' Tara said, only half-joking.

'It's pronounced latte,' Emily said, handing her the coffee. 'How was I supposed to know you'd be on time for once?'

'Touché,' Tara laughed, taking the cup.

Emily was twenty-three years old and had recently graduated with a BA in Psychology from Trinity College. She had a black bob haircut, a stud nose piercing and she dressed exclusively in vintage clothing from alternative thrift shops. The outfits she wore each day were rather provocative for an office setting, but Tara didn't dare infringe on her right to self-expression.

As a Trinity graduate herself, Tara liked the idea of taking Emily under her wing. Although truth be told, Tara wanted to be a mentor more than Emily wanted to be mentored. Sure, she couldn't be a mother, but she could still leave a legacy. She could still inspire women, uplift women, champion women. Even something as simple as a young girl seeing her thrive and saying, 'I want to be her when I grow up'. That would be enough. Enough to know that she, as a woman, had made a difference and left her mark.

She had learned rather quickly that Emily had nothing but apathy for the world of work and was merely hopscotching through internships in an effort to bulk out her CV. But Emily's star sign was Libra, the most compatible sign with Gemini, and Tara therefore excused her complete indifference to her role and let her get away with murder.

As an only child, Tara always longed for a sense of sisterhood in her life. She had female friends, of course, but they were all mothers now, and whenever she would call to catch up with them, they always seemed to have their hands full. She often felt like she had no one to talk to, no one to confide in. In many ways, Emily felt like the little sister she never had. And Tara admired how engaged she was with issues that affected her generation, specifically feminism, a field Tara was always trying to improve in.

Although she had studied business at Trinity College, Tara had taken a women's studies elective as part of a broad curriculum initiative. The module had changed her life. The patriarchy was suddenly everywhere. Her rose-tinted glasses of childhood had been replaced with bleak blue bifocals. There was no going back. She was ready to join the cause and become a trailblazing feminist icon, smashing the glass ceiling and dismantling the patriarchy. She had spent weeks writing a paper titled 'Girls Just Wanna Have Fundamental Rights: A New Theory of Synth-Wave Feminism'. But then, to Tara's horror, she only received third-class honours, or 49 per cent, to be specific. She was so devastated that ever since that grade, she found herself overcompensating in an attempt to prove that she was, in fact, a good feminist. How on earth had an elective on female empowerment given her an inferiority complex?

Tara took the first glorious sip of her triple-shot vanilla latte. Bliss.

'Don't tell anyone this, Emily, but the reason I'm early today is because I drove in the bus lane,' Tara said, still riding the high of her rebellious act.

'I know, it was on the news,' Emily said without expression.

'What?' Tara panicked. 'Did someone record me? Oh Jesus, did someone file a complaint?'

'Yeah, the guards asked me to wear a wire and record your

confession. They have the building surrounded,' Emily said sarcastically.

Tara felt a wave of relief. She should have known Emily was just winding her up, especially considering she did so every day. It was just so hard to read Emily's resting bitch face, an expression she had spent years perfecting in response to men telling her to smile more.

'OK, you got me,' Tara admitted. She couldn't help but notice Emily seemed taller than normal. She looked down to see a pair of knee-high patent leather boots.

'Emily, are those stripper boots?' Tara asked, raising an eyebrow.

'Well, you always say to dress for the job you want, not the job you have,' Emily said, showing them off.

'That's not exactly what I had in mind,' Tara said, bewildered. 'Anyway, how did your date go with that guy?'

Every Monday morning, Emily would debrief her on her latest hook-up stories and Tara was eager for the juicy details. With her own sex life dead as a dodo, she sometimes found herself living vicariously through Emily's youthful promiscuity, even if she secretly sometimes found the stories shocking.

'Ugh, he was so nice. It was awful. Why can't I just find a guy who'll ruin my life?' Emily said.

'Oh come on, nice guys don't always finish last,' Tara said.

'At least he got to finish. I swear, whenever a guy calls himself a cunning linguist, he always turns out to be icliterate,' Emily complained.

Tara nearly spat out her coffee at Emily's turn of phrase. She had a rather creative way of describing things. 'You young Millennials never cease to amaze me,' Tara laughed.

'Ew, I'm not a Millennial. I'm Gen Z.'

'Sorry, I always get those two mixed up.'

'Millennials are the ones who can't afford a mortgage

because they spend all their money on avocado toast. Gen Z are the ones who want to save the planet and have constant anxiety about failure,' Emily explained.

'Oh,' Tara said awkwardly.

'I'm actually thinking about quitting this job to pursue failure full-time.'

'Emily, it's only Monday morning and you've already mentioned quitting. Don't you like the experience? Don't you have a dream job you're working towards?' Tara asked, slightly concerned.

'Why would I dream of labour? Everyone in my generation just wants to be a viral internet star. Speaking of which, did you hear that crazy Mary woman on the radio? She's blowing up online,' Emily said, looking down at her phone.

'Oh my God, yes, it was hilarious!'

'Kinda makes me wish I was married just so I could cheat.'

'Emily! Don't say things like that,' Tara said, shocked.

'God, you are such a Mary,' Emily laughed as she rolled her eyes.

Tara was completely taken aback. In fact, she was downright offended! Tara wasn't one of those repressed prudes who calls *The Line* to complain about how Ireland is becoming too modern!

'EMILY!' Tara exclaimed, truly rattled by the comparison. 'I am not a Mary. I am shocked you would think that, let alone say it!'

'You have to admit there are some similarities.'

'Give me an example.'

'I don't know how to explain it. You're just so innocent . . . but also riddled with guilt. I think it's a Catholic thing. I feel like you're always about to bless yourself whenever I talk about sex. And I'm convinced you say the rosary in your head every time you see my outfits,' Emily laughed, signalling to her stripper boots.

Tara hated that Emily saw her that way. Her biggest fear had come to life. People at work really did see her as a dinosaur. 'Emily, you have me all wrong! I am a very fun, open-minded person,' Tara insisted.

'When's the last time you had sex?' Emily asked, never one for office decorum.

'EMILY!' Tara said, going puce.

'Wow . . . that long, huh?'

'You can't just ask someone that kind of thing!'

'Look at you, mortified by the mere mention of sex. That's big Mary energy right there,' Emily laughed.

'OK, maybe I've lost touch with my sexual side. But the past few months have been so draining. My husband and I are miles apart in bed every night,' Tara sighed.

'And what's been driving you two apart?'

'Well . . . I've never told you this but . . . I can't bear children.'

'Ugh, me neither. Like, all they do is cry. What's that about?'

'No, I mean, I can't physically bear children,' Tara explained.

'Oh,' Emily said awkwardly. 'Wait, that should mean you have more sex, not less.'

'Well, believe me, trying for a baby will drain your sex drive's battery. I feel like I need a jump start,' Tara sighed as she slouched into her chair.

'So the passion is just . . . gone? How long have you been together?'

'Together for eighteen years in total and married for seven of them.'

'Wow, that's a long time,' Emily said. 'That's almost as long as I've been alive.'

'Well now I really feel old,' Tara sighed. 'I don't know, maybe losing our passion was bound to happen eventually. Maybe it's just the seven-year itch.'

'Herpes?'

'No, Emily, it's a thing where couples lose their romantic spark after seven years of marriage. It's when most affairs happen, apparently.'

'You should join Fling then,' Emily suggested.

'Oh sweet Jesus. Me? Have an affair? You must be joking,' Tara said, going from puce to scarlet.

'Oh come on. Men are like shoes. You look silly with just one,' Emily said, trying to egg her on.

'That's all well and good, Emily, but what exactly would I do if my husband found out?'

'It's all anonymous so nobody would know. You can be a saint in the streets and a sinner in the sheets.'

'Absolutely not, I'd be found stone dead of shame,' Tara said, putting her foot down.

'OK, Mary,' Emily laughed as she left the room.

'I'M NOT A MARY!' Tara shouted after her.

Chapter 4

Colin arrived to work at 9.27 a.m., just as he did every day. His workday began at 9.30 and he had a knack for navigating the side streets of Dublin perfectly so that he was always on time. Like Tara, Colin spent his commute thinking about the world and his role within it. Now, at thirty-eight years old, he found himself trying to rediscover a sense of meaning within the meaningless chaos of existence.

There was no doubt about it.

Colin was having a mid-life crisis.

The past six months had felt like a perpetual purgatory. His marriage was falling apart and Tara didn't seem to have much interest in saving it. She seemed so apathetic, so numb to it all. They weren't in a fight but they also weren't not in a fight. He was tired of living his life in limbo. Colin would have preferred if they just addressed the elephant in the room that seemed to be getting bigger and bigger each day. He used to love their fights, the lovers' quarrels that always led to the best sex. But this insidious animosity was torture. It was death by a thousand cuts. At least a fight would clear the air. But Tara refused to have the very important conversation that loomed over their marriage.

She had given up on the idea of starting a family, and whenever he tried to have a reasonable discussion about it, she'd either change the subject, leave the room or stonewall him with a lecture about how it was her body, not his. She was searching for a new dream, she would say. But what Colin loved about his dream of having children was that it was an adventure to share with Tara. It was their next chapter. The way she talked about her destiny, it seemed as if he wasn't a part of it. Why was she so against the idea of asking Celine to call her fertility specialist friend? It could only help.

All he wanted was to be a dad. Not just a father but a proper loving, nurturing, compassionate, cringey, embarrassing dad. He wanted to wear socks and sandals. He wanted to say no to getting a dog but then eventually become the dog's best friend. He wanted to drag his family to the airport hours before the flight was even due to board. He even had a stockpile of dad jokes ready for the role he was destined to play. Most of all, he wanted to give a child the feeling of belonging that he never felt within his own family.

Colin had a father growing up, but he never had a dad. William O'Hara was a wealthy but withholding man who believed tough love built character. His mother Patricia, though slightly more affectionate, shared this belief. They were the type of stiff-upper-lip parents who said things like, 'When I was your age I had to walk ten miles to school barefoot in the lashing rain every morning.' Somehow, Colin always had difficulty believing such stories. It was as if they always wanted to see him struggle. He had vowed from a very early age that he would one day make a family of his own. He would raise his kids the very opposite to the way he had been raised. He had spent so many years saving money so that his children would want for nothing. Amazing Christmas presents, trips to Disneyland and, of course, the unconditional love he'd never experienced. He was willing to do anything for his dream of fatherhood to come true.

When he tried to explain this to Tara, however, she

completely blanked him. It was like his feelings didn't appear to have any bearing on their marriage any more. He felt constantly unheard. It was hard enough as a man to speak about his emotions, but when he finally found the courage to speak up, he was immediately shot down. She had even made some remark about his dream of fatherhood being an 'old-fashioned conservative ideal'. Old-fashioned? Was it really so terrible for him to dream of starting the family he'd always longed for as a child? And conservative? At heart, Colin was an anarchist. He used to be a rebel, raised on punk rock. He used to be a rolling stone that gathered no moss. He used to be a lone wolf howling at the moon. He even rode a Triumph Bonneville motorcycle back in the day as a youthful act of defiance against his parents.

On the night he first met Tara, he had waited for her on that very bike, smoking a cigarette outside O'Malley's. She said there was no way in hell she was getting on the back. But she had. She couldn't resist a walk on the wild side. Yet on the day they got married, the motorcycle had to go into the shed. 'I refuse to become a widow,' she had said. The same went for him smoking even an occasional cigarette. 'I won't let you pay a tobacco company to kill you,' she had said. So the lone wolf was tamed, the rebel was repressed and the rolling stone had become overgrown with moss.

Somewhere along the line he had adopted the mantra, you can be right or you can be happy. There were a million little things that he disagreed with Tara on, but he knew trying to prove her wrong was hopeless. And even if he ever did win an argument, victory was always only temporary. She would say 'That's fine,' and then revive the fight later with her favourite line 'I just think it's funny how . . .' So Colin had learned to bite his tongue, and for the sake of being happy he would let her be right. He convinced himself that the best way to win an argument was to choose not to have it in the first place.

But now, that mantra had failed him. Allowing Tara to be right in this instance made it impossible for him to be happy. After years of biting his tongue, he was at his wits' end. And yet, he couldn't blame Tara entirely. He had allowed himself to become too malleable, able to be hammered into any shape at the price of his own identity. He let Tara round off the very edges that made him a man. Now, he was an agreeable people-pleaser, putting the happiness of others before his own.

He had set himself on fire to keep others warm.

It would have been bearable if Tara showed some affection once in a while. Colin was a good-looking man and he saw the way other women looked at him. People often complimented his deep blue eyes and cheeky smile. He somehow still had zero grey hairs and, thanks to genetics from his maternal grandfather, his hairline wasn't going to recede anytime soon. He wasn't the most well-endowed man in the world but he was packing a full inch more than the global average, a fact he was secretly very proud of. Plenty of girls in UCD had made it abundantly clear they wanted to sleep with him back in the day. But he was always devoted to Tara. It was easy at the time because Tara was devoted to him too. They were unable to keep their hands off each other.

But how could he be expected to stay committed to one person sexually for the rest of his life if that person no longer had any interest in sex? For years, their lovemaking was reduced to its reproductive function, but since Tara's decision, their sex life had become extinct, preserved only in the amber of memory. Was that just the natural course of every marriage? To go from passionate lovers to sexually sedated companions? He found it ironic that less than a century ago, people got married so they could start having sex but now

45

they got married so they could stop. Colin didn't want a companion.

He wanted his wife back.

Colin couldn't cook so Tara was always the one who prepared the food when he did the weekly grocery shopping. But since their rift, those home-cooked dinners had become lukewarm microwavable meals. He had taken out a pair of steaks that morning as a way of breaking the cycle that had become all too symbolic of their marriage. He would open a bottle of wine, set the table and maybe, just maybe, they could re-connect. Still, he wasn't holding his breath. After all, Tara expressed no interest in reigniting their spark that had once burned so bright.

She had become some version of herself that Colin barely recognized. She was always dyeing her hair blonde and hiding the natural red he fell in love with. It was like she was constantly trying to hide the things he found beautiful about her. Even her gorgeous green eyes had gradually lost their seductive sparkle. The doppelganger that lay beside him in bed each night was not his wife.

She was a stranger.

He married a woman who was passionate, adventurous, optimistic and beaming with confidence. Where had these magnetic qualities disappeared to? Where was the joie de vivre that used to light up any room she was in? He missed the fiery redhead he had fallen in love with. He missed the Tara who had got on the back of his motorcycle. He missed the Tara who used to melt in his arms.

He wondered if he would ever find her again.

Colin checked his watched as he rode the lift to the second floor.

9.30 a.m. Like clockwork.

He worked as an actuary at McKenna & Co. Chartered

Accountants, helping other companies assess risk and calculate potential reward. The work wasn't gruelling but it didn't exactly invigorate him every morning either. He sometimes felt like a cardboard cut-out of a man, a middle-class stereotype of a middle-aged accountant. Even the office building was depressingly nondescript. It looked like a stock photo search result for 'dull, uninspiring office'. His twenty-year-old self would be ashamed if he could see him now. He had become the very antithesis of punk. Every day he woke up and did the same thing, a perpetual groundhog day, robbed of any excitement. He had once hoped to live for one hundred years. Now it seemed as if he was destined to live one year one hundred times. Like a hamster on a wheel, he had to just keep on keeping on.

Still, there were some perks that made his life easier. His childhood friend Rory McKenna was his boss and he had a laissez-faire approach to management, to say the least. When Colin opened the door to his office, he immediately saw Rory lying on his couch, wearing a pair of oversized sunglasses. It was clear from the mere sight of him that he was horrifically hungover.

'Colin, I'm dying,' Rory moaned, as if he was on his deathbed.

'Wow, hungover on a Monday morning again are we?' Colin laughed.

'You know I have a reputation to live down to.' Rory smirked.

Rory was eight years younger than Colin but held a superior position due to the fact that his father Michael McKenna owned the company. He was given the title of 'executive accountant', which didn't have a clear job description but technically meant he was Colin's boss, at least on paper.

The two had been neighbours growing up and always remained close despite their age difference. Rory was devilishly

47

handsome and oozed a nefarious kind of charm. He had neatly styled jet-black hair, sun-kissed skin and bulging muscles that made his shirts look like they were spray-painted on. He was a provocateur with no filter whatsoever, a true relic of a bygone era. But that was exactly why Colin liked him.

To the untrained eye, Rory appeared to be a narcissistic, entitled menace to modernity, but Colin knew it was all an act. Rory was always playing up his character for his own entertainment. He was a parody of himself, the real-life equivalent of an internet troll. He didn't believe half of what he said, he just loved winding people up and watching them go off. He considered life to be one big joke and he was more than happy to perform the part of the jester. It takes a very clever man to play the fool.

'And why are you recovering in my office, exactly?' Colin jeered, sitting down at his desk.

'I don't want Karen from HR to see me like this. She'll make me sit through another one of her "Office Etiquette" presentations. I'll have to avoid her all day,' Rory said, sitting up and taking off his sunglasses. 'Colin, man, you should have been there. I met these crazy girls from Amsterdam last night in town. Two gymnasts. You wouldn't believe how flexible these girls were. I took them home and showed them my black belt in Kama Sutra.'

Colin smiled. He knew to take Rory's wild stories with a grain, if not a barrel, of salt.

'Wish you were there, man, I would have given one of them to you,' Rory said. 'Lord knows you're not getting any at home.'

'You can say that again,' Colin said, his tone changing immediately, as if a cartoon rain cloud had just come over him.

'That bad, huh? How long has it been since you two even had sex?'

'Two hundred and ten days,' Colin replied a little too quickly. 'But who's counting, right?'

'Jesus, I don't think I could even go two hundred and ten hours without sex. God, that's over half a year. We should have done something for your six-month celibate anniversary,' Rory teased.

'Like a celibration?'

'I'm not usually one for your dad jokes, but that was actually good,' Rory laughed. 'At least let me buy you a lap dance or something.'

'So your solution for blue balls is more blue balls?' Colin asked, raising an eyebrow.

'Good point. This is why I've always said marriage is unnatural. I've caught a lot of things over the years, Col, but thankfully I've never caught mono.'

'Glandular fever?'

'Monogamy.'

Colin laughed. 'Never say never.'

'All I know is when women talk about tying the knot, they forget to mention it's a noose. It's like that Richard Mulligan guy was saying about his cheating app on the radio. Eighty-six per cent of people would cheat if they could get away with it,' Rory said.

'Did you say a cheating app?'

'Yeah, it's this new app called Fling where married people can find the perfect stranger online to have an affair with . . . '

Colin found himself intrigued by the idea. He was going to ask more about it but Rory was still talking.

'. . . I'm actually thinking of downloading it,' Rory continued.

'You just said it's for married people,' Colin said, confused.

'Yeah, but think about it. There must be all these sexually frustrated housewives out there not getting any satisfaction from their husbands. Supposedly a quarter million people have downloaded it already. I could just pretend I'm married and suddenly my options are doubled. Think of the MILFs, Colin,' Rory said, excited by the idea.

'This reminds me of when you were thirteen and you asked me if those porn ads about meeting local MILFs in your area were real,' Colin laughed.

'Well, maybe my fantasy is finally coming true! Actually wait, no . . .' Rory said, bursting his own bubble. 'It's all anonymous on the app. So you don't know if the girl is hot or not. That could be a recipe for disaster.'

'I know, imagine if you actually had to get to know a woman,' Colin said sarcastically.

'God, can you imagine?' Rory said, the sarcasm flying right over his head. 'Anyway, I'll be dying all day with a hangover so I'll be doing less work than usual.'

'What's less than nothing?' Colin said playfully.

'You tell me, you're the whizz accountant.'

'Technically you're the accountant. I'm an actuary.'

'Are you actuary?' Rory joked. He could never resist the low-hanging fruit.

'I think that qualifies as a dad joke,' Colin teased.

Rory peeked out of Colin's office door to see if Karen was lurking. 'OK, I think the coast is clear,' he said, putting back on his sunglasses. 'Should I get a stick and pretend I'm blind to Karen?'

'That would lead to about ten other etiquette presentations. Just keep the head down,' Colin said.

'Fair point,' Rory said, dashing across the hall.

Colin laughed to himself as Rory left. There was never a dull moment with him. The two complimented each other well as a result of their opposite personalities.

Colin was the angel on Rory's shoulder and Rory was the devil on his.

50

Chapter 5

By 11 a.m., Tara was still obsessing over what Emily had said. To compare Tara to that Mary woman was downright ridiculous. OK, maybe Tara hadn't had sex in over six months and maybe she hadn't had an orgasm in a lot longer, but to be compared to Mary? MARY?

Tara wasn't some holier-than-thou puritan. She was a modern woman. Wasn't she? It wasn't her fault her desires weren't being fulfilled. Granted, she had been brought up in Catholic Ireland and educated in a convent. The only sex education class she had ever been given was by a nun who managed to get through the entire talk without once using the word sex. Maybe she was a little repressed but she was not a prude.

She liked to think she didn't suffer from Catholic guilt but her late father had been a religious man and she had a recurring dream of him appearing in the form of a robin and saying, 'How long has it been since you went to mass?'

She tried to put the Mary comparison out of her mind. Emily was probably just winding her up. It wouldn't be the first time.

Tara headed into Insight's break room to make herself her third coffee of the day. She was the only one who called it the break room. It was officially called the 'Games Room' and its various pool tables, arcade games and TV screens were supposed to help employees overcome 'creative blocks'. When she walked in, she saw the Lads – Tommy, Mark and Rob – playing a game of table soccer, or foosball, as they called it. Tara didn't have anything against the three of them but they had the same energy as men on a stag party. Each of them was smart individually, but collectively their IQ seemed to plummet.

Tommy was without a doubt the best marketer of the three. He knew what sold well and he could schmooze his way to any deal with buzz words that didn't actually mean anything. His favourite go-to phrase was 'It's time to stop collecting the dots . . . and start connecting the dots'. For the life of her, Tara couldn't figure out what it meant.

Mark was decent enough at his job but he only spoke in sports metaphors and had enough grease on his head to fry chips. Tara had once ordered a café au lait in his company and, after misinterpreting her, he began the football chant 'OLÉ OLÉ OLÉ OLÉ!'.

Rob was the youngest of the three but he had a set of teeth that could eat an apple through a tennis racket and made wearing a lanyard his entire personality. To Tara, he was the human incarnation of the Comic Sans font.

As she approached them playing table soccer, they seemed to be in the middle of some kind of dirty joke.

'Well, lads,' she said, being polite.

The three of them paused their game and began to collect themselves. They were behaving like she was their teacher, catching them misbehaving. Tara hated when they did that.

'Hi Tara,' Tommy said apologetically, as if trying to avoid detention.

'What's so funny?' Tara asked, genuinely trying to join in on the banter.

'Oh, you wouldn't like it. Definitely NSFW,' Mark said, trying not to laugh.

Tara felt hurt. They were making the joke at work so they clearly didn't care about it being not safe for work. What they really meant was Not Safe For Women. She decided to change the subject.

'Were any of you listening to *The Line* this morning?' she asked.

'God, it was hilarious. That Mary woman was a real piece of work,' Rob laughed.

'Richard Mulligan is an absolute legend,' Tommy said. 'You know we have a pitch meeting with him tomorrow?'

'What?' Tara said, shocked. 'I have nothing prepared!'

'Oh don't worry, this one is a slam dunk for us. Not really your territory,' Mark said.

'What do you mean by that?' Tara asked, squinting her eyes at him. 'Women can cheat as well, you know? Last time I checked, it takes two to tango.'

'Of course but . . . you're not exactly the best person to pitch an ad campaign for it,' Tommy said carefully.

'Can you imagine?' Rob laughed, unintentionally snorting like a pig.

'And why not? Is the product not "pink" enough?' she said, making air quotes with her fingers.

'No . . . it's because you're . . .' Tommy said, struggling to find the best words.

'Oh spit it out!' Tara demanded.

'You're a bit of a Mary,' he finally said.

Tara was fit to be tied. Everyone had the completely wrong perception of her. The insinuation that she was some old prude who couldn't even handle an office joke was insulting. How could her self-perception be so dramatically different

53

from the way others saw her? Did people just write you off after a certain age?

She used to be a free-spirited bohemian who was wild at heart. She used to be the kind of girl who would get on the back of a stranger's motorbike. When did she lose her spark? When had she become a pearl-clutching, puritanical, finger-wagging MARY? She wanted to scream at the top of her lungs, but that was something a Mary would do. She refused to prove them right.

In fact, she would prove them all wrong.

'What time is Richard Mulligan coming in?' Tara asked calmly.

'11 a.m. But honestly, Tara, we've got this. You're just not the target market. You wouldn't download Fling in a million years,' Tommy said.

'Yeah, and if you don't know how to play the game, maybe you shouldn't be on the pitch,' Mark said.

'We'll see about that,' Tara said, turning adamantly to leave.

᭰

Tara stormed back to her office and pointed at Emily. It was clear she was on a warpath.

'My office. Now!' she said sternly.

Emily followed her through the door immediately, sensing something serious.

'Tara, is everything OK? You know I was just messing earlier about the whole Mary thing,' she said, worried her joke had gone too far.

'No, Emily, you were right. I am a feckin' Mary. The Lads just said the exact same thing. But I'm going to prove everyone wrong,' Tara said, handing her phone to Emily. 'Download Fling.'

'Wow, are you sure?' Emily said, taking the phone.

'Oh, I'm sure. Richard Mulligan is coming in tomorrow to hear a marketing pitch from the Lads. They seem to think I'm too much of a prude to contribute anything to the conversation, but they're going to discover otherwise,' Tara said, eager to wipe the smug grins off their faces.

Emily was immediately on board with the idea and searched for Fling on the app store.

'Found it,' she said instantly. 'It's number one on the apps chart. Looks like you're not the only cat that's in heat.'

'Emily, this is strictly market research for the pitch,' Tara insisted.

'Relax, it was a joke. Plus, I can hardly judge. I'm literally a nymphomaniac.'

'Oh don't say that. You know there's no male equivalent term for a nymphomaniac? A man just gets called a legend when he has a lot of sex. You're just a . . . a . . .'

'A libra?'

'Exactly! Well, the Lads think only men know how to sell sex in a presentation and we're going to prove them wrong,' Tara said, getting herself worked up.

'Alright, it's downloaded. It's asking if you want to turn on notifications for the app?'

'Absolutely not,' Tara said, afraid Colin might see a pop-up message by mistake and think she was having an affair.

'OK, we're good to go. Are you ready?'

'I'm ready,' Tara said, as she began to pace anxiously around her office. Emily opened the app.

WELCOME TO FLING

CLICK TO SIGN UP

The app had a gorgeous sky blue interface design, which was surprisingly aesthetic considering the seedy nature of the app itself. Emily clicked the icon which brought her to a new page labelled: RULES.

'OK, here we go. Welcome to Fling, the discreet cheating app to find an anonymous affair online. Discretion is key to the Fling experience, so there are some rules to ensure privacy is maintained,' Emily read aloud.

Tara felt surprisingly excited. It was as if she had entered some kind of secret club and she immediately wanted to learn more.

'Go on,' she said, continuing to pace.

'Rule number one. Never use your real name. Always use an alias,' Emily read.

Tara started to feel like some kind of double agent and was intrigued by the idea of being someone else.

'Rule number two. Do not send photos of your face. Face pictures could be used to blackmail you. Anonymity is essential.'

Tara was a little worried about this aspect. A person could literally be talking to anyone. And arranging to meet up with someone without seeing their face could potentially be dangerous. But that made it feel all the more exciting. There was something so sexy about a perfect stranger.

'Rule number three,' continued Emily. 'Always meet in a public place to determine if you would like to begin a Fling. Never go directly to your match's home, hotel room, etc.'

'OK, so it's kind of like a blind date,' Tara said. 'Go on.'

'Rule number four. When creating your profile, be honest about what you want. Our matchmaking algorithm needs reliable data about what you're looking for in order to find your matches.' Emily looked up from Tara's phone. 'OK, are you sure you want to do this?' she asked.

Although Tara tried to convince herself it was purely market research, she felt an unexpected rush of adrenaline.

Driving in the bus lane didn't even come close to this kind of high. She was in too deep to turn back now. 'In for a penny, in for a pound,' Tara said.

Emily clicked CREATE PROFILE on the screen and a new window popped up that said ALIAS and PASSWORD.

'OK, what do you want your fake name to be?'

'Hmm, I don't know. I love the name Blanche,' Tara suggested.

'No, makes you sound like you're in a nursing home,' Emily said, ruling it out.

'OK, what about Margaret?'

'Makes you sound like a ghost who's haunting a nursing home.'

'OK, OK! How about Claire? I love that name.'

'Claire ... yeah, it sounds young ... and feminine. I like it,' Emily said, typing it in. 'And what do you want your password to be?'

'Just use AbbaGold, all one word. Capital A and G,' Tara said. It was the same password she used for everything. It was honestly a miracle nobody had ever stolen her identity.

Emily entered the details and was brought to a new page where more information was required. 'Right, how old should we say you are?' Emily asked cautiously.

'Let's say ... thirty-three?' Tara said in a high-pitched voice.

There was an awkward silence.

'OK, fine, thirty-four,' Tara said unconvincingly.

Emily gave Tara a disapproving look.

'OK, FINE, I'M THIRTY-SEVEN! ARE YOU HAPPY NOW?'

'Let's say thirty-five so you're not a complete catfish,' Emily said, typing it in.

Although Emily's words were harsh, she wasn't wrong.

Tara couldn't pass for thirty-three. At times, she felt she looked older than thirty-seven. The past few years had aged her terribly, like her body had abandoned its youth. And Colin had stopped seeing her as a sexual being due to the friction, or lack thereof, in their marriage. But she couldn't lay all the blame on Colin either. Tara had begun to neglect even the most basic skincare routine. She even found it a monumental effort to wash her hair more than once a week.

Emily continued creating the profile. 'OK, so let's set your location to Dublin. For your body type let's say slim. 5'7. Blonde hair. Don't worry, I won't mention the greys.'

'WHAT?' Tara said mortified. There was no way she had greys, it had only been two weeks since she had got her colour done. Tara was a natural redhead but dyed it light ash blonde every six weeks, without fail. She wanted champagne blond but her stylist told her she needed the ash to tone down the natural red and prevent it from looking too brassy. Her decision to dye it from red to blonde came about several years prior when Celine said to Tara, 'You're so pretty . . . for a ginger.' The backhanded compliment had got under Tara's skin and sown the seeds of self-doubt. She hated that Celine lived in her head rent-free, but nevertheless her hair had been ashy blonde ever since.

But now Emily was saying she had *greys*? Impossible. She scurried over to the mirror in her office and saw what Emily was talking about. It was a clump of dry shampoo that Tara hadn't rubbed into her hair properly. 'Oh thank God,' Tara said, blending it in with her fingertips. 'It's not grey hairs, it's powder. No offence to diamonds but dry shampoo is a girl's best friend.'

'Not when it makes you look like a banshee,' Emily muttered.

'I forgot how brutally honest you can be,' Tara said, rubbing the last of the powder out.

'I'm an acquired taste. If you don't like me . . . acquire some taste.' Emily smiled. 'OK, that's that section done. Next up you need to describe yourself with five keywords.'

'Hmm . . . does it give a list of options?'

'Yes, but I'm not calling them all out. You describe yourself and I'll pick them if they're listed here.'

'OK, let's see,' Tara pondered. 'Well . . . I'm caring. My career is important to me so you could say I'm ambitious. Erm . . . I feel like what you see is what you get with me . . . So maybe I'm . . . genuine? Oh, and passionate! Definitely say passionate! And let's see . . . Oh God, I can't think of a fifth one.'

'I have caring, ambitious, genuine, passionate and . . . let's also say creative.'

'Aw thanks, Emily,' Tara said, chuffed.

'Now I need five keywords you find attractive in a man.'

'Oh, now this should be easy,' Tara said. 'Confidence is definitely number one. Good sense of humour also very important. Intelligence is a must. And I like a man who isn't afraid to assert himself, you know? And let me see what else . . . Oh, and loyal!'

'Loyal isn't listed here as an option,' Emily said.

'Why not?'

'I don't know, Tara, maybe because it's an infidelity app?'

'Good point,' Tara laughed. 'OK, then say . . . '

'Hung?'

'No, Emily! That's the last thing on my mind. Put down sociable. I like when a man is good with people.'

'Confident, good sense of humour, intelligent, assertive and sociable. Got it,' Emily said as she submitted the keywords.

'So now all we are missing is your bio. And it says here that your bio should say what you're looking for.'

Tara didn't know what she was looking for. She had been asking herself that for the past few months and still hadn't found an answer. She wanted to reclaim the years she had lost. She wanted her marriage to go back to the way it used to be. She wanted her husband back.

'Hey, scatterbrain! Stop overthinking,' Emily said, interrupting her thought process. 'Don't think, just speak. Go!'

'I want to feel like myself again. Like the woman I used to be. I want a man to kiss me without me having to ask him to. I want a man who knows what he's doing and knows when to take charge. I want him to grab me tight and make me melt in his arms. And I'm tired of feeling guilty for wanting that,' she said in one breath.

Tara had never said those words out loud before. But she obviously felt it subconsciously. Within her hard outer shell was a softer, more delicate woman who needed to be held. She had no idea where her life was headed, what her true destiny was any more, and all she wanted was for a man to take her in his arms and tell her everything would be OK.

After being confronted by her unconscious desires, Tara had the face of a saint who had just been decanonized. She felt guilty for admitting her fantasy out loud and she worried Emily would judge her.

'What's wrong?' Emily asked, seeing her worried expression.

'My fantasy just sounds so problematic out loud. You probably think I'm a bad feminist,' Tara admitted.

Emily laughed. 'Tara, being sex-positive makes you a good feminist. You're a control freak all day so of course handing over control in bed is sexy. You know what's not sexy? Shame,' she explained. 'Now we just have to get you out of those pantsuits.'

'What's wrong with my suit?' Tara said, suddenly feeling self-conscious.

'No, it's lovely. But do they make it for women?' Emily laughed.

'Well, I don't exactly want to wear pantsuits, Emily, but when a woman gets into a senior role, she has to blend in,' Tara said, defending her fashion sense.

'But wearing them when you don't like them only panders to the patriarchy by implying masculine traits are superior and that feminine identity expression needs to be suppressed in order to succeed. Constantly pining to be "one of the boys" can often be a sign of internalized misogyny,' Emily said in one breath. 'I think the feminist texts you've been reading are a little outdated. You're stuck in second-wave.'

'What wave are we on now?'

'Well, I'm very ahead of my time so I'm a seventh-wave feminist,' Emily said.

'What's that?' Tara asked, having never heard the term.

'That's when we convince men to go out and work all day to provide for us while we live off their labour,' Emily said. It was impossible to tell if she was being ironic or not.

'I guess women have really come full circle,' Tara said sarcastically.

'The point is, feminism is no longer about women growing a pair of balls. It's about women realizing they don't need balls to be powerful,' Emily explained.

Emily certainly had a point. Tara didn't like what she wore. She always felt like she was wearing a uniform, part of her tough external shell. She had this image of feminism in her head that she had to look like Rosie the Riveter shouting 'WE CAN DO IT!' while flexing her bicep. But all along she was pandering to the Lads so they would think she was 'Not Like Other Women'. Now that she thought about it, what

Emily said made perfect sense. She suddenly felt embarrassed for how long she had tried to fit in with a group of men she didn't even like.

Maybe she wasn't a bad feminist after all, she just had an outdated idea of the word. Maybe she could be a powerful woman and still fantasize about a powerful man. Maybe she could be dominant in the boardroom and still enjoy being dominated in the bedroom. Maybe she could wear the pants during the day and still want a man to strip them off her at night.

'You're right, Emily, I am a good feminist,' Tara said, putting words in her mouth.

'You know what would make you an even better one, though? Giving me a raise. I can hear the patriarchy shaking in its boots already!' Emily said, chancing her arm.

'Nice try,' Tara laughed.

'OK, but you know my motto. Minimum wage, minimum effort.' Emily shrugged. 'Now, back to finding your fantasy fling.'

'The funny thing is, the sex I fantasize about is the kind I had with Colin the first time. He was my first and I was so excited but also so terrified. I had no idea what I was doing so he was totally in control. It felt so good to hand my body over to him, you know?'

'Wait, does that mean you've only ever slept with your husband?' Emily asked.

'Yep, only ever Colin.'

Emily was shook. 'Well, no wonder you're so repressed. Life is literally an all-you-can-eat buffet and you've only ever had one cocktail sausage.'

'You certainly have a way with words, Emily,' Tara laughed.

'OK, your profile is ready,' Emily said. 'Goodbye Tara, hello CLAIRE, 35 – DUBLIN! Now let's find you some matches.'

She submitted Tara's profile on the app and an animation of a progress bar appeared.

MATCHING 1%————50%————100% COMPLETE

'OK, here's the moment of truth,' Emily said as she opened the list of matches. Tara began pacing around the room once again. Her heart was going ninety. She didn't intend on having an affair, so why did she feel so excited to see her matches? Where was all this adrenaline coming from?

'OK, first up we have Cormac, with a seventy-one per cent match. His profile says he likes long walks on the beach and hardcore bondage.'

'Oh for God's sake,' Tara said, making a face. 'Next, please.'

'OK, next up we have Eamon, with a sixty-five per cent match. Eamon likes cosy afternoons ... and has always wanted to make a sex tape.'

'NEXT!'

'We also have Ray clocking in at a fifty-three per cent match. OMG he just sent you a message!' Emily said.

'What did he say?' Tara said a bit too eagerly.

Emily tilted the phone towards Tara and showed her the message.

> **Ray:** Got any feet pics?

Tara winced at the screen. 'That's disgusting!'

'Keep an open mind. A feet cute could be the new meet cute,' Emily joked.

'Is this the best this app has to offer?'

'You do have more matches but they're all under fifty per cent.'

Tara was officially finished with Fling. If this was the standard, she didn't want to be part of its marketing campaign. It was yet another sleazy dating app designed by men, for men.

So why did she feel a little disappointed?

Was there something on the app that she was hoping to find? And why had she felt a rush of adrenaline while she was waiting for her matches to appear? The idea made her feel incredibly guilty all of a sudden. She was a married woman, for God's sake. Sure, her marriage was going through a rough patch, but she still loved Colin. She reminded herself once again that she had downloaded the app purely for research and that the experiment was officially over.

'OK, that's enough,' Tara said, grabbing back her phone and closing the app.

'Oh come on, they're not that bad,' Emily said, not wanting to go back to work.

'Sorry, Emily, but not a single one of those men are my type.'

'You're looking for an affair, not a blood donor.'

'Actually, I'm looking for neither. I hate to ruin the fun, but faceless perverts on the internet have nothing to offer me. The Lads can have the account,' Tara said, losing interest.

'Still, if I didn't know any better, I'd say you were disappointed you didn't find a good match,' Emily said with a knowing smile.

'Oh please, it was just research. Nothing more,' Tara said.

'Could have fooled me.' Emily smirked. 'I like this Claire persona. Seems like she has a lot of repressed desires bubbling under the surface.'

'Well, you can apply your degree in psychology somewhere else because I am not looking for an affair,' Tara insisted.

'I don't know,' Emily said, sauntering out of Tara's office. 'Even a dormant volcano can still erupt.'

Chapter 6

Colin spent the rest of that morning producing a few reports, with his brain on autopilot. He had done the job for so long that he didn't really have to focus his mind all that much. He often got that feeling you get when you've been driving for a while and then suddenly remember that you're driving.

His thoughts kept drifting towards Fling. He wished he had asked Rory for more information but he didn't want to appear overly interested. He wondered what the whole thing entailed. Was Rory exaggerating when he said a quarter million people had downloaded it? Would it be weird to talk to people without knowing what they look like? He felt guilty for having such an interest in an infidelity app. He was married to the love of his life, after all. What business would he have on such an app?

Then again, if everyone was talking about it, he didn't want to be out of the loop. There was nothing immoral about looking something up. Eventually, his curiosity got the better of him and he decided to search online to see what all the hype was about. He opened up his internet browser and typed in 'FLING'.

The first result was a dictionary definition that read 'a short period of enjoyment or wild behaviour (noun)' but as soon as he clicked on the news tab, he saw exactly what Rory had been talking about. He was bombarded with results.

FLING. THE CHEATING APP TAKING THE COUNTRY BY STORM, one headline read.

OPINION: MEN CAN RESIST ANYTHING ... EXCEPT TEMPTATION, another read, turning an Oscar Wilde quote into clickbait.

POLL: ARE YOU TEAM MARY OR TEAM JIM?

The list of results was seemingly endless. Everyone was talking about a woman named Mary who had apparently gone viral after throwing a fit on *The Line*. He kept scrolling until he found the most straightforward article headline.

EVERYTHING YOU WANT TO KNOW ABOUT FLING BUT ARE TOO AFRAID TO ASK

Bingo.

Colin clicked the link and finally got the information he was looking for. He learned that the app was exclusively for unhappy married people seeking discreet extra-marital affairs. The app was all anonymous and Colin was intrigued by the reduced risk of getting caught.

Still, an affair wasn't going to fix his unhappy marriage. It was a painkiller, not a cure. But then again, Tara had given up on searching for a cure to their problems. They both wanted children and had always planned to start a family together. That was the plan. The plan that Tara had just abandoned overnight because of some superstitious excuse about destiny.

What was he supposed to do with the rest of his life? He thought about the definition that had come up when he first googled the word 'Fling'. A short period of enjoyment or wild behaviour. Didn't everyone deserve that once in a while? Was he supposed to go another 210 days without sex? He felt like a lion who had been neutered and domesticated. Was he supposed to just accept that he would never roar again?

He took out his phone and searched Fling on the app store. There it was. Number one in the download charts.

Just a click away.

Colin took off his wedding ring and read the inscription on the inner band. 'Always and Forever,' it read, with Tara's inscription reading 'Forever and Always'.

His mind began to drift back to the night he proposed. Long before their time, there had been a trend for couples to meet before a date under the Clerys clock in the very centre of Dublin. Tara had always thought this to be an incredibly romantic notion and felt it was such a shame that the tradition had faded over time. And so they decided to keep the custom alive, but with their own unique twist.

Instead of Clerys, they always met for their dates under the Eason clock, directly across O'Connell Street. Tara liked to start their dates with a quick browse in the bookstore, although she often found herself buying more books than she actually had time to read. Finally, after countless dates and endless memories, Colin felt it fitting that he would propose to her where so many of their stories had begun. He had led her to the Eason clock, got down on one knee and asked her to start a new chapter with him. 'It's about time,' she had laughed, with tears of joy in her eyes.

They had nothing but time back then. It was all ahead of them. Now, he feared his best days were all behind him. What he would give to be able to turn the hands of that Eason clock backwards and reclaim his youth from time, irredeemable. He would do anything to escape the prison of the present, even for a brief moment. It was a terrifying thing, to feel trapped in your own epilogue.

While Colin was still deep in existential thought, Rory barged into his office without knocking. 'Col, let's get some lunch. I need some hangover food.'

Colin was caught off guard and nervously started minimizing his open tabs from researching Fling.

'Col . . .' Rory said, suspiciously. 'Why do you look like a teenager who's just been caught watching porn?'

Rory rushed over to Colin's desk before he could close everything. Seeing the articles on the screen, Rory knew exactly what was going on.

' "Everything you want to know about Fling but are too afraid to ask." Oh my God, look who finally grew a pair of balls,' Rory said, impressed.

'It's not what it looks like,' Colin said, embarrassed.

'You can't lie to me, Collie boy. Come on, show me your matches.'

'I don't even have the app yet.'

'Well download it! I want to see what all the fuss is about. And you obviously do too,' Rory said, rearing to go. The excitement seemed to have cleared the fog of his hangover.

'I can't do it to Tara.'

'Just because you look at the menu, doesn't mean you have to order.' Rory smirked.

For a brief moment, Rory's logic seemed to make sense to Colin, a rare occurrence. Even a broken clock is right twice a day. But still, downloading the app would be a betrayal.

'No, Rory, I'm not cheating on my wife,' Colin said.

Rory let out an ostentatious sign. 'You know . . . it's probably for the best. You're not exactly the type of man a woman would want an affair with anyway.'

'I know what you're doing. Trying to bait me into asking what you mean by that,' Colin said.

'You know I am a master baiter, Colin . . .'

'Ugh, fine. I'll bite. Why would a woman not want an affair with me, exactly?'

'Well, you're . . . God, I can't even say the word. You know

68

I hate political correctness man but this word is just too offensive to say out loud,' Rory said, pretending the word was making him gag.

'I'm a big boy,' Colin said, rolling his eyes.

'You've become . . . you've become . . .'

'Spit it out!'

'HARMLESS!' Rory yelled, finally getting the word out.

'Oh for God's sake, that's not the worst thing a man can be,' Colin said.

'Oh yes it is, Col. Go into any bookstore, walk towards the female erotica section and try to find a book titled *Seduced by the Harmless Man*. Spoiler alert, no such book exists. Because being harmless is the least sexy thing a man can be,' Rory explained.

'So what, I should try to be . . . harmful? Give me a break,' Colin said, brushing him off.

'The opposite of harmless isn't harmful, it's dangerous,' Rory explained. 'I'm a Scorpio, so women are naturally drawn to my inner shadow.'

'Oh don't tell me you believe in horoscopes too?' Colin said.

'Of course I don't. But women do. And we're talking about what women want. Col, I'm about to do something I've never done before.'

'Your job?'

'Don't be ridiculous,' Rory said. 'I'm about to give you some tough love. When I was eleven and you were nineteen, I used to think you were the coolest person to ever exist. You used to ride a Triumph Bonneville motorcycle for God's sake. You looked like a sex god! Now you drive a Nissan Qashqai. You went from man to mouse in just a few years. I wanted to grow up so fast so I could be just like you. Now I'm afraid

69

to grow up in case I become like you. It breaks my heart to say that but I think you need to hear it.'

Rory had a reputation for having no filter but this was the first time his words had had an effect on Colin. Because he was right. Colin used to be a rebellious non-conformist who answered to nobody. Now he worked a boring office job at an accountancy firm and came home to an unhappy marriage devoid of desire. Colin knew exactly why Rory's words cut so deep – the truth hurts.

'Download it,' Colin said, holding out his phone.

'Thatta boy!' Rory said, full of zeal. He had the app downloaded and opened in about five seconds, clearly a pro at online dating. Colin looked over Rory's shoulder as he opened the app.

WELCOME TO FLING, the app homepage read.

CLICK TO SIGN UP.

Rory clicked the button and started speeding through the sign-up process. 'Turn on notifications. Yes, obviously. List of rules, ugh boring. Let's see, number one, don't use your real name. Number two, no face pics. Number three, meet in a public place to see if you want to hook up. Got it. Number four, be honest about what you want. OK, boring parts over.'

Colin definitely felt like Rory skimmed over the rules too quickly, but he got the gist of them.

'OK, first things first, pick a fake name,' Rory said.

'I don't know. Something masculine,' Colin pondered.

'Max!'

'No, makes me sound like a Labrador. What about Kyle?'

'No, makes you sound like a skateboarder. I mean, I would let you use Rory but you just don't have the raw animal magnetism to pull it off,' Rory said.

'Thanks for the vote of confidence. I know! JACK! It's

70

manly but also not too fake either,' Colin said, happy with his choice.

'OK, Jack it is,' Rory said, typing the name. 'And for your password, I'll say RORY-IS-HUNG, all caps, hyphenated.'

Colin rolled his eyes but didn't object.

'OK . . . next we need some personal info. Let's say you're thirty-six . . . six feet tall . . . muscular . . .'

'I'm none of those things!' Colin said anxiously.

'Relax, we're not lying, we're just seasoning the truth,' Rory said, taking the reins.

'Ugh, fine.'

'Right . . . let's say you're based in Dublin . . . OK, now it's asking to pick five adjectives to describe yourself.'

'Hmm. Well . . . I'd say I have a good sense of humour . . . I'm fairly smart, if I do say so myself . . . I'm outgoing . . . I'm confident . . . and assertive!'

'Assertive? Really?' Rory said, raising an eyebrow.

'Well, I used to be. And I think it's time I started being assertive again!'

'That's the spirit! So I have good sense of humour, intelligent, confident, they don't have outgoing so I put down sociable, and assertive!' Rory said as he hit submit. 'Now, what five qualities do you find attractive in a woman? Maybe I should fill this section out on your behalf.'

'Absolutely not!' Colin laughed. 'You won't even mention her qualities!'

'I'm more into quantities, if you know what I mean,' Rory said. 'But fine have it your way. Go.'

'OK, let's see . . . well, I like a woman who's genuine, you know? A no-games kind of girl. And she has to be caring. And someone with ambitions too. Maybe a creative type. A woman who looks towards the future. And most important of all, she has to be passionate.'

'OK, so I have passionate, creative, ambitious, caring, genuine,' Rory said. 'Boring.'

'Don't put down boring!'

'No, I was saying your taste in women was boring.'

'And what's your type?' Colin asked. 'Lobotomized?'

'Of course not. Intelligence is very sexy!'

'That's good to hear,' Colin said. But he had a feeling there was some caveat coming.

'It takes brains to give head,' Rory smirked.

'There it is,' Colin said, rolling his eyes.

'OK, next section is your bio. This is where you say what you're looking for in an affair.'

Colin hadn't expected this question. 'What do I want from an affair? Well, I want to know that I have the power to take a woman all the way. I want a woman who knows that I call the shots and she can take it or leave it. When you're with me, I'm in control. If you're looking for someone harmless, then I'm not the man for you. I'm dangerous. This lion had been caged for too long. I'm ready to roar,' Colin said.

Colin felt as if something primal had awoken within him.

'I have some notes,' Rory said, taking him down a few pegs.

'I don't care. It's my bio and it's staying that way,' Colin said firmly.

'Wow, I'm liking this new assertive Colin. Or should I say, JACK – 36, DUBLIN,' Rory smiled. He hit the submit button and the progress bar began to fill as it searched for potential matches. They both looked nervously at the screen.

The suspense was excruciating.

'I probably won't get any matches,' Colin said, preparing himself for the worst.

MATCHING 1%————50%————100% COMPLETE.

A little jingle came from the phone, followed by a pop-up message:

100% PERFECT MATCH.

'A one hundred per cent match?' Colin said. 'Is that even possible?'

'Must be your lucky day. Now let's see who she is,' Rory said, clicking the profile.

CLAIRE – 35, DUBLIN

'OK, her name is Claire,' Rory said. 'She's thirty-five and lives in Dublin too. So far, so good.'

'Claire. That's such a sexy name. What does her bio say?' Colin asked, flustered.

Rory cleared his throat.

'I want to feel like myself again. Like the woman I used to be. I want a man to kiss me without me having to ask him. I want a man who knows what he's doing and knows when to take charge. I want him to grab me tight and make me melt in his arms. And I'm tired of feeling guilty for wanting that.'

Colin was shocked. She was looking for everything he was looking for. 'She sounds perfect! And a one hundred per cent match. Do you know what this means? The woman of my dreams is literally out there walking around Dublin some-where!' he said, gesturing out the window.

'Whoa, whoa, whoa,' Rory interrupted. 'You didn't down-load Fling to find the woman of your dreams. You're on here to give some housewife the old smash and dash. The old ride and glide. The old pump and dump—'

'Are you done?' Colin asked, unimpressed.

'The old hit and quit. The old tap and scrap. The old screw and shoo . . . I think there's one more . . . nope, I'm done.'

'But Rory, it's a one hundred per cent match. It doesn't

get more compatible than that!' he said, breathless with disbelief.

'Why don't you just start with a message before you begin falling head over heels? Let's not forget that you don't even know what she looks like. It could be saggy old Karen from HR for all we know!'

Rory had a point; Colin was jumping to conclusions. Still, though, he felt a rush. A rush he hadn't felt in years, so he allowed himself to enjoy it.

'OK, you're right. Let's start with a message. But what do I even say?'

'Use my classic opening line. Baby, if I could rearrange the alphabet, I'd put me in "u".'

'I don't think that's how that saying goes,' Colin laughed. 'I think I'm just going to keep it nice and simple.'

He began to type.

> **Jack:** Hey there, stranger ☺

Colin was happy with his message. It wasn't too forward and the flirty little winky face at the end made it clear he was interested.

'I guess now I just have to wait,' Colin said, feeling a bit of an anti-climax after sending the message.

'And that's our cue to go get some greasy hangover food,' Rory said.

As tempted as Colin was to indulge in some grease, he wanted to save his appetite for the two juicy rib-eye steaks he had taken out of the freezer that morning. 'You go on ahead. I defrosted some steak for tonight so I'm just going to get a chicken fillet roll for lunch.'

'OK, but you better not double text Claire while I'm gone. Women hate desperation,' Rory said.

'I won't, I swear. I'll let you know if there's a reply,' Colin said, putting his phone back in his pocket.

'I'm proud of you, man. You're back walking on the wild side where you belong,' Rory said, leaving Colin's office. After he left, he immediately stuck his head back in the door as if he had forgotten something. 'Give her the old nail and bail. I knew there was one more!'

Chapter 7

When Tara arrived home later that evening, she was greeted by the same old familiar emptiness. Although she had been living in the house for years, it had never truly felt like a home to her. It wasn't a mystery to her why she felt like this. She and Colin had bought the house to start a family but, ten years later, it was still just the two of them, haunted by the hallow halls. She owned the house of her dreams yet felt like she was living in the ruins of her life.

She missed their college days in the tiny studio apartment they used to share. Looking back, life seemed so easy then. They would have silly rows about whether Trinity or UCD was the better college. Although Tara always fought her corner well, at the end of the day, she always ended up wearing Colin's UCD hoody, even though it represented a kind of victory for him. She used to like when he won. She used to feel so safe in that hoody. Every day felt like a Sunday morning back then, and they would talk about all the things they would do one day.

But now, it seemed as if her marriage would never get out of this rut it was in. It felt deeper than a rut. It was a chasm. She used to feel so comfortable sitting in silence with him but recently, it was as if someone had increased the volume of the background noise, the sounds that lie beneath the threshold of life. She could hear the mechanical sounds underlying everything, like an unchecked engine, screaming to be repaired. Little things like his incessant snoring, his astronomical sneezes and his pronunciation of the word 'quinoa' as 'quinn-oh-ah'. All these small things became piercingly loud, like nails on a chalkboard. And then there was the unbearable small talk. Their attempts to fill the silence only amplified it. The cure was worse than the disease. The longer things were left unsaid, the more one thing became clear.

It was only a matter of time before the simmering silence came to a boil.

Tara was famished so she headed straight to the kitchen to get started on dinner. She opened the fridge to see what her options were but then she remembered the two rib-eye steaks Colin had taken out to defrost. She knew he had taken them out for her to cook. She did the cooking, after all. But Tara knew whether she would cook her husband a steak or not depended on one very important thing.

She opened the dishwasher.

Still not emptied.

Not a single plate or cup moved to the cupboard. Even though he had told her he would do it after she went to work. And this was no isolated incident. This was the new normal.

It hadn't always been like this. Before their rift, everything had always been 50/50. She cooked dinner, he did the weekly grocery shopping. She did the laundry, he took out the bins. She hoovered the house, he mowed the lawn. She loaded up the dishwasher, he emptied it the next morning. But now, he made no effort whatsoever.

Was there anything more irritating than a man who just couldn't be bothered?

She couldn't cook the steak. Even on principle alone, she refused to go above and beyond when all offered to her in return was the bare minimum. Marriage was a team sport, was it not? If her teammate was going to let her down, it shouldn't be her responsibility to pick up the slack.

Why, after all, should she be bothered?

Tara rooted around the fridge, finding a microwaveable chicken pasta bake. The dish served two and was going to expire the next day. Perfect. She would have half and Colin could have the other half if he wanted. And if he didn't want it, he could cook the damn steak himself.

She popped the meal into the microwave.

Microwaveable meals weren't her favourite thing in the world but she could never muster up the energy to cook these days. In fact, she found herself cooking less and less since her rift with Colin began. If he could just give her some kind of gesture that he still cared, that would be enough. She asked him every month to help her organize their garden shed but she might as well have been talking to a wall. Unless Colin gave her some indication that he appreciated her, it would be microwaveable meals for the foreseeable future.

There was a middle ground she could live with, however. A miracle had occurred in the culinary world with the surge in popularity of the air fryer. Everyone Tara knew had one and they loved to brag about the many different meals they could whip up with ease. But Colin, of course, had decided that an air fryer was just a fancy word for an oven and that they didn't need one. It drove her mental how frugal he could be.

Tara believed the trick to getting through life was to always have a holiday booked and a package on the way. But Colin never wanted to go abroad any more, and she had a secret agreement with their postman to only deliver her parcels when Colin's car wasn't in the driveway. He didn't have the power to stop her shopping, of course, but he took the fun out of it. And his refusal to go on holidays was because IVF was the only thing worth spending savings on, apparently. But what is life without something to look forward to?

For now, at least, Tara would have to rely on her trusty microwave while the air fryer remained a fantasy. Life is funny, she thought to herself. One minute you're dancing on a bar after one too many tequilas and the next you're daydreaming about air fryers.

While the food was heating up, she opened a new bottle of pinot grigio and sat down at the table. She filled her glass and suddenly realized that she had poured half the bottle in already. She used to be able to get four glasses of wine out of any bottle, but Tara's definition of one measure had gradually become bigger and bigger. She wasn't allowed to drink during IVF cycles, and Colin had recently taken to making passive-aggressive digs that she was 'making up for lost wine'.

She wondered what her glass would look like in another few years. Would she be one of those women who buy a comically large novelty wine glass as a joke and says things like 'Don't worry, I'll only have one glass' as they pour the entire bottle in? It didn't help that two months' worth of empty wine bottles were currently sitting in the utility room, waiting for Colin to take them to a bottle bank. 'I'll take them next week,' he said, every week. If anyone were to see them, they would undoubtedly think Tara had a problem. Perhaps she did need to lay off a bit.

The microwave beeped and snapped her out of her daze. She decided that she couldn't possibly give up wine because it was actually good for the heart once a person reaches a certain age. In a way, drinking fine wine would ensure that she too would age like a fine wine. She had a knack of being able to convince herself of anything. She took a sip and began to dish out her pasta bake.

Colin arrived home not too long after Tara. He had spent the rest of his workday thinking about Claire from Fling. Although they had got a perfect match, she had yet to respond to his message. He had opened the app every hour to check for a reply and hadn't once seen the little green light showing she was online.

But despite Claire's lack of reply, Colin had a new-found confidence as a result of his 100 per cent match. He had a certain swagger about him. His ego had been deflated for so long that he had forgotten what confidence even felt like. It took Colin very little to feel good about himself and he was determined to ride this high for as long as possible. He knew it was silly, needy even, but he didn't care. He felt like a king and was ready to feast like one.

He hung up his coat in the hall and walked into the kitchen just as Tara was sitting down to her meal.

'Oh, good timing,' she said, looking up from her pasta bake.

'What are you having?' he asked, squinting at her plate.

'Chicken pasta bake. It's really good, yours is cooling on the counter,' Tara replied, taking a large gulp of her wine to prevent Colin from seeing how much she had initially poured into the glass.

'I was defrosting steaks for today.'

'I know, but I wasn't really in the mood to cook. Mental day at work.'

Colin was more than just disappointed. He had purposely had a small lunch to build up an appetite for dinner. It wasn't that he hadn't got what he had wanted, it was more the fact that, as usual, she had made the call. He didn't even mind microwaveable meals, but they had eaten them exclusively for the past few months. It was more about convenience than enjoying the meal and it wasn't ever as hot as he wanted it to be. It was always just lukewarm.

Colin let out a deep performative sigh as he picked up the microwave dinner.

'Colin, if you want the steak then cook the steak. There's no problem,' Tara said.

'Sure,' Colin muttered. He didn't want to come across as brash but he had taken out the steaks for a specific reason: to get them out of the perpetual pattern of microwave dinners so things could go back to normal. He had planned to open a bottle of wine, but Tara had already poured half the bottle in her glass. It seemed as if they would be stuck in this loop forever. He put his half of the pasta bake onto a plate and threw the plastic container into the general waste bin.

'Colin, for God's sake, you know you're supposed to rinse them out and put them in the recycling bin,' she said, for the millionth time.

'Well, maybe if we ate less microwaveable dinners, we would produce less waste,' Colin said, putting his plate in the microwave to reheat it and slamming it shut a little too loudly.

'I just cooked that, why are you cooking it again?' Tara asked, confused.

'You didn't cook it, you microwaved it. There's a difference. It's not healthy to microwave everything,' he said, rambling.

'Well, if you hate the microwave so much, then I'm buying an air fryer!'

'An air fryer is just an Easy-Bake Oven for grown-ups! You can't fry air, it's a scam!' he said.

'OK, just so we're clear, you're annoyed that I'm not

81

spending enough time cooking you dinner? Is this really the hill you want to die on?' Tara said, trapping him.

'It's fine, forget it. I was just trying to break the cycle of microwave dinners every evening . . .'

Tara took another large gulp of wine and had a visible fury in her eyes. He saw the feminist switch flip within her. Her claws were officially out and Colin knew he had already lost the battle. But he still wanted to put up a decent fight. If only to prove he could.

'Well, why don't you start with the dishwasher cycle? Because you said you'd empty it this morning and it's still not done!' Tara began to rant. 'You don't lift a finger around here. I asked you to clean out the shed months ago and it's still not done. And trying to get you to go to the bottle bank with the wine bottles is like pulling hens' teeth!'

'Oh, so it's a game of tit-for-tat, is it?' Colin said. 'Well, I do plenty of other things around the house.'

'Do you? You don't do the laundry or the mopping or the dusting . . .' she said, listing them out.

'You never ask me to do those things!'

'I shouldn't have to ask.'

'Oh that's right, I forgot I'm supposed to be psychic. I'm supposed to just magically know what you want without you telling me,' Colin said, throwing his hands up in the air.

'I want you to want to do housework.'

'WHY WOULD I WANT TO DO HOUSEWORK?' Colin yelled, dumbfounded.

'Nobody wants to do housework, Colin, but you could offer!' Tara said.

'No, because you'd prefer to complain about nobody helping you than ask someone for help. Typical martyr complex. Like asking Celine to put us in contact with that fertility specialist. You're cutting off your nose to spite your face.'

82

'HA!' she laughed. 'What's Celine going to do? Give us a promo code for twenty per cent off egg retrieval? Give me a break.'

'She's an influencer, Tara. We should use her influence!' Colin said, trying to make her see reason.

'Having ten thousand followers doesn't make you an influencer!'

'Well, Jesus only had twelve followers and he had a fairly big influence!'

'Oh look who's suddenly a devout Catholic,' Tara said, rolling her eyes.

'There is no shame in asking for help. No man is an island.'

'Yeah, well, every woman is. I don't want any help from Celine and that's the end of it.'

'You know what, Tara? Green really isn't your colour,' Colin said.

'Are you implying that I'm JEALOUS? OF CELINE? Is that what this whole fight is about? You're annoyed I'm not a Yummy Mummy pushing out loads of babies and having your favourite dinner ready on the table as soon as you walk in?' Tara said, shocked.

'Ugh, you always do this. Stop turning everything into a feminist lecture,' Colin sighed.

'It's hard not to when my manchild of a husband throws a tantrum over me not cooking his favourite din-dins!'

'Anytime I offer to cook, you say no!'

'That's because the only meal you can make is chicken nuggets and chips!'

'They're chicken tenders, Tara, and you know that! You want me to do something and when I offer to do it, you say no. You're a barrel of contradictions!'

'Did you just call me a barrel?' Tara said, appalled. 'Well, seeing as I make more money than you, maybe you should have steak ready for me when I walk in the door. Now that I think of it, maybe I need a stay-at-home husband.'

'Salary isn't everything, Tara. I have investments. I work smart, not hard,' Colin said, folding his arms.

'Working smart? Is that what you call messing with Rory all day long? You know, I think he's rubbing off on you too much. You're starting to smell like toxic masculinity,' Tara said.

'Or maybe your lapdog just still has some bite left in him. Maybe I finally have the balls to address the elephant in the room,' he said.

'OK, so first I'm a barrel, now I'm an elephant?' Tara said, misinterpreting his point.

'You're not the elephant! The elephant is the fact that we're unhappy! I took out the two steaks so we could have a nice meal together! It's like you've given up on everything! Dinner, sex, the future, everything. It's like you've just checked out of this relationship.'

'I told you I'm at a spiritual crossroads, I'm trying to realign with my destiny!'

'I'm not letting you get away with those kinds of excuses any more, Tara. This isn't going to be like the time you rear-ended my car in the driveway and blamed it on some planet!'

'For the last time, Colin, Mercury was in retrograde! That's hardly my fault!'

'I'm not putting up with this nonsense any more. Your head might be in the stars Tara, but it's about time someone brought you back down to earth!'

The microwave dinged to signal Colin's food was ready.

'Oh look, my dinner is ready. A lovely, lukewarm dinner for our lovely, lukewarm marriage,' he said, taking it out of the microwave.

'You know, men should be careful telling women to get

back in the kitchen. That's where we keep the knives. Who knows, maybe my destiny is to be the focus of a true-crime documentary,' Tara said, taking a victory sip of wine as if the fight was over.

'I'll have dinner in the living room so my toxic masculinity doesn't accidentally smother you,' Colin said smugly.

'Great. And while you're at it, why don't you sleep on the couch tonight so my pillow doesn't accidentally smother you,' she replied peevishly.

Colin gave her a passive-aggressive smile as he left the kitchen.

Chapter 8

Tara and Colin spent the rest of the evening avoiding each other in a somewhat theatrical manner. When one entered a room, the other left dramatically. It seemed the built-up resentment had finally come to a head. Colin hadn't planned for things to escalate the way they did, but he was relieved that the underlying issues had finally been brought to the surface. He didn't think steak would be the tipping point that drove them both over the edge, but then again, it wasn't really about the steak.

Colin didn't mind sleeping on the couch, although it was a little dusty. He did, of course, have the option of sleeping in the spare room but the idea scared him a little. It seemed like a permanent solution to a temporary problem. He feared if he moved to the spare room, he would never move back to his own bed with Tara. That wasn't what he wanted. He loved her more than anything, after all. They were just in a rut and acknowledging that fact was the first step towards getting out of it. He grabbed a blanket from the closet and tucked himself in the couch.

As he lay there, he couldn't help but replay the fight in his head. Colin always found himself thinking of snappy comebacks after an argument had ended. He was hopeless on the spot. Tara had a sharper tongue, that had always been the case. When they were younger and Colin knew he was losing a fight, he would grab her and kiss her to shut her up. It was the only way to win against her. It was his trump card, the hidden ace up his sleeve.

Any tension between them was always of a sexual nature. Whenever they fought, there was a certain chemistry to it, an erotic undercurrent charging below. They were always able to harness that power into passionate sex and get the release they both craved. But Colin felt as if Tara didn't want to be grabbed and kissed any more. He wanted to make a move but her body language wasn't communicating that she wanted it. Now they were both trapped in a prison of their own design, desperate for a release that would never come.

His mind drifted to Claire once again. He wondered if she was also unhappy in her marriage. The fact that she was on Fling meant she would probably be able to relate to his situation. Colin opened Fling on his phone and saw that he had an 82 per cent match with SANDRA, 35 – DUBLIN and she had sent him a message.

> **Sandra:** Wow, 82% match. We must be perfect for each other hahahahaha

> Hello????? Are you there??????

> So . . . what are we?

Colin quickly unmatched with clingy Sandra. There was another message from a profile called MAGGIE, 43 – DUBLIN with whom he received a 62 per cent match with.

> **Maggie:** Hi Jack. I've always wanted to have sex in a graveyard. Would you be into that?

Colin was horrified. He didn't want to be judgemental but sex in a graveyard just seemed bonkers. He considered replying with a dad joke to be polite, but he couldn't decide between 'I hear people are dying to get in there' or 'Can't we start with a graveyard shift?' He eventually decided not to bother replying and hit the unmatch button once again.

After getting a 100 per cent match with Claire, it was hard to think about anyone else. He was an actuary, after all, and 100 per cent was the magic number in terms of probability, reporting, everything. But why hadn't she replied to him? It was like he'd hit the lucky jackpot but was then thrown out of the casino. Wasn't Claire at least curious about what made them a perfect match? Her silence was driving him crazy. Colin sighed and looked at the time.

11.06 p.m.

Time to call it. Claire obviously thought his opening line was stupid, or else maybe she just wasn't taking Fling too seriously. Either way, Colin couldn't help but feel his ego deflated by the lack of response. He got up and put his phone charging in the corner of the room. It was time to forget about Fling and get some sleep.

In the master bedroom, Tara was getting ready to put the day behind her. She wondered if tonight's fight was a once-off or if it was the first nail in the coffin of her marriage. With Colin not in the bed beside her, she felt the emptiness now more than ever. Being alone was one thing but feeling alone within a marriage was a much deeper kind of isolation. She and Colin had been a couple for eighteen years. Was the youth of their relationship coming to an end? Was it normal for what began as a sexual awakening to evolve into sexual anaesthesia? These questions tormented her.

After applying some Sudocrem on a spot she felt lingering under her skin, she got into bed. As she lay there, she thought about the things Richard Mulligan had said on the radio. Over two hundred and fifty thousand people had downloaded Fling, so maybe lots of people felt the same unhappiness she did.

Maybe she wasn't alone.

Tara realized she hadn't deleted the app from her phone earlier. For a moment she considered keeping it for market research, but she figured there was no point. The Lads had already poached the account anyway, and now that she knew the quality of men on it, she didn't want anything to do with it. She reached over to the bedside locker and grabbed her phone, eager to wipe all traces of Fling.

Just as her finger was hovering over the delete button, however, she paused for a moment and remembered some of the harsh things Colin had said. The cheek of him. The sheer audacity. Where did he get the nerve to treat her like that? She looked at the time on her phone.

11.11 p.m.

Although it was late and she was exhausted, she decided to spite him and have one last browse, as a secret act of defiance.

But when Tara opened Fling, she couldn't quite believe her eyes. She looked in disbelief at the on-screen animation that read: 100% PERFECT MATCH.

JACK – 36, DUBLIN

That's when it happened.

Something that made Tara feel more awake than she had been in years. Something that Tara had experienced only twice before. Something that Tara did not see coming.

Tara experienced a synchronicity.

She felt butterflies in her stomach, goosebumps appeared

all over her arms, the back of her neck began to tingle and she felt that familiar feeling of déjà vu. It was the gut feeling that had always given her the inexplicable knowledge that she was in the right place at the right time with the right person. The spiritual compass that she had believed to be broken.

Until now.

She felt her heart palpitating as she clicked on his profile to read more. She read Jack's bio and was immediately excited. He sounded like the man of her dreams, the kind of man she fantasized about. Then, she saw that Jack had sent her a message earlier that day.

Jack: Hey there, stranger ☺

Tara's heart started going ninety as she became completely flustered. What would she reply? It wasn't just that Tara was out of the game, she had never actually been in the game in the first place. Colin had been her first everything, and she was terrified of saying the wrong thing. She rattled her brain and eventually decided to keep it simple. Jack would probably be asleep anyway.

Claire: A stranger's just someone you haven't met yet x

In the living room, Colin's phone beeped. He got up off the couch and walked over to where his phone was charging. To his shock, the notification on his phone was from Fling and he immediately opened the app. He hoped more than anything that it would be Claire. He needed it to be her. Colin's face lit up when he saw the message.

Not only had Claire replied to him but she had texted back in a flirtatious way. He looked at her profile again which now had the illuminated green light that he had desperately craved to see all day. She had sent the message less than a minute ago so he knew he had to reply immediately, before she went offline again. Colin got back on the couch and began to type his response, or rather, his new alter ego Jack's response.

Jack: True 😊 I'm new to all this but I'm guessing a 100% match is a good place to start?

Claire: I know, 100% on a cheating test. There's a joke in there somewhere . . .

Jack: I guess we're good at being bad . . .

Claire: Well, we've certainly come to the right place then x

Jack: It seems so. I'm Jack 😊

Claire: I'm Claire x

So what brings you to Fling?

Jack: To be honest, I only just joined today and I'm still figuring out how it all works.

Claire: Same here. I wanted to see what all the fuss was about.

Did you hear about it on the radio this morning?

Jack: I missed it actually. But I heard that Mary woman had a conniption haha

Claire: I know, I'm so glad I'm not a Mary haha #TeamJim

But to be honest, I was just about to delete Fling when you messaged me

Jack: Oh . . . I hope you aren't still planning on deleting it . . .

Claire: Oh don't worry, I'm not. I just meant you caught me right in time.

Jack: Phew! I would have missed out big time

Claire: Oh yeah?

Jack: I can already tell you're a catch

Claire: Well, if you're my 100% match, I guess that makes you a catch too x

Jack: I like the way you think 😊

Claire: Haha if only my husband felt that way

Jack: Trouble in paradise?

Claire: More like paradise lost ☹

Jack: Tell me about it. I feel like the only one in the marriage.

Claire: Same! And it's like the more you do, the more you're taken for granted.

Jack: EXACTLY!

Claire: And we're expected to bend over backwards for them when they don't do the same for us!

Jack: Right? It's like, meet me halfway for God's sake!

And then they act like you're the problem.

Claire: Yes! Or make you think you're crazy!

Jack: Ugh, that's the worst!

Claire: Finally, someone who understands it. God, at times I thought I was the only one.

Sorry, I hope it doesn't seem like I'm complaining too much!

Jack: No, I completely get it. It feels good to talk to someone else who's unhappy.

Not that I'm happy you're unhappy!

Claire: Haha yeah, it makes me a little less sad that I'm not the only one who's unhappy.

Does that make sense?

Jack: Perfectly! It's nice to feel a little less alone.

Claire: And if you think about it, if they appreciated us more, we wouldn't feel the need to join Fling in the first place!

Jack: Yes! Like, there's only so much we can take . . .

Claire: It's like they want us to cheat . . .

Jack: We have no choice!

Claire: Haha. This is all so crazy.

We could pass each other on the street tomorrow and not even know it.

Jack: It's mad, isn't it? Probably for the best though

Claire: Why's that?

Jack: Because I'd probably grab you on the street and kiss you 😊

Claire: You don't even know what I look like haha x

Jack: I can tell you're beautiful

I can't explain it, I just get a good vibe from you 😊

Claire: I'm sure you'd probably prefer someone much younger . . .

With that bio, you must have loads of matches

Jack: Haha, a few did message me but they were a bit bizarre

Claire: What did they say?

Jack: One wanted to have sex in a graveyard!

Claire: NO WAY!

Jack: Yep. Call me old-fashioned but I don't think I could get mourning wood!

Claire: STOP HAHAHA Charming and funny, you're the whole package aren't you?

Jack: Thinking about my package already? ☺

Claire: Haha. Maybe I am . . . x

Oh my God, I can't believe I typed that!

Jack: I'm glad you did ☺

The algorithm seems to know exactly what I want ☺

Claire: And what's that?

Jack: You 😊

Claire: Careful, flattery will get you everywhere x

Jack: Oh yeah? Well, just imagine how much I could flatter you behind closed doors . . .

Claire: You're just going to have to tell me . . .

Jack: Well, first, I'd walk up behind you and kiss your neck . . .

Claire: Yes . . .

Jack: Then I'd take you in my arms and kiss you like you've never been kissed before

Claire: I bet I'd feel so small in your manly arms

Jack: Oh you would. So small that I'd pick you up and throw you on the bed

Then I'd start to kiss your neck and slowly move down your body.

Claire: Go on . . .

97

Jack: Then I'd start kissing all over your body, ripping off your clothes as I go.

Not even caring if I tear them

Claire: Oh yeah . . .

Jack: I'd put my hand around your neck and whisper in your ear that your pathetic husband isn't worthy of your body. It's mine now, not his.

Claire: Yeah, keep going . . .

Jack: Then I'd put my hand on your neck. Not tightly . . . gently.

Just enough pressure so you know that I'm the one in control

Claire: Yes! Then what?

Jack: Then I'd ask you if you were ready to know what a real man feels like.

Claire: And I'd say 'Teach me'

Jack: And I'd say . . .

Claire: Yes, tell me what you'd say, Jack . . .

Jack: Good girl 😊

Tara was breathless. She hadn't ever experienced this kind of titillation from texting before. She had read erotic novels, sure, but nothing compared to the fact that Jack was on the other end, sharing the experience with her. She felt completely immersed in the fantasy with him. Like she had just lived through everything he had described. Her legs were like jelly.

Jack: I hope that wasn't too much? I got a bit carried away.

Claire: No, it wasn't too much at all, I was just catching my breath.

Jack: I'd love to see what you look like right now . . .

Claire: That's against the rules . . .

Jack: True . . . but the rules only say no face photos . . .

Tara immediately began to panic. She wasn't completely green, she knew what Jack meant. He was asking for a photo of her body. But she didn't currently feel very sexy in her white granny knickers, with a face full of Sudocrem.

Claire: Well, maybe I'll have to take some photos tomorrow to give you a reason to come back x

Jack: I think that sounds like a plan

Claire: But I want to see some photos of your body too. Fair is fair

Jack: Deal. I just hope I don't disappoint ☹

Claire: After what you just described, I don't think you could possibly disappoint me

Jack: Well, in that case, chat same time tomorrow?

Claire: Definitely. 11.11 p.m. x

Jack: I'll be counting down the minutes

Sweet dreams, Claire ☺

Claire: You too, Jack x

Tara felt like something within her had come back to life. She was still short of breath after imagining Jack taking control. She couldn't remember the last time she felt this aroused. She was downright flushed. Her drought was over. Her clouds had burst. She had prayed for rain but Jack had unleased a sensual storm, a tempest of temptation.

There was something about him she couldn't put her finger on. Their connection was almost primal. And how right her instincts were when she got her gut feeling about him. It had been years since she last experienced a synchronicity and she had almost forgotten how powerful a sensation it was. Enough to conjure her spirit and set her soul on fire. Her spiritual compass had found magnetic north and it was pulling her towards Jack. Tara had spent the past few months desperately searching for her destiny.

But destiny, it seemed, had found her.

Chapter 9

Tara woke up the next morning not entirely sure if her online encounter with Jack had been reality or some kind of erotic dream. When she realized that it had in fact happened, she found herself smiling uncontrollably. She had always been one of those people who dreaded getting up in the morning. Yet here she was waking up naturally an hour before her alarm and practically bouncing out of bed. Her inner soundtrack of sad depressing notes had been replaced by the opening glissando piano slide of ABBA's 'Dancing Queen'. What a gift Jack had given her. Music. She had gone from a state of perpetual numbness to a kaleidoscope of emotion. It was as if months of anaesthesia had finally worn off.

She felt awoken.

What was it about Jack that made it impossible for her not to smile? She felt a fit of euphoric laughter taking over her body. She hadn't experienced this kind of sexual chemistry since meeting Colin for the first time. But what she had with Jack felt different. It felt deliciously obscene. Fate was fuelling a forbidden fire. It was a more mystical, transformative kind of chemistry.

It was alchemy.

Jack had turned her heavy heart from lead to gold, like some virtual Midas touch. She felt recharged with erotic energy, her libido fully loaded. Her battery was at 100 per cent, her vitality restored. It was as if Jack had fulfilled some secret wish that she hadn't even remembered making, at least not consciously. He had scorched her leaves with light and saturated her roots with water. She felt her body ripening for her new gardener's touch, as if she had saved all her summers just for him. That's when she remembered the simple word for this feeling she had long forgotten.

She felt alive.

With her extra time before work, she decided to ditch the dry shampoo and enjoy a lengthy hot shower. She washed, conditioned and blow-dried her hair in a manner that gave it a bounce that dry shampoo simply couldn't compete with. Afterwards, Tara dug deep into the trenches of her closet and picked out a Millennial pink pencil dress with short cap sleeves that she hadn't worn in years. She opened up an unused True U make-up pallet that the company had gifted her and applied just enough to highlight her features. She slipped into a pair of rose gold heels and put on some drop earrings to match.

When Tara finally looked at herself in the mirror, initially she felt like a whole new woman. But when she thought about it, she realized that she actually felt more like herself than ever before. For the past few years she had been a shadow of her former self, an imposter she didn't even recognize. But now, there in the mirror, was the woman she used to be.

After sneaking down the stairs and avoiding Colin on the couch, it was time to start her day with her fresh new glow-up. When she arrived at Insight, her revamped aesthetic was turning heads. She saw members of staff she barely knew pop their heads above their cubicles, like curious little meerkats. Some people looked at her as if she was a completely new employee they had never seen before. Was she really that unrecognizable? She couldn't believe she had spent so long in frumpy pantsuits. She finally felt comfortable and confident in the clothes she actually wanted to wear. Although she did wish the dress had pockets.

As soon as Tara entered her office, Emily did a dramatic double-take and spat out her coffee.

'Who are you and what have you done with Tara?' she asked, her jaw on the floor.

'I gave her the day off. Claire's in charge today,' Tara smirked, taking her latte from Emily.

'Wait a minute ... did something happen on Fling last night?' Emily asked, putting the pieces together.

'What makes you think that?' Tara asked coyly.

'Oh please, you're practically giddy. Come on, spill the tea!'

'OK, you're right! I got a match last night. But not just any match. A one hundred per cent match!'

'OMG, who is he? What's his name?' she asked, dying for the gossip.

'His name is Jack. He's thirty-six and he lives right here in Dublin!' Tara said, unable to hide her excitement.

'And is he hot?' Emily said, expecting to see some kind of photo.

'He's more than just hot. He's sensual, understanding and so easy to talk to. He's definitely an Aries, I can tell,' Tara said.

'Good, that means you're getting *rammed*.'

'Emily, behave!'

'Come on, show me his photo already!'

'Well ... I don't have one ... I don't actually know what he looks like.'

'You just said he was hot!'

'Well, I could feel his heat through the phone,' Tara said, thinking back to their steamy conversation.

104

'I suppose it's a glass-half-full situation. He could be a supermodel or he could be a goblin. Depends if you're an optimist or a pessimist,' Emily said.

'There's no way he's ugly based on his texting. Or should I say . . . *sexting*!'

'Shut up! You two sexted? I'm so proud. I love being a bad influence on you. Show me the texts!'

'Some things are best left to the imagination, don't you think? Let's just say he left me feeling very . . . flattered. But something strange happened when we matched. Emily, in your psychology course, did you ever study something called synchronicity?' Tara asked.

'We skimmed over it, why?'

'Well, right when I matched with Jack on Fling, I got my gut feeling.'

'Ugh, I have IBS too. There's a probiotic in my bag if you want one?' Emily said.

'No, I mean my intuition feeling. The same feeling I got when I met Colin. I felt a synchronicity with Jack, the strongest one I've ever felt.'

'Hmm, from what I can remember, Carl Jung said synchronicity was the connecting principle and that all coincidences have meaning. But it's considered a pseudoscience because you can't technically prove it's real. How would you describe the feeling?'

Tara took a breath and collected her thoughts. It was such a peculiar thing to explain, and people often looked at her like she had ten heads whenever she brought it up. She hoped Emily would keep an open mind.

'It's like a sudden moment of clarity. What's that word? Epiphany! Like a little wink from the universe telling me I'm in the right place at the right time. It feels like women's intuition mixed with déjà vu. I get goosebumps all over and this tingle down the back of my neck. And I can feel a kind of vibration running through me, followed by a release,' Tara explained, struggling to find the words.

Silence. Emily was looking her up and down.

'Tara . . . are you sure you didn't just have an orgasm?' Emily asked, smirking.

'Oh for God's sake, not everything is about sex, Emily,' Tara said, throwing her eyes up to heaven.

'Maybe I've read too much Freud and not enough Jung,' Emily laughed. 'Either way, this means that your one hundred per cent match with Jack might not be random. There must be something to it.'

Tara felt incredibly relieved. Colin always made fun of her for believing in such things. It was nice to explain it to some-one with an open mind.

'But we have a problem, Emily. Jack wants me to send him a body pic tonight. And I don't know what to do!' Tara said, pacing across her office.

'Don't worry, I'm an expert at taking nudes,' Emily bragged.

'*Nudes?*' Tara gasped. 'Emily, I'm not taking nudes!'

'Oh calm down, you won't be fully nude in them. What kind of lingerie do you have at home?'

'Literally nothing, just plain old white knickers.'

'Oh God . . . not those granny ones?'

'They're very comfortable!'

'Dear Lord. OK, I have a plan. Come on, follow me,' Emily said, heading towards the door.

'Follow you where?'

'Ann Summers.'

'Emily, that's a sex shop! I'd be mortified. What if someone sees us?' Tara panicked.

'That's funny, I was under the impression that you weren't a Mary,' Emily said, unimpressed.

'I'm not! But I have that pitch meeting with Richard Mulligan at eleven and I haven't prepared a thing,' Tara said, panicking.

'I thought you were leaving it to the Lads?'

'I was . . . but I have a lot more in-depth knowledge about Fling since yesterday.'

'You're right. So technically going to Ann Summers to get some naughty underwear for your virtual lover is just more market research,' Emily said with a cheeky smile.

Tara paused for a moment to consider Emily's logic. 'I'll grab my coat,' she said.

Chapter 10

Colin arrived to work that same morning with a grin on his face that his colleagues had never seen before. His confidence was soaring after his tantalizing conversation with Claire the night before. He still couldn't quite believe what had happened.

Colin had gotten his mojo back.

When Rory saw Colin's cheeky smirk in the hallway, he immediately clocked what had happened.

'I know that look!' Rory said, a little too loudly.

'Shh, I'll tell you in my office,' Colin said, trying to maintain some semblance of professionalism. They entered his office and Colin closed the door behind them.

'She replied!' Colin said the second the door was closed.

'Unreal!' Rory said, every bit as excited as Colin. 'What did she say? Give me all the filthy details.'

'Well . . . she started flirting . . . so I started flirting back. And let's just say things eventually got pretty steamy,' Colin said, his grin now a coy smile.

'Nice one, so you had cam sex?'

'What? No.'

'Then how was it steamy?'

'Well, we were chatting and then I started telling her all the things we'd do in bed. I said I wanted to kiss her neck, whisper in her ear, throw her on the bed. It was pretty hot, if I do say so myself,' Colin said smugly.

'It sounds pretty soft-core, but I suppose you've been sex-starved for months,' Rory said. 'What's that old Irish saying? Hunger is the best sauce.'

'I'm telling you, it was raunchy,' Colin boasted.

'Either way, I'm just glad you're finally letting Colin Junior out on an adventure! He's still alive down there!' Rory crouched down and began trying to whack Colin in the crotch. Colin tried to block Rory's attack while playfully trying to whack him in his own crotch.

While the two were engaged in their boyish tomfoolery, Karen from HR walked past the window and caught a glimpse of what was happening. She let out a gasp and immediately opened the door.

'What is this? I smell horseplay!' Karen snapped. She was a short stout woman who had an asymmetric blond bob with unblended tiger-stripe highlights, a side-swept fringe and a spiky cut at the back.

'No horseplay at all Karen. Although I am hung like a horse if that's what you're asking,' Rory said, winding her up – his favourite pastime.

'Not a word out of you, Mr McKenna!' Karen yelled.

'Karen, I apologize on Rory's behalf,' Colin said before Rory could dig a bigger hole for himself. 'It's just a misunderstanding. I'll keep him in check.'

'Lickarse,' Rory coughed.

'JUST BEHAVE!' Karen said, slamming the door behind her as she stormed out.

'You see what I'm always saying, Colin. She's like the PC police. She's trying to take horseplay away from us!'

'You're lucky your surname is written on the front of the building – at least you can't be fired,' Colin said.

'Anyway, back to your midnight mistress,' Rory said. 'What does she look like? Let's see some pics.'

'We . . . haven't actually seen each other yet.'

'Yikes, you better be careful you're not getting catfished, man. She could be some ugly old hermit.'

'Hey, don't call her ugly,' Colin said, defending her honour.

'Fine, she could be . . . aesthetically challenged then. What if she's tricking you into liking her? Even I've been catfished, man. This one girl was a ten online but only a six when I met her in person.'

'Imagine how she felt when you told her ten inches online but only had six in person.'

'Joke all you want, Col, but I'm just trying to protect my boy from getting hurt,' Rory said, briefly revealing an inner tenderness.

'I appreciate it but there's no need to worry. We're exchanging pics tonight. But just bodies because face pics are against the rules. That's where I need your help. I've never taken a photo of my body in my life. What should I do?' Colin said. He barely used the camera on his phone for anything, let alone taking sexy self-portraits.

'You've come to the guru for this kind of thing, Colin. So here's how to make your body look good in photos. The first thing you do is put your right leg out . . .' Rory said, putting out his right leg.

Colin mimicked his movement.

'. . . then you pivot your body towards the door . . .' he continued.

Colin did the same, expecting that this would frame his body is some kind of way. 'OK, now what?'

'. . . and then you go to the gym, you fat bastard,' Rory said, collapsing into laughter.

'Oh for God's sake, I'm being serious, Rory. I need help!' Colin said, frustrated.

'You should have seen your face,' Rory said, still laughing.

'But I'm actually being serious. Grab your jacket, we're going to the gym across the road.'

'I can't just leave right now, I have too much on my plate,' Colin said, making excuses.

'Yeah, that's exactly the problem,' Rory said, pointing at Colin's midsection.

'You're hilarious,' Colin said, unimpressed. 'I don't even have any gym gear.'

'You can use my spare gear. Plus, I'm your boss and it's an order.'

'But I really need—'

'Remind me what your name is on Fling again?' Rory said, interrupting him.

'Jack.'

'Exactly. So grab your coat and let's get JACKED!'

Chapter 11

When Tara arrived outside Ann Summers, she popped up her coat collar and put on a pair of sunglasses to disguise herself.

'Good God, who are you hiding from? The other Marys?' Emily asked, mocking her.

'Emily, I can't just waltz into a sex shop in broad daylight! This is so out of character for me!' Tara whispered.

'WHY ARE YOU WHISPERING?' Emily yelled, drawing attention to them.

'OK, fine! Let's go in,' Tara said, taking off her shades and lowering her collar.

'Right, let's head to the lingerie section,' Emily said as they stepped inside. As they walked down the centre aisle, Tara saw some of the sex toys on sale. She didn't know what half of them even did but she could guess what the more phallic objects were used for. She was genuinely mortified even seeing the most common of sex toys, which was a testament to her naivety. She truly didn't know where to look and kept averting her eyes. Emily, on the other hand, strutted down the aisle like it was a runway.

'I feel like I'm doing the walk of shame,' Tara blushed.

'I call it the stride of pride,' Emily smirked.

As they walked through the store, they passed a sign that read 'Good Vibrators Only' and Emily stopped momentarily to see if any new arrivals had come in. 'See one you like?'

Tara nearly lost her life. 'Absolutely not. I wouldn't even know how to turn on a vibrator.'

'They're supposed to turn *you* on, silly.'

'We should go, Emily, I'm scarlet.'

'I thought you wanted to be a good feminist? If men wouldn't have burned you during the Salem witch trials then you're probably not living life to the fullest,' Emily insisted. 'Where is all this repression coming from anyway?'

'I grew up in Catholic Ireland, Emily. It was very different to the Ireland you grew up in,' Tara tried to explain.

'But even still. You're thirty-seven, not seventy. Something doesn't add up.'

'I don't know where it stems from. Maybe it was the nuns who gave me the sex education talk. And my dad was very Catholic too. I guess I've just been programmed not to break the rules.'

'Well, look at it this way,' Emily said. 'If you don't sin, Jesus died for nothing.'

They arrived at the lingerie section and Emily began to look on the rack for something suitable. As she was looking, a sales assistant came up behind them.

'Can I help . . . ?' the sales assistant said, startling Tara and causing her to make a shriek that drew the eyes of the other women in the store.

'Oh my God, you frightened the life out of me,' Tara said, catching her breath.

'My apologies, miss. My name is Ava, just let me know if you need help with anything,' she smiled.

'No, it's OK. We're not looking,' Tara said, embarrassed.

'Yes, we are,' Emily interrupted. 'My friend here is looking for some lingerie that says: "pin me down and make me yours".'

'EMILY!' Tara shrieked.

'We have just the thing,' Ava said. 'Follow me.'

They followed Ava into the back of the store where a mannequin was wearing a stunning lingerie set made up of a cherry-red lace plunge bra, lace panties and a velvet suspender belt connected to red silk stockings.

'We call this the Venus, for the woman who knows what she wants,' Ava said.

Tara stood in awe. It was like a work of art. It somehow felt so dominant and submissive at the same time, like a gift demanding to be unwrapped.

'We'll take it,' Emily said on Tara's behalf.

'EMILY!' Tara said, in shock. 'I can't pull this off. This is for a woman oozing with confidence. I'll look like a stuffed ham in it.'

'Will you stop putting yourself down. You said Jack is expecting a photo tonight. Do you really think he'll text back when he sees your granny knickers?'

'Well, if you're looking to impress a man with some erotic photos, the Venus will certainly get his attention,' Ava added.

Tara knew if she didn't buy it today, she never would.

'OK,' Tara said, daring herself. 'I'll take it!'

When Ava rang the items up at the till, Tara almost had heart failure once she heard the price. 'One hundred and twenty-six euro?' Tara gasped. She had never spent more than ten euro on underwear in her life.

'It's a special occasion, Tara,' Emily said, trying to justify it to her.

Although Tara was shocked, she knew she couldn't present herself to Jack in her usual undergarments. Anyway, she had spent years not feeling sexy and she deserved a day off from Catholic guilt. She put her card into the machine and entered her pin.

'Perfect. Here's your receipt,' Ava said, handing it to her along with the bag of lingerie.

'We're going to be using your fitting rooms before we leave. This woman has some selfies to take.'

'Of course, right down at the back,' Ava said. Emily headed down towards the fitting rooms and Tara chased after her with her bag of lace.

'Wait, we're taking the photos here? We're supposed to be at work! I'm supposed to be your mentor!' Tara said, chasing after her.

'Well, today I'm the mentor and you're the student so get in there and lace up!' Emily said, pointing to an empty stall.

Tara didn't resist any further because she was secretly dying to try on the items. She entered the dressing room and started to change. After a few minutes of figuring out where everything went, Tara pulled back the curtain to reveal a body worthy of sculpture.

'Oh my God! Clean up on aisle ME!' Emily shouted throughout the store.

'Shh,' Tara said, embarrassed by the attention. Tara walked out of the dressing room and looked at herself in the full-length mirror. She was every bit as shocked as Emily. It was like looking through a window to her past. She looked good. And she felt good.

'Jack, eat your heart out,' Tara said, taking in her own image.

'I'm starting to like Claire more than Tara,' Emily said. 'This Jack has turned you into a whole new woman.'

'There's something about him, Emily. It's like he sees me. The real me.'

'Well, he's definitely about to see the real you with these pics.'

'OK . . . so now what do I do?'

'Nudes are all about the angles. Everybody looks better from a high angle, looking down. So hold your phone up high and take a selfie facing downwards. But don't forget to crop out your face. Never send full body nudes or believe me, somebody will leak them. You can't trust anyone,' Emily explained, with an air of experience.

'Oh God, did someone leak yours?' Tara asked, concerned.

'Oh, I leaked my own nudes. I can't even trust myself,' Emily laughed.

Tara followed Emily's instructions and held her phone up high to take a selfie. She obscured her face and pointed the camera at her breasts. They looked exquisite in the red lace push-up bra, if she did say so herself.

She was beaming with confidence at this point and she took about a dozen other pics from different angles, showing off the lingerie in all its glory. After a few minutes, and plenty of instructions from Emily, she was confident she had got the perfect pic for Jack.

'That's it, that's the money shot!' Emily said, seeing the final image. 'I'm calling it The Rebirth of Venus and hanging it in the Louvre.'

'Well, that's a bit generous, Emily, but thank you,' Tara said, flattered. 'Although I still can't quite believe I had the confidence to walk into a sex shop and not care what people think.'

'Tara, can I let you in on a little secret?'

'By all means.'

'Confidence isn't just when you stop caring what people think. It's when you stop thinking that people care. Usually when you think people are judging you, it's all in your head.'

'You're right,' Tara said, looking around. 'I have nothing to be ashamed of.'

'Then my work here is done. The student has become the master. Or should I say . . . the mistress,' Emily said proudly.

'Thanks so much for your help, Emily. I hope this is still valuable experience for your CV.'

'Content creation is a very important skill these days.'

'OK, let me just change out of this before we go,' Tara said, pulling the curtain closed.

'Nope,' Emily said, pulling the curtain back open. She grabbed Tara's pair of granny knickers off the floor. 'These are going in the bin.'

Chapter 12

As Colin put on Rory's gym gear in the locker room, he found it to be a little tight around his waist. 'Aren't gym clothes supposed to be comfortable?' he asked, frustrated.

'No, rookie mistake,' Rory explained. 'The gym is where I pick up most women. It's full of raw sexual instinct. We're in the wild here. Pure Darwinian natural selection.'

'I don't think women even really care that much about muscles.'

'They say they don't, which means they do. I didn't invent jungle law, Colin. I just obey it. And if my gym gear is too tight, don't be discouraged. Try and keep your chins up.'

'I'm not fat!' Colin said defensively.

'Oh stop taking everything I say so seriously, I'm only winding you up. You're actually in decent shape. But we need to get you a good pump for these pics.'

Rory led Colin on to the gym floor. It wasn't overly busy but Colin was still intimidated by all the v-shaped backs and rock hard abs. He had got into weightlifting in college and gained an impressive amount of strength in the one year he attended the college gym. But his testosterone levels would have been a lot higher back then so he would likely be starting from scratch now.

'OK, so first things first, we need to discuss your problem

areas,' Rory said when they arrived in the free weights section.

Colin looked in the mirror as Rory circled him, scanning his body for flaws.

'Right, so the overall problem is that you have a dad bod,' Rory concluded.

'How can I have a dad bod? I'm not even a dad!' Colin said, annoyed by the term.

'Doesn't stop you telling dad jokes, does it? Look, you're not fat, but you're not exactly toned either. But don't worry, you're giving me a lot to work with here. I see a lot of potential.'

'This feels like that show *Queer Eye* that Tara watches. Except you're a flaming heterosexual.'

'The good news is, you're in a very good position to tone up,' Rory continued. 'We just need to focus on burning some fat. Think of your fat as a marble sculpture, we just need to chisel some off to reveal the muscle underneath.'

'I think that makes sense.'

'Now, personally, the only cardio I do is sex,' Rory said, raising his voice so an attractive woman in leggings would hear. 'But that's not really an option for you. Instead, I think you should focus on good old-fashioned heavy lifting.'

Colin was intimidated by the idea, considering how long it had been since he was last in shape. Still, Rory did have a great physique and he was willing to trust his advice. Personal trainers were expensive after all, and Colin was essentially getting one for free.

Rory had even set up his own PT business when he was twenty-five that he claimed would 'change the face of fitness'. He had bought a van, filled it with gym equipment and began travelling door-to-door, taking the gym directly to his clients.

It was a good idea on paper, but in retrospect, the brand name 'Jehovah's Fitness' may not have been the best the decision.

'OK, teach me more, guru,' Colin said, inflating Rory's ego.

'We're going to start with the foundation of all body-building. The bench press,' Rory said, putting a towel over a bench to mark his territory. 'Now, some guys will tell you that squats and deadlifts are more important, but trust me, women care more about a big chest than big thighs. It's the law of the jungle. And I'm the expert on jungle law. I'm the alpha.'

'Calling yourself the alpha doesn't sound like something an alpha would do,' Colin said, trying to humble him. An impossible task.

Rory began stacking weight plates onto a steel barbell above the bench.

'Watch my movements,' he said, sitting down and gripping the barbell. 'Arch your back. Arms shoulder-length apart. Firm grip on the bar. Bring it down to your chest slowly. Then slowly push it back up.'

Rory put the barbell back down on the rack and got up off the bench. 'You're up,' he instructed.

Colin lay back on the bench and gripped the barbell. He knew the basics from college but he still wanted to make sure his form was correct.

'OK, arch your back,' Rory coached him. 'Firm grip, lower the bar slowly. And push back up. Good. Now repeat eight times.'

Colin completed eight repetitions and didn't feel very challenged.

'Nice one. So that was thirty kilos, let's try forty,' Rory said, loading two more small plates.

'That seemed kind of light though, can we double it?' Colin asked.

'Wow, OK, big man, let's double it to sixty then,' Rory

said, adding the extra plates. Colin performed eight reps of sixty kilos with surprising ease. He felt a little resistance on the last rep but it was nothing too intense. But he most certainly felt the pump Rory had mentioned. He could feel the blood coursing through his chest and it made it look significantly bigger in the mirror.

'OK, now that you've got a nice pump going, it's time to take some pics. Take out your phone and get closer to the mirror. Close enough to the camera in the photo,' Rory instructed.

Colin approached the mirror so that he could only see his body on screen. He sucked in his stomach, held his breath and took the photo. Rory leaned over to see it.

'Straighten up, you have the posture of a question mark,' Rory said, hyperbolic as always.

Colin straightened his spine and put his shoulders back.

'Better,' Rory said, examining him intensely. 'But widen your frame a bit more. You want to make your upper body appear bigger than your waist. So stick out your lat muscles.'

'Which ones are my lat muscles again?' Colin said, clueless.

'Your side muscles on your back, stick them out and widen your back.'

Colin widened his back and immediately saw a difference in his appearance. He had a far manlier frame just by changing that one thing. That, coupled with his new pump, made Colin appear quite attractive on his phone's screen. He took a few photos in this position, feeling very happy with the result. He only hoped that Claire would feel the same.

Rory grabbed his phone and had a look at the photos.

'Not bad, let's just filter these.'

'Why do they need to be filtered?'

'Because your pasty Irish skin makes you look like a milk bottle. We need to make you look like you've seen the sun at least once in your life.' Rory worked some kind of magic on Colin's phone and he suddenly had a nice golden tan in the photo.

'See, now Claire will think you're just home from a two-week trip to Bali.'

Colin had no idea how Rory had done that on his phone but he wasn't going to question it. Filtering a photo was an alien concept to him. He had no social media presence what-soever so his self-image wasn't something that ever crossed his mind. Plus, this was the first 'dating' app he had ever used and the idea of appearing attractive online was very new territory for him. But now that he saw his idealized self on the screen, he liked what he saw. It was like a mirror that reflected things not how they were, but rather how they could be.

'These look great,' Colin said. 'I just hope Claire likes them.'

'Oh she will. And they'll give you the perfect opportunity to ask her to meet up this weekend.'

'This weekend? Isn't that a bit soon?'

'With women, you have to strike when the iron is hot.'

'But where should I take her? What if she says no?' Colin panicked.

'You have to go big or go home if you want to impress her. You need to invite her to The Vine on Dawson Street. No woman can resist it. She'll be like a moth to a flame.'

'There's no way I'm going to get a table for this weekend. They're always fully booked weeks in advance,' Colin said disheartened.

'Yeah, but yours truly happens to be a very valued cus-tomer. Don't worry, I'll be able to get Jack a table for two,' Rory said with full confidence. 'Now, let's move on to bicep curls.'

'Can I try a heavier weight on the bench press first? Sixty kilos didn't feel very heavy,' Colin said, eager to prove himself.

'Right then, Mr Universe, let's give you eighty kilos to kick you off your high horse,' Rory teased, adding the weight.

'Bring it on,' Colin said, gripping the bar.

He lowered the weight down towards his chest and pushed back up. Admittedly, he felt a lot more resistance with this weight, but it was nothing he couldn't handle. He finished his eighth rep and still didn't break much of a sweat.

'I'd say you're wrecked after that,' Rory said hopefully.

'Not really, I still didn't feel much strain,' Colin said, hungry for more.

'Are you serious? Eighty kilos is a very heavy weight. That's like two hundred and twenty pounds!'

'That conversion is definitely wrong,' Colin said, running the numbers in his head. 'Just give me one hundred kilos.'

'Have you lost your mind?' Rory shrieked. 'My one rep max is only ninety.'

'Afraid I'll embarrass you by beating your personal record?'

'I'm afraid you'll hurt yourself. Even one rep of one hundred is too heavy.'

'Wanna bet?'

'As a matter of fact, I do. What are the terms?' Rory said confidently.

Colin thought about what he wanted from Rory. He was already the most laissez-faire boss imaginable so anything Colin wanted at work he could get from him anyway. He suddenly remembered Rory bragging about his new golf membership at the Imperial Dublin Golf Club. Colin wanted to become a member but had put the money towards IVF instead.

'OK, if I'm able to do one single rep with one hundred kilos, you have to let me play at your fancy new golf club,' Colin said.

'My membership only allows one player and one caddy,' Rory said.

'I know. Which is why I'm going to play and you're going to caddy. And I get to choose when I get to play, regardless of your schedule.'

'Ugh, fine! But if I win, you have to tell Karen in HR that her bone structure gives your bone structure,' Rory said, smirking at the idea.

It took a second for Colin to wrap his head around Rory's sentence. Once he made sense of it, the thought of saying it to Karen was horrifying. On any other day, Colin wouldn't have taken the bet, but his new confidence convinced him he could lift the weight.

'You're on,' he said, lying down on the bench and gripping the barbell. Rory stood over him, ready to catch the bar.

Colin pushed the weight up and immediately realized that the resistance was too much for him. Still, the bar was now in the air and he only had to perform one rep to win the bet. Colin lowered the weight down towards his chest where he held it for a second. He wasn't sure if he had the rep in him, but then he imagined Claire watching. He imagined how much it would turn her on if he picked her up like this weight and threw her onto the bed as if she was a feather. The pressure on his arms was becoming greater and greater. If he didn't push the weight now his arms would give out. He decided to give it everything he had. For Claire.

To Rory's shock, the barbell began to rise back up as Colin gave out a massive grunt that made other gym-goers look over. He pushed until his arms were fully extended and the weight was secured back on the rack. Rory stood in disbelief as Colin got off the bench. The pump he felt earlier was nothing in comparison to this. He felt as if his entire body was erect.

'How is that even possible?' Rory said, visibly fuming. 'You don't even have big chest muscles! You don't even lift.

It's beginner's luck. Your body obviously kicked in some adrenaline response and went into overdrive. That's the only explanation for how you could lift more than me.'

Rory was out of breath from pure annoyance.

'Well, I'm no expert on jungle law,' Colin said. 'But I think this makes me the alpha.'

Chapter 13

Tara strutted back to the office with the unbridled confidence she had once believed was exclusive to women in their twenties. She loved the feeling of the lace lingerie underneath her pencil dress. It was a far cry from granny knickers and shapeless pantsuits. When they arrived back to Insight, Emily wished Tara good luck as she sashayed into the boardroom, looking and feeling like a million dollars.

'You don't mind if I sit in, do you?' she said, emitting a charismatic aura the Lads had never seen before.

Tommy, Mark and Rob looked at her in complete and utter shock. She knew by their faces alone that she had already proved the point she was trying to make: Tara was not a Mary.

'Tara . . . we've already started. I'm afraid you're a little late,' Tommy said, trying to exclude her.

'Am I?' she said. 'Or did you boys just come early?'

At the back of the boardroom, Tara heard a quiet laugh from Richard Mulligan. He looked different than Tara had imagined. He was older than his voice had portrayed, maybe around forty-five. He was exceptionally well groomed but he had one of the worst receding hairlines Tara had ever seen, undermining his attractiveness. And his was definitely a face for radio.

Tara sat down on the opposite side of the desk to the Lads.

She had every right to be there – and Tommy was still on the first slide of his presentation. 'Shall we?' she said, signalling him to continue.

Tommy began with a slideshow presentation of their proposed marketing strategy. As usual, Tara hadn't been consulted on any aspects of their pitch so she had no idea what was coming. It was typical of the Lads to exclude her when products were considered masculine.

'Well, Tara, we were just congratulating Mr Mulligan on his impressive launch,' Tommy continued. 'I don't think there's a person in the country who hasn't at least heard of Fling by now.'

'Thank you,' Richard said, his face not showing any emotion.

'Although just some feedback, Mr Mulligan, if I may?' Rob said out of nowhere. 'I joined Fling to . . . analyse the customer experience . . . but I discovered a glitch within the app.'

'My tech team eradicated all glitches in beta testing,' Richard said confidently.

'Well, they must have missed one because when I joined, I didn't get any matches. Not a single one,' Rob said with an awkward laugh.

'That sounds like a "you" problem, not a "tech" problem,' Richard said, silencing him.

Tara laughed to herself and noticed Richard smirking when he saw her reaction.

'As I was saying,' Tommy said, giving Rob a dirty look, 'you've certainly hit the ground running . . . but we think it's just the beginning for Fling. That's why we've put together a marketing strategy and advertising campaign that is going to take your app to the next level.'

Tommy clicked to the next slide to reveal an image of a scantily clad woman against a dark background. She was holding one finger against her red lips as if she was telling the viewer to keep a secret. Tara rolled her eyes at the image's lack of originality.

'This game-changing marketing campaign will be targeting married people exclusively, to ensure you get the most bang for your buck. The sexually suggestive images we'll be using will arouse a very physical response for the target market and communicate the idea of temptation. We all know that sex sells, and that's how we get them to click the ad and download the app. It's not enough to think outside the box, we need to think outside the cube.'

Tara cringed. Another one of Tommy's catchphrases that didn't mean anything. And using sex to sell to men wasn't thinking outside the box, let alone the cube. Tommy continued through his slideshow for what felt like a lifetime. The campaign was a tasteless, tacky attempt to arouse men enough to want to cheat. Tommy eventually wrapped up with his proposed slogan. 'You have the wife . . . now all you need is a mistress,' he said, genuinely proud of his work.

Rob and Mark began to applaud Tommy when he had finished. She wasn't surprised. They were the type of people who clap when a plane lands: any excuse to make noise. But once they had stopped, a sudden silence came over the room. Everyone looked towards Richard Mulligan as he leaned back in his chair.

'No,' he said nonchalantly.

'I'm sorry?' Tommy said, certain he had misheard.

'I hate it,' Richard said unapologetically.

'Mr Mulligan, we can tweak any aspect of the pitch that you'd like,' Tommy responded, beads of sweat appearing on his forehead.

'No, I think I'd better get going. Unless . . . you have anything better to add?' Richard asked, turning to Tara.

All eyes were suddenly on her. She was their colleague and she didn't want to insult their proposal. But she had been asked a direct question and she needed to answer. She considered saying as little as she could to end the meeting quickly, but something told her to speak her mind. She had been a little too quiet for a little too long.

Tara had downloaded Fling and got a 100 per cent match. If anyone knew how to pitch it, it was her. Anyway, the Lads had already lost the account, so she had nothing to lose and everything to gain. Under normal circumstances, Tara would never have felt confident enough to pitch an idea completely on the fly. But she reminded herself that she had given Tara the day off.

It was Claire's time to shine.

'As a matter of fact, I do,' Tara said, standing up.

Tommy almost choked on the sip of water he'd just taken. Richard Mulligan leaned back in his chair once again. The spotlight was on her.

It was time to reel in a big fish and prove she was still on the top of her game.

'Well, although I can see where my colleagues were coming from,' Tara said, as she began to saunter around the room, 'they missed the target. Quite literally. Mr Mulligan, I'm willing to bet that when you look at your user data, you have a lot more men on the app than women. The advertising proposal you just saw would only make that problem ten times worse. Your challenge isn't going to be getting men to join, it's about making sure there's a perfect match for everyone. And to do that, you need women. The campaign you saw panders to the male gaze and, quite frankly, makes it seem like an escort service. The women who join Fling aren't the models in those stock photos. They're regular women who feel trapped in their own lives. Women who feel that the more they do, the more they're taken for granted. Women who feel completely alone in their marriages. She doesn't want to leave her husband, but maybe her match on Fling will awaken something in her. Maybe her match will make her feel like the woman she used to be. Maybe her match will make her feel alive. She's already found Mr Right but maybe she needs Mr Wrong, even just for a night. Mr Mulligan, you don't need a big controversial advertising campaign. Everyone is already talking about Fling. Your strategy shouldn't be to outrage the Marys of the world. It should be about showing them that it's OK to be someone else for a day. To take a break from your own life. To have a day off from being unhappy. I don't have a fancy presentation ready for you right this minute, Mr Mulligan, but if you were to give me the chance to put one together for you, I'd start with that. Women are flowers. And your target market are the ones who are wilting.'

The room went silent for several excruciating seconds as everyone absorbed Tara's improvised pitch. She had no idea what the reaction would be, and held her breath in anticipation. Richard was looking at her intently, the way a lion looks at a gazelle.

'Yes,' he said at long last. 'Finally, someone who gets it.'

Tara was shocked. She let the breath she was holding leave her lungs. She had pulled it off.

'I'm happy to give Insight the account,' he said, getting up.

'Can't wait to work together, Mr Mulligan!' Tommy said, sticking out his hand, trying to imply that he had landed the deal.

Richard looked blankly at Tommy's extended hand and then back at his face.

'Under one condition,' he said, turning to Tara. 'I want you to take the lead.'

The Lads were visibly raging. Richard smiled and extended

130

a handshake to Tara. She was in shock at what she had just pulled off. She hadn't imagined doing anything like that when she entered the meeting. Was it the dress? Her make-up? The lingerie? No, it was something deeper, like an inner confidence that had finally been unlocked. The clothes and make-up may have been the key but the power had always been within her, waiting to be unleashed.

She had spent so long trying to be one of the Lads that she had stripped down every aspect of her femininity to get a seat at the table. She always thought gaining power meant acting like a man but she had just been proven wrong. Here she was after closing a deal in a pencil dress, with a full set of lace lingerie underneath. It was her secret coat of armour that gave her the confidence to charge into battle. After four long years, she had finally proved she still had it.

'Tara, let's schedule a full pitch meeting in two weeks. I'll want to see specific targeting, creative copy, advertising strategy, the works. Have your assistant arrange somewhere nice for us to have lunch and you can give me a full rundown. But Tara, you've set my expectations very high so I expect this pitch to be a knockout. Shouldn't be difficult for you,' he said flirtatiously.

'I promise, Mr Mulligan, you won't know what's hit you,' Tara said, excited.

'Please,' he said, with a carnivorous smile. 'Call me Dick.'

Chapter 14

To celebrate landing the Fling account, Tara decided to do a little shopping on her way home from work. She bought a sign that said 'Live, Laugh, Love', just to spite Colin. She also bought one that read 'Don't Worry, Be Happy' as a not-so-subtle dig for his whinging over not getting his preferred dinner.

But the most deliciously spiteful thing that Tara bought was her very own state-of-the-art air fryer. She chose the most obnoxiously large one she could find, to ensure it didn't go unnoticed. It wasn't cheap but it was a small price to pay to prove a point. Colin still hadn't unloaded the dishwasher, so she would be cooking for one for the foreseeable future. She had bought herself a week's worth of food that was all air-fryer friendly, most notably her favourite thing in the world: cheesy garlic bread. Tara normally avoided such an indulgence but after such a successful day, it was time to treat herself.

When Tara and Colin finally sat at the kitchen table for their separate dinners, they were both hell-bent on letting each other know that they were having a wonderful day and completely unbothered by their fight the night before.

Colin began to dig into his meal which consisted of the two rib-eye steaks, sweet potato fries and onion rings. He cracked open a can of cold beer in such an exaggerated manner that the noise rippled through the entire house. 'Ahh,' he said, taking a big slurp directly from the can. 'Fit for a king.'

Tara's blood began to boil at the sound of his slurping, but she'd sooner take her grave than let Colin see he was getting to her. Tara poured herself her usual generous glass of wine but this time she did it without an iota of guilt, humming a chirpy tune. She had air-fried a Cajun chicken breast, a bed of vegetables and three pieces of cheesy garlic bread in under ten minutes. Now was the moment of truth. She took her first bite into her garlic bread and began moaning euphorically.

'Oh my God,' she said in an almost orgasmic manner.

'I didn't know garlic bread was an aphrodisiac,' Colin said, raising an eyebrow.

'Not just any garlic bread. Air-fried garlic bread.'

'Sounds like you can really taste the air.'

'Mmm . . . Better than sex,' Tara said with a smug grin. 'And it's such a healthy way to cook.'

'I'm not sure if it air-fries the calories out of the food. But you know best, darling. You're the garlic breadwinner after all,' Colin said sarcastically.

'Well, I might as well eat whatever I want considering I'm a barrel.'

'Not sure if those were my exact words.'

'No, I remember it perfectly. Elephants never forget,' Tara said with a spiteful smile.

Colin knew what Tara was doing. He hadn't called her a barrel or an elephant. She was choosing to misinterpret what he said so she could play the victim. He wasn't having any of it. He looked to his left to see Tara's new kitchen sign. The four words were stylized in a confusing, artistic way with an awful squiggly font.

'Don't Be Happy . . . Worry?' he said, squinting at the sign.

'It's Don't Worry, Be Happy!' Tara said, letting her

133

frustration show a bit too much. She took a breath and re-adjusted herself. 'Just wanted to make the kitchen a bit cosier. You know, seeing as it's where I belong.'

'I should actually put my vintage beer signs up in my man cave,' Colin said, ignoring her dig.

Tara nearly choked. 'I'm sorry, your . . . what?'

'Man cave. Seeing as the couch is where I belong, that's the room's new name.'

'Is that like a working title? Because last time I checked it was called the living room,' Tara said, rolling her eyes.

'I think my pub signs are in the shed actually . . . I must go out and get them,' Colin said, knowing well that Tara hated his collection. When they had first moved into the house, Tara had forbidden them, just as Colin forbade tacky kitchen quotes. At the time, they had compromised and agreed to only hang wall art with no text on it. But now, Tara had broken the truce so Colin was ready to fight fire with fire.

'Great, why don't you clean the shed while you're out there?' Tara suggested.

'I think I'll focus on redecorating the living room first,' Colin said smugly.

'Well, let's hope you don't die in there from bad taste.'

'That would be ironic.'

'What would?'

'Dying in the living room,' Colin replied, taking another gulp of beer. 'I have to say the couch is incredibly comfortable. I had one of the best night's sleep in years.'

'That's so funny, I was about to say the exact same thing. I woke up so recharged. I had forgotten what it was like to sleep in a room without constant snoring,' Tara said, adding a fake laugh for an extra touch.

'It's nice to wake up on the right side of the bed for a change, isn't it?'

'Finally, something we both agree on. Then again, you know what they say. If a man agrees with you, you've probably said something stupid.'

'I couldn't agree more . . . babe.'

Tara had many pet peeves but at the very top of the list was being called 'babe'. Colin knew that and she knew that he knew. She resisted every urge within her to scream. She refused to give him the satisfaction. Thankfully, Colin had a pet name he despised as well.

'Glad to hear it . . . honeybun,' Tara said, intently locking eyes with him.

Colin had to use every bit of his willpower not to wince. He returned Tara's intense gaze. He felt as if he was in a spaghetti western, engaged in a pistols-at-dawn-style stand-off with his own wife.

Tara knew that their tit-for-tat farce would only lead them in circles, so she took out her phone to appear uninterested. She opened Fling to see if Jack was online. Even though his green light wasn't on, she decided to send him a text to build some anticipation, almost like foreplay before the main event that night.

Claire: Excited to show you some pics tonight x

Tara put her phone down and took a big sip of wine, feeling satisfied with herself. She loved that Colin had no idea that she had taken erotic photos for another man and was now texting him in plain sight.

Colin felt his phone vibrate silently in his pocket. He took it out and read the message from Claire. He felt his heart rate increase. He loved the danger of texting Claire while his wife was in the room. He was living a double life right under

135

her nose and the rush was intoxicating. He began to type his reply, hiding the phone under the table, just out of Tara's view.

> **Jack:** It's all I've been thinking about all day. I took some for you too 😊

Tara looked back down at her phone and saw Jack's message. She began to laugh audibly in a girlish way to irritate Colin. She wanted to make it clear she had checked out of their dinner conversation. She began to reply to Jack.

> **Claire:** Can't wait to show you x My husband is driving me up the wall!

> **Jack:** I feel your pain! But living a double life with you is keeping me going 😊

> **Claire:** Same time tonight? x

> **Jack:** 11.11. I'll be there 😊

> **Claire:** Chat then x

Tara closed the app and let out one more theatrical laugh to annoy Colin. A part of her couldn't believe her actions. Sexting her virtual lover while having dinner with her unsuspecting husband felt so transgressive, so bold. But she knew exactly what Jack meant. It turned her on too. The sheer

136

recklessness of it all was so irresistible. 11.11 couldn't come quick enough.

After finishing her meal, Tara grabbed her wine and walked towards the door.

'Enjoy your night, honeybun,' Tara said, making it clear her night didn't involve Colin.

'You too, babe,' Colin replied, making it clear he didn't care.

Chapter 15

While waiting for the clock to strike 11.11, Colin decided to make good on his promise to hang up his vintage pub signs in his man cave. He went out to the backyard and opened the shed door. He was immediately greeted by a wall of dust and made a mental note to take an antihistamine later. He rooted through the many boxes in the shed, unable to remember which box contained the signs. That was the main reason Tara had been nagging him to clean the shed for so long. All of her boxes were labelled but Colin didn't share her knack for storage organization.

As he was looking, he saw a large dust sheet laid across something big. Colin pulled off the sheet to reveal his 1988 Triumph Bonneville motorcycle. He had almost forgotten how beautiful it was. And sitting right on the seat was a crate containing his vintage pub signs.

Jackpot.

Colin kicked some boxes out of the way and wheeled the bike out of the shed, into the light. She was a beauty, but sadly an ageing one. She was a vintage Bonneville and he had nicknamed her Bonnie. He, of course, was her Clyde. There was some rust on her body despite her being kept in storage and it was clear she needed a lot of work. Like himself, she hadn't escaped the cruel hands of time. Colin began to think about how far he had drifted from his rebellious nature. The bike that had once made him feel like an untameable renegade had spent ten years in a suburban shed. It didn't feel right.

Maybe there were still some miles left on her tyres. She wasn't beyond repair, though, and Colin could tell looking at her that she could be saved with some tender love and care. Due to the bike's age, procuring parts wasn't the most straightforward process, but it was a challenge Colin was up for.

He killed an hour giving the bike a shine and taking note of which parts needed replacing. After he was finished, he decided to leave Bonnie in the back garden to give her some air. She had been locked up for far too long. And a part of him wanted Tara to see the bike out of the shed.

He grabbed the crate of pub signs and brought them into his man cave. When he was finished hanging each of them up with adhesive strips, he stood in the middle of the room and admired the rustic saloon-like vibe they gave the room. It now felt like a proper man cave. 'Guinness is good for you', one sign read. 'This Bud's for you', read another.

There were about twenty of them in total, each one a unique collector's item in its own right. As he looked around the newly decorated room, he felt a sense of pride in his work. Not because the work was particularly challenging but because he had done something he wasn't supposed to. It was a small act of rebellion but an act of rebellion nonetheless.

After his revolutionary evening faded into night, Colin lay down on the couch, ready to chat with Claire. Tara was now in bed for the night so the coast was officially clear.

Claire's online light turned green at 11.11 exactly and Colin's face lit up with anticipation. He could see the moving ellipsis that indicated she was typing. After an entire day of counting down the minutes, their late-night rendezvous was about to begin.

Claire: Hey there, stranger x

Jack: Hey sexy, how was your day? 😳

Claire: I had an amazing day thanks to you x

Jack: Oh really?

Claire: Yeah, I woke up thinking our conversation last night was a dream

But then I realized it wasn't x

Jack: Well, that's good to hear because I couldn't stop thinking about you all day

Claire: Oh really? What were you thinking about doing to me? x

Jack: All sorts of sordid things 😊

I was thinking about you especially when I was lifting in the gym

Claire: Oh, you're into bodybuilding?

Jack: Yeah, it's a passion of mine

Claire: You just keep getting better and better. I bet your muscles are huge x

Jack: I'm not usually one to brag but I benched 100kg today. All because of you

Claire: Because of me?

Jack: I've never lifted a weight like that before.

But when I was about to lift it, I just pictured you sitting on top of me and I was able to lift it 😊

Claire: You don't even know what I look like haha

Jack: Oh yeah haha

We better fix that . . .

Claire: Well, I really hope the photos I took live up to the image of me you have in your head

Jack: Oh don't worry, I know they will . . .

Claire: Can I ask a favour?

Jack: Of course

Claire: Can you send your photos first? I'm kinda nervous.

I've never done anything like this before, it's all still so new to me x

Jack: I understand. And just so you know, this is all new to me too so please don't feel nervous.

I took these pics in the gym today. I hope you like them . . .

Claire: I know I will x

Jack: Image Delivered

Image Delivered

Image Delivered

It was the moment of truth, and every second she didn't reply felt like an eternity. He thought he looked good, but for all he knew, Claire had extremely high standards for men. He regretted saying he was passionate about bodybuilding. He had only gone once for heaven's sake. And Rory said he had a dad bod! She hadn't responded in about sixty seconds and Colin was sure she had lost interest.

142

Jack: If I'm not your type, I understand . . .

Claire: Are you serious? I was trying to catch my breath again.

You have a habit of leaving me breathless x

Jack: Phew, I thought you were about to block me or something haha

Claire: Block a guy with a body like THAT? I don't see that happening!

You're so masculine. Your back is so wide.

Ugh and that tan. It's obvious you're no stranger to sun x

Jack: You got me, I love to travel 😊

Claire: Ugh same x

Jack: Imagine me and you escaping to a tropical island somewhere . . .

White beaches, cocktails 😊

Claire: How do you always know the right thing to say?

Jack: Haha seems like we just both want the same things

So . . . I guess it's your turn to send a photo . . .

After seeing Jack's photos, Tara felt even more nervous sending hers. She was shocked when she saw Jack's body pic in the gym. He was exactly how she fantasized he would be. She wished she could see the face attached to his body but she knew it was against the rules.

Now it was her turn. She hoped to God he would like her pics. They were genuine photos of herself, albeit an artistic interpretation of her body. But Jack made her feel like the best version of herself and that's the version she wanted to show him. And isn't that what nudes have been for centuries? A way of expressing the beauty of the human body? What was once done with a paintbrush was now done with a smartphone, but the principle remained the same. Tara hit send on her risqué photos.

Claire: Image Delivered

Image Delivered

Image Delivered

Jack: IS THAT REALLY YOU?

Claire: Of course, I took those pics today x

Jack: I'm speechless . . .

Claire: In a good way?

Jack: YES IN A GOOD WAY! YOU'RE PERFECT!

Claire: I warned you, flattery will get you everywhere x

Jack: You're even more beautiful than I imagined. That lingerie is such a turn on 😊

Claire: I bought it today, just for you x

Jack: Really? 😊

Claire: Yeah. I'm not usually a very 'sexy' person but I wanted to be . . . for you x

Jack: As much as I love looking at it, I'd have even more fun tearing it off 😊

Claire: Well, it's a gift to you so it's only right that you unwrap it however you want x

Jack: The real gift is what's underneath the wrapping

Your husband doesn't deserve that body

Claire: He doesn't even notice it x

Jack: I don't know how he can't see what's right in front of him

But all the better for me 😊

Claire: It's yours x

He could never lift a 100kg weight

Jack: I wish I could break into your house right now and take you.

I wouldn't even stop if he walked in on us.

I'd look him dead in the eye and keep going 😊

Claire: Why is that such a turn on? I'd give anything to have you beside me right now.

I keep looking at your gym pic. Your wife is a very lucky woman

Jack: She's lost all interest. I could be standing there fully naked and she wouldn't notice

Claire: I know what it's like to feel unseen 😦

Even when me and my husband fight, all I want is for him to grab me and kiss me

But he's completely oblivious to what I really want

Jack: I'd grab you and kiss you, Claire 😊

Claire: I know you would, Jack. And I wouldn't even have to ask you

You'd just know how much I want you to take me x

I have this burning desire for you x

Jack: I feel exactly the same.

It's like I've known you my whole life 😊

Claire: Honestly, I joined Fling just to prove something to myself

I never actually expected to find someone like you

Let alone want to meet you x

Jack: Well, I mean, that's what Fling is for. Once we like each other, the next step is to meet in person and see if we feel the connection in real life 😊

Claire: You're right x

Oh my God, are we crazy? x

Jack: I'm crazy about you, that's all I know 😊

Claire: It feels so risky, meeting publicly in person

But it's all I want to do x

Jack: How about this Saturday. The Vine. 8 p.m.

Claire: Wow, The Vine? You sure know how to impress a girl x

But will you be able to get a table at such short notice?

Jack: Let me take care of everything 😊

Claire: Ugh, you always know what to say x

My husband wouldn't take me to The Vine if his life depended on it

Jack: Well, while he's taking you for granted, I'm taking you for drinks 😊

What do you say?

Claire: My brain is telling me that this is completely crazy and that I should be locked up

But my body is telling me I have to meet you. Even if it's just to see if our connection is real x

Jack: Exactly. We need to know

Claire: OK. Yes x

Jack: I'll make all the arrangements.

Claire: You certainly know how to sweep a girl off her feet x

Jack: Leave it all to me. All you have to do is be there 😊

Claire: Today is only Tuesday. The anticipation is going to kill us all week haha

Jack: Well, we're just going to have to continue our late-night rendezvous every night until then

Claire: 11.11 p.m. every night work for you? x

Jack: I wouldn't miss it for the world 😊

Chapter 16

The moment Tara woke up on Saturday morning, she immediately began preparing for her date with Jack that evening.
She thought back over their multiple late-night rendezvous
over the week, which played like a montage in her mind. She
loved getting to know Jack on a deeper emotional and sexual
level each night. Although they were two faceless strangers
on the internet, their connection felt more and more real with
every interaction. Their conversations at 11.11 each night
felt like a completely different world, an escape into a shared
fantasy.

Things with Colin had remained the same during the week.
They both avoided each other as much as physically possible
while living in the same house. They had continued their
game of pretending that everything was wonderful and that
they were much happier not spending time together. But in a
way, Tara felt like she wasn't pretending. Everything really
did seem wonderful with Jack in her life. He had re-vitalized
her, spiritually and sexually. She knew it was possibly just a
form of online escapism, but her emotions felt so authentic.

Now Saturday had finally come and her fantasy realm was
about to collide with reality. She knew it would either be
cosmic bliss or a complete catastrophe.

They had agreed to stick to the rules of Fling and not
exchange face pictures before meeting. She was to meet Jack

at The Vine at 8 p.m., just for a casual drink. She did, of course, feel a pang of guilt for meeting another man, but she kept reminding herself that it was just a drink. She felt she wasn't actively trying to cheat on Colin, she was merely trying to discover the meaning behind the synchronicity. She felt herself being spiritually drawn towards Jack and she needed to know why. He was an itch she had to scratch.

Tara needed to pull out all the stops to make a good first impression. After finishing shaving in the shower, she slipped on a royal blue bodycon dress and a pair of D&G silver heels. She always had to hide the heels from Colin. He would have a fit if he knew how much she paid for them. But she loved the idea of wearing them for Jack, sneaking out for their secret date in her very own pair of glass slippers. She applied the final touches of dark rouge on her lips and a splash of Gucci Bloom on her neck and suddenly the entire look came together. But as stunning as she looked, Tara still found a way to home in on her insecurities the moment she looked in the mirror.

She didn't like her neck. It made her seem older than she actually was. Why hadn't she spent her life up until now loving her neck? Because now there was nothing she could do about it. She had diagnosed herself with EOTN, or Early-Onset Turkey Neck, a condition she invented in her head after discovering it didn't exist on WebMD. She had tried every neck cream under the sun to fight EOTN but nothing worked. She had even considered Botox but learned it was really only a temporary solution that required more treatments every few months. She was afraid that if she got Botox once, she would be paying the piper for the rest of her life.

And then there was the pouch. That stubborn piece of fat that refused to leave her lower stomach. In her desperation, Tara had even bought several exercise gadgets she saw on teleshopping channels. But to her shock, the PerfectCore didn't give her a perfect core and Six-Second Six-Pack didn't give her a six-pack in six seconds. Trends made it easy enough to conceal the pouch with the right outfit, but she still lived in perpetual fear of low-waisted jeans coming back into fashion. But in the bodycon dress she was wearing, there was nowhere to hide the pouch. It didn't help that she was bloated either. Why had she eaten so much cheesy garlic bread this week? She had completely ballooned. Maybe she should wear a black dress instead, it would be much more forgiving.

'No,' Tara said aloud, in an attempt to snap herself out of her critical daze. She had spent her twenties thinking she wasn't attractive enough and then spent most of her thirties wishing she was as attractive as she was in her twenties. If she didn't break the cycle of self-criticism now, she never would. Emily had told her during the week that when women look at themselves, they focus on what they like the least. But when men look at women, they focus on what they like the most. If Jack really was the man Tara thought he was, he wouldn't care about her neck or her pouch. Their connection was deeper than that.

Tara looked at her watch. 7 p.m.

The date wasn't for another hour but she knew she'd go mad if she sat around waiting. On top of that, Colin had left the house hours ago to get a haircut and he still wasn't home. It was perhaps the first time Colin had gone to the barbers without Tara begging him to. If she left now, maybe she could avoid having to make up an excuse for where she was going so dolled up.

Tara ordered a taxi on an app and saw that it was two minutes away. Perfect.

She hurried downstairs and took one last look at herself in the hallway mirror. But as she brushed a piece of her hair behind her ear, she suddenly became hyper-aware of the fact that she was wearing her wedding ring on her finger. It felt strange to wear the symbol of her eternal bond with Colin while meeting another man behind his back. She took off the ring and looked at the inner inscription.

Forever and Always.

She felt a lump in her throat as she realized how impulsive the entire situation was. She was jeopardizing her marriage for a date with an anonymous stranger she had met online. But even when confronted with the sheer audacity of her actions, she was still willing to risk it all. What was it about Jack that was so intoxicating? How had she become so drunk with reckless abandon?

But this feeling wasn't completely alien to her either. It was the exact same feeling she felt before getting on the back of Colin's motorbike all those years ago. Although she knew that she was playing with fire, she had to trust her intuition. Her gut feeling had never led her astray before and she needed to know why she was feeling the way she was feeling. There had to be a rational explanation for her irrational behaviour. She slipped her wedding ring into her handbag.

Tara opened the front door and, to her shock, saw Colin standing on the other side with his keys in his hand. She had come so close to avoiding him.

'Colin!' she said, caught off guard.

'Wow, look at you,' he said, acknowledging her appearance for once. 'Where are you off to?'

'Oh . . . I'm just off to meet . . . Emily from work . . . for ladies' night,' Tara improvised.

'Oh, that's handy because I'm actually meeting Rory for boys' night,' Colin said. 'Which bars are you heading to?'

'Oh well . . . we were thinking . . .' Tara's taxi pulled up outside and beeped. 'That's me! Gotta run,' she said, gunning it out the door as fast as her heels would allow.

ॐ

Colin raced upstairs the second Tara's taxi drove off. For once, he was completely behind schedule. He had gone to get a quick trim that would impress Claire but the line in the barbers was practically out the door and it took him ninety minutes to get a nine-minute haircut. And it wasn't even worth the wait. It was far too short and made Colin look more boyishly cute than ruggedly handsome. But, of course, when the hairdresser had asked him if he was happy, he had replied, 'Oh yeah, that's perfect, thanks.'

He jumped in the shower, shaved his face, brushed his teeth and picked out a pair of dark blue chinos and a bright blue shirt. The entire process took about fifteen minutes. Traffic had been bad on his drive home from town so he figured getting the Luas tram would be the fastest way to make the date on time, especially as it stopped on Dawson Street, right across from The Vine. He power-walked to the stop and, by some miracle, he got on the tram just as it was about to leave. For once, Murphy's Law had cut him some slack.

On the journey into the city, Colin wondered where the night would go. The possibilities were endless. Claire had told him that she didn't want to rush into a sexual affair and that tonight was really about getting to know each other in person. He respected her decision and hoped the date went well enough to warrant a second in-person rendezvous.

Still, if their textual chemistry became sexual, he wondered if he would cross that line. He had enjoyed the moral ambiguity of their digital infidelity but things were moving fast. He felt guilty for what he was doing but he was inexplicably drawn to Claire's mystery, her sensual allure. It was as if she was a siren, calling his ship to shore. He knew her song might be his ruination but he had no control over the wheel. It was just a drink, he reminded himself, to ease his conscience. Two people meeting for a drink technically wasn't an affair.

But regardless of what happened, Colin was just excited to see the woman he had spent all week getting to know. He only hoped she wasn't expecting perfection. He had painted himself as a bodybuilder but he had literally been to the gym once. He straightened up his posture and widened his back in the reflection of the Luas glass window.

It wouldn't be long now before all was revealed.

Chapter 17

Tara arrived at The Vine at 7.50 p.m. When she got out of the taxi, she saw a few men lingering around the street and she wondered if one of them was Jack. She made eye contact with each of them but they all gave her a confused look in return. She wished she hadn't been the first one to arrive. She was always fashionably late and now she seemed like the more eager one. She was oscillating between feelings of incredible excitement and crippling nervousness. One moment she would feel liberated for going behind Colin's back, the next she would feel overwhelming guilt. She felt like a pendulum swinging between pride and shame. She only hoped it would swing in the desired direction when the clock struck eight.

She looked across Dawson Street at the bookshop Hodges Figgis, a place she had spent many a college day in search of that elusive new-book smell. It was like catnip to her. She began to wonder if that was what she was seeking on this date with Jack. The satisfying scent of beginning a new story and escaping into a different world.

'Can I help you?' the hostess asked, seeing Tara daydreaming outside the doors to The Vine.

'Oh, hi there. I'm meeting someone here for drinks but I think I'm the first to arrive,' Tara said.

'Do you know what name the reservation was made under?'

'I think it was Jack. It's kind of a blind date so I don't have the last name,' Tara admitted, half embarrassed.

'That's OK, there's only one Jack on my list. Party of two. Your table is just here on the veranda, follow me.' The hostess smiled.

Tara wondered if she should have waited at the door for Jack but it was quite chilly out. She hadn't worn a coat in the hopes Jack would get the full impact of seeing her in the dress. Emily had told her that people decide if they're attracted to someone in less than three seconds. A frumpy coat could have jeopardized her potential meet cute with Jack. She was freezing and the veranda looked wonderfully snug with multiple outdoor gas heaters.

'This is you,' the hostess said when they arrived at the table. 'Can I get you anything to drink while you wait?'

'Oh . . . yes, actually. I'll have a glass of Malbec, please,' Tara said.

'Perfect,' she said before walking away.

Tara sat down and relaxed into her chair. The veranda was so romantic, with candles lit everywhere and a warm, electric atmosphere. It was the type of place Colin would never take her. 'A veranda in Ireland? Notions,' he would probably say. There were about ten other couples around her and she felt a bit odd being the only person sitting by herself. But Jack would arrive any minute and that would change. The suspense was killing her. She didn't know if she was about to meet a supermodel or a dungeon troll. She felt so nervous and excited at the same time. The pitter-patter of her heart was unbearable. That glass of wine couldn't come quick enough.

That's when Tara saw something that knocked the wind right out of her.

On the passing Luas, Tara could see Colin through the glass window, approaching the Dawson Street stop! The tram was stopped at a red light and she was in his direct line of sight.

This couldn't be happening.

Colin began to turn his head towards The Vine and she quickly held her menu up to cover her face from him. If Colin saw her, she'd be caught in a lie. She was not out on some ladies' night. She was quite clearly in a romantic candlelit restaurant on a date! She had thrown caution to the wind but now it was blowing right back in her face. Tara peeked over the menu to see the light had turned green and the tram was slowly passing the restaurant. It was possible that Colin wasn't going to get off on Dawson Street, wasn't it? But then again, that's where a lot of the best bars in town were, and Rory did have expensive taste.

Only one person would know what to do. Tara pulled her phone out of her bag with lightning speed and immediately began to dial.

'Tara, is everything OK?' Emily answered. 'You know phone calls aren't good for my anxiety.'

'Your anxiety? Try my anxiety! I'm at The Vine waiting to meet Jack and I just saw my husband passing by on the Luas!' Tara whispered loudly into the phone.

'Oh my God, what are you going to do?'

'That's why I called you! You're always getting into crazy date scenarios. What would you do?'

'OK, did he get off the Luas at Dawson? He might just be passing through to another part of the city,' Emily said.

'Let me check,' Tara said, peeking over her menu once again. She could see the Luas was now stopped at Dawson Street and Colin was no longer in his seat.

He was walking up the road towards The Vine. And he was closing in!

Tara's heart was in her mouth.

'Christ, he's walking in my direction!' Tara said in a complete fluster.

'Abort mission. I repeat, ABORT MISSION!' Emily shouted into the phone.

Tara stood up immediately but heard a sudden shriek behind her. The hostess had brought her glass of Malbec but Tara's sudden movement had knocked the tray out of her hands.

The red wine spilled all over Tara's dress, followed by the painful sound of the glass smashing on the ground. It all happened so fast that Tara didn't have time to process the fact that her dress was destroyed. She needed to get as far away from The Vine as possible. Even though she hadn't even said hello to Jack, it was time for an Irish goodbye.

'Miss, I'm so sorry,' the hostess said.

'I need you to get me out of here. Is there a back door?' Tara said, in crisis management mode.

'Eh . . . yes . . . but please, let me . . .'

'There's no time. I need to leave right now,' Tara insisted.

'Follow me,' the hostess said, leading Tara inside just in time to avoid Colin's line of sight.

The hostess brought Tara back through the kitchen to an emergency fire exit.

'Miss, I'm so, so sorry. Please don't leave a bad review. I'll be fired,' the hostess pleaded.

'I won't – it was my fault, really. But could you do me one favour,' Tara said.

'Anything,' the hostess replied.

'If my date asks for me, pretend I was never here. This whole thing was a huge mistake,' Tara said, walking out the back door.

Tara felt like she had avoided a car crash by a millimetre. Her heart was still racing. Her real life and her fantasy life had almost met in a head-on collision that would have proved fatal to her marriage. The thought alone made her feel sick. She knew she couldn't meet Jack now. Not just because she was covered in red wine but because she realized she was playing too dangerous a game. Dublin was a small city, you couldn't just openly have an affair on a veranda and expect no consequences. What had she been thinking? She waved down a taxi that was passing through the side street she found herself on. She got into the back seat and immediately reached into her handbag. She pulled out her wedding ring and put it back on her finger where it belonged.

'Where ya headed, love?' the taxi driver asked.

'Home,' she said, looking out the window as if she was in a Hollywood movie. 'I'm going home.'

'Sure I don't know where ya feckin' live,' the taxi driver said, bringing her back down to earth.

'Oh, sorry. Hillcrest Grove, please.'

Tara knew that any minute Jack would message her asking her where she was. She couldn't bear the thought of reading it. She took out her phone and without even opening the app, she deleted Fling.

She let out a sigh of relief. How on earth had she almost risked her marriage to meet a complete stranger? The idea suddenly seemed beyond ludicrous. She had become intoxicated by her fantasy affair but she had sobered up fast. Although Jack had brought an end to her drought, his storm had almost left destruction in its wake. She was lucky to have got out unscathed.

৺৩

Colin stood outside The Vine, looking around for any woman that might be Claire. He made eye contact with a few women passing by but they all just smiled awkwardly and kept walking. He asked the hostess if anyone had checked in under the name Jack, to which she replied, 'No, sorry, I'm afraid not.'

Colin looked at his phone every thirty seconds to see if Claire's green light would illuminate.

But it never did.

He stood there like a fool, desperately searching for someone who simply wasn't coming.

> **Jack:** Hey there, stranger. I'm outside now.

> Text me when you're here ☺

> Is everything OK? It's 8.30, are you on your way?

> I'm getting worried, are you not coming?

> So, it's almost 9, am I wasting my time waiting?

After the longest hour of his life finally passed, Colin took the hint and walked away.

He should have known it was all too good to be true. Claire was nothing more than a mirage brought on by a terrible thirst. He knew a pint of Guinness was the only thing that would quench any kind of thirst now. He had always believed that one shouldn't drink to feel better, only to feel *even* better. Tonight, however, all Colin wanted to do was drown his sorrows.

'Pint of plain,' he said, taking a seat at the bar of the nearest pub. 'And keep 'em coming.'

After reflecting over the events of the week, Colin concluded that Claire was probably a catfish like Rory had said. For all he knew, Claire was some creepy old hermit woman using stolen lingerie photos to manipulate him. He felt like a fool. Murphy's Law had prevailed again. He should have seen it coming.

After a few pints too many, Colin hopped in the back of a taxi and headed back to Hillcrest. When he arrived home, he could see most of the lights in his house were still on. He opened the front door and braced himself for a lecture from Tara about the amount of alcohol he had consumed. As he walked into the kitchen, he saw Tara sitting at the kitchen table with a glass of wine, already in her pyjamas.

'Well, how's the head?' she asked in a surprisingly friendly tone.

'I'm not as think as you drunk I am,' Colin said, one of his favourite dad jokes.

'Good night with Rory?' she asked.

'Well . . . honestly I'm kinda glad to be home. Did you have fun with Emily?'

'I'm kinda glad to be home too,' she replied, smiling.

'Did you wait up for me?'

'Yes, actually . . . I wasn't able to open this jar of pickles. Would you mind?' she said, sliding a mason jar towards him. Colin was no fool. He knew she hadn't waited up this late just for a pickle. This was her roundabout way of telling him she needed him.

'Sure,' Colin said, picking up the jar. He twisted the lid off with ease. 'But I still don't know how you can eat those things.'

'Well, every marriage has one person who loves pickles and

one person who hates them,' Tara joked as she ate one. 'I take it you were on the Guinness all night?'

'Yeah . . . reminded me of the first time we met.'

'Well, nobody pulls a pint better than me.'

'I miss that time,' Colin smiled.

'Me too,' Tara said, smiling back at him.

A silence came over the room but it wasn't an awkward one. It was the kind of warm silence they used to share.

'Colin, I don't know how we got here but whatever it is that's broken between us, I want to fix it. I know it hurts that we can't have children but we can't lose each other because of it. We have to fight for what we have,' Tara said.

'You're right,' Colin said. He realized he wasn't just saying she was right to appease her. He meant it.

'I found us a marriage counsellor. I booked an appointment online for Monday evening,' Tara said.

Colin was hesitant at first but he knew these were Tara's terms. After just risking his marriage to meet a complete stranger online, he knew he was lucky he still had a marriage to save.

'OK, Tara,' he said. 'Whatever it takes.'

'Thanks, Colin. I'll see you in the morning,' Tara said, before heading upstairs to bed.

Colin knew his marriage was far from fixed. He was still sleeping on the couch, after all. But there was hope. And that made anything possible. He was willing to do whatever was necessary to make things work.

And so Colin finally unloaded the dishwasher.

Chapter 18

On Monday evening, Colin sat beside his wife in the office of Dr Mildred Burke, the therapist Tara had found online. He was struggling to get comfortable on the avant-garde couch which seemed out of place in the warm mahogany room. He didn't like the idea of therapy. In his house growing up, people simply didn't talk about their problems. He wanted to fix his marriage himself, not with some therapist who didn't understand the nuances of their relationship.

Still, he promised himself he would at least try to keep an open mind. Tara had supposedly found 'the best therapist money can buy', although that remained to be seen. If she was the best, how had they been able to get an appointment so quickly? Colin had informed Tara that the most expensive doesn't necessarily mean the best quality. This had inevitably led to bickering about not being able to put a price on saving a marriage so he left it alone. But €300 an hour? Really? A few sessions a month would cause significant financial stress. He felt like he was paying a therapist to *give* him anxiety.

Colin had spent Sunday repairing his motorcycle and, after a good day's work, Bonnie was officially restored to her former glory. He had fixed her up, revved her engine and taken her for her first spin in years. But even as Colin had felt the breeze of freedom as he rode, it didn't give him the feeling of fulfilment he had been expecting. Bonnie gave him no sense of triumph.

His mind was still fixated on Claire.

He had even bought a pack of cigarettes and lit one up as a way of feeling like he still had some sense of control in his life. But as he'd taken his first drag in years, he immediately felt like being sick. Perhaps the idea of a cigarette was always better than the cigarette itself. He tried to convince himself that the same logic applied to Claire. If she could just give him some kind of closure, maybe then he could move on.

At work, before he had come to therapy, he found himself checking Fling every few minutes like an addict, desperate for his fix. Even Rory said he had a problem, which said a lot considering his own addictive personality. But Colin couldn't help himself. He was obsessively searching for Claire's green light to illuminate the darkness.

But her light never appeared.

Dr Burke sat down in her chair across from them, ready to begin the session.

'Tara, Colin, you're both very welcome. My name is Dr Mildred Burke and you're—' she began.

'Oh, you don't need to introduce yourself, Dr Burke,' Tara interrupted. 'I was reading your book *Manifesting Marriage* all day yesterday and let me just say . . . WOW!'

Colin's feathers were immediately ruffled.

'What is this, a book signing? *Manifesting Marriage*, that sounds like witch-doctor carry-on to me,' he said sceptically.

'Colin, stop embarrassing yourself. I was just trying to hit the ground running,' Tara said, mortified.

'No, you were doing homework so you could be the teacher's pet,' he said, folding his arms.

'Let's just take a breath,' Dr Burke said. 'As I was saying, my name is Dr Mildred Burke and my area of expertise is healing broken connections so that compromise and catharsis can be achieved for all those involved.'

'Well, for three hundred euro an hour, you could at least offer a massage chair or something,' Colin pouted, still struggling to get comfortable.

'In my experience, a couch is always best for couples. That way, there's room to meet in the middle.' Dr Burke smiled.

'Oh my God, I love that,' Tara said enthusiastically. 'You're a Libra, aren't you?'

'No, actually, I'm not,' Dr Burke said.

'Sorry, I meant Virgo. Obviously!' Tara said, correcting herself.

'Afraid not.'

'Aquarius?'

'No.'

'Capricorn?'

'Well . . . yes, technically . . .'

'I KNEW IT!' Tara yelled.

'This is what I'm dealing with, Dr Burke,' Colin complained. 'She tries to use astrology to explain everything.'

'If star signs aren't real then why do all Taurus men not believe in star signs? Explain that!' Tara said.

'It's called a self-fulfilling prophecy. When you were a teenager you probably read in *Vogue* magazine that Geminis are always fashionably late and, lo and behold, you've been late for everything ever since.'

'I didn't base my entire personality on a magazine, Colin,' Tara said defensively.

'Oh yeah? Then why do you have a new issue every month?'

'At least I'm not an atheist who doesn't believe in anything.'

'Yes I do. I believe in science. The world is made up of protons, electrons and neurons.'

'And morons, apparently,' Tara muttered. 'What are you

going to do at your funeral when you're all dressed up with nowhere to go?'

'I'm trying to focus on my life right now, not my death.'

'Oh really? Then why did I hear you revving up your motorbike's engine yesterday?'

'I just took her for a little spin.'

'I knew it! Dear God, why do men only feel alive when they're on the brink of death? I know you were smoking too, by the way,' Tara said, splitting him with a dirty look.

'No I wasn't,' Colin lied.

'Your nostrils flare when you lie,' Tara said, watching his nose like a hawk. 'So you're back smoking and riding a motorbike. This is exactly why women live longer than men.'

'Or maybe it's because women nag us to death. And I seem to recall you getting on the back of that bike the night we first met.'

'We were different people back then,' Tara sighed.

'Yeah, that's the whole problem,' Colin replied.

'If I could jump back in . . .' Dr Burke said. Colin had completely forgotten she was there.

'Sorry, Dr Burke. Please continue,' Tara said, embarrassed.

'As I was about to say . . . I like to start all of my session with a little exercise,' Dr Burke said. 'I'm going to give you both a pen and paper and I'd like you to write down the reasons you married each other.'

Dr Burke handed them each a pen and notepad and sat back in her chair.

'Please don't overthink it, I'm looking for the first things that immediately pop into your heads, so I'm just going to give you sixty seconds,' Dr Burke explained.

Colin tried to write on his notepad but discovered his pen wasn't working.

'My pen is broken,' he said, frustrated. 'Is this some kind

of psychological test? Let me guess, the pen is supposed to be a phallus?'

'No, Colin, sometimes a pen is just a pen. Here's another one,' she said, handing him a replacement.

Colin began to write down the reasons he married Tara, but his mind immediately began to wander. Claire kept creeping into the crevices of his brain. Although he had no idea who she was, he couldn't quite purge his thoughts of her. Why had she stood him up so ruthlessly and not even bothered to explain why? Did their late-night conversations mean that little to her?

For a moment, he wondered if something bad had happened to her. Was she in danger? Had someone abducted her while she was on her way to their date? Did she need his help?

No, he decided. There was no elaborate damsel-in-distress scenario in which he would save her. That was just his brain's way of trying to pretend he was still the hero of his own life. Claire wasn't a princess trapped in a tower. She was just some woman who didn't want him. It was a harsh truth but it was one he had to accept. He needed to erase any memory of Claire from his mind and focus on the task at hand.

'OK, that's about sixty seconds,' Dr Burke said. 'Tara, would you be so kind as to read what you wrote?'

'Sure. Reasons why I married Colin. One, we fell for each other the moment we met each other. Two, we used to be very sexually compatible. Three, we both used to be very career-driven. Four, he used to always make me laugh non-stop. And five, he used to always make me feel seen and heard,' Tara said.

'Are you joking? That's just a list of sly digs,' Colin said, annoyed.

'Colin, could you read what you wrote, please?' Dr Burke asked.

'I didn't make a big list. I just wrote that I married Tara so we could start a family together,' Colin said, holding up his bare notepad.

'Oh, so people only get married to start a family, do they?' Tara asked.

'Well, marriage is technically two people coming together to make a family, so yes,' Colin said.

'That's not what marriage means to me,' Tara said, turning away from him.

'Yeah, you made that clear when you refused to take my name.'

'Because I didn't want my name to be Tara O'Hara! It sounds like an Irish nursery rhyme character!'

'Tara, I'd like to focus on what you wrote,' Dr Burke jumped back in. 'Most of your points appear to be written in the past tense. Why do you think that is?'

'Well . . . sometimes it feels like our best years are behind us. We never go anywhere. Or do anything. We've become strangers.'

'Why do women want to do things all the time?' Colin sulked.

'Because I want us to make new memories. I want us to fill our lives with joy,' Tara explained.

'Tara, you make a good point. Marriage is like a piano. You have to play it in order to keep it in tune. And both of you have to want to hear the music,' Dr Burke said.

'Well, we've been out of tune for a long time,' Colin said. 'Do you think it's really possible for us to love each other the way we used to?'

'That's the age-old question. Can two people fall back in love once they fall out? In my experience, the answer is yes.

But you have to stop viewing each other as opposing forces. When two people want different things, it can cause conflict. But when two people want the same thing and don't realize it, it can cause war. Most of my clients come to me at war with one another. I help them remember that the goal of war isn't victory. It's peace.'

'I love that, Dr Burke,' Tara said, like a goody-two-shoes.

'Oh please, like butter wouldn't melt in her mouth,' Colin muttered as he rolled his eyes.

'Colin, I want to hear from you,' Dr Burke said. 'Tell me about the most recent fight within your marriage.'

Colin didn't like being put on the spot but he was glad to give his side of the story before Tara overcomplicated it. 'Well, our most recent fight was the perfect example of how our marriage works. I wanted steak, she wanted pasta, so we compromised and had pasta,' he said.

'Oh, that is such an oversimplification of what happened!' Tara said.

'OK, Tara, your turn. What do you think the problem to be?' Dr Burke asked.

'Well . . . I think you've already witnessed part of the problem, Dr Burke. It feels like we're talking but we're not really communicating,' Tara said, sounding a little too rehearsed.

'Tara, that's a word-for-word quote from my book. I want to hear from you, not myself,' Dr Burke said.

'See? She's trying to win at therapy. Unbelievable!' Colin said, throwing his hands up.

'OK, fine,' Tara said, embarrassed for being called out. 'Our marriage hasn't been the same since we got some rather devastating news. We found out that we can't have children . . .'

'That is not what happened,' Colin butted in. 'We failed three rounds of IVF, but lots of couples do. There's no medical reason we can't have kids. You've just given up.'

'I didn't give up, I accepted reality. There's trying and then there's just putting yourself through hell for no reason. You know how devastated I was every time we failed. How many times are you willing to put me through that?' Tara said.

'But you won't even consider other options. You've just turned your back on the whole idea of being a mother, even though I know it's what you really want deep down,' Colin pleaded.

'Jesus, can society please normalize women wanting more than just a husband and a baby?' Tara said, exhaling dramatically.

'Oh no, don't turn this session into another feminist lecture,' Colin said, seeing where the conversation was going.

'In case you couldn't tell, Dr Burke, my husband isn't a feminist and that's a big part of the problem.'

'For the millionth time, I'm an equalist. I believe men and women are equal,' Colin explained.

'That's the literal definition of a feminist.'

'No it's not, feminism is about hating men.'

'Are you really mansplaining feminism to me right now?' Tara asked, putting him on the spot.

'No, I'm just trying to make you understand things from a man's point of view,' Colin said defensively.

'Great, so now you're mansplaining mansplaining,' Tara said, at her wits' end. 'You know, men should really be grateful women want equality and not revenge!'

'All you do is complain about men even though I'm literally the most perfect husband anyone could possibly ask for!' Colin said.

'And so humble,' Tara said, rolling her eyes.

'Why are you rolling your eyes? I'm literally the most humble person in the world!'

'Yeah . . . clearly.'

'In every argument you play the victim because you can't take any kind of personal criticism whatsoever,' Colin said.

'YES I FECKIN' CAN TAKE CRITICISM!' Tara screamed.

'Yeah . . . clearly. I can't remember a single time you admitted you were wrong.'

'Well, I'm not always right but I'm never wrong.'

'You see, Dr Burke? I can't win.' Colin shrugged. 'She emasculates me because she failed feminism in college and has something to prove.'

'I did not fail, I got forty-nine per cent and I was unfairly marked!'

'Aww, would you like some dip for that chip on your shoulder?'

'Name one way I emasculate you!' Tara demanded.

'It's the little things. Like wanting me to sit down every time I pee, for example!'

'Well, that just means a cleaner bathroom for everyone.' Tara shrugged.

'And then, of course, there's the time you made me get my foreskin cut off,' Colin said.

'Colin, it wasn't a foreskin, it was a fiveskin!' Tara said. 'And it looks so much better circumcised.'

'But you said we would have more sex after I got circumcised, which turned out to be a complete lie,' Colin said.

'That brings me to my next question,' Dr Burke said. 'How are things in the bedroom?'

'Not good, doctor,' Tara answered a little too quickly.

'Finally, something we agree on,' Colin said, throwing his arms in the air. 'I'm practically married to a nun.'

'Oh that is so unfair. I am a very sexual person!'

'Then why haven't we had sex in two hundred and seventeen days?'

'Jesus, do you have a spreadsheet for all the days we don't have sex or something?' Tara said, shocked.

'No I don't. Because nothing is getting spread in our sheets,' Colin pouted. 'You just lay there. Dr Burke, one time she said "try not to wake me". Can you believe that?'

'That's because you wanted to have morning sex. You know I like a lie-in on the weekends,' Tara said, trying to justify herself.

'It's not just mornings. Anytime I want it, you never do! I'm expected to be a mind-reader.'

'You don't have to read my mind, Colin. You have to read my body. I'm an open book.'

'I'd have a better chance at understanding *Ulysses*! There's no rhyme or reason for women being so complex,' Colin sighed.

'It's not some big mystery, Colin. We need to feel desired and appreciated. And a bit of spontaneity goes a long way.'

'Well, you need to tell me what you want so I can plan something spontaneous in advance.'

'That defeats the whole purpose! It has to come from you. Even simple things like buying me flowers.'

'I'm allergic to pollen!'

'Well, I'm allergic to excuses. You used to always buy me flowers for our anniversary. A bouquet once a year wouldn't kill you. But now you're so cheap you won't even pay attention to me. And then you whine about how stingy your father used to be when you're exactly the same! Make it make sense!'

'Do not compare me to my father,' Colin said sternly. 'You know, Tara, you really don't know how good you have it. So many men go out and drink their money or gamble it away or put it straight up their nose. I put my money away so our children would never be disappointed on Christmas morning.

A little appreciation would be nice. And let's not forget that I'm the one who paid for IVF.'

'I do appreciate all that, Colin. I just need to feel like you care. Any kind of gesture to make me feel desired. You have to admit you stopped seeing me in a sexual manner as soon we started trying for a child,' Tara said.

'Oh, that's not true.'

'Isn't it? The moment we started trying it was like you were racing to the finish line as soon as possible. You just completely forgot that I was having sex too! Honestly, I would have had more fun using a turkey baster trying to get pregnant.'

'I'm sorry I wasn't turned on by all the talk about ovulation and hormones and menstrual cycles . . .' Colin babbled.

'Oh, have a bit of empathy, Colin. You know, just once I wish men could menstruate! Admit it. When you started seeing me as the mother of your potential children, you stopped caring about pleasuring me,' Tara said matter-of-factly.

'That is actually quite common,' Dr Burke interjected. 'Freud called it the Madonna–Whore Complex. It is when men either see women as virginal mothers for procreation or fallen women for pleasure. It is an outdated view of female sexuality, but many men still view women in this binary. A lot of men even cite it as the reason they seek extra-marital affairs. They want the Wife and the Other Woman.'

Colin knew that Dr Burke had a point. Maybe he did have the complex she described. Maybe that's why he had joined Fling. It just seemed as if Tara had no desire to be taken the way he wanted to take her. With Claire, he could always feel her desire radiating through his phone. She was just as turned on by their rendezvous as he was. They both felt a mutual lust, bound by shared sin. Maybe it was because it was so wrong that it felt so right. Maybe guilt made sex that little bit more appealing. Maybe he was a good Catholic after all.

'OK, I hear what you're saying,' Colin said. 'But Tara, you always said that I was "husband material" not "one-night-stand material". I think women divide men in that way too. Why is there no complex for women?'

'I thought you said women were already too complex?' Tara said, raising an eyebrow.

'I see your point, Colin,' Dr Burke said. 'But if both of you are seeing each other in this desexualized manner, it begs the question of whether or not either of you have been unfaithful . . .'

The room immediately fell silent.

Colin felt his pulse begin to race. He hadn't actually gone through with the affair, so technically, he had nothing to hide. But he had to choose his words carefully. If his nostrils started flaring, Tara would get suspicious.

'I've never slept with anyone other than my wife,' Colin finally said.

'And I've only ever had sex with my husband,' Tara added.

'That's great. But I'm assuming there have been instances of temptation for you both?' Dr Burke pried.

'Well, fantasizing about other people isn't cheating,' Colin said.

'No, but it could lead to wanting that fantasy to become a reality. Love is to have and desire is to want. That is why marriage takes effort. It's difficult to desire what you already have. Desire is fuelled by the forbidden,' Dr Burke explained.

'But then how do we do we get back the chemistry we used to have?' Tara asked.

'Well, when we talk about chemistry between two people, we're actually talking about the chemicals released in the brain,' Dr Burke began. 'When we experience sexual attraction, our body releases hormones: testosterone or oestrogen. This fuels our sex drives in a feeling we commonly call lust. When that attraction grows into something more, the brain releases the hormone dopamine. What we consider romantic love is really just a chemical fix of dopamine you receive from someone. But of course, this fix isn't infinite and once the so-called honeymoon phase ends, dopamine levels start to drop and it's replaced with what's called oxytocin. This chemical is what causes a bond between two people, feelings of closeness, belonging. Oxytocin is wonderful but nothing beats the kick of dopamine. The question is if two people can return to the honeymoon phase and experience that initial rush of first love again. I have developed a strategy that helps with this. It's all outlined in my book *Romanticizing Romance*.'

Colin rolled his eyes again. He just knew Tara would buy this book too. They needed advice, not a reading list. 'Feel free to spoil the ending on us,' he said sarcastically.

'Romanticism is the perception of life the way it ought to be, not the way it is. To see life in soft focus, through rose-tinted glasses. When you first arrived in my office, you were both very eager to point out the other person's flaws instead of their virtues. My point is that you both have a choice in the way you look at your partner. Do you home in on their minor imperfections or do you celebrate the things that made you love them? Sometimes we need to take a trip to the past to revaluate our present and rediscover hope for the future. That's what it means to romanticize romance,' Dr Burke explained.

'I think we can both do that,' Tara said, smiling at Colin.

'I'm going to give you an assignment for this week.'

'A reading list *and* homework?' Colin sighed.

'Don't be so immature, Colin,' Tara said, slapping his arm.

'Don't worry, your assignment is simple. It's to have a

romantic date night. Colin, imagine you've lost something in the past and so you're building a time machine to get it back. It's not about living in the past. It's about bringing the magic of the past back into the present.'

Colin didn't like Dr Burke explaining it to him as if he was a child, but admittedly her metaphor did actually inspire some excitement.

'OK,' he conceded. 'But how do we bring the past into the present?'

'By watching a very important film,' Dr Burke said.

'If you say *Mamma Mia*, I will set myself on fire,' Colin said.

'The film I'm referring to is your wedding video,' Dr Burke elaborated. 'So many people record wedding tapes then let them gather dust for the rest of their marriage. People don't realize that nostalgia is a powerful aphrodisiac. I want you to see on screen the people you used to be. The couple you used to be.'

'OK, that's doable,' Colin conceded.

'After watching your wedding video, I want you both to make love. Not as a way of getting pregnant like you're both used to, but rather as a way of expressing your love for one another. Even if you don't feel incredibly in the mood, be open to seduction. Sex is sometimes like a skydive. You might not always feel like making the initial jump but, once you land, you're glad you made the leap. Your bedroom should be a safe space where you can both share your fantasies with each other.'

'OK, that makes sense,' Tara said, keeping an open mind.

'And finally,' Dr Burke said, 'I don't want either of you to start an argument between now and our next session. If at any point you find yourself on the verge of a row, count to ten and let it go. I'll be checking back in on this next time we meet. Do you think you can both do that?'

Tara and Colin looked at each with a hopeful smile.

'Yes,' they said in unison.

Chapter 19

As she prepared for her romantic evening with Colin, Tara found herself troubled by something Dr Burke had said. She didn't feel she could share her fantasy with her husband because it didn't involve him. It involved Jack and their illicit online romance. She hoped Dr Burke's suggested strategy would help reignite the flame, but was there really a way of reliving the physical rush of first love?

Back then, Colin was the bad boy who had tempted her onto his motorbike, but now Jack was the forbidden fruit she couldn't resist. Perhaps Colin had made a point about women dividing men in their minds. Like she had said in her pitch for Fling, she had found Mr Right but she found herself lusting for Mr Wrong.

But Tara had stood Jack up without offering him any explanation. She knew she should have been feeling guilty for almost cheating on her husband but she found herself plagued with guilt for ghosting Jack. She couldn't stop thinking of him, standing out in the cold, waiting for her to arrive. The image tormented her. Had he moved on already or did his thoughts still linger on her, the way hers did on him?

She tried to tell herself that she and Jack were just ships passing in the night, yet her gut was telling her to grab the wheel and sail after him, even if it was into uncharted waters. There must have been some kind of meaning behind the synchronicity she felt when they matched. It had to be more than just a coincidence. Her brain and her gut were divided against one another, each one trying to steer her in opposite directions.

But still she knew she couldn't save her marriage and have an affair at the same time, and she wasn't going to choose a man she'd never met over her partner of eighteen years. That would be completely off the wall, even for a Gemini.

For now, at least, she had to extinguish her burning desire for Jack and channel all her energy into reigniting the spark with Colin. And to do that, she had to pour her heart and soul into date night.

Everything was set. They had ordered a delivery from their favourite Chinese takeaway, bought an expensive bottle of Malbec and rooted out their wedding video in the attic. Colin dished out the food as Tara uncorked the wine. They were both determined to make sure everything went perfectly. After all, their marriage depended on it.

'OH FOR GOD'S SAKE!' Colin yelled out of the blue.

'WHAT?' Tara yelled back.

'They forgot the bloody prawn crackers,' he sighed.

'Jesus, Colin. You frightened the life of me!'

'This happens every time! You know what, I'm going after the delivery guy,' Colin said, heading for his jacket.

'Colin, he's probably long gone on his scooter by now.'

'Well ... then I'm calling them,' he said, taking out his phone.

'Colin, for God's sake, it's a bag of prawn crackers. You always say I'm too picky when I ask for salad dressing on the side in a restaurant. Let it go.'

'They should at least refund me,' Colin said, stubborn as ever.

'It's one euro for prawn crackers, Colin. I'll give you a euro if you're that out of pocket over it. Dr Burke said you need to stop being so stingy, remember?' she said.

'She never said that!' Colin snapped.

'She didn't need to say it, Colin. It was needless to say,' Tara said.

'Yet here you are . . . saying it,' Colin muttered.

'Can we just continue with our nice evening, please? We're not allowed fight, remember?' Tara said, diffusing the situation. She pulled the cork out of the wine and began to pour.

'OK . . . you're right,' he said, cooling down. He took a deep breath and continued to dish out the rest of the food. He handed Tara over her tub of chicken curry, only to hear a shriek immediately after.

'OH FOR GOD'S SAKE!' Tara shouted.

'What's wrong?' Colin asked frantically.

'I asked for no onions!' Tara said, distraught.

'Jesus, you nearly gave me a heart attack, Tara.'

'This is a disgrace! Ring them!'

'You just told me not to ring them!'

'Well . . . it's different now,' Tara said, knowing well it wasn't.

Colin raised an eyebrow in disbelief. 'Oh, because it affects you? You can eat around the onions and still enjoy your meal. Dr Burke said you need to be more adaptable, remember?' he said, giving her a dose of her own medicine.

'She never said that!' Tara shrieked.

'She didn't need to say it, Tara. It was needless to say,' he said, smirking.

'Yet here you are . . . saying it.' Tara smirked back.

Tara and Colin looked at each other and laughed. It was their typical tit-for-tat behaviour at its finest, and in that moment they chose to appreciate the humour of the situation rather than let it escalate into an actual fight.

181

'I actually feel bad for Dr Burke having to put up with us,' Tara laughed.

'Well, at three hundred euro an hour, I wanna make her work for it,' he joked.

'The wine is amazing by the way, great choice,' Tara said, taking a sip.

'Thank you, but this meal looks like it's missing one thing,' Colin said, comically scratching his head as if he didn't know.

'If you say prawn crackers, I'll scream,' Tara said.

'No . . . but I would love to try some of your famous air-fried garlic bread,' he said.

Tara knew this was Colin's way of apologizing.

'Coming right up,' she said.

❧

After their meal, Tara cleaned up and Colin tried to figure out how to get their DVD player to link up to their TV, so they could watch their wedding video. When Tara walked into the living room to join him, she realized it was the first time she had properly entered Colin's man cave.

'Oh my God, it smells like a man in here,' she said, after getting a whiff of the room's new scent.

'There's no such thing as a man smell,' Colin said, still rooting at the DVD player.

'Oh trust me, there is.'

Colin was clearly struggling with setting up the machine. She knew that it was the perfect time to subtly give the room a woman's touch while he was distracted. She took some scented candles from the kitchen and began placing them around the room. When all the candles were lit, the room suddenly had the perfect romantic atmosphere for date night.

But the smell of manliness still lingered. Colin was still

rooting away behind the TV so she took out a new incense kit from the coffee table drawer. She had been saving it for a special occasion and now seemed like the perfect time. Colin probably wouldn't even notice it. She set the kit up on the little wooden stand and lit an incense stick. She immediately loved the aroma. She was a sensual woman and she wanted all her senses to be stimulated as much as possible during their romantic evening.

'Do you smell smoke?' Colin asked, concerned.

Busted.

'It's not smoke . . . it's just some incense,' Tara said, trying to downplay it.

'Oh for God's sake, Tara. You know well incense irritates my nose,' he sighed.

'I read somewhere that incense can actually be good for sinus issues,' Tara said, making it up as she went along. 'I don't see what the big issue is with having a nice smell in the room.'

'It smells like a church.'

'We're about to watch our wedding, so it might help make it more immersive. It'll be like we're really there.'

'It smells more like a funeral than a wedding. Put it out,' Colin said as a final word.

'Fine,' Tara said, blowing out the incense stick and putting the kit away. She was disappointed, of course, but she knew she had pushed her luck. And now that Colin had got his way about the incense, he didn't even notice the candles she had secretly lit. Celebrate the small victories, she told herself as she sipped her wine.

She looked around the room at the vintage beer signs now littering her walls.

'GUINNESS FOR STRENGTH', the one nearest to her read. She desperately tried to ignore them. *Don't mention them, don't mention them, don't mention them*, she repeated to herself.

'I see the beer signs are still up,' she inevitably said.

'They sure are,' Colin said. 'Is that a problem?'

'No, it's fine,' Tara said, biting her tongue. *Don't say it, don't say it, don't say it.* 'I just think it's funny how—'

'Nope! Don't even start with your "I just think it's funny how" crap. We're having a nice evening, remember? And anyway, you're always saying how much you believe in signs,' Colin slagged her.

'I mean signs from above, not signs from the pub,' she said, rolling her eyes.

'You never know, pub signs could have a deeper meaning,' he said.

'Do you remember that old Guinness ad that said a woman needs a man like a fish needs a bicycle? You should get that sign,' she said playfully.

'Women need men to connect the DVD player to the TV to watch their wedding video, don't they?' Colin joked.

'OK, I'll give you that one. But you'd want to get a bloody move on,' she said, impatiently.

'It should be on HDMI one, I don't know why it's not showing up.'

'It would probably work if you paid the TV licence inspector, instead of hiding behind the couch every time he comes around. It's not even that expensive.'

'It's not about the price, it's about the principle! You don't drive a TV. Anyway, this has nothing to do with having a TV licence, it's about finding the right input.'

'I'm telling you, Colin, he saw you hiding behind the couch and probably turned off our HDMI.'

'That couldn't possibly make any less sense.'

Tara grabbed the remote and pressed the source button.

The TV changed to HDMI 2 and the menu for their wedding video suddenly appeared on the screen. Colin's face dropped.

'That was just a fluke,' he said.

'Or maybe all it needed was a woman's touch. Just like this room,' Tara teased.

'Oh yes, like you secretly lighting the candles.'

'But doesn't it make everything so much more romantic?'

'I think they pair perfectly with my pub signs. It's like our own little private shebeen.'

'It would be even nicer if it wasn't in my living room,' Tara said as she sculled her wine. 'Time for a refill. You get cosy, I'll bring in the bottle for us.'

Colin sat down on the couch and made himself comfortable. Tara brought the bottle of Malbec in from the kitchen and refilled both their glasses. For a split second, the image of the hostess spilling Malbec all over her dress flashed into her mind. What would have happened if she stayed at The Vine instead of fleeing out the back? What if she was destined to meet Jack but had ruined everything by running?

No, she couldn't let those kind of intrusive thoughts in. She had to focus on making date night with Colin a success.

'I can't get over how good this wine is,' she said, bringing the glass to her nose to smell the aroma. 'I'm getting undertones of cherry and oak. What are you getting?'

'Hammered,' Colin joked as he took a generous gulp.

'Aww this is nice, isn't it? We haven't had a movie night together in ages.'

'Yeah, because we can never agree on a movie. You always say "you pick" and then every time I pick something you say "not that one".'

'But you always pick the right one eventually,' Tara smiled.

'And then you fall asleep five minutes into the movie and I'm left watching some rom-com on my own!' Colin whined.

'Oh stop whinging. You're not the most fun person to watch movies with either, you know,' Tara said, slagging him back.

'What's that supposed to mean?'

'Every time you see an actor you recognize, it's always, "What was he in before? Yer man with the face",' Tara said, imitating Colin. 'Then you spend the next ten minutes on Wikipedia looking up some B-list actor's entire filmography instead of actually watching the feckin' film!'

'Thankfully we're watching our wedding video so I'll know everyone on the screen,' Colin said picking up the remote.

Colin put his arm around her and hit play on the DVD menu. A title card appeared on screen that read 'This video is to celebrate the holy matrimony of Colin O'Hara and Tara Fitzsimons'. The title card faded to an opening shot outside a stunning cathedral that people in formal wear were entering. There were some vox-pop-style interviews outside the cathedral with messages to Tara and Colin.

Rory suddenly appeared on screen, full of energy. He was in his early twenties and had some not-so-mysterious white powder on his septum.

'Good God, was Rory off his face at our wedding?' Tara asked, shocked.

'Would you expect anything less?' Colin laughed.

'True, he was born with a silver spoon up his nose.'

Rory began to speak directly to the camera on the screen. 'Cameraman, what do you call a funeral for two people?' The cameraman didn't respond. 'A wedding!' Rory said, laughing hysterically.

'He really is one of a kind,' Colin laughed.

'I certainly hope so,' Tara said.

'I still think there's a woman out there for him somewhere,' Colin said, sipping his wine.

'God help her.'

186

Tara's former boss Tom O'Malley appeared on screen.

'Oh my God, look at Tom,' Tara said, her heart filling up.

'Now listen here, Tara,' Tom began to say playfully to the cameraman. 'I know you work in Dublin now at your big fancy job but when are you coming back to visit me in O'Malley's?'

'Aww bless him,' Tara said. 'I feel so bad – I haven't gone to see him in years!'

Colin fast-forwarded to Tara pulling up in a vintage white car and walking towards the church doors.

'Oh my God, I was so SKINNY!' Tara screeched in disbelief.

'You still are skinny,' Colin laughed.

'Oh please, I'm a beached whale now compared to then. I didn't even have a pouch! That's it, I'm starting that keto diet,' Tara decided.

'Isn't that the no-carb one? What about your cheesy garlic bread?' Colin asked.

'I'll just have to air-fry some cucumber until the pouch is gone.'

The video cut to the inside of the church, capturing Colin's face as Tara walked down the aisle.

'Oh my God, you were so handsome!' Tara said.

'Sorry . . . I *was* so handsome?' Colin said.

'Oh, you know what I mean,' Tara said, brushing it off.

'Imagine if I said, "You *were* so pretty!" It would be World War Three,' Colin said.

Tara knew Colin had a point. She hadn't meant anything by her statement, but if the shoe was on the other foot, she would have used it to give Colin the boot. She knew well that Colin was still handsome. She saw the way other women looked at him, even the likes of Celine. The stress of IVF hadn't aged his body the way it had aged hers. Sometimes she wished he was a little less handsome. On some occasions, she actually felt quite jealous of the attention he would receive, though her pride always prevented her from expressing it out loud.

'OK, you're right. You were boyishly handsome back then but you're more ruggedly handsome now. Is that fair?' she said.

'I can work with that. But for the record, men need to be complimented once in a while. Literally one compliment a year will keep us going,' he joked.

The video cut to Tara walking down the aisle with her father by her side, giving her away. Tara felt a pang of loss seeing him alive on screen.

'Are you OK?' Colin said, sensing her sadness.

'Yeah, just weird seeing him. He was taken far too soon,' Tara said.

'At least he got to give his only daughter away. I'm sure that meant a lot to him,' Colin said, tightening his grip around her.

On the screen everyone had turned around to see Tara walking down the aisle. Everyone except Colin's mother Patricia. Tara's sadness was replaced by shock.

'Look at that! Your mother didn't even turn around. I told you she hates me,' Tara said, pouting.

'She doesn't hate you, she was just focusing on my reaction,' Colin said, unconvinced.

'Typical Irish mother, obsessed with her golden boy,' Tara said, sipping her wine.

'Let's just skip to the vows,' Colin said, trying to change the subject. He fast-forwarded until he saw Tara's younger self begin to read her vows on screen.

'Colin. When you walked into O'Malley's for the first time, I didn't see a stranger. I saw someone I had known my whole life but just hadn't met yet. You know I've always been superstitious, but the gut feeling I experienced when I saw you was love at first sight. Of all the pubs, in all the towns, in all of Ireland, you had to walk into mine. And when you did, I knew there was a reason for everything. It was like we were together in a past life and had been reunited once again. And I know that even when we eventually lose each other in this life, we will find each other once again. We will always find each other, Colin, no matter what. Because our flame has been burning from the beginning of time. Destiny will always find a way of bringing us together and keeping our eternal flame burning. I love you, Colin. Forever and always.'

Tara looked at Colin on the couch beside her and could see there was a tear in his eye.

'Oh my God, are you crying?' she said, shocked.

'No, my eyes are sweating. Probably from that stupid incense,' he said defensively.

'I thought it irritated your nose, not your eyes,' Tara slagged him as she sipped her wine.

On the screen, Colin was about to speak.

'Tara, the night we met, I knew there would never be another woman who could make me feel the way you did. For you, it was love at first sight but for me, it was love at first fight. As soon as we started driving each other mad, I knew we were madly in love. I don't know what made you get on the back of my motorbike that night but I know that if you hadn't, my life wouldn't have been the same. At this moment in time, there's no place I'd rather be than standing in front of you, in front of all our friends and family, about to start our next chapter together. Thank you for making me the luckiest man in the world. I love you, Tara. Always and forever.'

'I forgot how much I loved your vows,' Tara said, welling

up. She cosied up closer to him on the couch. 'OK, I want to see our first dance next.'

Colin zipped on to their first dance on screen. Their wedding song, 'Eternal Flame' by The Bangles, began to play as they met each other in the middle of the dance floor. It was the song that had been randomly playing in the restaurant on their third date, when Colin officially asked Tara to be his girlfriend.

'Oh my God,' Tara said, hearing the music. 'Our song.'

Colin stood up and gestured for her to join him in the dance. Tara took his hand and stood up. He brought her close and they began to slow dance, just as they were doing on screen. He kissed her gently but with intent. Dr Burke had been right. Nostalgia was certainly a powerful aphrodisiac.

'I think it's time you stopped sleeping on the couch,' Tara said, her head on his chest.

Then, without her needing to ask, Colin picked up his wife and carried her upstairs.

෴

As he kissed his wife's body, Colin loved how soft she was. Unfortunately, however, so was he. Once he became aware that he wasn't erect, his penile stage-fright kicked in, exacerbating the problem.

'I'll be right back,' Colin said, rushing into the bathroom. He opened the medicine cabinet and took out his secret stash of Viagra that Tara was still unaware of. He hated having to take it but the pressure of trying for a baby over the past few years had given him some kind of psychological block.

As he looked at the blue pill in his hand, Colin decided to try a little experiment. He opened up Fling on his phone and clicked on Claire's profile. As expected, she was still offline.

Colin scrolled back through their text conversations, back to where they had exchanged photos. After scrolling back far enough, he found the photos of Claire in her red lingerie. He imagined himself ripping the lingerie off Claire's smooth body and taking her in any manner he pleased. He looked down to see that his performance anxiety was no more, so he put the little blue pill back in its box.

While waiting for Colin in the bedroom, Tara was trying to find a seductive pose for when he returned. She wasn't sure why he had gone to the bathroom but she hoped it was to put on a cologne of his that she liked. She had bought him Sauvage by Dior one Christmas but it irritated his nose too much to wear. She prayed he would wear it just this once. There was something about the scent that really got Tara going.

Colin, on the other hand, was a strictly visual lover. He wanted to see as much as possible. Tara had tried to explore various erogenous zones on his body years ago, but after much research, she discovered he only had one. Colin suddenly rushed back, like an actor who had missed his curtain call.

'Now, where were we?' he said, picking up where he had left off. He began kissing her neck which she audibly enjoyed.

'Yeah, you like that?' Colin said.

When it came to orgasms, Tara believed in the mantra 'fake it till ya make it'. She had to act it out at first in order for it to happen for real. But it had been forever since Tara's last performance. She would have to pull out all the stops.

'*Yeah, just like that,*' she moaned, half passion, half performance.

Colin ripped off her clothes in a surprisingly aggressive manner. She liked it. If he had asked her permission to rip off her clothes, she'd probably have said no, but she liked Colin taking charge for once. He began to caress and kiss her inner

191

thigh, one of her more erogenous zones. She loved that he was taking initiative, exploring new uncharted lands.

For a moment, Tara wished she was wearing her red lingerie so that Colin would be met with an unexpected surprise. But she had bought that lingerie for Jack and wearing it for Colin didn't sit right with her. It was as if the lingerie was tainted by her illicit behaviour and didn't belong in her marital bed.

They were suddenly embracing each other's naked bodies and Colin began kissing her neck as he thrust inside her. Tara was loving the sensation but found herself imagining it was Jack's lips on her neck. She imagined it was him inside her, taking her in any manner he saw fit. She wanted Colin to pull her hair or spank her a little, but having to ask spoiled the fantasy. Jack wouldn't need to be asked. Jack would have done as he pleased. She imagined Jack's hand resting gently on her neck, applying just enough pressure to let her know he was in control. Then, Tara suddenly began to feel she was on her ascent towards the summit.

'OH YEAH, KEEP GOING,' she roared.

As Colin continued thrusting, his mind oscillated between the highly erotic image of Claire's red lingerie and the emasculating image of her green light being extinguished forever. He focused his mind on the former in order to maintain the erection. Tara's moans were also driving him wild, and he knew she was getting close.

In the missionary position they currently occupied, he was limited to stimulating her neck and lips, but he suddenly thought about her ears. He began to breathe heavily into them, his grunting getting deeper as he followed her towards climax, hoping not to overtake her.

'*Oh yeah, almost there,*' she moaned, tantalized by the aural stimulation. She dug her nails into his back as if she was holding on for dear life. He gave one last thrust of energy and they both let out a loud moan in unison that felt seismic in comparison to the glacial lovemaking of the last few years.

It had been a long time since Tara had been satisfied, and even longer since they had climaxed together.

Their satisfaction, however, was bittersweet.

There was an invisible layer of deceit to their lovemaking. Their bodies had connected but their guilty minds betrayed them.

Tara felt as if Jack had just given her an orgasm and Colin felt as if his climax belonged to Claire. It wasn't Tara's eternal flame that lit up Colin's life any more. It was Claire's green light. He was more turned on by a mere headless photo of his online mistress than his completely naked wife beside him. Perhaps Dr Burke had been right about that complex.

Although Colin had taken her all the way physically, Tara knew Jack had done it mentally, emotionally and spiritually. The fantasy of the perfect stranger, ravishing her, that's what took her there. Why did her mind have to cruelly divide love and lust into opposing forces? Would she spend the rest of her life loving Colin but lusting for Jack? Longing for the man she never met? It felt like a cruel, twisted fate.

She wished there was some way to have one's cake and eat it too.

Chapter 20

On Tuesday morning, Tara sat in her office brainstorming for the Fling advertising campaign. But no matter how hard she tried to focus, she couldn't get her creative juices flowing.

It was no mystery where her mental block was stemming from, of course. During her pitch, she was speaking from her heart about why she fantasized about infidelity. At the time it was easy because Fling was the perfect escape from her humdrum existence. Jack had rescued her from the tower of unhappiness. But now that Jack was gone, she felt more trapped than ever. The emptiness in her chest had come back with a vengeance, the void desperately calling out for him.

She had gone snooping that morning and discovered Colin's secret stash of Viagra, which explained why he ran to the bathroom in the middle of their lovemaking. It made her feel strangely insecure, like her body wasn't desirable without some form of medical assistance. She knew Jack wouldn't need Viagra. One look at her body and he'd be ready to go. She missed the excitement of having him in her life, even if it was reckless. While her brain begged her to see reason, her body was begging for his carnal touch.

All day yesterday, Emily had been eager to hear the gossip about Tara's date with Jack. But Tara didn't want to discuss it. She wanted to pretend it didn't even happen. And to be fair, there was nothing to tell. She hadn't even met Jack, and now, after deleting Fling, she had severed her only connection to him. She knew she needed to put Jack completely out of her mind but it was proving to be damned near impossible. She wished she had never heard about Fling in the first place. Pandora's box had been opened and she knew it would be impossible to get the lid back on. She had already bitten the apple and discovered her nakedness. The problem was, she liked it. The apple tasted like more. She was insatiable.

Coming up with a campaign for Fling suddenly felt like an insurmountable task. Jack was the electrical current that had been supercharging her with confidence. Now, she felt like her battery was right back at 1 per cent. Was she destined to spend the rest of her life as a lonely heart, forever wondering *what if*?

She found herself scrolling aimlessly through social media in an attempt to distract herself. Celine had a story post up saying, 'So a lot of you have been asking for my skincare routine . . .' Tara rolled her eyes. Nobody had asked her for her skincare routine. Still, it wasn't as bad as the time Celine had put on a full face of makeup for a #NoMakeUpSelfie. Celine had recently given birth to a third baby boy and was oversharing every aspect of it online. Out of politeness, Tara had quickly commented 'Congradulations' on her post, to which Celine replied, 'You mispelled congratulations, haha.' Tara got extreme pleasure in replying, 'You misspelled misspelled, haha.' It was perhaps the pettiest exchange Tara had ever had with Celine and she vowed to never comment again. She dreamed of the day she would be able to unfollow Celine, but she knew it would result in passive-aggressive digs as long as they remained neighbours.

And it didn't help Tara's mood that she was currently following the ketogenic diet to try and get her wedding-day figure back. She had read online that she was allowed to eat fats but not carbohydrates. But it wasn't even noon and Tara felt herself in a slump with zero energy. She felt so irritable. It was torture. How did so many women do the keto diet and make it seem so easy? After only five waking hours without carbs, Tara was willing to kill for a slice of white bread.

She had to find a way to concentrate on the campaign. She had promised Dick Mulligan a full presentation and she was due to pitch it to him in less than a week. Tara remembered that she had tasked Emily with making the lunch reservation for Dick and herself. But Emily had a habit of not following through with clear instructions.

'Emily, can you come in here?' she said, paging Emily's desk phone.

Emily walked in, cautiously. 'Am I in trouble?' she asked.

'Of course not. Why?'

'I don't know, it just seems like you've gone back to the old Tara. You wouldn't spill any tea yesterday about your date with Jack.'

'There's no tea to spill,' Tara shrugged. 'My husband almost caught me, I called you in a panic, I spilled wine all over my dress and bolted out the back door. That's all there is to the story.'

'Fair enough. But you still haven't asked me about my weekend hook-up story. It's our tradition!' Emily sulked.

'I'm sorry, Emily,' Tara laughed. 'How did it go?'

'Another trainwreck,' Emily sighed. 'He had a Soviet Union banner as a headboard. It was a big red flag.'

'Yikes.' Tara winced.

'Still, most guys don't even have a headboard these days. Glass half full right?' Emily shrugged. 'Anyway, what was it you wanted to see me about?'

'Oh yes, I was just wondering if you booked a table at Al Fresco for my pitch with Dick Mulligan?'

'No, you never asked,' Emily said, confused.

'I emailed you twice about it.'

'Oh, all my work emails get marked as spam.'

'Why?'

'Because I mark them as spam,' Emily said, deadpan.

'Emily, please be serious!' Tara snapped.

'OMG calm down! Stress isn't good for the baby!' Emily said, taken aback.

'WHAT BABY?'

'ME! I'M THE BABY!' Emily yelled.

Tara let out a laugh with relief. 'Sorry, Emily, I'm a mess today. I just really want the entire pitch to go well but I have a creative block from all the pressure.'

'Diamonds are formed under pressure, Tara. You taught me that. We both know why you're really annoyed,' Emily said cheekily.

'What do you mean? I'm just stressed over the pitch, I swear,' Tara lied.

'Swear on ABBA,' Emily demanded.

Tara couldn't do it. 'OK, fine! I miss Jack, are you happy now?'

'I should have warned you. If a man's name begins with J, you're in for an emotional rollercoaster.'

'But that's the problem, Emily. I miss the rollercoaster. I want to get back on. I can feel this emptiness coming back into my chest. Jack made me feel so alive. I've been trying to get him out of my mind, but last night, while Colin and I were . . . you know . . . I was fantasizing about Jack the entire time! He's all I can think about. He's like a song I can't get out of my head,' Tara said, flustered.

'In my experience, the only way to get a song out of your

head is to sing it all the way through. You need to text him,' Emily said.

'I wish I could but it's too late. I stood Jack up and deleted the app in the heat of the moment. My profile is gone,' Tara said, putting her face in her palms.

'No it's not. You just need to sign in again once you re-download it. Here, give me your phone,' Emily said, holding out her hand.

'Oh my God, Emily, are you serious?' Tara said, handing over the phone.

'That's literally how all apps work. I swear, you're hopeless with technology.' Emily had Fling re-downloaded in a few seconds. 'OK, let's see ... Alias Claire ... password Abba-Gold and ... look at that, we're in,' she said, handing Tara back her phone.

Tara was in shock. She had just assumed that by deleting the app, she had lost Jack forever. It was yet another example of her being behind the times when it came to technology. But now, as she looked at her phone, she could see that Jack was still there in her inbox. She opened their conversation to see the several heart-breaking texts Jack had sent while waiting for her outside The Vine.

'Oh my God, he waited outside The Vine for over an hour!' Tara said.

'What are you waiting for? Text him back already!' Emily said.

'But Colin and I are in couples therapy to try and save our marriage. And I can't do that while having an online affair. God, I used to be a good person,' Tara sighed.

'Good people are just bad people who've never got caught. Send him the text already before I download Fling and steal him from you,' Emily said.

'OK, here goes nothing,' Tara said, typing out the message.

Claire: Hey there, stranger x

I'm so sorry I disappeared on you

Can we chat at 11.11 tonight? x

Tara didn't know if Jack would be willing to forgive her for standing him up, but even if she never heard from him again, at least she would know she tried. Still, the idea of him not replying was terrifying for some reason. The mere thought of Jack rejecting her was devastating.

'Oh my God, what am I going to do if he doesn't reply? What if we were meant to be together and I ruined everything?' Tara panicked.

'Tara, I'm all for you meeting Jack, but don't you think you're getting a little emotionally involved? This should really be a no-strings-attached kind of thing,' Emily said, concerned.

'I hear what you're saying, Emily, but there's just something about Jack. We have this strange connection,' Tara said, staring off into space.

'Yeah, it's called Wi-Fi. He's still a stranger on the internet, remember? Let's reserve judgement until you know what he actually looks like.'

'It's not even about looks, Emily. Neither of us know what the other one looks like but we really see each other, you know?'

'You need to stop romanticizing men online. I made that mistake on that sugar daddy website.'

'What happened?'

'He took me for lobster but I ended up with crabs,' Emily said, shrugging her shoulders.

'Yikes. But Jack is different, Emily, I can feel it in my bones.'

'I'm just saying, lower your expectations. Better to be pleasantly surprised than utterly disappointed.'

'OMG!' Tara yelled suddenly. 'I've just realized I have a new problem. Colin is no longer sleeping on the couch. And I can't talk to Jack if Colin is lying in bed beside me! What the hell am I going to do now?'

'That's easy, just start a fight with him,' Emily said.

'I promised our counsellor that I wouldn't start any fights. And if I do, Colin will use it against me in therapy. And I don't want to give him any ammunition,' Tara said.

'Then you make him start the fight . . .' Emily said deviously.

'I'm listening . . .'

'You're going to have to peeve-bomb him.'

'What the hell does that mean?'

'Peeve-bombing is a strategy I made up to get men to lose interest in me. It's when you use all of their pet peeves against them at once. For example, if I'm with a guy I don't like, I won't dump him directly. Instead, I'll ask him what exact time he was born at so I can do a full astrological birth-chart reading. Do you catch my drift?' Emily explained.

'OK, that's clever, actually,' Tara said, intrigued by the idea. 'What other kind of things should I do?'

'Try to take over his space in the house as much as possible. Make him feel like the couch is the only place he can have some peace and quiet.'

'Got it. What else?'

'Hmm, let's see . . . I bet he'd hate it if you said you were going vegan.'

'Oh, that's a good one,' Tara said, making a mental note.

'But the best way to annoy any man is to ask him this one hypothetical question.'

'What question?'

'Ask him if he'd still love you if you were a worm,' Emily said with an evil smirk. 'Trust me, he'll lose it.'

Chapter 21

Colin sat at his office desk on Tuesday, unable to perform the most basic of spreadsheet tasks, even on his usual auto-pilot mode. His mind was adrift in a sea of uncertainty. He had opened Fling a total of thirty-four times that morning to check to see if Claire would appear online. Searching for her green light had become a borderline obsession.

He even had to turn off his phone notifications temporarily. Every time his phone made any kind of noise, he checked it frantically in the hopes it would be Claire. So far, however, his cold-turkey approach wasn't working. His infatuation with her was like an open wound. He wanted to touch it constantly. But he had to let the wound heal.

Colin knew he needed to focus all his energy into saving his marriage with Tara. The only problem was that he couldn't imagine a future with her that didn't involve children. They had spent many a night in their youth having pillow talk about starting a family in the future. Well, now it was the future and it was time to take action. There were still so many options open to them. Surrogacy, adoption, foster children; why wouldn't Tara even consider these? And there was still a very good chance of IVF working, especially if Tara would swallow her pride and ask Celine to refer them to her fertility specialist friend.

Maybe that was the next move. Tara was too proud to ask

Celine. But what if she didn't have to? Perhaps it was up to him to take initiative. Being too proud to ask for help had always been Tara's tragic flaw. He had seen her completely burn out on more than one occasion because she thought asking for help implied weakness. Maybe it was his duty as her husband to recognize her inability to ask for help and bite the bullet for her. Perhaps it wasn't about what Tara wanted, it was about what she needed.

Colin decided to ask Celine himself. He found her number in his contacts and took a deep breath as he hit the call button.

'Hello?' Celine answered.

'Hi Celine, it's Colin, from across the road,' he said awkwardly, having never called her before.

'Oh Colin, what a surprise! Don't tell me my dogs got onto your lawn again!'

'No, no, nothing like that. I was calling about something you said a few months back. You mentioned that you were friendly with some IVF doctor?'

'Oh yes, Dr Guillermo Ferreira-Hernández. He's the top fertility specialist in the country.'

'How do you spell that?' Colin said, reaching for a pen to look him up.

'Oh goodness, I don't know off the top of my head. Most people just call him The Brazilian because he makes your lady parts feel brand new. I know a woman who was forty-nine when she went to him and she got pregnant on the first round. Hand to God,' Celine said.

'Well . . . I was wondering if there was any chance you could put in good word for myself and Tara?' Colin asked.

'I'd only be delighted to, Colin. I'm surprised you didn't ask me sooner! Now, he's usually booked months in advance but I can certainly get you on his waiting list right away.'

'That would be amazing, Celine.'

'But Colin, I have to ask. Why isn't Tara the one calling me?' Celine asked curiously.

'Well . . . Tara has given up hope on IVF. But I think it's worth one last try. Tara doesn't know I'm calling you, so if this could stay between us for now, I'd really appreciate it,' he explained.

'Colin, my lips are sealed. And you were right to call me. I'll text you when I hear back from him.'

'Thank you so much, Celine. Chat soon,' Colin said.

'Bye,' she said, hanging up.

As he took the phone from his ear, Colin had mixed feelings about what he had just done. Although he had taken action, there were still so many things beyond his control. There was no guarantee Tara would open up to the idea, and even if she came around, it was still just a spot on a waiting list, when time was of the essence. He tried to conjure up a sense of excitement but he couldn't find the energy. He had hoped that calling Celine would be the bandage his wound needed, but it didn't change the fact that he was still in pain. He slammed his head down on his desk in hopelessness.

Rory opened the door to Colin's office to discover the pity party that was taking place.

'Oh don't tell me you're still moping over Ciara,' Rory said, seeing Colin's face on his desk.

'Her name is Claire!' Colin snapped.

'Remembering a woman's name? Jesus, you're obsessed with her!' Rory said, slamming his hand down on Colin's desk. 'I've never seen you like this.'

'I can't help it. I have no control over my life any more. I don't know what to do.'

'Have you tried whining more? I hear that always works,' Rory said sarcastically.

'This is your fault, you know? You're the one who told me to join Fling in the first place,' Colin said, sitting up.

'Yeah, to find a *fling*! Not to get your heart broken by a woman you've never even met. It's time to get back in the saddle,' Rory said.

'Well, I'm sorry I can't just flip a switch in my head and forget about her. Tara and I had sex last night, but the only way I was able to get it up was by looking at Claire's lingerie pics. And I'm pretty sure Tara went snooping and found out I need Viagra to have sex with her,' Colin said.

'Wow, she must be taking it hard,' Rory smirked.

'Oh shut up,' Colin said, trying not to laugh. 'But one look at Claire's nudes and I was a horny teenager again. And now she's just gone.'

'Col, the only way to get over someone is to get under someone new. We need to get your body count up to two,' Rory said.

'My body count?' Colin said, horrified by the term.

'Sex is just a numbers game, Colin. My goal is to sleep with one hundred women before I die. I won't rest until I become a centurion,' Rory bragged.

'What number are you on now?' Colin inquired.

'I don't know my exact number, Colin. What am I? Some kind of human calculator?' Rory said defensively.

'Yes, you're an accountant.'

'Well, I obviously lost count of the women, Colin. It's called being a stud,' Rory bragged.

'Yeah, you're a stud, just without the U,' Colin joked.

'Haha very funny,' Rory said sarcastically. 'But the joke's on you because I'd rather catch chlamydia than catch feelings like you. There must be so many bored housewives on Fling dying for a dick appointment.'

'Is that what the kids are calling it these days?' Colin laughed.

'As a matter of fact it is. Now stop acting like an old man and go sow your wild oats. Open up the app right now and see if you have any other matches,' Rory said.

'Fine,' he said, taking out his phone. 'Just to prove to you that I'm not interested in anyone else.'

Colin opened Fling and, to his shock, saw that Claire's green light was on. Not only that, but she had messaged him.

Claire: Hey there, stranger x

I'm so sorry I disappeared on you

Can we chat at 11.11 tonight? x

Colin almost dropped the phone in shock. 'Oh my God, Claire replied. She said she's sorry and she wants to chat tonight. What should I say? Should I tell her how much I missed her?' Colin asked, with the face of a dog whose owner had just come home.

'Dear Lord, man. I have second-hand embarrassment just from hearing you say those words. She stood you up, now it's time to stand up for yourself. Be a man,' Rory demanded.

'OK, you're right,' Colin said, puffing out his chest as he began to type.

Jack: I'm not the kind of man who tolerates getting stood up

Colin immediately began to panic the moment he sent the message.

206

'Oh God, maybe that was too harsh,' he said.

'Relax. She wants you to put your foot down,' Rory said confidently.

'Are you sure?' Colin asked, still flustered.

'If you can't stand up *to* a woman, you can't stand up *for* a woman,' Rory said. 'And if a woman knows she can walk all over you, she'll walk away from you.'

'I hope you're right,' Colin said, biting his nails.

Colin's phone beeped.

Claire: I deserve that, Jack . . .

But I'm begging that you'll let me make it up to you x

Maybe I should be punished . . .

Colin was shocked. Rory's advice had apparently paid off. Not only was she apologetic, she was begging to make amends.

'You see?' Rory said, seeing the message. 'She wants you even more because you stood up to her. Because she knows you're not harmless. Women are always attracted to the idea of taming a wild man. But once they tame him, their attraction disappears.'

'Well, I'll show Claire just how wild I can be tonight,' Colin smirked as he began to type a coy reply.

Jack: I think that can be arranged at 11.11 tonight.

Don't keep me waiting . . .

When the message sent, Colin suddenly realized there was a rather significant obstacle in his way. Tara had forgiven him for their fight and he was now sleeping in bed beside her once more. But if he was in bed beside Tara, he couldn't text Claire.

'New problem. Tara and I aren't fighting any more so we're back sleeping in the same bed. But if I'm not sleeping on the couch, I can't text Claire,' Colin panicked.

'So start a fight and make Tara send you to the couch.'

'Our therapist told us we're not allowed to start fights,' Colin sighed.

'So make Tara start the fight,' Rory said.

'Hmm . . . yeah, I see what you mean,' Colin said. 'But how do I pull that off?'

'You're telling me you've been with Tara for eighteen years and you don't know how to get under her skin?' Rory asked, raising an eyebrow.

'You're right. I know exactly how to push her buttons,' Colin said, pondering.

'Good. So all you have to do is push them . . . all at once,' Rory said with a mischievous smile.

Chapter 22

Colin spent his drive home making a mental note of Tara's pet peeves. She had a long list of things that bothered her but he needed to focus on the ones that would really drive her up the wall. A part of him did feel a little guilty for what he was about to do, but he couldn't miss his rendezvous with Claire. And texting Claire while in bed beside Tara simply wasn't an option. He knew he had to commit to his mission of getting banished to the couch.

When he finally arrived home, however, he could smell that something was burning. He followed the scent and, when he opened the door to the living room, he was blindsided by what he saw. Tara was meditating in the lotus position, right in the middle of his man cave. She was surrounded by burning incense sticks, something she knew he absolutely despised. She had moved all the furniture around in such a way that the room was unrecognizable.

'What the hell is this?' Colin said.

'Yoga,' Tara said, not opening her eyes.

'Yoga is just stretching with notions,' he said, frustrated by the sight before him.

'Shh . . . I'm meditating.'

'I can see that . . . but why are you doing it in my man cave?'

'Well, I was reflecting on some of the things Dr Burke said. Like how there needs to be no boundaries between us . . .'

'I think you're paraphrasing.'

'. . . and it got me thinking,' she continued, getting up from her yoga mat. 'This is *our* living room and the term "man cave" is just so outdated. Sexist even! So I moved the furniture around to improve the room's feng shui and renamed it the zen den.' Tara put her hands together and bowed like a Buddhist monk. 'I'm so glad we're learning to compromise!'

Colin felt like banging his head against the wall. But if he started a fight now, he'd be the bad guy and Tara would play the victim in therapy. He needed Tara to start the fight, not him. He had to bite his tongue and stick to his plan.

'No problem . . . babe,' he said, overemphasizing the word she hated so much. Colin headed into the kitchen and looked around for an opportunity to vex her in any way possible. He noticed that the recycling bin was full and needed to be emptied but the regular waste bin was only half full.

Bingo.

Colin picked up the recycling bin and poured half the rubbish into general waste. The rattling of the waste made plenty of noise and he knew it would get Tara's attention.

'What are you doing?' Tara said, storming in.

'Oh, the recycling bin is full so I'm just making some space,' he said, provoking her.

'Are you serious?' she snapped. 'You can't mix the two!'

'Well, I'm just so glad the general waste and the recyclable waste are finally learning to compromise,' Colin said smugly.

'That's not how it works, Colin. If we just dump everything, it'll end up in the ocean and kill the turtles,' she said frantically.

'Yeah, but I was thinking . . . what have the turtles ever really done for me, you know?' Colin said, taking pleasure in annoying her.

Tara's blood was boiling but she wasn't about to let Colin make her lose her temper.

'Whatever you say, honeybun,' she said with a smile that almost killed her.

Colin began walking towards the fridge for some food. When he opened the door, he was greeted by a fully stocked jungle of fruits and vegetables. There wasn't a single space on the shelf that didn't have something green on it.

'Why does our fridge look like a farmer's market stall?' Colin asked, confused.

'Because, honeybun ... we're going VEGAN!' she said, clapping her hands together like a toy monkey holding cymbals.

'I'm sorry?' Colin said in shock.

'Yes, it's official. We're stopping eating all animals and animal products.'

'If humans aren't supposed to eat animals, then why are they made of food?'

'Honeybun, it seems like you're a little hangry. Would you like me to air fry you some Brussels sprouts for dinner?'

'No thank you, babe. I've suddenly lost my appetite,' he said, closing the fridge.

'Don't worry, I'm not going to be one of those vegans who keeps talking about being vegan all the time,' she said.

'You mean like you're doing now?' he said snidely. Colin knew he had to up his game. He rattled his brain for something that had driven Tara up the wall in the past.

Then, suddenly, a lightbulb.

'As much as I'd love to go vegan, babe, now's just not a good time. I need all my vitamins and minerals for growing my beard.'

'Your ... beard?' she asked, taken aback. 'Colin, you tried to grow a beard before, remember?'

'Yeah, but I didn't really commit to it. I should have given it more time.'

'You gave it six months and it was just random patches of black, grey and ginger hair. You looked like a registered sex offender!' Tara said, petrified that he was serious.

'But this time, I'm going all in. I'll need to give it a good year. It'll all be worth it in the end. Now, if you'll excuse me, babe, I'm going to go watch the match in my man cave,' he said, heading into the living room.

'I THINK YOU MEAN ZEN DEN!' she yelled after him.

Tara realized she wasn't getting anywhere. He seemed to be playing some kind of game of his own. Or perhaps he was playing her at her own game, she couldn't tell.

Either way, it was time to up the ante.

'You get comfortable and I'll make you a nice cup of tea,' Tara called into the living room, boiling the kettle. Colin took his tea in a very specific way, with the teabag soaking for at least sixty seconds and with barely a thimble of full-fat milk. There was nothing he hated more than weak, milky tea. Once the kettle had boiled, Tara put the teabag in Colin's least favourite mug and stirred it for less than five seconds before taking it out. She then filled the mug up with the newly purchased almond milk until the tea turned white.

Having rearranged the furniture back to normal, Colin was already watching Manchester United play Liverpool on the TV. He faintly heard Tara creep into the room like a silent assassin. He knew she was up to something but he couldn't figure out her endgame. Only one thing was certain.

They were engaged in a battle of wits.

'TEA TIME!' she shouted, nearly lifting him off the couch.

'JESUS! You certainly know how to keep me on my toes, babe,' he said, taking his cup of tea.

The second his lips touched the hot liquid, he knew something was wrong.

'How is it, honeybun?' she said, smiling like a parody of a fifties housewife.

Colin wanted to spit the disgusting contents of his mouth out all over the room, but he was determined to keep his composure. 'Just perfect, babe,' he replied, not giving her the satisfaction.

He placed his mug down on the coffee table, directly beside one of the coasters, something he knew would drive Tara crazy. Tara almost winced when she saw what he had done but she bit her tongue and feigned a painful smile instead.

'I hope you don't mind, but I called your mother earlier to find out what time you were born at.'

'And why exactly did you do that?' Colin asked, genuinely puzzled.

'So I could give you a full astrological birth-chart reading, silly!' she squeaked, as she took out her phone.

'Let me guess? Mercury is in Lucozade again?'

'It's retrograde, honeybun,' she said, opening a zodiac app on her phone. 'So we know your sun is in Taurus but did you know your moon is in Leo? Makes so much sense now that I think about it. And listen to this. Uranus is in Cancer!'

'What is this? A colonoscopy?'

'Think of it more as a Colinoscopy. It's all about what makes you, you,' Tara grinned.

'Well, better to have Uranus in Cancer than Cancer in Uranus,' Colin smirked. 'You know, it's too bad you didn't marry the Zodiac Killer, babe. He would have loved all this stuff. I bet he was a Gemini.'

Colin put his feet directly up on top of the coffee table, something he was sure would get a vocal reaction. Tara still didn't react. She refused to. She needed him to be the one to snap.

'Do you not get bored watching the ball go back and forth?' she asked, looking at the match on the screen.

'That's not what football is about. It's about strategy. It's about outwitting the other team.'

'I think Liverpool will win.'

'ARE YOU JOKING?' Colin yelled, a die-hard Manchester fan since he was five.

Tara knew that asking stupid questions during a match was Colin's biggest pet peeve and she had finally got a more vocal reaction out of him. She was on to something. Thankfully, Emily had suggested just the question that she knew would infuriate him.

'Colin,' Tara said softly as she moved closer to him. 'I have to ask you something.'

'What?' Colin said, still watching the match.

'It's important, Colin!' she said, trying to get his undivided attention.

'OK, OK, what is it?' Colin said, turning to her.

'Would you still love me if I was a worm?' Tara said, her tone deadly serious. A part of her wanted to laugh but she couldn't break character now. She had to commit to the question.

'Excuse me?' Colin said, thinking he had surely misheard her.

'Like if I turned into a worm, would you still love me?' Tara said.

'What kind of a stupid question is that?'

'It's not a stupid question, Colin. It's a very important question.'

'How on earth is that important?'

'Because if I turn into a worm someday, I want to know if

214

you're just going to get up and leave me!' Tara said, pretending to be hysterical.

'Why would you turn into a worm?' Colin said, getting visibly more irritated that the match was being ruined on him.

'Just answer the question, Colin!' she said, now in full-swing histrionics.

'Dear Jesus, if you were a worm, I wouldn't know it was you, so I would probably squash you by accident.'

'No, you would know it was me,' Tara said, as if it was the most obvious thing in the world.

'How on earth would I know it was you?'

'I'd still be able to talk.'

'Then . . . no,' Colin said, now calm and collected.

'No, what?'

'No, I wouldn't still love you if you were a worm. Because if you could talk, you'd spend all day asking me stupid questions while I tried to watch the match,' Colin said matter-of-factly.

'Wow . . . and here I was thinking you were loyal,' she said, pretending to be hurt. 'So you'd just throw me in the bin, would you?'

'Babe, of course not,' he said calmly.

'Really?'

'I'd recycle you.'

'You can't recycle worms, Colin!' Tara snapped.

'And what about me? Would you still love me if I was a worm?' Colin asked, turning the question back on her.

'You already are a worm!'

'Great, we can be worms together,' Colin said as he took another sip of tea, forgetting it tasted horrible. He was almost at boiling point but he cooled down his internal temperature by focusing on his objective. He had one more play. There was nothing Tara valued more than her beauty sleep. If Colin could get in the way of it, she would surely banish him to the couch immediately.

'Oh, I forgot to tell you, I'm reading this new book that says successful people wake up at five a.m. every morning, without fail. You don't mind if I set an alarm for five, do you, babe?' Colin said, knowing victory was in sight.

'Five a.m.?' Tara laughed. 'You're not waking me up at five a.m.!'

'You're always telling me I should read more books to help me work on myself. I'm just trying to make you happy,' he said, shrugging.

'Getting up at five a.m. is just pure madness!'

'Well, you know what they say about madness and genius. I guess that's why so many CEOs get up at five a.m. Early bird gets the worm! Oh, you can be my worm, babe!' Colin said, in an annoyingly chirpy tone.

Colin could see the vein on Tara's temple protruding like a river of rage.

Her blood had officially come to a boil.

Checkmate.

'WELL, IF YOU'RE GOING TO BE WAKING UP AT FIVE A.M., YOU CAN GO BACK TO SLEEPING ON THE FECKIN' COUCH!' Tara screamed as she stormed out of the room, defeated.

Manchester scored a goal on-screen and Colin leaped out of his seat with excitement. He had beaten Tara in their little battle of wits and he was now free to chat to Claire at 11.11 every night.

Chapter 23

Jack: Hey there, stranger 😊

Claire: Jack, I owe you a huge apology

I'm so so sorry for standing you up

Please don't hate me x

Jack: I could never hate you. But it did hurt when you didn't show up.

What happened?

Claire: Long story short, I felt like I was about to be caught.

I just completely panicked and deleted the app.

I think maybe we rushed into meeting

Can you forgive me? x

Jack: I forgive you, Claire, but you do need to be punished 😊

Claire: Punish me, Jack, make me pay for what I've done x

Jack: Oh, we'll get to that . . . Making you wait is part of your punishment 😊

Claire: I haven't stopped thinking about you 😊

Even when I'm with my husband, it's you that's taking me all the way x

Jack: Only a real man like me can take you all the way 😊

When I'm with my wife, all I can think about is you in that red lingerie . . .

Claire: My husband doesn't even know I own that. It's for you and you only x

Jack: Still, your husband is one lucky man getting to enjoy the body underneath the lingerie

Claire: Too bad he doesn't appreciate it 🙁

Jack: If it were me, I'd be making sure your body was appreciated every single night . . .

Not just appreciated . . . worshipped 😊

Claire: Ugh, there you go again knowing the exact right thing to say x

I wish you could just break in and save me x

Jack: I'd give anything . . .

Claire: Do you ever feel like you're trapped in your own life?

Jack: Constantly. Sometimes I feel like I'm not really living . . . I'm just existing

Claire: Yes! I had a terrible void in my chest for so long

It only goes away when you're in my life

I guess that's why I missed you x

Jack: Honestly, I really thought I'd lost you.

I checked every day to see if your little green light would appear

Claire: I thought when I deleted the app, my profile was gone forever

As soon as I realized I could sign back in, I came back x

Jack: I'm so glad you did

Life felt so empty without you 🙁

Claire: Maybe we were lovers in a past life x

Jack: Maybe I was an old Irish king and you were my queen

220

Claire: Or maybe you were a Greek sculptor and I was your muse x

Jack: No, I'd be too greedy . . .

I'd keep all your sculptures to myself so I wouldn't have to share that perfect body 😊

Claire: You're the one with the amazing body!

Sometimes I see a man in gym gear on the street and I wonder if it's you

Jack: I always wonder if we've crossed paths or met in real life

Claire: We definitely haven't

Jack: What makes you so sure?

Claire: Because if we had met, we would have had an affair ages ago x

Jack: You're right haha

Our chemistry would have erupted 😊

Claire: It certainly has in my fantasies x

Jack: Oh you've been fantasizing about me have you? 😊

Claire: It's hard not to. You're all I can think about x

Can I tell you a secret? x

Jack: Of course 😊

Claire: I love the idea of you taking me any way you want

Walking up behind me and grabbing me in your big arms

Kissing me like you own me

In total control x

Jack: You'd fight your feelings at first

But I'd whisper 'Let go' in your ear

And you'd give in to the pleasure

Claire: It feels so good to be able to talk like this

I always feel ashamed for having that kind of fantasy x

Jack: You should never be ashamed of pleasure

And a woman like you deserves all the pleasure in the world ☺

Claire: I know you'd give me what I deserve x

Jack: All night long ☺

Well, my schedule happens to be open every night at 11.11 ☺

Claire: What a coincidence . . . so is mine x

Now . . . tell me how you're going to punish me for missing our date . . .

WEDNESDAY — 11.11 P.M.

Jack: Hey there, stranger ☺

How was your day?

Claire: I was very bad today . . .

223

Jack: Oh really? 😊

Claire: I left work again to go buy some new lingerie . . .

Just for you x

Jack: I think I might just be the luckiest man alive 😊

Do I get a sneak peek?

Claire: Well, it would have been a waste of money if I didn't show it off . . .

But it's just my body again, no face pics x

Jack: Don't worry, I know the rules 😊

Claire: Image Delivered

Image Delivered

Image Delivered

Jack: OH MY GOD!

The blue one is even sexier than the red!

How do you keep getting hotter and hotter? 😊

Claire: I guess you just get me all steamed up x

Jack: I wish I'd taken some more gym photos for you, but I wasn't there today

Claire: Don't worry, I love showing off for you x

If my colleagues knew I was taking lingerie pics on my lunch break haha

Jack: Can you imagine if it turned out we worked together?

Claire: Oh God, if you were one of the men I work with, I'd run a mile haha

Jack: Are they awful?

Claire: They're not that bad but sometimes I feel they don't take me seriously

They have this image of me in their head that isn't the real me

Jack: I'm going to come to where you work and sort them out

Claire: Haha that's against the rules

But the thought of it does turn me on, I won't lie x

Jack: Any man that crosses you will have to deal with me

Claire: My own personal bodyguard. Now you're really turning me on x

Jack: I don't know how I got so lucky with you . . .

You're literally my fantasy come to life 😊

Claire: So are you, Jack. I feel so drawn to you

Not just sexually . . . spiritually too

Jack: I'm just so glad you're back in my life

You don't even know how crazy I was going without you

226

Claire: Is your wife that bad?
Haha

Jack: She's just become a
different person

It's like I don't even recognize her
any more ☹

Sorry, I don't mean to be a
downer

Claire: No, I like that we can talk
about this kind of stuff

I know exactly what you mean.
My husband just doesn't make me
feel the way he used to

The way you currently make me
feel x

Jack: Not to sound selfish but I'm
glad he takes you for granted

Gives me a chance to worship you
the way you deserve to be ☺

Claire: I like that you're selfish.
You take what you want and you
don't apologize x

Jack: The real man you deserve 😊

Claire: But I can't even fully blame my husband either

Sometimes I don't like the person I've become 🙁

Sorry, you probably have no idea what I'm talking about

Jack: No! I do! Like you've become a stranger to yourself?

Claire: Yes! That's exactly it!

Jack: Sometimes I think my younger self would be ashamed if he saw me now

Claire: It's crazy how we allow ourselves to become so far removed from our true selves

Jack: But here's the even crazier thing. I feel fully myself talking to you on this app

Like I'm back to being me again

Claire: I know what you mean! I had become this version of myself I didn't even like

I swear you brought the old me back to life x

Jack: I wish you could have seen the old me back in the day. I was a proper rebel

And I know you like a bad boy 😊

Claire: You're still that rebel, Jack

I mean, everything about our relationship is rebellious if you think about it x

Jack: True haha I sometimes forget how scandalous it is for us to even be talking

Claire: It takes courage to refuse unhappiness

I was so numb before we matched

You saved me from drowning just in time x

Jack: Now that makes me think of a very hot role-play scenario

Claire: Tell me all about it . . . Lifeguard Jack x

THURSDAY — 11.11 P.M.

Claire: Hey there, stranger x

Jack: Hey sexy, I have a surprise for you . . .

Claire: Oh yeah? x

Jack: Image Delivered

Image Delivered

Image Delivered

Claire: My God, you've been working out hard, it seems

Jack: Haha, you like?

Claire: Oh yes. You look so sexy in that gym gear of yours

I'm jealous of those dumbbells
getting picked up by you x

Jack: Well . . . there's one muscle
on my body only you can work
out 😊

Claire: Now that would be one
vigorous workout x

Jack: Claire, I have something I
want to ask you

But I hope it's not too soon

Claire: You can ask me anything,
Jack x

Jack: All week, my feelings for
you have been getting stronger

And I was wondering . . .

What do you think about trying to
arrange another date?

I know you said we rushed into
it last time but if you're ready, so
am I 😊

Claire: Don't get me wrong, I absolutely want to x

But there's just one fear holding me back . . .

Jack: You can tell me . . .

Claire: My fear is that we'll meet up but that afterwards . . .

I'll never hear from you again ☹

Jack: Claire, I would never. I swear.

Claire: I know, I know, but it's just an irrational fear I can't control.

It's just that most men only want one thing ☹

Jack: But I'm not most men, Claire

I would never in a million years hurt you

What we have is too important

Claire: That feels so good to hear x

Jack: So what do you say?

Should we try meeting again?

Claire: It feels so risky but I can't fight my feelings any more . . .

Let's do it! Let's meet for a drink x

Jack: Amazing! Where would you like to go? ☺

Don't say The Vine, they'll never give me another reservation haha

Claire: Haha! How about Elixir? It's a cocktail bar on Harcourt Street x

Jack: Perfect. Does tomorrow work for you?

Claire: Yes! Say 8 p.m.?

Jack: Perfect. Elixir on Harcourt Street, Tomorrow at 8 p.m.

You have no idea how excited I am!!!

Claire: Me too! My heart literally just started beating out of my chest!

Jack: Just please don't stand me up again haha

Claire: I won't, Jack.

I'll be there x

Chapter 24

When Friday arrived, Colin found himself smirking uncontrollably in the hours leading up to his date with Claire. He had been too excited to concentrate on his work that morning so he decided to cash in his winning bet with Rory, who had no choice but to agree. A luxury game of golf felt like the cherry on top of a perfect week. Colin took a deep breath of fresh air and felt more alive than ever.

'You know the only thing better than a game of golf?' Colin asked Rory as he lined up his shot.

'Please don't say it,' Rory pleaded.

'A free game of golf,' Colin said as he took a strong swing that sent his ball flying halfway down the fairway.

'This is ridiculous. You don't even need a caddy,' Rory whined as he carried Colin's golf clubs on his back.

'Yeah, but it makes my victory all the more sweet.'

Colin began to walk down the fairway towards where his ball had landed as Rory trailed awkwardly behind him. As he sauntered along the grass, his imagination ran wild with all the possible outcomes of his date with Claire. He found himself more enthralled by her than ever. He knew there was no guarantee that she would find him attractive, or even vice versa, but the two had shared so many intimate moments on Fling each night that not feeling anything in real life seemed damn near impossible. What they had was too real.

On the app, they were merely two disembodied personas, yet Colin felt more in touch with his true self than ever before. It almost felt as if Colin was his mask and Jack was who existed beneath. Perhaps when he woke up in the morning, he put on his person-suit to play the role he thought he had to. But every night with Claire, he felt like he could take off his guise and be his deeper, primal self. The virtual realm they created together had no shame. It was a judgement-free erotic space with no inhibitions.

Now it was time for the veil to be lifted.

Although it only began as an empty threat to annoy Tara, Colin had started growing a beard. Tara had been right when she said his previous attempts at facial hair had been a mistake. He always believed he didn't have the genetic potential. But now, after only three days of not shaving, Colin had stubble he was quite proud of. It gave him a more rough-and-ready look and he even noticed a few women on the street giving him a second glance. His confidence was at an all-time high.

'So what's the game plan for meeting Claire tonight?' Rory asked when they arrived at Colin's ball.

'No games. Just two people meeting each other for a drink,' Colin said, squinting at the green to determine which club to use. 'Three-wood please.'

Rory let out a grunt and handed Colin the club. 'So where are you taking her exactly?'

'She requested Elixir. We're meeting there at eight p.m.'

'Nice one. Which hotel did you book?'

'What?' Colin said, confused. 'I didn't book a hotel.'

'Hold on, you don't have a room to take her back to afterwards?' Rory said, shocked.

'Of course not, she just said she wanted to meet for a drink at Elixir. She didn't mention any hotel,' Colin said.

'Yeah, Col, she chose Elixir because it's on Harcourt Street. And what else is on Harcourt Street? A bunch of hotels. Does she really have to spell it out for you? If she chooses Elixir, she's hoping he licks her,' Rory said, forcing the pun.

'Only your filthy mind would think of that,' Colin laughed, brushing off the idea. He lined up his shot and sent the ball flying right onto the green. 'Anyway, I don't even know if she'd be up for having sex on the first date.'

'How many times do I have to tell you? It's not a first date, it's an affair. The normal rules don't apply. Nobody has an affair to have less sex. That's what marriage is for!'

'Well . . . our conversations are always very sexual . . . but she never specifically said she wanted to sleep with me tonight,' Colin said.

'Of course she didn't explicitly say it. That's your job. You have to master the art of the *Bold Move*,' Rory said, emphasizing the phrase.

'And what might that be, exactly?' Colin asked.

'When you're seducing someone, you need to make a leap of faith in order to take things to the next level. No woman wants to have to ask a man to kiss her. She wants the man to just do it already. She wants you to make a bold move. But the two of you are married so you can't really just grab her and kiss her in public. Dublin is too small for that. People might recognize you. Your bold move is finding the right moment to whisper in her ear that you have a bottle of champagne on ice in a hotel room nearby . . .'

'And what if she says no?'

'Then fine, her loss. But what if she says yes and you don't have a room to take her to? Talk about leaving her high and dry,' Rory said.

Colin thought about it for a moment. He wasn't sure about Rory's logic, but his relationship with Claire was already quite sexual. After all, they had spent many nights talking about their deepest desires. If she wanted to take things to the next level, Colin wanted to have that option available. It did feel a little presumptuous to book a room in advance, however. And being frugal to a fault, Colin didn't like the idea of paying for a room that might not even be used.

'Can't I just book the room after we have a drink?' Colin said, wanting the best of both worlds.

'A last-minute room? On Harcourt Street? On a Friday night? Yeah, good luck with that.' Rory laughed.

'OK, fine! I'll book a bloody room,' Colin said, taking out his phone. Colin searched online to get a good rate on Harcourt Street hotels but saw that most of them were booked out.

'The cheapest room available is a suite in the Gibson Court Hotel but it's two hundred and sixty euro,' he said, wincing.

'Look, it's your call, but if Claire says she wants to bang, what are you going to say? Follow me baby, I know a quaint little ditch around the corner?' Rory said, painting a horrifying picture in Colin's mind.

Even though Rory was being hyperbolic as usual, what he was saying did make sense. Better to have the room and not need it than need the room and not have it. She had told him constantly on Fling that she loved how dominant he was, how much control he seemed to have. Maybe she would want this bold move.

Either way, Colin was happy to keep all his options open.

'Well . . . it's technically cheaper than therapy,' he said, as he clicked the BOOK NOW button on his screen. After a few more clicks, the room was officially secure, he just had to pay at check-in. Colin felt a rush of adrenaline flood his brain. He was excited just to meet Claire, but now there was the possibility of their online sexual fantasies being realized.

238

As they arrived at the green, Colin felt a sliver of guilt creeping in. Had he really just booked a hotel room for him and another woman? Rory was always the devil on his shoulder but maybe he was walking down the path of no return. A part of him would have loved to have spent the night in the hotel with Tara. The old Tara. The Tara he fell in love with. But she wouldn't want a bold move the way she used to. The Tara that had wanted him to grab her and kiss her on Nimmo's Pier eighteen years ago was gone. Now it was Claire who wanted him. And everyone deserves to feel wanted, do they not?

Colin suddenly realized he would be arriving home late after his date which would undoubtedly raise some alarm bells.

'I'm going to need to come up with an excuse to tell Tara. Something she will believe,' Colin said, worried.

'Keep it vague,' Rory said. 'Otherwise you'll trip yourself up.'

Colin took out his phone and sent Tara a text saying:

> Working late, not sure what time
> I'll be home.

It wasn't the most original lie but it was simple and to the point. After he sent it, he noticed that he had an unread text from Celine that had been delivered that morning. Colin opened the message.

> **Celine:** I got The Brazilian for you.
> And don't worry, I won't say a
> thing to Tara 😊

Colin had almost forgotten about asking Celine to be put on the fertility doctor's waiting list. He had asked her in a moment of desperation about his future. He couldn't think about the idea of having kids with Tara right now, it made him feel too guilty.

'What's the matter?' Rory said, seeing his expression.

'Nothing. It's just a text from Tara's friend Celine. I asked her a few days ago to help us get on the waiting list for this fancy fertility doctor,' Colin explained.

'I thought Tara ruled out IVF?'

'She has. I went behind her back thinking she would come around eventually.'

'Yeah, that's not going to backfire at all,' Rory said sarcastically.

'I didn't think it all the way through. It's just hard to let go of the idea of being a father. Don't you ever think about kids?'

'Nah, I'm more of a daddy than a dad.'

'I think it's pronounced caddy,' Colin slagged him.

'Hilarious,' Rory said, rolling his eyes. 'But anyway, you need to forget about the future and focus on living in the present with Claire.'

'Yeah, but the funny thing is, when I do think about the future, I see it with Claire,' Colin admitted. 'Is that an awful thing to say?'

'Yes, awfully stupid. You don't even know what she looks like!'

'I know she has the hottest body I've ever seen.'

'Yeah, but what if she's a butter face?' Rory asked.

'What the hell is a butter face?'

'It's when a girl has a hot body . . . but her face . . .' Rory said, grimacing.

'Oh, that's just mean. Even if she's not a model, I'll still treat her with respect and dignity. Two new words for your vocabulary,' Colin said, teasing him.

'I still don't understand why you're so obsessed with her.'

'I'm not obsessed. I just feel like I can truly be myself with her. I don't have to pretend to be someone I'm not,' Colin explained.

'You met her on an anonymous affair app under a fake name. The whole point is to be someone else!'

'Well, maybe I like being Jack more than I like being Colin.'

'Now is not the time for an existential crisis, Col. This is about sex, not premature e-*Jack*-ulation,' Rory said.

'You'll understand how I'm feeling one day, Rory,' Colin said.

'It's nothing a healthy dose of post-nut clarity wouldn't cure anyway.'

'What's that?'

'It's when your feelings for someone magically disappear after you've had sex with them. Just wait and see, it'll happen after you get with Claire tonight,' Rory said.

'Not if the sex is life-changing,' Colin said as they arrived at his ball on the green. 'Putter.'

Rory sighed and took Colin's putter out of the bag. 'Put her in any position you want, you'll still lose your feelings for her after you do the deed. And if you don't, well, then it must be love,' Rory said, handing him the club.

'Time will tell. I guess now all I have to do is enjoy my well-earned game of golf while I wait for this evening,' Colin said, gripping his putter in his hand. He tapped the ball and watched it roll into the hole. 'Good thing we've got seventeen more holes to go.'

'I thought we agreed nine holes!' Rory said, fuming.

'You're the one who's always saying every hole's a goal,' Colin smiled.

'I WASN'T TALKING ABOUT GOLF!'

Chapter 25

Tara spent her Friday lunch break getting the one thing that can give any Irish woman the confidence to do anything.

A curly blow-dry.

She didn't often indulge in such a treat but she was determined to make the best impression possible with Jack later that night. When she arrived back at her office, her hair bounced with limitless volume.

After each late-night rendezvous that week, Tara felt closer and closer to Jack. He told her about how his wife didn't let him be the man he truly was, but that with Claire, he felt he could be his true masculine self. And Jack made her feel so comfortable in her femininity. She felt like she had accessed some higher plane of existence where she could embody the divine feminine. It was a feeling of sensual power.

She wasn't planning on sleeping with Jack but the thought had certainly crossed her mind. After all, he made her feel things she hadn't felt in years. The way Colin used to make her feel. Tara had given herself to Colin completely on the first night they met but it didn't feel rushed. It felt right. And somehow, she felt the same way about Jack. But she knew that didn't make any sense considering she didn't even know what he looked like. Anonymity was sexy in the fantasy realm of Fling, but there was no way to be anonymous on a real date. The blindfold had to come off. And yet, her instincts told her that her feelings for Jack were real. She felt completely aligned with her destiny, ready to take a leap of faith to discover her fate.

But first things first, Tara still had work to do. Her pitch for Dick Mulligan was on Monday morning so she asked Emily to help her put the final touches on the slides. Everything was pretty much ready but she still hadn't come up with a catchy slogan to tie the campaign together. It was still missing a hook.

'What about . . . "You have the ring, now find a fling",' Tara said.

'Hmm, it feels a bit forced. And I don't think it needs to rhyme,' Emily said, unimpressed.

'OK, what about "Have your cake . . . and eat it too",' Tara suggested.

'It kinda just makes me want cake.' Emily shrugged.

'Ugh, me too. And I haven't eaten a single carb all week,' Tara sighed, suddenly remembering how hungry she was.

'I saw you eat a biscuit this morning,' Emily said, calling her out.

'Don't tell me there are carbs in biscuits? I thought they were full of fat?'

'You probably should have researched this diet more,' Emily laughed to herself.

'OK, well, today can be my cheat day then,' Tara decided. 'Wait, would that be a good slogan? "Everyone needs a cheat day"?'

'It makes me think that there's a specific day of the year to cheat. But that's actually not the worst idea in the world. One day a year where you're allowed to have an affair without any consequences. Like a national holiday,' Emily said, thinking out loud.

'I think launching a national holiday is beyond the scope

of our marketing campaign, Emily,' Tara sighed. 'God, why is it so hard to come up with this slogan?'

'Stop focusing on the outcome and think about the customer journey. You're about to take your fling from the app to reality. How are you feeling?' Emily asked.

'Nervous. Excited. Free. Reckless. Empowered. Guilty. Worried. Insane. I'm feeling a million different things. Like, I'm not trying to cheat on Colin. But I spent so long feeling sedated that I'm living for the rush. And I need to know why Jack is making me feel this way, why I felt the synchronicity. Colin's been on the couch all week so Jack and I have been having plenty of late-night rendezvous. We've acted out some really steamy role-plays. Like where he's a lifeguard and I need CPR,' Tara said cheekily.

'Oh Tara, you're so adorable. The fan-fiction I wrote when I was thirteen sounds steamier than that,' Emily laughed. 'But I'm glad you're finally learning to use your biggest sex organ.'

'Emily, behave,' Tara said playfully.

'What? I'm talking about your brain,' Emily said.

'Oh.' Tara laughed. 'Actually, I better text Colin to say I'll be home late. I don't want him getting suspicious.' Tara took out her phone, and when she unlocked her screen she saw Colin's text:

> Working late, not sure what time I'll be home.

Perfect.

'Phew, Colin is working late so I don't have to make up an excuse. One less thing to worry about,' Tara said, relaxing her shoulders.

'So are you going to let Jack take you down to pound town?' Emily asked cheekily.

'EMILY!'

'Tara, aren't we past the point of me saying something out-landish and you being shocked by it?'

'OK, fair enough,' Tara laughed. 'But the feelings Jack and I have for each other are more than just lust, Emily. He's not just thinking about sex.'

'Tara, he's a man.'

'Well, nobody's perfect,' Tara shrugged. 'Let's just say I'm open to seeing where the evening takes us.'

'Just don't do anything I wouldn't do,' Emily joked, pre-tending she was a beacon of virtue.

'I think that gives me a lot to work with,' Tara laughed.

'And while he's on top of you, ask him for some slogan ideas.'

'I might have to,' Tara sighed. 'I've hit a wall. I'm going to take my tablet home over the weekend in case I come up with something. Did you have any trouble getting the reservation at Al Fresco?'

'What reservation?' Emily asked nonchalantly.

'EMILY! THE RESERVATION FOR MY MEETING WITH DICK!' Tara screeched.

'Will you calm down. I'm messing with you. I got you a table on the outside terrace and I even put your appointment with Dick in your work calendar,' Emily said.

'Wow, Emily, you actually did your job? That means a lot to me. How can I ever repay you?'

'Money is fine,' Emily said, deadpan.

With that, the door to Tara's office opened and in walked Tommy, Mark and Rob. They all had a strange swagger about them and Tara didn't like it one bit.

'Can we help you, boys?' she said, folding her arms.

'We just stopped by to see how the big pitch is coming along,' Tommy said.

'Couldn't be going better. Myself and Emily are almost finished. Now if you'll excuse us—'

'The three of us were doing some thinking,' Tommy said, interrupting her.

'First time for everything,' Tara replied, smiling.

'We think the three of us should join you for your pitch meeting,' Mark said.

'And why would I let you do that?'

'Well . . . based on Dick Mulligan's public persona, we're not sure if you should be alone with him,' Rob said carefully.

'We think he's not as interested in your idea as he is in . . . you,' Mark added.

'Wow. Is it really that hard to accept that my pitch was better?' Tara said, taken aback.

'It's in your best interest if we come with you,' Tommy said.

Tara was furious. It felt like a threat. 'In my best interest? What is this, some kind of mob shakedown?' she asked.

'No, it's us trying to have your back. You know you're one of the Lads,' Tommy said.

'Oh please, for years the three of you have pushed me out of big accounts because I'm not a man. Well, guess what? I don't want to be one of the Lads. This campaign is a job for a woman,' Tara said, standing tall.

'Well, "lads" is technically a gender-neutral term,' Rob said.

'Oh really? How many *lads* have you slept with?' Tara said to Rob. He was suddenly silent.

'We're just trying to look out for you,' Mark said.

'No, it seems more like you're showing up at the last minute to take credit for all the work that I've done. Sound about right?' Tara said.

'You know what,' Tommy said calmly, 'we've said what we came here to say.'

'Well, thank you so much for stopping by, but it's not my job to hand out participation trophies for ideas that didn't make the cut. Why don't the three of you go back to foosball. Some of us have actual work to do,' Tara said smugly.

Tommy turned and left Tara's office, followed by Mark and Rob.

Emily looked at Tara in complete awe. 'Oh my GOD!' she yelled. 'I wanna be you when I grow up.'

They were the exact words Tara had always wanted to hear. The words that made her feel that she, as a woman, had made a difference.

'Never underestimate the power of a curly blow-dry,' she said, flicking her hair back over her shoulder.

Chapter 26

As Tara sat in the backseat of the taxi on the way to Elixir, she found herself riddled with nerves yet giddy with anticipation, the feeling one gets just before going on stage. She couldn't wait to perform the role of Claire, but she was still anxious about Jack's review.

She reminded herself that she was currently looking better than she had in years. After work, she had changed into a black satin dress with a cheeky thigh-high slit. Emily had tried to set off the fire alarm when she saw the sultry transformation. Tara was looking fabulous and she knew it. But her appearance wasn't the source of her confidence. Her erotic energy was radiating outwards from within, her core supercharged. She took pride in knowing that with a little bit of effort, the image in the mirror was capable of reflecting how Tara saw herself on the inside. She had always been her own worst critic and the fact that she had impressed herself meant she could impress anyone.

With her mind at ease, Tara relaxed her shoulders and told herself to enjoy the present moment. The excitement, the curiosity, the wonder – all these feelings were rare in Tara's life and she wanted to relish them. It was as if she had rediscovered some of her favourite records in an old dusty attic and she was finally allowing a needle to release the symphonic melodies they contained. Music was back in her life once again.

Out of nowhere, the taxi driver suddenly jammed on the brakes and jolted Tara back to reality.

'Jaysus, feckin' jaywalkers. The bane of my existence!' the taxi driver yelled as he stopped in front of a man crossing the street. When Tara sat up and looked out the front windscreen, she saw something completely unexpected.

It was Colin.

He was crossing the street in front of her cab and turning onto Harcourt Street. Not only that, but he was dressed rather stylishly and looked impeccably well groomed. The stubble she wanted to hate made him look annoyingly handsome. He was a downright hunk!

But Colin had texted her earlier to say he was working late. After he had crossed the road, he began to walk down Harcourt Street. What was he doing so far from his office?

She had to know.

'Excuse me, I know this is a strange request but would you mind following that man?' Tara asked.

'Who? The lad who walked out in front of me? Do ya know him?' he asked.

'He's my husband. And he's supposed to working late,' Tara explained.

'Hmm ... I always say jaywalkers can't be trusted,' he said. 'I'll follow him.'

The taxi driver tailed Colin as he walked down Harcourt Street and past Elixir. At least he wasn't going to the same place that she was due to meet Jack. He continued walking for about four hundred metres until he turned into a building. Tara looked at the sign and saw it was the Gibson Court Hotel.

'What the hell is Colin doing in a hotel?' Tara said, thinking out loud.

'Do I have to spell it out for ya, love?' the taxi driver replied.

'No, I'm sure there's a logical explanation for why my husband would lie about working late and go to a hotel room instead,' Tara said to the taxi man. But as soon as she heard the words aloud, she realized how ridiculous they sounded.

'Right, anyway, that'll be twenty-five euro, my dear,' the taxi driver said.

Tara rooted through her handbag and handed him the exact amount.

'And there's a twenty per cent private investigator fee for following your fella,' he said.

'Are you serious? You only drove an extra few metres!' Tara snapped.

'Relax love, I'm only winding ya up. You have enough to be worrying about. Good luck,' he said.

'Thanks,' Tara said, getting out of the taxi. She stood outside the hotel, not knowing what to do. She desperately tried to think of reasons why Colin would have gone into that hotel. Maybe he was attending a work event and that's why he said he was working late. Maybe the hotel was hosting an accounting conference. Was that a thing? Or maybe it was a co-worker's going away party and they were having a send-off in one of the hotel's function rooms.

She wanted to give Colin the benefit of the doubt, but she knew that if she didn't solve this mystery, it would ruin her date. She couldn't focus on Jack if her mind kept drifting to the things Colin may or may not be doing in a hotel. She looked down the street to her left where Elixir was located. She checked her watch.

7.50 p.m. She was early for her date with Jack. She had time.

Time to get answers.

She walked slowly through the front door of the Gibson Court Hotel and looked to her right towards the check-in desk. She could see Colin talking to the receptionist. She hid behind a pillar and peeked out to see what was going on.

She couldn't hear what they were saying but she could see Colin paying for something with his credit card. Was he getting a room? Tara tried to convince herself she was imagining things but when she saw the receptionist hand him a key card, she knew there was no denying it. Colin turned around and Tara tucked behind the pillar again, narrowly avoiding his gaze. Her back gripped the wall as he walked past her and up the stairs.

Tara followed Colin up the stairs and just about caught a glimpse of him turning left down the first-floor corridor. She crept up behind the wall and peeked down the hallway. Colin inserted his key card into one of the doors, about halfway down, and closed it behind him.

Tara was bewildered by what she was seeing; her brain couldn't process the images her eyes had sent to it. Never in a million years would she have considered the possibility that Colin was cheating on her. Yet that was certainly how things appeared. Maybe he was getting the room with Rory and they were going to bar hop on Harcourt Street? No, Rory lived in the city centre. If they were having a night out, they would have stayed at his apartment.

Even though her head was spinning, Tara began creeping down the hall towards the room Colin had just entered. She put her ear to room 117 and tried to listen for anything suspicious. She could hear a little bit of movement but it sounded like Colin was alone. If he was having an affair, where was the woman? Was he one of those men who paid for sex? Was there a sex worker on the way to meet him?

As she was listening at the door, Tara heard the lift open

down the hall and the sound of rickety wheels approaching. It was a porter with a room service tray. She composed herself and began to act naturally as she walked towards him. She didn't want to be caught spying on one of the hotel's guests.

As she passed the boy on the corridor, she noticed the contents on his tray. There was a bottle of champagne in an ice bucket and two champagne flutes, each of which contained a sliced piece of strawberry. Tara reached the end of the corridor and, once again, hid behind the wall that led to the staircase. When she peeked her head out, her worst fears were confirmed. The server was knocking on room 117. The door opened and he wheeled the trolley in.

Tara felt a sharp pain in her heart, as if a blade had just pierced through her back. Colin no longer deserved the benefit of the doubt. The writing was on the wall.

Colin was having an affair.

She felt a fury rise within her. She wondered how long it had been going on under her nose, how long she had been made a fool of.

The bellhop exited the room with his empty cart and returned to the lift. Although she knew it would be incredibly difficult, Tara decided to call Colin and ask him where he was. She wanted to hear him lie. She wanted to see how low he would stoop. She took out her phone and called him.

'Tara, this isn't really a great time,' Colin answered.

'Oh, are you still at work? I just saw your text about working late,' she said.

'Yeah, I am. Rory messed up an audit for a client so I'm here trying to fix it.'

'Oh, so you're at the office now?' she said, giving him just enough rope to hang himself.

'Yeah, yeah, it's gonna be a long one. I could be here all night,' he said unconvincingly.

'I'm actually in town at the minute. I'll swing by your office and bring you a coffee.'

'NO! No, honestly, I just got a coffee so no need. Thanks for offering though!' Colin said, his voice cracking.

There was a long pause on the call.

'I'll see you at home,' Colin said, eager to hang up.

'Oh . . . you most certainly will,' Tara said, ending the call.

Tara was on the verge of breathing fire. She had given him a chance to explain, but now everything was clear. The lies, the hotel room, the two champagne glasses, there was no way to misinterpret the situation.

Her husband was cheating on her with another woman.

Sure, she was on the brink of cheating on him, but her actions seemed more innocent by comparison. She was merely meeting a man for a drink, but here was Colin, meeting some woman in a hotel room for what could only be sex. Who was the woman? Was she some random sex worker? Or worse, was it a woman that Tara knew? Was he planning on running off with her?

She felt dizzy with all the questions that raced through her mind. She composed herself and looked at her watch. 7.55 p.m. She had been so blindsided by this chance occurrence that she forgot she had a date in less than five minutes. But she knew she couldn't meet Jack now. She still wanted to, out of spite, but her entire confidence had shattered. Just a few minutes prior, she had felt unstoppable.

Now, she was at an all-time low.

Her husband no longer wanted her, it seemed, and it felt like a rejection of her as a wife, as a lover, as a woman. The knife in her back cut deep, to the core of her very being. And because of that rejection, she had to reject Jack, at least for now. Even though all she wanted was to be held by him, to be taken by him, to be worshipped by him, she knew it was not his duty to stitch up her wound.

She left the hotel and hailed a taxi. She decided she would text Jack in the cab explaining she couldn't meet. She only prayed he would understand. There was only one thing Tara could focus on right now. When Colin returned home, she would be ready.

Ready for war.

Chapter 27

Colin looked around the room he had just prepared. The champagne was chilling, the lights were dimmed and the thermostat was set to the perfect temperature. He had even sprinkled some rose petals on the bed for that final touch. Everything was perfect.

And yet, suddenly it all felt wrong. Tara's call had made the situation far too real. He was lying to his wife while in a hotel room he had booked for another woman. It made him sick to his stomach. The guilt was too much.

He decided that booking the room was a mistake. Rory had gotten into his head and convinced him a bold move was the right approach. But if he felt this guilty before such a move, going through with it would surely leave him riddled with guilt for the rest of his life. It would be a step too far.

He had arranged to meet Claire for a drink. And that was what he intended to do. A drink was not an affair, he reminded himself for the millionth time. He would meet her to see if what they both felt was truly real and figure things out from there.

Colin checked the time on his phone and saw that it was 7.58 p.m. He stood up and looked at himself in the mirror. He was ready. As Colin reached for the door handle, he heard a beep from a notification on his phone. He took it out of his pocket to see the notification was from Fling. He opened the app to see a message from Claire waiting.

> **Claire:** Jack. I'm so sorry. I've just got some devastating news.

> I can't meet you tonight.

> Please don't hate me x

Colin stared at the message, reading it over and over. He didn't believe her. He knew she hadn't received any devastating news. If she had, why would she wait until one minute before their date to tell him? She was simply standing him up again, another cold rejection. He never should have given her a second chance. Now, he was a fool once again. But this was the last time, he vowed. He didn't want to hear her fictional excuses. He didn't want to hear from her at all.

Colin closed Fling and deleted the app from his phone.

He opened the bottle of champagne and brushed away all the rose petals before sitting on the bed. He suddenly felt so embarrassed for putting them there in the first place. But it was also a tremendous relief. The sickness in his stomach was gone. The crushing guilt was letting up.

He thought about how Tara had called him to ask if she could bring him a coffee while he was working late. And yet he was here, on the verge of jeopardizing everything he had built with her. He had been so intoxicated by Claire's siren call that he had almost wrecked his ship on her rocky coast. And all along, she was leading him on for her own sick amusement. Although Claire had hurt him once again, he could only blame himself.

He may have lusted after Claire but it was Tara he loved. He felt an overwhelming desire to collapse into her emerald eyes. She was the one he had chosen since day one, and even though the currents of life had dragged them apart, he needed to swim back to her shore. Tara was his rock. His home. And that's exactly where he wanted to be. He took a swig of champagne and said goodbye to his double life.

When Colin arrived home to Hillcrest, he got out of his car and stared up at his house. To think, he had risked the life he had built for some fleeting fling. '*Is glas iad na cnoic i bhfad uainn*,' the plaque above his door read, and only now did Colin fully appreciate its meaning. Claire's faraway hills may have appeared greener but there truly was no place like home. He thanked his lucky stars that Tara had no idea about his online infidelity. Colin took his golf clubs out of his car from the game earlier and opened the front door.

'Tara, you home?' Colin said, his voice echoing through the house. There was no answer.

Colin opened the door to the living room and saw the room was in darkness.

'Tara?' he said again.

The lamp in the corner of the room suddenly turned on, revealing Tara to be sitting on an armchair holding a glass of wine.

'Hello, honeybun,' Tara said, taking a sip.

Colin immediately got a bad feeling. She looked like a femme fatale in an old film noir. The kind of woman who's looks could kill. All she was missing was a cigarette. And she had called him "honeybun". She was obviously annoyed about something. But what? His alibi had been air-tight.

'Tara, is everything OK?' Colin asked, setting his golf bag down against the wall. He turned on the main light to remove the ominous atmosphere in the room.

'Colin, I'm going to give you one chance and one chance only to tell me where you've been,' Tara said, deadly serious.

Colin was struck with fear. How could she have possibly known he wasn't working late? Had she called Rory? No, Rory would have covered for him. Had she called his office reception? No, there was nobody at the front desk past five, so she wouldn't have got through to anyone.

She had to be bluffing.

'I already told you, I was working late,' he said calmly.

Tara looked him dead in the eye for a solid ten seconds, their spaghetti-western-style face-off had begun again.

'Interesting . . .' Tara said, walking towards the room's back wall. Tara looked at Colin's collection of beer signs that were still hanging up. She scanned through them, as if she was choosing one for something. Colin had no idea what was going through her mind.

Then, with unrelenting force, Tara ripped a Guinness sign off the wall.

'WRONG ANSWER!' she roared as she flung the sign directly at Colin's head. He blocked the sign with his forearm just before it could hit his temple. Thankfully the signs were made of aluminium and not real steel, so it wasn't too painful.

'WHAT THE HELL IS GOING ON?' Colin yelled in complete and utter shock.

'You tell me, Colin,' Tara said, her eyes widening. 'Now I'll ask you again. Where have you been?'

'Tara, I was working,' he insisted.

'YOUR NOSTRILS ARE FLARING, HONEYBUN!' Tara shouted. She ripped off a Heineken sign and aimed it directly at Colin's head. 'YOU LYING BASTARD!'

'Tara, STOP,' Colin pleaded, but she threw it anyway. He ducked just in time as it flew over his head. 'What are you, crazy?'

'Oh don't you dare call me crazy. YOU HAVEN'T SEEN CRAZY YET!' she screeched.

Colin knew the jig was up. He had been caught. But he hadn't technically cheated. How on earth was he going to explain the complexity of the situation?

'Tara, let's just talk this out, OK? Let me explain everything . . .' he said.

Tara tore another sign off the wall. 'Who is she? What is this TRAMP'S name?' she said, with a firm grip on the sign, ready to propel it at any moment.

'I swear nothing happened,' Colin said.

'Nothing happened? So you booked a hotel room with a woman to do what, exactly? Play Scrabble?' Tara asked sarcastically.

'I swear I didn't cheat on you, Tara,' Colin said, actually telling the truth. 'I'm flabbergasted you would think that!'

'People only use the word flabbergasted when they're LYING!' Tara screamed, flinging the sign at his shoulder.

'Can we just talk about this like adults?' Colin begged, ducking again to avoid the sign.

'Oh look who's suddenly ready to grow up. I want to know the name of this trollop! Oh God, do I know her? Oh sweet baby Jesus, please don't tell me I know this home-wrecking tart!'

'Tara, for the love of God, I didn't cheat on you!'

'Prove it. Give me your phone. If you're not cheating on me, then give me your phone!' Tara said, holding out her hand.

Colin was reluctant to hand over his phone to Tara but then he realized he had deleted Fling. The app that had all the evidence of his affair was gone. Thank God he had made the decision to wipe all traces of Claire. He might just come out of this fight alive after all.

'OK, fine!' Colin said, taking out his phone. 'You won't find any evidence of me having an affair because I'm not having an affair. I have nothing to hide.'

Tara snatched the phone out of Colin's hand. She looked through Colin's apps to see what she could find. Colin held his breath but felt confident that there was nothing incriminating. He hadn't screenshotted Claire's nudes or any of their erotically charged conversations.

He was clean.

'OH MY GOD!' Tara screamed. Her scream was otherworldly. He felt like he was hearing a banshee prophesizing his own death.

'What's wrong?' Colin asked, not knowing what she had found.

Tara faced Colin's phone towards him. That's when he saw what she had seen.

The mother of all misinterpretations. The final nail in his coffin.

> **Celine:** I got The Brazilian for you. And don't worry, I won't say a thing to Tara 😉

Colin wanted to die there and then. He hadn't a hope of explaining this one.

'CELINE?' Tara roared. 'YOU'RE CHEATING ON ME WITH CELINE?'

'Tara, please. It's not what it looks like!' Colin said, begging her to see reason.

'Well, it looks like Celine texted my husband to tell him

she got a Brazilian bikini wax a few hours before he booked a hotel room and pretended to be working late!' Tara said, all in one breath.

'I know this looks bad! But you're jumping to the wrong conclusion,' Colin tried desperately to explain. But he knew it was no use. She was already drunk with rage.

'Do you think I was born yesterday? Of all the women to cheat on me with. CELINE?' She was completely unhinged.

'Tara, I'm not sleeping with Celine! You're being crazy!'

'DON'T YOU DARE GASLIGHT ME!' Tara screamed. 'I won't be made a fool of. This is a betrayal of biblical proportions!'

'Oh don't be so melodramatic, Tara!' Colin snapped. He knew the moment he said it, he had made a fatal error.

'Melodramatic? Oh, I'll show you melodramatic!' Tara said, walking past Colin and into the hall. She grabbed Colin's nine-iron out of his golf bag and stormed out the back door of the house.

'TARA, STOP!' Colin yelled, chasing after her. When he got outside, he could see Tara holding the golf club in the sky above the motorcycle he had finally repaired.

She looked like an ancient goddess of war.

'Not the Triumph, Tara!' Colin said helplessly reaching out his hand.

Tara brought the golf club down and whacked the bike's engine.

'Tara, stop this madness right now!' Colin demanded.

'Oh I'm sorry, did my back hurt your knife?' she asked. She took another almighty swing and smashed the bike's headlight.

'Tara, please listen! Celine wasn't talking about a bikini wax! The Brazilian is the IVF doctor that Celine knows. Dr Guillermo-something. You can look him up, I swear I'm

261

not lying. I asked Celine to help us get on his waiting list. I thought maybe you were too proud to ask for help so I did it for you,' Colin said desperately.

Tara continued to hold the golf club above her head as she tried to process what Colin had just said. She put down the nine-iron for a moment while she thought. Then the look in her eyes changed, indicating she had made up her mind about how she felt.

'THAT'S WORSE THAN CHEATING!' she said, whacking the front wheel and causing it to fall over.

'How is that worse than cheating?'

'You went behind my back and did the one thing I asked you not to do. I made it clear that I wasn't trying IVF again and that I didn't want Celine's help. What was your big plan, Colin? To harvest my eggs while I wasn't looking?' she asked.

'I thought you might be open to it further down the line. I just wanted to be on the waiting list, in case you changed your mind,' Colin said honestly.

Tara was finally starting to calm down.

'That still doesn't explain why you got a hotel room and why there were two champagne glasses on that porter's trolley!' Tara said.

'What porter? Wait, how do you know that?' Colin asked, confused. 'Did you follow me?'

'You're damn right I followed you,' she said unashamedly.

'We're supposed to trust each other, Tara!'

'Oh please, I wouldn't trust you as far as I'd throw you. And wasn't I right to follow you in the end? I smelled a rat and I caught a rat.'

'Tara, it was a stupid mistake and I'm sorry,' he said, genuinely meaning it.

'Oh please, men are only ever sorry they got caught. You

wouldn't be apologizing if I hadn't seen you check in to the room,' Tara said.

'Well, maybe I wouldn't have checked in to a hotel room if you hadn't checked out of our marriage!' Colin said defensively.

'Don't you dare pin this on me! I didn't drive you into that tart's arms. Well, when I find out who that tramp is, God help her,' Tara said, glistening with rage. She dropped the golf club and began to walk inside.

'Where are going?' he asked.

'I'm going to go find a real man and have an affair of my own!' Tara said, slamming the back door behind her. She wasn't actually leaving to go and have her own affair, of course. She was just trying to hurt Colin in the heat of the moment. As much as she would have liked to, she couldn't just run into Jack's arms. She didn't know who he was. And she had stood him up for a second time. She had got a second chance she didn't deserve and she had ruined it. There was no way Jack would give her a third chance. But it didn't matter. Because Tara didn't need a man to kiss her better. Tara needed the one person who could always heal her pain.

Tara needed her mother.

Chapter 28

Tara drove for almost three hours to Galway, singing ABBA heartbreak songs at the top of her lungs. When she finally arrived home to the cottage she grew up in, it was too dark to see the beautiful lush green fields that surrounded her. But as the light from the cottage kitchen window lit up her face, Tara knew she had made the right decision by coming home.

'TARA!' her mother Shannon screamed as she opened the door and saw her daughter. Shannon Fitzsimons was a psychic healer by trade and, although she was now seventy-five years old, she still had quite the reputation when it came to spiritual advice. Any medical doctor in the country would denounce her so-called cures as old wives' tales, but nevertheless, people travelled from all over the country to seek her guidance. Now, for the first time in her life, Tara was about to ask for help. And if there was anyone who could help her, it was certainly her mam.

'Hi Mam!' Tara said, leaning in for a hug.

'What a surprise!' Shannon said, taken aback. 'Come in, come in.'

Tara walked into the small cottage.

'What are you doing here so late?' Shannon asked, leading her into the kitchen. 'Oh my God, don't tell me. YOU'RE PREGNANT!'

Perhaps her psychic abilities weren't what they used to be.

264

'No, Mam. It's not good news, I'm afraid,' Tara said with tears in her eyes.

'Oh God, pet, is everything OK?'

'I can't even find the words to say it,' Tara said, embarrassed that Colin had betrayed her.

'Sit down,' Shannon said, pulling out a kitchen chair. 'I'll put the kettle on. Everything is always a bit easier with a warm mug of tea in your hands.'

As she sat down, Tara looked around at all the knick-knacks and trinkets that occupied the room. It had an inner chaos that made her feel so at home. It was noisy. Alive.

'I know the house could use a bit of a clean,' Shannon said, seeing Tara gawking around the room.

'No, Mam, it's perfect,' she said.

'Your old friend Tom O'Malley does be asking for you non-stop by the way,' Shannon said, as she waited for the kettle to boil.

'Aw, how is he? Do you be talking to him much?' Tara asked, her spirits momentarily lifted.

'He was here with me today. I had to give him the cure of the sprain,' Shannon said.

'Oh, is he OK?' Tara asked.

'Oh God yeah. Just a sprain in his groin. I dipped a piece of string in butter and I knotted it into a circle for him to wear. Sure wasn't the sprain gone in a matter of minutes,' Shannon said, smiling.

Tara smiled back. It was exactly the kind of cure Colin would ridicule, even though Shannon had once removed a wart from his knee just by giving him a penny. The kettle finally boiled and Shannon began making a pot for the two of them to share. She let it sit and finally filled Tara's favourite mug.

'My little mug,' Tara said, remembering how much she

used to love it. She took a sip of her tea and it felt like a tonic. There was just something about the way mothers made tea.

'Oh God, I really needed this, Mam. I mostly drink coffee when I'm in Dublin,' she said.

'Well, you were a fair tea-aholic when you lived here. You used to come down from your room every evening holding six or seven mugs for the wash,' Shannon joked.

'The Irish walk of shame, as you called it,' Tara laughed back. Her laughter quickly faded, however.

'It's alright, pet, let it out,' Shannon said, touching her hand.

Tara took a deep breath. Why did she feel ashamed for being cheated on? Why was she struggling to get the words out? But she knew the answer on a subconscious level. It was because, in a way, she couldn't really judge Colin. She had no right to throw the first stone. She too had been planning to have an affair. Perhaps Colin's betrayal had forced her to hold a mirror up to herself.

But then again, Tara was merely going to meet a man for a drink. Colin had gone to a hotel room to have sex. Yes, they both had guilty minds, but he had committed the guilty act. He had done the deed. Her actions, however scandalous they may have been, seemed a lot more innocent that Colin's. She was wounded by what he had done. And she needed her mother to heal her.

'Colin cheated on me,' she finally said.

'WHAT?' Shannon snapped. 'You're joking. There's no way, Tara.'

'I saw him, Mam. He lied to me about working late but I saw him going into a hotel room. I don't know who the woman is, but God help that trollop if I ever find out her name,' Tara said.

'Between two stools a man falls to the ground. But I just can't imagine Colin with another woman, Tara. You two have always been so in love. I know you fight like cats in a bag but sure the best relationships are often like that,' Shannon said.

'We've been drifting apart since we started IVF. It just sucked all the life out of us,' Tara admitted.

'Didn't I tell ya not to be going down the immaculate conception route? I always said you'd have a child when the time is right,' Shannon said.

'Mam, I'm thirty-seven years old,' Tara sighed. 'The odds are against me.'

'Oh would ya give up with that kind of talk! I had you at thirty-eight and you turned out fine, didn't ya? What's meant to be, will be,' Shannon said.

'You always told me there's a reason for everything. But what reason is there for Colin cheating on me with another woman? Where's my silver lining?' she asked desperately.

'Tara, the tricky part about life is that we have to live it forwards. But it can only be understood backwards. Maybe Colin has met someone new because you're supposed to meet someone new,' Shannon said.

'Jack,' Tara whispered to herself.

'Who?' Shannon asked.

Tara didn't know where to begin. She was exhausted after the day she had put in. 'Mam, I have a lot to tell you but I feel like I'm about to collapse. I have a knot in my stomach after everything that's happened. Can I tell you the rest of the story in the morning?' Tara asked.

'Of course, pet. You tumble into bed and in the morning, I'll have breakfast ready for you,' Shannon said.

'Thanks, Mam.' Tara smiled.

Tara headed down the hall and opened the door to her old bedroom. It was exactly how she had left it, albeit a lot dustier. She looked at the walls covered in vintage posters of ABBA and tried to smile through the pain she was feeling.

She undressed, got into her old bed, and suddenly she was a teenager again. Shannon opened the door and came into the room.

'Here, pet,' she said, handing her a glass filled with a clear liquid. 'Drink this. It's the cure of the stomach.'

'What is it?' Tara asked, sitting up.

'It's just flat 7up,' Shannon smiled. 'It'll get rid of the knot in your stomach.'

'Thanks, Mam,' she smiled, taking a sip.

'You'll be a whole new person in the morning,' Shannon said as she turned off the light.

Before going to sleep, Tara opened Fling to see if Jack had replied to her.

Nothing. No text and no green light. But she knew he had every right to ignore her. She had stood him up twice for heaven's sake. She typed a message in the hope he would see it next time he opened the app.

Claire: I hope you can forgive me
Jack x

I need you x

Chapter 29

The next morning, Tara arose to a heavenly sound and smell of sizzling grease. She rubbed the sleep out of her eyes and opened Fling to see if Jack had replied. Still nothing. Give him time, she told herself. She headed into the kitchen to see her mother whipping up enough food to feed an army. There were eggs, sausages, bacon rashers, baked beans, white pudding, black pudding, fried tomato and a seemingly endless supply of toasted white bread.

'Jesus, Mam, you didn't need to go to this effort,' Tara said, seeing the spread.

'Oh will you give up, you need to eat. You're skin and bone since the last time I saw ya,' Shannon said, dishing the food onto Tara's plate.

Tara sat down and reached for a slice of lightly toasted buttered white bread. She took a bite out of it and experienced pure ecstasy. Just like tea, there was something about the way mothers made toast.

'Oh my God, Mam, you have no idea how much I needed this. I've been off carbs all week,' Tara said, savouring the magnificent taste.

'You need to stop with them fad diets, Tara. Women aren't designed to not eat white bread. Why would you choose to suffer?' Shannon asked rhetorically.

Tara knew she had a point. Her five days off carbs had

made her an irritable mess. She wondered if she would have taken a golf club to Colin's bike if she had eaten white bread earlier that day. Probably not.

Shannon dished out the rest of the food onto Tara's plate. The only way to describe the meal was mountainous. She quite literally couldn't see the plate underneath the food.

'Mam, this is too much,' Tara said.

'Oh start eating, will ya!' Shannon insisted. 'Now, if my memory serves me well, you were about to start telling me about someone called Jack.'

Tara laughed to herself. A doctor had told Shannon several years ago she carried the gene for Alzheimer's, but her mother seemed sharper than ever.

'So much for that doctor saying you'd lose your memory.' Tara smiled.

'Oh yeah, I forgot I had Alzheimer's,' Shannon laughed. 'Now, who is this Jack character?'

Tara took a deep breath. If anyone could advise her on the impossible situation she was in, it was her mother. 'OK. Here it goes. So things haven't been good between me and Colin since our last failed attempt at IVF. I told him I couldn't go through it all again. But ever since then, Colin and I have been drifting away from each other. And while I was drifting from him, I started to drift towards someone else,' Tara said.

'Go on, who is he?' Shannon asked.

'So that's where things get complicated. There's this new app out called Fling, you probably haven't heard about it.'

'Of course I've heard about it! Everyone in the country heard Mary Muldoon on *The Line*. She visited me three weeks ago looking for the cure of the shame.'

'What's the cure of the shame?' Tara asked, curious.

'A vibrator.'

'MAM!' Tara said, shocked.

'She didn't react well when I told her that either,' Shannon laughed. 'Anyway, get on with your story, pet.'

'OK, so I joined Fling, to prove I wasn't like that Mary woman and to research the app for work. But the day I joined, I got a one hundred per cent compatibility match with a man. A man named Jack,' Tara explained.

'One hundred per cent – that's certainly something,' Shannon said, sitting back in her chair.

'But here's the craziest part, Mam. You know how both of us get our gut feeling?' Tara said.

'Of course. Your granny had it too. It's our intuition. Like a sixth sense.'

'Well . . . when I matched with Jack on Fling, I got my gut feeling. A full-on synchronicity. The very same feeling I got when I first met Colin in O'Malley's,' Tara said, knowing her mother would understand.

'My God, this is serious. Keep going,' Shannon said, already heavily invested in the story.

'So I've been chatting to Jack for the past while but we've never actually met. It sounds so stupid I know, but I've developed feelings for him even though I don't even know what he looks like. Because one of the rules on Fling is to not use face pictures before a meeting, it's all anonymous.'

'And you haven't tried to meet him yet?' Shannon asked.

'I have, but I stood him up twice. And now I think I've lost him. He hasn't replied to me and I don't think he's going to. I should be thinking about my husband and how he cheated on me, but all I can think about is Jack. It's beyond irrational,' Tara said.

'Matters of the heart are never rational, pet. In a way, it's quite beautiful that you've developed feelings without seeing him. Maybe it means it's more than lust. And the synchronicity must mean something.'

271

'Do you really think Jack could be my destiny?' Tara asked.

'I don't have the answer, pet. But I think I know where we can find it,' Shannon said.

After finishing their monumental breakfast, Shannon led Tara out into the back garden. Tara wasn't sure where she was being taken and the garden looked unrecognizable from the last time she was home. They walked towards the back corner and into a little floral area, enclosed by trellises.

'What is this, Mam?' Tara asked.

'It's a little memorial garden I made for your father,' Shannon replied.

As Tara stood looking around at the stunning greenery, she realized how much she missed her dad. She had been very close with him, particularly when her mother would be fully booked with people coming to their house for various cures. She had gone through all the stages of grief and had come to peace with his passing. But he had left a void in the world. The wake had lasted four full days, that's how loved the man was.

'It's beautiful, Mam. You must miss him every day,' Tara said.

'Yes, but he's not really gone, pet. Energy is never destroyed, it's only transferred. And your father's energy is everywhere in this garden,' Shannon said, looking at all the flowers.

'That's a nice thought. I try to think like that too.'

'He spent most of his life being my gardener. It feels nice to do the same for him. As long as this garden lives, so does he,' Shannon said, smiling.

'That's beautiful,' Tara said.

'But now, it's time to take a glimpse at your destiny. Step

272

into my office,' Shannon said. She led Tara into a gazebo-like structure built from old wicker. Plants grew throughout the hut's walls, lending an other-worldly feel to it. There was a table in the centre and two large beanbags on each side.

'What is this place?' Tara asked, having never seen it before.

'I had it built recently, pet. It's a Yoni temple.'

'And what is that, exactly?' Tara asked, confused.

'Well, the word "yonic" is the opposite of the word "phallic". Patriarchal society is so obsessed with phallic buildings, I decided to build a yonic one, a representation of the female reproductive system, specifically the womb,' Shannon explained.

'Wow, back in my mother's womb after all these years. I guess nine months wasn't enough,' Tara joked.

'I actually carried you for nine and a half months. You were late for your own birth, imagine,' Shannon teased.

'Fashionably late,' Tara laughed.

'Anyway, this is where I do all my readings now. Including yours,' Shannon said, shuffling a deck of tarot cards in her hand.

'Sure, I'll take all the guidance I can get at this stage,' Tara said, sitting down on the large beanbag.

Shannon spread the deck of cards face down on the table in front of Tara. 'OK, pet, pick your first card.'

Tara sighed and picked a card at random from the spread deck. She put the card down, face-up, and saw that it read 'Wheel of Fortune'.

'OK, card number one is the Wheel of Fortune. Upright. The first card is a reading of your past. It represents fate and destiny. With this card, there is no random chance but rather a sense of things that are meant to be.'

'Oh my God. That could be about Fling. The one hundred per cent match with Jack,' Tara said, perking up.

'Choose your next card,' Shannon instructed.

Tara chose another card at random and placed it down face-up to reveal 'The Two of Swords'.

'OK, your second card is the Two of Swords. Upright,' Shannon said. 'It represents your present. Here you see a woman who is blindfolded and holding up two swords in front of the sea. The blindfold suggests this woman is hood-winked and cannot see what is right in front of her. This woman is at a crossroads, unsure of which path to take. She is trying to balance two swords. These could be interpreted as phallic. Perhaps she is trying to balance two men.'

'OK, this is getting a bit scary,' Tara said in shock.

'Choose your third card, pet. The third card represents your future,' Shannon said, waving her hand over them.

Tara took a deep breath. This was the card that might give her some kind of guidance. Knowing her luck, the card would probably say 'Death'. She closed her eyes and reached of a card. When she opened her eyes once more, she saw the card read 'The Lovers'.

'Ah yes, The Lovers. Upright,' Shannon said. 'It represents inner harmony through perfect union. This is the card of kin-dred spirits bound by fate. This is the card of soulmates.'

Tara was speechless.

'So in your past, I see a wheel of fortune spinning in your favour. In your present, I see a woman struggling to see what is right in front of her. And in your future, I see two lovers discovering each other. Does that resonate with you, pet?' Shannon asked, knowing well that it did.

'YES, IT RESONATES!' Tara shouted, blown away by the reading. 'But now what am I supposed to do? The cards are telling me I'm supposed to be with Jack but he still hasn't responded to me on Fling!'

'Tara, pet, he's a man. They never last long at giving us the silent treatment,' Shannon said with a smirk.

'But then there's Colin. I hate him right now but I still love him. Isn't the whole idea of finding The One that there's only one of them?'

'I used to think that too, pet, but recently I've started seeing things a little differently,' Shannon said, coyly.

'What do you mean?' Tara asked, raising an eyebrow.

'Well . . . you know how much I loved your father. And I always will. But he's been gone six years now and I find myself being courted by another man,' Shannon said, unable to stop herself from smiling.

'Mam, that's amazing. Who is he?' Tara asked, delighted.

'Tom O'Malley,' Shannon said.

'TOM O'MALLEY! You're joking! I thought you said he was only visiting you to cure his sprained groin.'

'How do you think he sprained his groin in the first place?' Shannon laughed.

'MAM!' Tara said, mortified.

'Oh lighten up, pet. I don't know where you got all that Catholic guilt from. It must have been from your father because it certainly wasn't from me,' Shannon said.

'It was definitely from Dad. And the nuns,' Tara laughed.

'Well it's time to stop feeling bad over things that make you feel good!'

'You're right. It seems like everyone is getting the ride except me! Even my mother has more sex appeal, apparently!' Tara laughed.

'Well, maybe you should go and shake what your mama gave ya,' Shannon laughed.

'You're right. I'm not going to let Colin's betrayal define me. I'm a strong feminist and I'll rise above this,' Tara said confidently.

'Ah, pet, you're not still a feminist after all these years, are ya?' Shannon asked.

'Mam, of course I believe that women are equal to men!' Tara said, shocked.

'But, pet, that doesn't mean men are equal to women. I'd hate for us women to have to lower ourselves down to equality with men,' Shannon smiled.

'You had me worried there for a minute, Mam,' Tara laughed.

'Well, your worrying stops now. After that tarot reading, it's clear what you have to do.'

'I have to meet Jack. I have to find out who he is,' Tara said with certainty.

'And never forget what I've always taught you, pet,' Shannon said, wise as ever. 'Everything happens for a reason.'

Chapter 30

While Tara was receiving spiritual advice from her mother, Colin found himself waking up to the mother of all hangovers. His head pounded like a hundred drums at once and his mouth felt like a bag of sand. He got up off the couch and immediately began gulping down as much water as he could from the kitchen sink. His condition improved slightly but he was still far from over The Fear.

He had drunk himself into a hole when Tara had stormed off and the events of the night before were suddenly coming back to him. The things Tara had said came flooding back and he wasn't sure whether or not she had come home after storming off.

'Tara?' he shouted through the empty house. There was no reply.

He knew things must have been bad if she hadn't come home. He remembered her last words before she left. Something about her going to have an affair of her own. Surely that was just an empty threat to try and hurt him. Still, where the hell was she?

Colin took out his phone and immediately called her. The call rang once and then went straight to voicemail, as if she had denied the call.

'Hi, you've reached Tara. Leave a message and I'll get back to you,' her voicemail said.

'Tara, it's Colin. Where are you? Please come home so we can talk through this. I love you,' Colin said, before hanging up.

When he walked back into the living room, he registered the pub signs on the floor and remembered that Tara had thrown them at him. He knew the least he could do was take down the rest of the signs and dismantle his man cave. He needed to fix the mess he had made. He had to do everything in his power to save his marriage to the love of his life. He gathered them all up and stacked them into a pile.

While carrying the signs to the shed, Colin saw his motorbike lying sideways on the ground and remembered that Tara had tried to destroy it. Although she had given it a few decent whacks, he knew it had survived. He wasn't sure, however, if the same was true for his marriage. His wife had disappeared without telling him where she was going and he honestly wasn't sure if she was coming back. She would return to the house eventually, of course, but he wondered if she would return to him.

Even though he hadn't slept with Claire, he knew the optics of the situation didn't help his case. Tara had witnessed him go into a hotel room while lying to her with an alibi of working late. If a jury was to assess the situation, he wouldn't have a hope. He may not have been guilty, but that didn't make him innocent. Despite not believing in a higher power, Colin felt as if he was experiencing some kind of divine punishment. He had not committed adultery but he had coveted his neighbour's wife. The fact that two of the ten commandments were about cheating meant there was no escaping judgement.

He felt an overwhelming sense of regret. The entire idea of Fling suddenly seemed so sordid. The fact that he had put his marriage on the line for another woman, and one who had stood him up twice, made him breathlessly angry, winded by his own self-contempt. And yet, he still couldn't banish thoughts of Claire from his mind. Her siren call was still ringing in his ear despite the fact she had already destroyed his ship. He wanted to punch a stone wall and break every bone in his hand. The hand that had downloaded Fling in the first place. The once idle hand that had become the devil's plaything.

Colin put his stack of pub signs on the bike's seat and wheeled the remnants of his manhood back into the shed from whence it came. He leaned it up against the back wall and sat down on the floor beside some old storage boxes. He wondered if there was any chance of Tara forgiving him. She was hurt, and she did have a tendency to nurse grudges. 'I forgive but I don't forget,' she would often say.

He considered telling her everything when she came home. From downloading Fling, to matching with Claire, to trying to meet her for a drink and booking the hotel room just in case she wanted to have sex. But as he thought about the events in chronological order, it made him seem like a monster. His actions suddenly seemed so premeditated. If an affair had just happened in the spur of the moment, it might have been more understandable, but Colin had come upon many junctions to turn off the road to ruin.

He just hadn't taken them.

To his left, Colin could see a storage box that read *Tara: College*. He dragged it towards him and opened the box. The first thing he saw in the box was Tara's old Magic 8 Ball. He used to make fun of her for having so much faith in the plastic oracle. He smiled as he picked it up and pondered what he would ask it.

'Is Tara the love of my life?' he said, shaking the ball.

YES, DEFINITELY, the ball read.

'OK . . .' Colin said, pondering once again. 'Are my feelings for Claire real?'

279

YES

'Are me and Tara supposed to stay together?'

WITHOUT A DOUBT

'Are me and Claire supposed to be together?'

IT IS CERTAIN

'Will my marriage to Tara last forever?'

YOU MAY RELY ON IT

'Should I have an affair with Claire?'

ALL SIGNS POINT TO YES

'This thing doesn't have a clue,' Colin said, throwing the Magic 8 Ball across the shed.

He rooted through the box again and found a whole host of memorabilia that she had kept from her college days. Notepads from her lectures, her O'Malley's work uniform, the box was seemingly endless. She had kept their Interrail passes, all the ticket stubs from the concerts they had gone to together, old photos of the two of them and his UCD college hoody that Tara used to wear constantly. He picked up the hoody that he himself had only worn a handful of times. He put it on over his clothes and discovered that it still fitted him. He smelled her scent on it and his brain was flooded with memories. He used to love seeing her wear it.

He even found Tara's paper titled 'Girls Just Wanna Have Fundamental Rights: A New Theory of Synth-Wave Feminism'. It had 49% written on it in red pen, the grade that crushed Tara, even to this day. He picked up a photo of the two of them on their Interrail stop in Paris. The Eiffel Tower stood behind them as Tara planted a kiss on Colin's cheek.

They looked so happy.

Colin then realized this box he was rummaging through was essentially a shrine to their relationship. A time capsule he never even knew existed. He had never been the sentimental type but the items in the box pulled at his heartstrings and inspired an idea. He stood up and looked around the small shed.

Maybe there was still time to turn off the road to ruin and onto the road to redemption.

He knew what he had to do, although it certainly wouldn't be easy. It seemed as if Tara would be gone for the rest of the weekend, and when she came home, he knew he wouldn't be able to tell her how sorry he was. He would have to show her.

It was time to get to work.

Chapter 31

After a rejuvenating weekend with her mother, Tara decided it was time to head back home. She made a promise to herself that she would visit Galway at least once a month. The long drive was a small price to pay for the tonic of a mother's love. She had arrived on the verge of a breakdown but she was leaving full of hope. It was Sunday evening and she had her lunch meeting with Dick Mulligan in less than twenty-four hours. Even though she was currently dealing with the heartache of infidelity, she was still determined to land Dick as a client, if only to prove to the Lads that she could.

Before she got on the motorway towards Dublin, however, Tara had one little stop to make. She drove into the heart of Galway, heading straight for O'Malley's pub. As she sauntered down Shop Street, Tara could feel the electric energy of the city all around her. She always felt at home here, like she could relax her shoulders and just exist. She saw the usual tourists wandering around, taking photos of the colourful bars and bronze statues. Galway just had a certain magic about it. It was like a living, breathing postcard.

When she finally reached O'Malley's, it looked exactly the same as it always did. Not even a fresh coat of green paint on its rustic exterior. When Tara opened the door, she was thrilled to see the interior still hadn't changed one bit either. It was one of Galway's smallest pubs but this meant it always had a warm, full feeling. It never looked empty. Even now on a Sunday evening, it vibrated good energy. Tara wasn't in the door five seconds when Tom O'Malley spotted her.

'TARA FITZSIMONS!' he shouted from behind the bar.

'TOM O'MALLEY!' Tara shouted back, walking over to him. 'You shouldn't still be working at your age!'

'Sure who'd run O'Malley's only O'Malley himself.' Tom laughed. He had aged quite a bit since Tara had last seen him, but he was right. The place wouldn't be the same without him.

'But you must be in your seventies at this stage, Tom?' she said.

'That's very kind of you, Tara, but I actually turned eighty a few weeks back,' Tom said, flattered.

'Oh my God, Tom, and you're still working away?'

'Well, you know what they say, retirement is the number one killer of old people. Once you have a job, you have to stay alive to do it,' he said, laughing. 'What brings you back to Galway?'

'Oh, long story. Big fight with my husband. Just needed to get away,' Tara said, taking a seat at the bar.

'I always say fight fire with fire. If your marriage is on the rocks, you need a whiskey on the rocks,' Tom said, producing a bottle of Jameson.

'I wish I could, Tom, but I have a three-hour drive ahead of me. Just a 7up for me, please,' Tara said.

'Coming right up,' Tom said, opening a bottle and pouring it into a glass. 'You know, the regulars still say that you pulled the best pint of Guinness back in the day.'

'Glad to hear my legacy lives on. I used to love working here Tom. I think about the laughs we used to have all the time. I'm so glad you haven't changed the place one bit.'

'I've been asked by some people to take down some of the more outdated signs, but I refuse. This one is my favourite,'

Tom said, pointing at a sign above the bar that read 'GUIN-NESS FOR STRENGTH'.

'My husband has that same sign hanging in our living room,' she said. Tara looked around the pub and saw that all of the signs Colin owned were also hanging in O'Malley's. 'God, that's a weird coincidence. Colin has all of these signs, actually.'

'Well, he certainly has a keen eye – lots of these are very rare. Not easy to track down. I'm just going to change a keg, my darling. Back in a minute,' Tom said, heading into the back room.

As she sat alone at the bar, Tara began to think back to the first time she met Colin, in this very spot.

November 11th. She hadn't even seen him walk into the bar, she had been busy restocking shelves. Then she had heard a voice behind her ordering a Guinness and when she turned around, there he was. It was the first time Tara had ever experienced a synchronicity. But she hadn't been confused by the feeling, she had known exactly what was happening. She knew in that very moment he was The One.

He had been so cheeky back then, complaining about the Guinness, knowing well it would send her into a long-winded rant.

'What time are you finished your shift?' Colin had then asked her.

'What business is that of yours?' she had replied.

'Just wondering if you'll be too tired for another shift after this one,' Colin had said, playfully.

She had told him that he was a complete and utter chancer and that he shouldn't wait for her under any circumstances. But of course, as soon as she left O Malley's that night, there he was, sitting waiting on that motorbike with a cigarette in his mouth.

'You waited,' she had said in pure shock.

'Of course I did, you told me not to,' Colin had said, starting his engine. 'Get on.'

'There's no way I'm getting on that feckin' motorbike,' Tara had told him.

'Well, you can either get on now or spend the rest of your life wondering what would have happened if you did,' Colin had said back to her.

'Of all the pubs in all the towns in all of Ireland, you had to walk into mine,' she had told him as she climbed aboard.

As Tara sat in O'Malley's now, she wondered, if she could live her life over, would she still get onto that motorcycle? What would her life have been like if she never did? If she hadn't got on, she wouldn't have experienced the best years of her life. But she also felt wounded by the fact that she had given the best years of her life to a man who stopped loving her somewhere along the line. Was it better to have loved and lost than to never have loved? Was it better to feel pain than to feel nothing at all?

There was a part of her that felt incredibly jealous. Colin had found a new flower to garden. Were her roots younger? Her petals prettier? Could she bear fruit unlike Tara? She desperately wanted to know what this woman had that she didn't. But she also knew she had no right to judge Colin. She knew exactly what motivated a person to cheat.

It was the desire to feel alive.

Colin had been right. If she hadn't got on the back of that motorbike, she would have spent the rest of her life wondering what would have happened if she had. But now she was afraid that if she didn't meet Jack, she would forever wonder what she missed out on. Even though she would always love Colin, now it was Jack's motorcycle she wanted to climb aboard. Just like back then, her rationality was telling her not to do something so reckless, but something deep within beckoned her to risk it all. It felt like a new adventure, a fresh start, the enticing smell of a new book.

But she found herself tormented by so many unanswered questions. Where had Jack gone? Would he ever respond to her? Would his green light ever illuminate again? She had tried several times to delete Fling but she couldn't bring herself to do it this time. She and Jack had too much unfinished business. His profile hadn't been deleted, so there was still some hope. But that very same hope was torture. If he told her their online romance was over, she would accept it and move on. It was the silence that was killing her. She began to type yet another message into the abyss.

Claire: Jack, please talk to me . . .

You have no idea how much I need you right now x

Tara put her phone back in her bag as Tom returned from changing the keg.

'So what's this I hear about you courting my mother?' she said, teasing him. 'It seems you've become quite the tomcat in your old age.'

'So that's why you're here. For a good old-fashioned shake down,' Tom laughed.

'Don't worry Tom, you have my blessing. I haven't seen her in this good form since my dad,' Tara said, tipping her glass to him.

'Oh, that's music to my ears, Tara. It warms my heart to know I make her happy.'

'You're doing something right anyway. She's acting younger than I am these days,' Tara laughed.

'Well, I've always believed that every flower deserves to bloom,' Tom said.

That was it. The slogan for Fling Tara had been searching for.

Every flower deserves to bloom.

It was the exact idea she had been trying to communicate but couldn't find the words.

'Tom, you're a genius. I have to get home. You've just inspired me,' Tara said, before downing her 7up.

'Ah, darling, you only just sat down,' Tom said.

'I'll be back for another visit soon Tom, I promise. Me, you and Mam should go out to dinner.'

'Ah, that would be lovely, darling.'

'Behave yourself while I'm gone, tomcat. No more spraining that groin of yours,' Tara teased as she headed towards the door.

'No promises!' Tom laughed.

෫෧

After a three-hour-long drive, Tara finally got home to Hillcrest just after 11 p.m. She was utterly exhausted after the journey and she was in no mood for any kind of confrontation with Colin. Thankfully, when she peeked into the living room, she saw him passed out cold on the couch. She couldn't help but notice that there were specks of paint all over his body and his hands looked rough and calloused. It seemed as if he had been working non-stop on some home improvement project but, as she looked around, any improvements remained to be seen. She did notice, however, that the pub signs had been taken down and the man cave was back to looking like her living room. His beard had grown quite a bit more in the two days she hadn't seen him, and she hated that it actually suited him. She closed the door quietly and tiptoed upstairs to the bedroom.

She still had to update the presentation for Dick Mulligan with the new slogan but she was completely wrecked. She could barely keep her eyes open. She decided she would wake up early the following morning and make the changes with brand new eyes. Tara got into bed and said a silent prayer that everything the following day would go according to plan.

Chapter 32

Tara awoke bright and early for what she hoped would be a career-defining day. Everything had to go perfectly – too much was riding on this pitch. One hiccup and all could be lost. All going well, Dick Mulligan would be one of the most high-profile clients Insight had ever landed. Even if he was public enemy number one, he was still a big fish and Tara was determined to reel him in. She needed to prove to the Lads, and the board of directors, that she was still on top of her game.

She went downstairs to the kitchen, took her tablet out of her handbag and brewed some coffee. She looked out the kitchen window and adored the blush pink colour of the morning sky. She couldn't help but notice there were some tools lying around the outside of the shed and she figured Colin must have been mending the damage she had done to the bike.

As her coffee was brewing, she poked her head into the living room and saw that Colin was still out like a light. Ideal. She couldn't handle a fight with him right now. Tara poured her coffee and spent the next thirty minutes perfecting her presentation. She went through each slide and added the slogan 'Every flower deserves to bloom' in small font under the logo. It was the cherry on top of the entire campaign. All thanks to Tom O'Malley, of all people.

When the presentation was finally ready, however, Tara

noticed that the tablet's battery was low, and she would need it for the pitch. She saved the file and plugged the tablet into a charger on the kitchen counter. It was only 7.30 a.m. so there was still plenty of time to charge it up.

Now Tara just had to get her own battery back to 100 per cent.

She knew she needed to resurrect every last ounce of confidence still left within her. She couldn't let Colin's infidelity get in the way of this huge career opportunity. She had razzle-dazzled Dick during the first pitch meeting so the bar was set high. Now she would have to outdo herself.

Tara showered, applied her best make-up and dressed up in a tantalizing red dress and a pair of black four-inch heels that gave her the confidence she needed. Admittedly, the dress was a little short and Tara wondered if it was office-appropriate. But as she looked in the mirror, she realized she looked good. Great, even. Dick Mulligan was, after all, the founder of an infidelity app. He needed to know she had sex appeal in order to sell her marketing strategy. Her pitch was all about women unlocking their desires and reclaiming their vitality, so it was kind of on-brand that she wear a dress that radiated an erotic aura. Now more than ever she had to embrace the divine feminine.

Colin may have cheated on her and Jack may have been ghosting her but she wasn't going to let a man dictate her mood on such an important day. She stood up tall, threw her shoulders back and walked confidently back downstairs. When she returned to the kitchen, however, she was struck by the image of Colin preparing a bowl of cereal. He was pouring the milk in first, like a madman.

'Tara!' he said, looking up in shock. 'I didn't know you were here.'

'Well, here I am,' she said without emotion.

'I didn't hear you come home last night. I have something to show you,' Colin said, getting up.

'Colin, I'm in a rush this morning,' she said, picking up her handbag.

'You're definitely going to want to see this. Come on, it's in the shed,' Colin said, like an excited child.

'Colin, I don't care if you cleaned the shed after me asking you for months. I have more important things to think about today,' she said.

A look of devastation came over Colin's face. 'What's more important than our marriage?'

'Having an affair, apparently,' she snapped.

'Well, the last thing you said to me was that you were going to have an affair of your own. Is that where you've been all weekend?' Colin asked.

'Wouldn't you like to know,' Tara said, trying to hurt him.

'You're awfully dolled up for someone who's about to go to work,' he said, looking her up and down. 'It looks like you're going on a date.'

'Maybe I am,' Tara said, twisting the knife.

'You're only saying that to hurt me,' Colin said, refusing to believe it. He was right, but Tara didn't want him to know that.

'Believe whatever you want. Either way, I'm not having this conversation,' she said, putting her handbag over her shoulder. She walked out of the kitchen with her head held high. She wasn't about to let Colin ruin this day.

&©

Colin heard the front door slam as Tara stormed out. Surely she was bluffing. There was no way she was going to have an affair. Then again, he had thought she was bluffing when she confronted him about his own affair and he had been dead

291

wrong. And she did look incredibly glamorous for just a regular Monday at the office. Who was she trying to impress? He sat back down to eat his cereal.

Colin suddenly heard a beeping sound in the kitchen that wasn't coming from his phone. He looked around to see Tara's tablet vibrating and lighting-up on the kitchen counter. Colin walked over to mute it but when he got closer, he was shocked by the notification he saw on the screen.

TODAY AT 12 P.M.: DICK APPOINTMENT

AL FRESCO, DUBLIN

Colin was in complete and utter shock. There was only one possible explanation he could think of. Tara wasn't bluffing. She actually was having an affair. It all made sense now. Disappearing for the entire weekend. Sneaking home in the middle of the night. Getting all dolled up for work. And now, a DICK APPOINTMENT in her calendar. She used to schedule reminders for SEX with Colin in her calendar when she was ovulating. But scheduling an affair! It was obscene.

Who did Tara think she was? Was she really that hell-bent on revenge that she would sleep with someone out of spite? Or worse, did she have feelings for this man? Was she planning on leaving him?

Colin felt short of breath. He had heard Rory use the term 'dick appointment' before and he knew it meant a casual hook-up, nothing serious. Colin didn't know the next plan of action, but he knew Rory would have a strategy.

෨

Emily was waiting for Tara when she strutted into the office.

'Oh my God,' Emily said, seeing how well she looked. 'I feel like I should throw money at you.'

'It's not too much, is it?' Tara said, referring to the dress.

'Of course not. I mean, you're pitching a campaign for an infidelity app. You have to look the part. You have to become the Anti-Mary.' Emily smiled.

'That's exactly what I was thinking,' Tara said, feeling reassured. She put her handbag down on her desk and took a seat. 'I found the slogan by the way. "Every flower deserves to bloom." What do you think?'

'Sexy and poetic; I like it,' Emily said.

'I made the changes this morning. Actually, would you mind proofreading my presentation?'

'Tara, in that outfit, I don't think Dick is going to notice any typos in your pitch deck,' Emily teased.

'Don't be silly – Dick is only interested in my idea. He has no interest in me,' Tara said, brushing off the notion.

'Still, isn't it strange that he insisted on you pitching to him over lunch instead of here in the office like the Lads did?' Emily asked, slightly concerned.

'It's a little . . . unusual, I suppose. But in a way, it's better. More casual, less pressure. You can deliver the pitch with me if you want?' Tara said.

'Me, pitch something? With my anxiety? I'd rather take a bath with a toaster,' Emily said, deadpan.

'OK, but will you please still proofread my presentation? You know I seldom ask you to do your job,' Tara said, guilt-tripping her.

'Fine, give me your tablet,' Emily whined.

'Thanks, Emily,' Tara said, reaching into her handbag. She rooted around for five seconds until the penny finally dropped. Her face turned pale as a ghost. She had left her tablet charging on her kitchen table.

'Oh my God,' Tara said. 'I FORGOT MY TABLET! I can't give Dick the pitch without my slides!' She began to pace around her office, hyperventilating.

'Relax. When's the last time you saved it?' Emily asked.

'This morning. When I made my final changes,' Tara said, gasping for air.

'Then it's probably saved in the cloud,' Emily said calmly.

'What cloud? We have a cloud?'

'You and technology,' Emily laughed. 'Wait here, I'll grab my tablet.' She walked to her desk and returned holding her tablet. 'So let's see, your email is tara@insight.com and I'm guessing your password is AbbaGold and . . . oh look at that, I'm in.'

'Is my presentation there?' Tara asked frantically.

'Yep. Fling Pitch Deck. Last updated this morning. Here, take my tablet for the presentation,' Emily said, handing it to her.

'Oh Emily, you're a saint!' Tara said, beyond relieved.

'Take that back,' Emily joked.

'Seriously, you're literally my silver lining in the cloud! Will you please let me take you for drinks after I finish?' Tara said.

'OK, but I'm waiting in the car until the pitch is over,' Emily insisted.

'Deal. God, I feel so relieved,' Tara said, catching her breath once again. 'I just really need everything to go perfectly today.'

'Tara, don't worry. I read the Gemini horoscope for you today and it said something big was going to happen,' Emily said, smiling.

❧

When Colin opened the door of his office, he found Rory sprawled across his couch. It was Monday so, naturally, he was hungover once again.

'Tara's having an affair,' Colin said, bursting in.

'JESUS!' Rory said, sitting up immediately. 'Are you sure?'

'Well . . . no. But I can't think of any other explanation.'

'Start from the beginning,' Rory said, eager to get up to speed.

'OK, so first of all, Tara found out about me going to the hotel room to meet Claire. Then she confronted me about it and disappeared for the entire weekend. Then this morning when I woke up, she was back and dressed to the nines in a short dress that she's never worn before in her life. Then after she left, I found a notification on her tablet for a dick appointment. Tell me I'm crazy, Rory! Tell me there's another way to interpret that!' Colin said, out of breath from talking so fast.

Rory paused momentarily as he digested the information. 'Colin, I know everything there is to know about women. And there is no other way to interpret this information. Tara is having an affair,' he said without any doubt whatsoever.

'Oh my God,' Colin said, collapsing on his office couch. 'What the hell am I going to do?'

'Are you joking? You have to fight for her! What did the notification say?' Rory asked.

'It said "dick appointment". Today at twelve p.m. at Al Fresco, Dublin.'

'Al Fresco, I know the place. It's a little outdoor restaurant in Dalkey. We have to be there at noon to catch her in the act.'

'You're right! We need to see who she's meeting. I have to know! She must think I'm some fool. She's only having an affair because she thinks I had an affair! She's only doing this to get back at me!' Colin ranted.

'She's trying to make a cuckold out of you. She thinks she can get away with it because she thinks you're harmless!' Rory said, riling him up.

'Well, I have news for her. I'm not the kind of man who turns a blind eye to his wife having a dick appointment!'

'I'm coming with you. If the guy she's with tries to start something, I'll be your back-up,' Rory said, puffing out his chest.

'I'm gonna show this guy that he picked the wrong man's wife to sleep with,' Colin said, ready for battle.

Chapter 33

Colin and Rory pulled up across the street from Al Fresco around 11.50 a.m. They had a clear line of sight from Rory's car but there was no sign of Tara in the restaurant.

'Are you sure we're in the right place?' Colin asked, squinting towards the restaurant.

'There's only one Al Fresco in Dublin. Relax, we're early,' Rory said, turning off the engine of his Range Rover.

'I can't believe my marriage has come to this. My wife cheating on me in broad daylight!' Colin said.

'She's obviously trying to get back at you. You said she saw you meeting Claire?' Rory asked.

'She didn't see me with Claire, thank God. But she saw me going into the hotel room. The hotel room *you* told me to get by the way!' Colin said snidely.

'Oh come on, how was I supposed to know Tara would find out! What kind of psycho follows someone to catch them cheating?' Rory asked.

'You mean like what we're doing right now?'

'No, this is totally different,' Rory said. 'You're reclaiming your manhood. You're fighting for your wife!'

'Yeah. I'm trying to stop her from making a mistake she's going to regret. I didn't even technically cheat. I decided I couldn't go through with an actual affair while I was in the hotel room. But if Tara goes through with this, our marriage might be beyond repair. And I'll be damned . . .'

As Colin was speaking, Tara's blue Nissan Micra passed by Rory's side window.

'THAT'S TARA'S CAR!' Colin said, ducking down in the passenger seat. Rory ducked down with him to avoid detection. They both peeked above the dashboard. Thankfully, she hadn't noticed them. She indicated to her right and began to park on the same side of the street, just one car in front of them. She moved forward and tried to reverse into the spot.

'Oh God, we could be here forever. Tara can't parallel park,' Colin sighed.

'Is there someone else in the car with her?' Rory asked, thinking he saw someone in the passenger seat.

'I can't tell,' Colin said, squinting.

After a few clunky manoeuvres, Tara eventually got into the parking space, although she wasn't exactly inside the white line. She got out of her car and crossed the quiet street towards Al Fresco.

'Look at her, all dressed up for her mystery man. I feel sick,' Colin said, watching her. They had a clear view of the entire place: they could see Tara checking in with the hostess and then being seated at the table by herself.

'Hmm, no mystery man so far,' Rory said.

'I'm going to call her,' Colin said, taking out his phone.

'What? Then we lose the element of surprise!' Rory said.

'I'm not going to tell her we're here. I'm just going to ask her where she is. Maybe there's a reasonable explanation for her being here,' Colin said. He pressed her name in his contacts and waited for her to pick up. In the distance, he could see Tara reaching into her bag and taking out her phone. She looked at the screen and winced when she saw who was calling her. She answered the phone and put it to her ear.

'I'm at work, Colin, don't call me again,' Tara said, hanging up before Colin even had a chance to say anything. He was in shock.

'What did she say?' Rory asked, curious.

'She said she was at work and then she just hung up. Well, we know that's a lie. We can see that with our own eyes. She's clearly not working. And working is what I said I was doing when I was really meeting Claire at the hotel!' Colin said, furious.

'Did you see her face when she saw you were calling her? She is out for vengeance. Hell hath no fury like a woman scorned,' Rory said.

'*Look!*' Colin said, pointing.

A man in a black suit approached Tara's table and she got up to greet him. He gave her a kiss on the cheek and put his hand a little too low down on the small of her back for Colin's liking.

'Who the hell is that creep?' Colin said, squinting.

'I can't make him out. Use your phone and zoom in on the camera,' Rory suggested. This was clearly not his first private investigation.

Colin opened the camera on his phone to get a closer look. The image wasn't crystal clear but it was certainly better than Colin's eyesight.

'Who is he?' Colin asked.

'I'm not sure, but his suit looks expensive. Whoever he is, he looks like a big shot,' Rory deduced.

Colin could see a smile on Tara's face unlike any smile he'd seen in months. He seemed to have made some kind of joke and Tara was laughing just a little too hard for it to be natural.

'She's doing that flirty laugh thing women do,' Rory said.

'I need to know who he is,' Colin said, furious.

Rory looked intensely at the image on the phone screen. 'Hmm . . . he looks rich. A little older than you, I think. Strong jaw but weak chin. We'd need binoculars to see how far back his hairline goes. Poor guy has a fivehead,' Rory said.

'What the hell is she doing with him then? It would make more sense if he was better looking than me!' Colin said, confused at Tara's taste.

'I guess she's so mad at you, she's willing to downgrade,' Rory said.

'I'm going in for a closer look,' Colin said, putting his phone down on the dashboard.

'OK, let's go,' Rory said, reaching for the door handle.

'No, you stay here. Keep an eye on the situation,' Colin said, opening his door.

'Ugh, fine. But give me a signal if you need back-up!' Rory said, eager for some action.

Colin left the car and walked diagonally across the street towards the restaurant, out of Tara's line of sight.

Rory continued watching the scene unfold for a few seconds when he saw the passenger door of Tara's car open suddenly and a good-looking young woman getting out. He was immediately enthralled by her.

'I knew there was someone in there!' Rory whispered to himself.

To his surprise, he could see the young woman was approaching his car.

'What the hell is going on?' Emily asked, opening the passenger door.

'What do you think you're doing?' Rory said, shocked.

Emily got into the passenger seat and closed the door behind her.

'I know you are spying on Tara. I could see you through the make-up mirror of Tara's car,' Emily said.

'You mean the rear-view mirror?' Rory said, horrified.

'Why are you spying on her?'

'It's a private matter between Tara and Colin,' Rory said, refusing to tell.

'So that's Tara's husband. The plot thickens. Among other things,' Emily said, looking at Rory's protruding crotch.

'He gets excited in chaotic situations!' Rory said, trying to hide it.

'START TALKING!'

'You just broke into my car! I should be the one interrogating you!'

'Go ahead. My safe word is *harder*,' Emily said, smiling.

'OK, I'll tell you everything – under one condition. You have to agree to a three-course dinner with me,' Rory said, enamoured with her chaotic sexual energy.

'I'm only interested in one course,' Emily countered.

'Which one?'

'Intercourse.'

'Dear God, I think I'm in love,' Rory said. 'OK, we have a deal.'

'Now tell me what's going on!' Emily demanded.

'Colin is spying on Tara because she's having an affair and he wanted to catch her in the act. He saw a notification on her tablet this morning that said she had a dick appointment today at noon so we followed her to catch her cheating,' Rory explained.

Emily realized that she was partly responsible for the mix-up. She was the one who had entered the words 'Dick Appointment' into Tara's calendar.

'Oh God, I know what happened. I manage Tara's calendar. She doesn't have a dick appointment! She has an appointment with Dick!'

'You're speaking in riddles!' Rory said.

'Dick is Richard Mulligan! The CEO of Fling!'

'The guy who was on the radio?'

'Yes, and Tara's just about to make the most important pitch of her career to him,' Emily said frantically.

'And Colin just went to confront her about having an affair!' Rory said, realizing the gravity of the situation.

'WELL, CALL HIM AND STOP HIM!'

Rory took out his phone and immediately called Colin.

'It's ringing,' he said.

'Thank God!' Emily said, relieved.

Colin's phone began to ring on top of the car's dashboard.

'Oh God, Colin forgot to take his phone,' Rory said, panicking. 'Come on, we have to try and stop him, before it's too late!'

⁗

As Tara was walking Dick through her slides, she found his gaze fixated on her chest rather than her presentation.

'So the theme of a flower blooming brings the entire campaign together. So many women feel trapped in their own lives and Fling can offer them a fantasy, a way to reconnect with their erotic selves,' Tara said, trying to keep Dick's attention.

'Mmhmm,' he said, clearly not listening.

'The campaign is all about showing women that having desires is nothing to be ashamed of. It's about showing them they deserve their desires,' Tara said, swiping to the next slide.

'Tara, I'm sure the rest of the pitch is wonderful,' Dick said, taking the tablet and resting it down on the table. 'But I want to know about *your* desires.'

'Me? Well, I think I'm no different to any woman really,' Tara said nervously.

'Oh, you are very different to other women,' Dick said, putting his hand on her knee.

Tara laughed awkwardly, not knowing what to do. 'I'm not sure what you mean,' she said.

'Well, you're just oozing sex appeal, I knew that much the moment I laid eyes on you,' Dick said, moving his hand from her knee to her thigh. Tara felt frozen with fear. It was as if she had sleep paralysis, yet she was wide awake and what she was experiencing wasn't a lucid dream but a waking night-mare. 'And this dress you have on is driving me wild.'

'Ehh . . . Richard, I—'

'Please, call me Dick,' he said, putting his hand up her dress.

'GET YOUR HANDS OFF OF MY WIFE!' Colin shouted, barging across the terrace and towards the table.

Tara was in complete and utter shock. Colin's sudden appearance had jolted her out of her paralysis but she couldn't understand where he had come from.

'Colin, what are you doing here?' she said, getting up of her chair.

'What am I doing here?' Colin snapped. 'What the hell are you doing here with this creep?'

'Listen here, buddy—' Dick said defensively.

'I'm not your buddy! Who do you think you are putting your hands all over my wife?'

'COLIN, STOP TALKING!' Tara screamed.

'Oh I'm sorry, am I interrupting your little date? Your little *dick appointment*?'

'Colin, I can explain. Please listen . . .'

'Oh, I'm done listening. You think you can just make a fool of me, do you? Well, this dirtbag chose the wrong man to cross!' Colin roared.

At this point, everyone on the terrace was staring at the

spectacle Colin was making of himself. Several members in the crowd began taking out their phones and filming.

'Who are you calling a dirtbag?' Dick said, getting up off his chair.

'I'm calling you a dirtbag! I saw you put your hand up my wife's dress!' Colin yelled.

'When a woman wears a dress that short, she's begging for a hand up it,' Dick said unapologetically.

Colin took an almighty swing and punched Dick Mulligan square in the jaw, knocking him out and sending him flying back onto the table.

'COLIN!' Tara screamed.

The crowd let out a huge gasp but continued to record every second of the mess unfolding in front of their cameras.

'When a man says things like that, he's begging for a punch in the face!' Colin said to Dick's unconscious body.

Rory and Emily arrived on the scene, a moment too late.

'Colin, stop, it's not what you think,' Rory said.

'Oh yes it is. This is Tara's dick appointment!'

'IT'S NOT A DICK APPOINTMENT! IT'S AN APPOINTMENT WITH DICK! YOU JUST PUNCHED RICHARD MULLIGAN!' Tara screamed.

'Who?' Colin said confused.

'He was going to be the biggest client I ever landed. I'm not having an affair with him. This was a business meeting!' Tara said, dizzy with rage.

'Then why did he have his hand up your dress?' Colin said, still dumbfounded.

'He ... well ... I ...' Tara began. But she stuttered with anger. She was angry with Colin for storming into her meeting but she was also furious with Dick for his appallingly inappropriate behaviour.

Dick Mulligan regained consciousness and got up off the table. He was still dizzy and his nose was pumping blood.

'Mr. Mulligan, there's been a misunderstanding,' Tara said, approaching him.

'DON'T COME ANY CLOSER!' Dick roared. 'Don't you or anyone at Insight ever contact me again.' He turned to Colin with venom in his eyes. 'And as for you, you ape! If I ever see you again, I'll sue you for every cent you have!'

Dick turned around and stormed inside to clean his bloody nose.

Tara, Colin, Rory and Emily stood there in the wreckage, each of them at a loss for words.

'Tara, I'm—' Colin said eventually, knowing his words were feeble.

'Don't you say a word. Whatever hope you had of me forgiving you for cheating is now gone. What, was destroying our marriage not enough? You just had to derail my career too? Go home, Colin. Go home and pack your stupid bags, your stupid pub signs and your stupid motorbike,' Tara said, practically frothing at the mouth with fury.

'Tara . . .' Colin begged.

'It's over.'

Chapter 34

Tara sat in Dr Burke's office on a Saturday afternoon in October, waiting for her husband to arrive. She wasn't there for a therapy session, however. Dr Burke was now their mediator, aiming to help them draw up a separation agreement. Tara had texted Colin telling him this, but he was already ten minutes late.

Tara hadn't gone back to work since the fiasco at Al Fresco, choosing to use up her annual leave sooner than face the Lads. She had hoped she could sweep the whole thing under the rug but she quickly learned that wouldn't be possible.

One of the onlookers who recorded Colin punching Dick had uploaded the video online and, thanks to Dick Mulligan being so publicly hated, it became an overnight viral phenomenon. Thousands of people were still sharing the video. Dick Mulligan was publicly disgraced and was forced to step down, with the Fling board of directors electing a woman to take his place as CEO. But even though he had gotten his comeuppance, Tara still felt mortified by the entire situation and she knew the Lads would have a million different jokes ready when she returned to work. She wanted to crawl under a rock and hide for the foreseeable future. It was embarrassing enough having the crowd in the restaurant watching, but

306

now it seemed as if the whole country was laughing at her. The more she thought about it, the angrier she got at Colin.

And yet, there was a deeper part of her that wanted to forgive him. He had, after all, saved her. She hated thinking of herself as a damsel in distress, but when Dick put his hand up her dress, she was paralysed with fear. Colin had appeared just in time, like her knight in shining armour. If he hadn't shown up, who knows what Dick might have done next. Colin had finally been the hero she needed him to be.

The problem was that Colin hadn't shown up to the restaurant to save her, he had shown up because he thought she was having an affair. It wasn't heroism that drove his actions. It was spite. She was torn by the question of whether it was OK to do the right thing for the wrong reason. She had kicked him out of the house and hadn't seen him in person until now. She kept reminding herself that even before he punched Dick, he had cheated on her. And then to make a national embarrassment out of her?

No, the damage was done.

The door opened and Colin strolled in. He looked dishevelled, like he had just rolled out of bed. His beard was now fully filled in and, even though the facial hair suited him, it was due a trim. He sat down on the couch beside Tara and turned towards Dr Burke.

'OK, let's get this over with,' he said, slouching back.

'Excuse me?' Tara said, shocked at his devil-may-care attitude. 'This is a very important meeting.'

'Well, I don't see how meditation is supposed to help our marriage. You know I hate yoga,' Colin said, folding his arms.

'It's marriage mediation, not meditation, you dope! We're here to organize a separation agreement,' Tara replied.

'Your text said marriage meditation,' Colin said. He took out his phone and opened the message. He shoved his phone in front of her face and she could see that he was right, she had misspelled the word. Tara was silently furious she had made a typo.

'Well, my phone must have auto-corrected, Colin. You should have known it was mediation after everything that's happened!' she said.

'Hold on, so we're getting divorced?' Colin said, genuinely shocked.

'No, we're separating. Divorces take a long time.'

'Do I need a solicitor? You've completely blindsided me with this. I didn't prepare anything.'

'That's why we have Dr Burke as a mediator. To help us agree on everything.'

'And we couldn't have found a cheaper one?' Colin said, throwing his hands in the air. 'She charged us three hundred euro to tell us to re-watch our wedding video.'

'That strategy usually works for couples,' Dr Burke shrugged.

'I guess nostalgia ain't what it used to be,' Colin muttered. 'Is she even qualified to be a mediator?'

'Dr Burke, I apologize for him,' Tara said. 'Actually no! I no longer have to apologize for him. Because he's no longer my problem.'

'Hallelujah!' Colin rejoiced.

'That's OK, Tara,' Dr Burke said calmly. 'Colin, to put your mind at ease, I have ten years' experience as a licensed mediator and I am authorized to draw up legally binding separation agreements on behalf of my clients. Mediation is designed to help couples negotiate their own separation terms while making sure everyone's needs are met. It's a long process; we could be here for a few hours.'

'Jesus, I think I actually would have preferred yoga,' Colin sighed.

'You know, Colin, you have a lot of nerve to be cracking

jokes after the stunt you pulled. You practically derailed my entire career!' Tara snapped.

'Oh please, I made a simple mistake.'

'A simple mistake? You followed me to try and catch me having an affair!'

'You mean the way *you* followed *me* to catch me having an affair? What was I supposed to think when you left for work in a cocktail dress and eight-inch heels?'

'God, men really have a warped view of how big an inch is, don't they? Dr Burke, allow me to explain what we're talking about,' Tara said, turning to her.

'There's no need, Tara, I saw the video online,' Dr Burke said with a faint smile.

'Oh for God's sake, even you've seen it? Emily was right, it's gone viral. Congratulations, Colin, you've turned me into a complete laughing stock!' Tara snapped.

'You're barely even in the video, Tara, I'm the one they were recording. And for the record, most of the comments are saying I'm very heroic for what I did,' he bragged.

'You're lucky you're not in jail, Colin! You can't just go around assaulting people!'

'I can when they're feeling up my wife! I cannot believe you're siding with the man who put his hand up your dress. You see, Dr Burke, my wife isn't a feminist and that's a big part of the problem,' Colin said, mimicking Tara's words from their one and only therapy session.

'I AM A FEMINIST!' Tara screamed.

'Well, according to the comments on the video, I'm the new face of feminism,' Colin said, taking out his phone. 'Let's see . . . ah yes, here we are. The top comment says, "This is what a feminist looks like #ImWithHim", and the second one says, "We need more men like him to stand up to misogyny #HeFor-She". See, I'm a feminist icon.' He was revelling in the moment.

Tara felt as if steam was about to come out of her ears. All she wanted was to be a feminist icon who inspired women, and now Colin was the bloody poster boy for women's liberation! It didn't make any sense! She had spent eighteen years trying to get Colin to say he was a feminist and now all she wanted was for him to shut the hell up.

'I won't let you distract me from the facts, Colin. We were fighting before Al Fresco, remember? Or have you forgotten the fact that you slept with another woman?' Tara said.

'How many times do I have to say it? I didn't have sex with anyone else! Look at my nostrils. Are they flaring? No!' Colin said, genuinely telling the truth.

'I saw you go into that hotel room with my own two eyes, Colin. Most likely with a sex worker!'

'She wasn't a sex worker!'

'She might as well have been. Dr Burke, let the record show that my husband cheated on me due to his incurable Madonna–Whore Complex,' Tara said, expecting her to write it down.

'I never actually made that diagnosis,' Dr Burke said.

'Well, whoever that home-wrecker was in that room with you, at least I didn't barge in and punch her in her face!'

'Oh yeah, you just waited at home in the dark so you could attack me with pub signs! Dr Burke, let the record show that my wife threw dangerous objects directly at my head,' Colin said.

'Oh please, nothing could put a dent in that thick skull of yours,' Tara said, turning away from him.

'I would like it stricken from the record that I met a sex worker.'

'You do realize we're not in court and there is no record?' Dr Burke said.

'Did this tramp know you were married?' Tara asked.

'Yes. She's married too.'

'Well then, I should track her down and sleep with her husband. Give her a taste of her own medicine. Come on, what's her name?' Tara said.

'She's nobody. She was just a woman who made me feel good about myself. She was kind, gentle and she actually wanted me to be happy.'

'WELL, WHY DON'T YOU JUST MARRY HER THEN?' Tara yelled childishly.

'MAYBE I WILL!' Colin said, every bit as immature.

'You know what? That actually makes me feel better,' Tara said, calming down. 'When a woman steals your man, the best revenge is to let her keep him.'

'Great. So where's this separation agreement? I'm ready to sign and become a free man.'

'Well, we haven't actually begun the mediation process yet,' Dr Burke chimed in.

'Let's get on with it then,' Colin said, slouching back in his chair.

'Anyway,' Dr Burke said, finally able to proceed. 'Today is about coming together in order to divide. It's not a divorce, it's more of an uncoupling.'

'Oh just call a spade a spade,' Colin muttered.

'After this meeting, I'll go and draft up the separation agreement for you both to sign and it will lay everything out clearly if you want to begin formal divorce proceedings. So first things first. Assets and liabilities.'

'Well . . . there's the house,' Tara said. 'I'm currently living there. Colin is staying with a friend.'

'Which makes no sense considering it's a three-bedroom house!' Colin said, getting slightly heated again.

'I think a little bit of space is a reasonable request, all things considered.'

'So I'm supposed to just keep paying half the mortgage, am I?'

'Of course not. It doesn't make sense to keep the house. It's probably worth a lot more now than when we bought it. We'll be able to pay back the banks and make some money for ourselves,' Tara said with sadness in her voice. She knew selling made the most sense but she did still feel an emotional attachment to the house. She had her gut feeling the first time she saw it that told her she would live happily ever after within its walls. But life hadn't been the fairy tale she had hoped it would be. Perhaps it was time to pack up and move on. 'I say we sell the house and I'll stay in it until it's sold.'

'I can't stay on Rory's couch, it's bad for my back.'

'Well, my back's a bit sore from the knife you lodged in it, so I'm staying. Let's not forget who the breadwinner is,' Tara said, trying to hurt Colin.

'I thought you were off carbs?' Colin said, mocking her.

'Whoever stays in the house will have to decorate it for an open house so we can sell it. Naturally, I'm the right person for the job.'

'Oh please, in a week you'll have "Live Laugh Love" plastered on every single wall in the house!'

'Well, you'd end up turning every room into a man cave. Not happening! I'm staying and that's the end of it,' Tara scoffed.

'Fine, but don't come crying to me when you find a spider in the sink you're too afraid to kill,' Colin sulked.

'I'd rather live with a spider in the sink than a snake in the grass!'

'Tara. Colin,' Dr Burke said, interrupting their fight. 'We are leaning back into marriage counselling territory here. Remember, this is marriage mediation. It's about agreeing on how best to separate.'

'OK, let's keep going,' Tara said.

☙

After about three hours of bickering, Colin and Tara had finally agreed on the terms of their separation. Tara would stay in the house until it was sold, and Colin would stay with Rory while he searched for his own bachelor pad in the city.

After the house was sold, all the assets within the house were to be divided up in a ridiculously peevish manner. If Tara wanted the lamps, Colin wanted the light bulbs. Tara could have the bed but Colin insisted on the mattress. Colin got the couch but Tara got the cushions.

But eventually, the tit-for-tat saga was over and Dr Burke had finally compiled all the information for the separation agreement.

'OK,' Dr Burke said. 'I think that just about covers everything. I will have the agreement drawn up this evening and posted to your house tomorrow.'

'Thank you, Dr Burke,' Tara said as she and Colin stood up. Colin headed straight for the door without even saying goodbye.

'Sorry about him,' Tara said, embarrassed.

'Remember you don't have to apologize any more,' Dr Burke said.

'Oh yes, sorry,' Tara said, realizing she had just apologized again.

'Can I just say one thing before you go?' Dr Burke asked Tara politely.

'Of course, doctor,' Tara said.

'Take your time before signing the agreement. Make sure it's really what you want. I know it might feel like you hate him right now, but love and hate are two sides of the same coin,' Dr Burke said, touching her shoulder.

'Thank you, Dr Burke, but sadly, I think our story has come to an end.'

Chapter 35

As she left the building and walked towards her car, Tara realized that this was it. Separation may not be as final as divorce but it was a means to an end; her marriage was essentially over. It would only take two signatures to solidify everything. She felt a sudden pang of loneliness come over her. Was she doing the right thing? Was Colin's lapse in judgement forgivable? Why was she still holding on to false hope for Jack? He still hadn't texted her back, and she found herself checking the app to see if her knight in shining armour would appear.

She wanted Jack to save her, the way only he could.

If it had been Jack who punched Dick Mulligan, she would have been his forever, there and then. And maybe if Colin hadn't already cheated on her, she would have felt the same for Colin. But she was still so hurt by his betrayal. She tried to remind herself that she was unhappy long before Colin punched Dick. That was the final domino to fall, not the first. But even after she had got what she wanted in the separation agreement, she felt no sense of victory, only defeat.

When she got to the car park, she could see Colin about to get onto his motorcycle, seemingly now his main mode of transport. Her whacks with the golf club obviously weren't hard enough.

'Not even a goodbye?' she said.

'You're the one who wants to say goodbye, not me,' Colin said, turning around to face her.

There was a silence between Tara and Colin, the likes of which they had never experienced before. It was a mournful moment of silence for their love. Tara began to feel as if she had made a terrible mistake. She didn't know how she would get through this heartbreak alone.

'You know, I really thought we were gonna make it, you and me,' Colin said, trying to hold himself together.

'So did I.'

'So much for forever and always.'

Tara didn't know what to say. She was breaking. 'Maybe stars that burn the brightest . . . shine for half as long,' she finally said.

Colin didn't say anything for a few seconds. She stood there, desperately wanting to dress the wounds she had given him. But she was wounded too. She had to stitch up her own heart before she bled out.

'If you could do it all again, would you still get on the back of my bike?' Colin asked her.

Her eyes were heavy. It was an impossible question. She didn't regret getting on that bike, but it had led her to this moment in time, a moment of heartbreak and despair. 'I don't know how to answer that,' she said at last.

Colin looked devastated by her answer. 'Of all the pubs, in all the towns, in all of Ireland, I had to walk into yours,' he said, trying to hold back the tears.

A tear ran down Tara's cheek, even as she did everything to maintain her composure. She felt the emptiness in her chest return, a void she feared would consume her this time. It had only just hit her now that this was the end. She was fighting the tears with every ounce of her being, desperately trying to prevent the dam from breaking.

'Before you sign the separation agreement, take a look in the shed. I left something for you to remember me by,' he said.

Colin gave her one last bittersweet smile as he put on his helmet and started the bike's engine. As she watched him ride off into the sunset, she completely broke down. Ten minutes ago there was no doubt in her mind that she was making the right decision, and now she was questioning everything. She started her car and prayed the tears wouldn't blind her on the drive home.

When she finally arrived back to Hillcrest, Tara felt the cold, empty house mocking her, the walls whispering of her failures. Tara suddenly realized that this was the first time in her life she was truly alone. The gravity of the situation was crushing her and the isolation threatened to drag her into the depths of melancholia. She felt as if her life had lost all meaning, as every strand of her complicated belief system had been proven wrong.

She had wanted it all. To be married to the man she loved, in the house of their dreams with a beautiful baby and a thriving career. Now, she had nothing. No marriage, no children, a derailed career and a home soon to be sold. She realized it was her match with Jack that had set off the series of events that led to her ruination. She had downloaded Fling and just a few short weeks later, she had lost everything. The synchronicity that always acted as her spiritual compass had seemingly led her to her doom.

Was this cosmic cruelty the destiny she deserved?

No, there had to be something more to it. It couldn't all

just be random. If it was, then what was the point of any-thing? She had to believe there was some deeper meaning to all the chaos. Now, more than ever, she needed to have faith in fate.

She opened Fling and saw all of the messages she had sent to Jack that he had not responded to.

Ghosted. Exactly what she deserved.

She felt a little embarrassed about him ignoring her, but then she saw that he had not been online in two weeks. Maybe he wasn't ignoring her, per se. Perhaps he just hadn't opened the app. Or even deleted it. But his profile was still there, which meant there was a chance. A slim chance but a chance nonetheless. It was Saturday evening and she had tomorrow free.

She had to try one last time. If she didn't, she would always wonder *what if*? She would forever wonder why her life had played out this way. She decided to throw herself to the mercy of the universe. After all, what had she left to lose? If it was meant to be, it would surely be.

Destiny would decide.

Claire: Hi Jack, I know you probably hate me and you might not even see this message. But I want you to know how sorry I am for standing you up again

I don't deserve a third chance, I know that

But I'll be at Dún Laoghaire Harbour tomorrow at 3 p.m.

Halfway down the West Pier, there's a quiet walkway

I know there's probably no chance you'll show up. But I'll be there, Jack

I promise I'll be there x

Chapter 36

'You said we were going to a bar,' Emily sighed as she and Tara were getting pedicures in Oscar's Hair and Nail Salon.

'Technically, I didn't lie. It's a nail bar,' Tara said, knowing well she had misled her.

'Well, I'd rather be getting hammered.'

'Emily, it's Sunday morning.'

'Exactly. Have you never heard of bottomless brunch?'

'Come on, I need you here for moral support. I want to look perfect for Jack from head to toe. And Suzanne here gives the best mani–pedi in Dublin,' Tara said to Suzanne, who was currently working miracles on her feet.

'Aw, thanks, hun,' Suzanne said, smiling up at her.

'So let me get this straight. You're here getting all done up to meet Jack at Dún Laoghaire Harbour even though he didn't respond to your messages and you have no idea if he'll even show up?' Emily asked.

'Yes.'

'Jesus, that is some next level Gemini shit,' Emily laughed.

'Oh come on, Emily, you're telling me you've never gone somewhere on the off-chance a man would be there?'

'Hmm . . . touché,' Emily said. 'Still, I hope you don't put all this effort in for Jack, just for him to stand you up.'

'I'm not doing it for Jack, I'm doing it for me,' Tara explained. 'I need to feel like myself again. And if he doesn't appear, then I'll know it wasn't meant to be and I can move on with my life.'

'Fair enough,' Emily said, looking back down at her phone.

'How many views does the video have now?' Tara asked, her curiosity getting the better of her.

'Do you really want to know?'

'Well, I need to know how many people in the country are laughing at me.'

'One point two million.'

'WHAT?' Tara said, accidentally walloping Suzanne in the face with a kick. 'OH MY GOD, I'M SO SORRY, SUZANNE!'

'Jesus, Tara, I thought it was your husband who was going around knocking people's blocks off. Not you,' Suzanne said playfully.

'Oh God, you've seen the video too?' Tara said mortified.

'Your reaction to the punch is even funnier than the punch itself. Look,' Emily said, showing her screen.

On Emily's phone, Tara could see a close-up of her reaction at the moment Colin punched Dick Mulligan. It was the most unflattering photo that Tara had ever seen of herself. It was an image of pure shock caught on camera. People online were making memes by adding different captions to the image of Tara's face. One read, 'When you realize you left the immersion on.' Another read, 'When you stub your toe on the corner of the bed.'

'Oh my God. I'm a meme!' Tara sighed. 'This is a complete and utter disaster!'

'Tara, going viral is a good thing. You've literally stolen my dream of becoming an internet celebrity. And it proves you're a good marketer because your clients will definitely see you know how to get something trending,' Emily said, seeing the positive side.

'Are people still calling Colin a feminist icon?'

'I mean, he did punch the face of modern misogyny. That comment Dick made about you wanting a hand up your dress? I would have punched him too. But it was so much hotter seeing Colin do it. I heard he's single now. Do you think I have a shot?' Emily teased.

'Don't even think about it,' Tara laughed as she handed Emily back her phone. She had seen enough memes of herself for one day.

'Didn't it turn you on just a little bit to see Colin defend your honour?' Emily pried.

'Of course it did,' Tara admitted. 'But he did it for the wrong reason, Emily. He wasn't trying to defend my honour, he was trying to publicly expose me having an affair. Now if Jack was the one who punched Dick, that would be a different story. But the way it all went down makes me so mad.'

'You're not mad at me for writing "dick appointment" in your calendar, are you? I mean, how was I supposed to know that my actions would have consequences? That's not the way the world works,' Emily said.

'No, I'm not mad at you,' Tara sighed. 'I'm just dreading the slagging I'm going to get from the Lads when I go back to work on Monday. My career is practically over.'

'Tara, I think you've got them all wrong. They've been asking me how you've been doing, non-stop. They were horrified at what Dick said in the video. I think they were being genuine when they tried to come with you to the pitch meeting,' Emily said.

'Ugh, you're right. They weren't trying to take credit. They were just trying to protect me,' Tara said, realizing she had misjudged them. She thought about the events that led up to Colin punching Dick and saw she had nobody to blame but herself. 'You know what? This entire situation is my fault.

It's karma. I should have just let them do the pitch alone. This entire series of events started because I tried to take the account off them. All I wanted was to prove I wasn't a Mary and now I'm all over the internet. I'm literally the new Mary!'

'I love that journey for you,' Emily laughed. 'Well, if it makes you feel any better, at least you're not the number one trending topic any more.'

'Oh yeah, what knocked me off the spot?' Tara asked.

'The number one hashtag at the moment is #Yummy-Mummy. Everyone is talking about that influencer Celine Loftus.'

'Ugh, she's my neighbour. Everyone in Hillcrest worships the ground she walks on. Don't tell me the rest of the country is obsessed with her now too,' Tara said, horrified at the idea.

'No, quite the opposite. A journalist went undercover as a Yummy Mummy and just published an article exposing the business as a pyramid scheme. Everyone is demanding that Celine give them their money back. She's losing all her followers. Look,' Emily said, handing her the phone. Tara's face lit up as she looked at all the comments.

Celine needs to answer for her years of FRAUD. Give back the money you scammed or else! one comment read. Celine has made millions robbing women in plain sight. OFF WITH HER HEAD! read another.

Tara felt like crying tears of joy. She had been right all along. It was the most euphoric sense of relief she had ever experienced.

'Emily, you have no idea how happy that news makes me. I always had a hunch Celine was rotten to the core but everyone made me out to be crazy! You literally just made my day,' Tara said, relaxing back in her chair.

'All done,' Suzanne said, as she finished Tara's pedicure. 'You're getting your hair done as well, is that right?'

'Thank you so much, Suzanne. Yes, I am,' Tara said, getting up.

'Perfect, just take a seat on one of the salon chairs and Oscar will be over in a few minutes,' Suzanne said.

Tara and Emily went over to the hairdressing section of the salon and took their seats.

'So if Jack shows up, what are you two going to do after the pier?' Emily asked, suggestively.

'I haven't planned that far ahead to be honest. I'm just going to follow my intuition. I know it's crazy, but these past few weeks the universe has been pointing me away from Colin and towards Jack. My whole life has crumbled around me and it all started with Fling. I have to believe it's all happened for a reason. I have to listen to my gut.'

'I still think it's just IBS,' Emily joked.

'Have you never felt as if you were destined to meet someone?'

'Well, it's funny you should say that actually, because I recently met someone special and I'm meeting him later today,' Emily said, clearly smitten.

'Emily, that's wonderful! I knew there was someone out there for you somewhere! Well, spit it out! Who is it?' Tara demanded.

'Your husband's friend Rory,' Emily said as if she was bragging.

'RORY! No, no, no, anyone but Rory! He's literally the worst person I've ever met!'

'I know, he's perfect!'

'His inner thoughts are just "Mr Brightside" by The Killers on a loop 24/7,' Tara said frantically.

'The world's best wedding song,' Emily said, daydreaming.

'Emily, if he gets the clap one more time, it'll be an applause!'

'Oh, I built up an immunity to that years ago.'

'But he's basically the male version of a nymphomaniac!' Tara said, before suddenly realizing that they might actually be a good match. 'OK, now I get it.'

'The term is satyromaniac, I looked it up.' Emily smiled. 'I thought they were just a myth. I can't believe I actually found one in the wild.'

'I guess Colin was right, there really is someone for everyone. And you're a Libra, so the more I tell you not to sleep with him, the sooner you will,' Tara said, giving up.

'And he's a Scorpio. It's going to be the most toxic relationship in history,' Emily said, excited.

'And they say romance is dead.'

'There's a lot more to him than meets the eye. I can see through his façade. Most men these days are wolves in sheep's clothing. But Rory is a sheep in wolves clothing,' Emily said warmly.

'Still, good luck getting past his commitment issues.'

'Oh please, men don't have commitment issues. They have abandonment issues. Once you realize that, they make a lot more sense.'

'OK, you win. I guess he's perfect for you. So when are you meeting him?'

'Right after my bikini wax,' Emily smirked.

'If you see Colin at all while you're meeting Rory, will you tell me how he looks? If he's taking care of himself?' Tara asked, concerned.

'You need to stop thinking like Tara and start thinking like Claire. Colin is the past, Jack is the future. Well . . . if he shows up,' Emily said.

Tara's hairstylist Oscar approached them.

'Tara, great to see you. Curly blow-dry, same as last time?' Oscar asked.

'No, she needs a whole new look,' Emily butted in.

'Oh, looking for something new, are we?'

'Not necessarily something new, Oscar, but . . . I want to feel like me again,' Tara said. 'Is there something that can give me even more confidence than a curly blow-dry?'

'Hmm . . . do you trust me?'

'With my life,' she said.

'OK, then put this on,' Oscar said, taking a cold gel eye mask out of a mini fridge.

'Oh, I hear these are great for under-eye bags,' Tara said, putting it on. She noticed that it almost completely obscured her vision.

'Yeah, and it'll make you keep your eyes closed while I do my thing. Now just sit back and relax.'

'Have fun, Tara,' Emily said. 'I'm off to get waxed within an inch of my life.'

'I can't believe I'm paying fifty euro for you to get a Brazilian wax for Rory McKenna,' Tara sighed.

'Hey, it's not my fault it's a total rip-off,' Emily said, shooting Oscar a look.

'Look at it this way, ladies. You get what you pay for,' Oscar joked, causing Tara and Emily to erupt in laughter.

After a nerve-wrecking hour in the chair letting the dye set and telling Oscar the entire story about Jack, it was finally time to take the gel mask off and see the result. Tara took a deep breath. She had no idea what to expect. Oscar took the mask off and Tara looked at her reflection in the mirror. She nearly collapsed in pure shock.

She was a redhead once again.

Her first instincts were to not like it. But when she looked closer, she realized it was the most luscious shade of red she had ever seen. It was the kind of red you see on Hollywood starlets. This was Academy-Award-winning red. It was the colour of summer wine with the hue of a fiery sunset. It was like her natural colour but a more enhanced, vibrant shade. As she saw her true reflection in the mirror for the first time in years, she came to a beautiful realization.

Tara had become herself.

'Oscar, you're a miracle worker,' Tara said, giving him a hug.

'Well, we've been fighting the red for years with that ashy tone. It was time to let the real you shine through.'

'Thanks, Oscar,' Tara said. 'I hope Jack likes it as much as I do. If he even shows up, that is.'

'If he doesn't appear, Tara, it'll be his loss,' Oscar smiled.

Chapter 37

When Tara arrived home and pulled into her driveway, she could see a moving van outside Celine's house and dozens of cardboard boxes on her lawn. Tara got out of the car and looked across the street to see Celine arguing with the van driver. The other mothers on the street were standing outside their homes, watching Celine pack. She spotted Tara looking at her and began to rush towards her. Tara tried to avoid her gaze but she was already halfway across the road.

'Tara!' Celine cried. 'Tara!'

Tara turned around. 'Everything OK, Celine?' she asked.

'Tara, my life is falling apart. Everyone is calling me a con artist. We have to sell the house to refund all my ambassadors or else they're going to sue me for fraud. We have to move to . . .' Celine began to gag on her own words. '. . . we have to move to . . . THE NORTHSIDE!'

It took every ounce of Tara's willpower not to laugh.

'Is there anything you can do to help?' Celine begged. 'You work in marketing. Is there a way we can spin the story to make me look good? We're both girl bosses. And boss babes need to support each other. I mean, you know I don't belong on the Northside. I'm the one who put Hillcrest on the map! It won't be the same without me.'

'Amen to that,' Tara smiled.

'Excuse me?' Celine said, taken aback. 'I will not stand here and be judged by you or anyone else for that matter!'

'Well, good for you not caring what people think. I've always admired your confidence,' Tara said, giving Celine a dose of her own backhanded compliments.

Celine let out a grunt and stormed back to her house to finish her argument with the van driver. Tara took out her phone and opened Celine's social media profile. She was down to only 410 followers from 10k. Then, in what was one of the most cathartic moments of her life, Tara hit the Unfollow button. The Wicked Witch of the South was now the Wicked Witch of the North and she was no longer Tara's problem. She only wished this had all happened sooner, before she and Colin had agreed to put the house on the market. She wished she could have got to experience Hillcrest now that Celine's spell had been lifted.

Tara headed inside to perform a quick outfit change before meeting Jack. She felt a million dollars and she already knew exactly what she was going to wear. When she opened the front door, she saw a large envelope lying on the hall floor and she immediately knew what it was.

The separation agreement had arrived.

She picked it up and carried it to the kitchen. When she opened the envelope, she saw that the document itself wasn't that big. Her entire life with Colin, summarized down to a few pages. It didn't feel right for their story of eighteen years to be reduced to so little. She flicked through the pages and saw the section where she was supposed to sign. She took a pen out of her handbag and held it in her hand.

As the pen kissed the paper, Tara felt a knot in her stomach. She was temporarily back on keto and she hadn't eaten a carb in twenty-four hours, just to ensure she wasn't bloated meeting Jack. But this didn't feel like hunger. It was something different. Colin's words suddenly echoed in her mind. He had told her that before she signed the separation agreement that she should look in the shed. Something to remember him by was waiting there, he had said. She looked out the kitchen window. She knew she was no match against her own curiosity.

As she approached the shed, she wondered what could have possibly been so important in there. If Colin thought organizing a few boxes after months of her asking was going to fix anything, he was very much mistaken. She opened the door and could barely see a thing. The shed had no windows so it was in complete darkness. She considered turning away there and then, but she owed it to Colin to see what was inside. She walked blindly into the darkness towards the general area of the light switch. Colin had installed it on the back wall instead of by the door like common sense would have dictated. She felt around and finally – eureka! – she found the switch. Tara turned on the shed lights and almost collapsed with shock at the image before her eyes. Every inch of the room was suddenly illuminated. At first, she thought she was hallucinating. But as she looked around, she realized what he had done.

Colin had transformed the shed into a replica of O'Malley's pub.

It wasn't as big as the real O'Malley's, of course, but it was an authentic scale model that captured the essence of one of her favourite places in the world.

The place they had fallen in love.

The bar, which was made up of two standing pallets and a large plank of wood, had been painted mahogany, just like the real thing. It even had a Guinness tap. Above the bar hung a makeshift sign that said 'O'Malley's'. All of Colin's vintage pub signs were hanging up on the walls, in exactly the same positions they hung in the real O'Malley's. It was only then that Tara realized why Colin had begun his collection in the first place.

On each wall, he had stuck dozens of photos of the two of them during the best years of their lives, their smiles glimmering on every wall. Photos of them in different European cities on their Interrail trip, photos of them in their old studio apartment – the walls were covered with pictures. Old concert tickets, wristbands from music festivals, boarding passes. He had even hung up hundreds of fairy lights that looked like fireflies in the night.

The room was alive with their love.

Tara walked over to the bar and pulled gently on the tap. To her further surprise, a drop of Guinness came out. He had even installed a real tap connected to a real keg. The middle of the room had a small wooden table and chairs. On the table and all along the bar were wine bottles with large candlesticks stuck inside. The wine bottles that Colin had never taken to the bottle bank suddenly looked so beautiful. Behind the bar, he had framed her old work uniform as well as the paper she had written about Synth Wave Feminism. He had got a red pen and changed her 49 per cent grade to 149 per cent, with an added note that said '*Feminist icon*'. She began to laugh as the tears fell down her face.

How had he done it?

It felt like a miracle beyond her comprehension. The amount of work it would have required to magically re-create O'Malley's was enormous. She had only been gone for one weekend and apparently Colin had spent every one of the forty-eight hours working on rebuilding the place they first met. That must have been why he had passed out on the couch, covered in specks of paint. And that morning he had asked Tara to come to the shed with him. It was all making sense now. But still, it seemed as if Colin had done the work of three men. Having revisited O'Malley's so recently, she could see the attention to detail was impeccable. It was a living, breathing replica. But it was more than that.

It was a museum of their memories, a monument to their marriage.

Then what Tara saw on one of the bar stools broke her. It was Colin's UCD college hoody. The hoody she had claimed as her own. The fabric that hugged her body whenever she missed him. She wanted to put on the hoody and belong to him again. But how could she? She was no longer his.

Tara felt the knot in her stomach tighten as a wave of nausea came over her. In that moment, she would have given anything to turn back time. If only she could go back to the moment when she and Colin had lost each other. She wanted nothing more than for him to hold her in his arms.

But what did Colin want?

As the tears rolled down her face, ruining her make-up, she thought about Colin's dream of being a father. His dream that hadn't come true. Starting a family was all he ever wanted and, as much as she wished otherwise, it hadn't happened. He was still young and handsome. He would find someone new with ease. Maybe the person he was meeting in that hotel room had feelings for him. Maybe she could make him happy. Maybe she could give him a family.

Although it hurt that Colin had found a new flower to tend to, maybe he deserved one that could bear his fruit. She knew he would be the best father imaginable. A proper dad, as he described it. The kind he never had and always vowed he would become. It would kill her to see him with another wife and a family, but this this wasn't about her. She had been selfish. She had become so obsessed with discovering her destiny

331

that she hadn't once paused to consider Colin's fate. If ever a man was destined to be a dad, it was him.

She thought about that old adage that if you love someone you should set them free, and if they come back to you, it was meant to be. She loved Colin and, despite everything, she didn't begrudge him a thing. All she wanted was for him to be happy, and if she couldn't do that, she had to let him go.

He deserved to be happy.

She wished she could be the one to make him happy, but maybe that was beyond her control. And if she ran to Colin now, she would forever be tormented by the idea of Jack. Why had she experienced the synchronicity? Why had her entire life crumbled around her as a result? She couldn't live the rest of her life without answers to these questions. She knew going to the pier was the only way to get her answers. And she knew she couldn't stop herself. She needed some kind of closure.

Tara went back inside and looked at the unsigned separation agreement. She knew signing it now would be too emotional and she couldn't risk ruining her make-up any further. She stuffed the papers into her handbag and checked her watch.

2.01 p.m.

She was due to be there in less than an hour and she dared not be late. She pulled herself together and went upstairs to get ready. She reminded herself that everything had been leading up to this very moment. And even if that moment didn't happen, it would still give Tara the answers she needed to close the chapter on Jack.

He still hadn't replied to her message so the chances of his showing up were essentially zero. But it didn't matter. Because even if she didn't have a date with Jack, one thing remained the same.

Tara had a date with destiny.

Chapter 38

Colin sat slouched on Rory's couch in his pyjamas, eating a large bowl of cereal. This was what most of his free time consisted of since his separation from Tara. His new beard had gone from stylish to wiry and he lacked any motivation to get out of his rut. It wasn't quite rock bottom but it did feel that way at times. He lost the love of his life and the home they shared. But worst of all, he lost his future with Tara. His current situation was only temporary, of course, but it was hard to see past it.

Rory's apartment was essentially one big man cave in the form of an open-plan loft. There were vintage *Playboy* covers unapologetically hung on the wall, a fully stocked bar in the living room and an eighty-inch TV, a dream to watch any match on. It was impeccably clean, but at the same time, Colin suspected if he saw the room under an ultraviolet light, he would go blind. There was no doubt that if those walls could talk, they'd scream.

'Are you still in bed?' Rory said, coming out from his bedroom.

'I'm not in bed, I'm on the couch,' Colin said defensively.

'Yeah, but you're sleeping on my couch, which technically means you've been in bed all day. Get up, we're playing a game of pool.'

'I'm not in the mood.'

'I wasn't asking. If there's one thing I can't stand, it's people feeling sorry for themselves. Now get up already.'

Rory was right. Colin couldn't lick his wounds forever. And to be fair, he was very fond of Rory's red suede pool table, the perfect addition to any bachelor pad.

'OK, fine,' Colin said, getting up. 'I'm still just feeling a bit lost.'

'I get it, man,' Rory said, racking up the balls. 'But you have to get back up on the horse. There are plenty of women out there waiting for a man like you.'

'But I don't want other women, I want Tara back,' Colin said, breaking the balls and sending two of them flying into the pockets.

'Well, for the record, I still can't believe Tara left you because you punched that creep. You looked like a champ in that video!'

'Thank you! And everyone in the comments agrees I was a hero.'

'Exactly! And I looked pretty heroic too, backing you up like that,' Rory said, hitting a ball into one of the pockets.

'You didn't lift a finger!' Colin snapped.

'It's called being a hype-man, Colin. I didn't interfere because I wanted to let you have your moment,' Rory said unconvincingly.

'Yeah . . . right,' Colin laughed.

'But my point is, there are hundreds of women on the internet talking about how heroic you are. Now is not the time for a pity-party on my couch. Now is the time to put yourself back out there. The timing couldn't be better for you!'

'Hmm . . . maybe you're right,' Colin said. He hadn't really thought of it like that before. If it was his fifteen minutes of fame, perhaps he should make the most of it.

'I'm always right,' Rory said. 'I mean, why haven't you

downloaded Fling again? Now that Tara is gone, there's nothing stopping you getting with Claire.'

'Claire doesn't want me either,' Colin sighed. 'She stood me up twice. If she wanted me, she'd have met me by now.'

'When's the last time you chatted with her?'

'When I was in the hotel room, she messaged me and said she wasn't coming to Elixir. So I deleted Fling. I haven't been on it since. Cold turkey.'

'No offence, but cold turkey isn't a good look on you,' Rory said, looking at his wiry beard and pyjamas. 'At the very least, download Fling again and see what new matches you have. Even for an ego boost.'

'I'm not going to get a better match than one hundred per cent, Rory. Claire was the only woman apart from Tara who really made me feel something.'

'Then tell her you're the hot-shot everyone is talking about online! You don't need to hide your identity any more. Once she sees that video, she'll be dying to meet you. And not just for a drink either.'

Colin was officially out of excuses. He didn't feel that Claire truly wanted him the way he wanted her. But perhaps it was worth a shot. There was nothing stopping him sending a face picture now. He was heartbroken, but maybe putting his heart on his sleeve was the step towards healing it.

After everything that had happened, what did he have to lose?

'OK, fine. I'll download Fling,' Colin conceded.

'Thatta boy!'

Colin took out his phone and downloaded the app once again. When he hit the icon, he was greeted with the log-in page. He entered the name JACK.

'What was the password you used again?' Colin asked.

'RORY-IS-HUNG, all caps and hyphenated.' Rory smirked.

Colin rolled his eyes and logged into his account. When the homepage opened, he almost dropped the phone in shock. He had a massive amount of messages from Claire waiting for him. The most recent messages appeared first.

> **Claire:** Hi Jack, I know you probably hate me and you might not even see this message. But I want you to know how sorry I am for standing you up again

> I don't deserve a third chance, I know that

> But I'll be at Dún Laoghaire Harbour tomorrow at 3 p.m.

> Halfway down the West Pier, there's a quiet walkway

> I know there's probably no chance you'll show up. But I'll be there, Jack

> I promise I'll be there x

Colin was speechless as he stared at his screen. His brain couldn't quite comprehend what he was reading. He had no idea what to do. All he really wanted was Tara back but she had made her decision. She didn't want him any more. But

Claire did. And he so desperately wanted to be wanted. Was it some kind of cosmic sign? He didn't believe in that sort of thing, but for a brief moment he wondered: had everything happened for a reason? Had his marriage with Tara fallen apart because he was supposed to be with Claire? Her siren call had been his ruination. Could it also be his redemption? His mind was going a mile a minute.

'What the hell is the matter?' Rory said, seeing his expression.

'It's Claire! She wants to meet at Dún Laoghaire Harbour!'

'No way! When?'

Colin squinted at his phone and saw that the message about meeting tomorrow was sent yesterday. 'TODAY! SHE WANTS TO MEET TODAY! Oh my God! She said she'd be there at three – what time is it now?'

'It's half two!'

'HALF TWO!' Colin panicked. 'I'll never get to Dún Laoghaire in that time!'

'NOT WITH THAT ATTITUDE!' Rory screamed.

'OK, OK,' Colin said, trying to gather his thoughts. 'Clothes, I need clothes!'

'Go to your suitcase and get jeans and a shirt! And tame that beard! Then brush your teeth. And deodorant!'

Colin rushed into Rory's room where his suitcase was. He rooted through it and found a dressy pair of dark jeans, a blue shirt, a brown belt and brown boots. After he was dressed, he ran to the bathroom, brushed his teeth and combed his beard with some beard oil to make it less wiry. He sprayed deodorant on his pits and some cologne on his neck. He checked his watch.

2.36 p.m.

There was practically no chance he would make it.

But dammit, he had to try.

337

'Do I look OK?' Colin asked Rory when he was just about to leave.

'Well, it's not bad for six minutes,' Rory said.

With that, the door buzzer rang.

'Oh, that's Emily. Right on time for her dick appointment,' Rory said.

'Please don't use that phrase around me, I still have PTSD,' Colin said, eager to forget the memory.

As Rory let Emily in, she immediately jumped on top of him and began devouring him alive. Rory stepped back into the apartment, holding Emily up as he aggressively kissed her back. Emily suddenly saw Colin in the corner of her eye.

'Oh, I forgot you had company,' she said, composing herself.

'You must be Emily,' Colin said. 'I've heard a lot about you.'

'You can't prove any of it,' Emily smirked.

'Anyway, I have to run!' Colin said, dashing towards the door. 'WAIT! I never texted her to say I was coming!'

'There's no time, Col! Just go!' Rory yelled.

'Right! Wish me luck!' Colin said before rushing out the door.

'Godspeed my friend!' Rory said, closing the door after him. 'Now, where were we?'

Rory and Emily began devouring each other once again as they moved into the middle of the loft.

'Where's Colin off to in such a hurry?' Emily asked. She wanted Rory all over her body, but she also wanted to get some gossip for Tara.

'Oh, it's a long story,' Rory said, still kissing her neck. 'He just found out he has a date in like thirty minutes at Dún Laoghaire Harbour. I really hope he makes it on time. Poor guy needs a win.'

'Wait a minute, Colin has a date at Dún Laoghaire Harbour?' Emily asked curiously. 'That's weird, so does Tara.'

'That'll be awkward,' Rory laughed as he unzipped the back of Emily's dress.

'Well, I don't know if I'd call it a date. Tara's going there in the hopes this guy called Jack will show up. Which he probably won't. Anyway . . .' Emily ripped open Rory's shirt, felt his bulging pecs and began kissing him again.

'Hold on,' Rory said, pulling back. 'Did you say . . . Jack?'

'Yeah, that's the guy she's been texting,' Emily said. 'They met on that app Fling.'

'Oh my GOD,' Rory said, putting the pieces of the puzzle together.

'What?'

'By any chance . . . is Tara's name on Fling . . . Claire?'

'Yeah, how did you . . .' Emily said. Then realizing what was going on, 'OH MY GOD!!! COLIN IS JACK?'

'TARA IS CLAIRE? So they've been talking to EACH OTHER for the past few weeks?' Rory said in complete disbelief.

'They must have been! OMG, we have to call them!' Emily said, taking out her phone.

'WAIT!'

'Wait for what? There's no time!' Emily said frantically.

'Hear me out,' Rory said, thinking everything through. 'Why don't we just sit back and see what happens? I mean, who are we to get in the way of Jack and Claire's first date?'

'Hmm . . . that's a good point, actually,' Emily smirked. 'And I've just realized we have a far more urgent problem that needs fixing.'

'What's that?' Rory asked as he lifted Emily up against the wall.

'I've never done it on a pool table . . .'

Chapter 39

Colin leaped onto his Triumph Bonneville motorcycle.

He only had twenty minutes to get to Dún Laoghaire Harbour. The odds were against him. But he was never one to let the odds stop him.

He rolled on the throttle and revved up Bonnie's engine. He zipped out of the car park of Rory's building and sped onto the street. This wouldn't be a calm and steady Sunday ride. This was all or nothing. He had messed things up with Tara. He couldn't do the same with Claire.

He drove through the city centre streets, swerving in and out of traffic. Bonnie was truly being pushed to the limit but this was the journey she was born to make.

He came upon a lane of bumper-to-bumper traffic that was going nowhere.

'Not today,' he said, turning into the middle of both lanes and zooming past the traffic jam. Some drivers beeped at him bending the rules but he didn't care. There was too much at stake.

He finally got out of the city centre and arrived at a red light.

He hit the brakes and checked his watch.

2.45 p.m.

Getting there was still improbable.

But it wasn't impossible.

And that was good enough for Colin.

The light turned green and he twisted the throttle harder than ever.

৪৯

As she walked along Dún Laoghaire Harbour, Tara felt queasy. The nausea she had felt in the shed had evolved into sea-sickness as soon as she saw the water, even though she was on firm land. She told herself it was normal to have a knot in your stomach before a blind date, so she took a deep breath and tried to relax. Although she really had no clue whether or not her blind date was actually on his way.

For a split second she considered turning around and running a mile from the entire situation, but she thought better of it. She remembered her second tarot card of the blind woman in front of the sea and here she was, at the sea, ready to remove the blindfold. She had got The Lovers as her future card reading. That had to mean something. She had to trust her intuition now more than ever.

She finally reached the end of the walkway and rested on the barrier as she looked out to sea. She put her handbag down and leaned over the railing, allowing the breeze to catch her newly dyed red hair in the wind. It was a warm, mild day for October, so she had changed into a sleeveless white sundress with a chunky brown belt and gladiator sandals. It was the kind of look she had only ever worn on holidays, never in Ireland. But as the wind hit her, she immediately regretted not bringing a jacket.

She prayed Jack would see the message and come to her. The tapestry of events that had led to this moment all appeared completely chaotic and random, but Tara needed to believe there was some underlying plan for her, that she was still on the right track. It was synchronicity that had led her down this road and it was finally the moment of truth. If Jack didn't show up, she would know it wasn't meant to be. But if she and Jack weren't meant to be, was anything meant to be? Would that mean her synchronicity was meaningless? The question terrified her, but she still needed the answer.

She looked down at her watch.

2.59 p.m.

She would have her answer soon.

Tara looked out to sea and waited patiently for fate to find her.

Colin could see the water.

He knew he was close.

The problem was he didn't have any GPS navigation on his motorcycle and he wasn't entirely sure which turn he was supposed to take. But with the ocean in his view, he was surely almost there.

But that's when he heard the chucking sound. Like someone had thrown a spanner into Bonnie's engine. Then the smoke appeared.

'No, no, no, no, no!' Colin said. 'Not now!'

Bonnie began to slow down as her engine gave out. Had he pushed her too hard? She was almost as old as him and perhaps she simply wasn't up to the tumultuous journey Colin had just put her through. But she had been repaired so recently. Then again, Colin had repaired the motorbike himself and maybe he wasn't the mechanic he believed himself to be. Plus Tara had whacked the bike with a golf club.

He pulled Bonnie over to the side of the road and turned

off her engine. He wanted to inspect her and see if he could fix the problem but he knew he couldn't.

Time was of the essence.

He checked his watch.

3.08 p.m.

He was already late. But surely Claire would give him a few minutes' grace period. He looked to his left and his face lit up with hope.

He could see the pier. Practically a stone's throw away. He could still make it if he ran fast enough. And that's exactly what he planned on doing.

Colin began to sprint towards the pier with every ounce of his being. He needed to make it. Otherwise his entire life would have fallen apart for nothing. He ran out onto a main road separating him from the pier. The cars whizzed past him and beeped him out of it for jaywalking. He had never run this fast in his life and he was becoming breathless. But maybe the adrenaline of the situation would give him the push he needed to make it.

Finally, his feet arrived on the harbour. He stopped for a moment to catch his breath. The pier stretched down before him and there were plenty of people out enjoying their Sunday. How would he know which one was Claire? What had she said in her message? Something about a walkway, halfway down the pier.

That was it.

Colin looked to the walkway stretching into the middle of the harbour. He hadn't even caught his breath when it was taken once again. At the end of the path, he could see the figure of a beautiful red-headed woman looking out to sea, as if she was longing for him. Her back was turned to him so he couldn't see her face. But she was the only person on the walkway.

He knew it was Claire.

The siren for which he had willingly wrecked his ship, just to get a glimpse of her majesty. It made perfect sense that she was a redhead. They had always been his weakness.

Colin smiled and moved forwards down the pier. As he approached her, he felt a strange feeling of familiarity. When he had been talking to Claire over the past few weeks, he felt as if he had known her his entire life and now, as he closed the distance between them, he felt it more than ever. Her red hair flew in every direction like untameable flames in the wind. A part of him was afraid to blink in case the ethereal fantasy would disappear. She appeared like a mirage in the desert of his life, an oasis of possibility.

He suddenly became hyper-aware of the fact that he would need to speak in just a few seconds. What could he possibly say that would live up to the moment? How would he sound? She was attracted to his masculinity, but Colin didn't have a particularly deep voice. He decided he would deepen his voice by one octave, so he cleared his throat in anticipation.

But what would he do after speaking? He and Claire had spoken on such a deep emotional level online that small talk just wouldn't be good enough. He began to think about his late-night conversations with Claire. Her deepest desire, she had told him, was for a man to walk up behind her, take her in his arms and kiss her like she was his. She didn't want to have to ask a man to enrapture her in his arms, she wanted a man who knew she was his, even without her saying a word.

As he stepped onto the walkway, he knew what he had to do.

ॐ

Tara looked down at her watch for the last time.

3.14 p.m.

It was time to call it. If Jack wanted her, he would have appeared by now.

She felt a little silly for going to the pier in the first place. It suddenly dawned on her how ludicrous it all was. Going to meet a man who hadn't even responded to your messages? It was downright absurd.

But at least now she knew. She had her answer. An answer that made her question her entire belief system. An answer that meant everything she had ever believed in was a lie. An answer that made her lose all hope.

But then she heard the footsteps.

They were behind her and getting closer.

For some inexplicable reason, she knew it was Jack. She could feel his masculine energy approaching.

The suspense was killing her. She wanted to turn around, but she wanted to wait until he was right there behind her. Finally, the footsteps stopped.

'Hey there, stranger,' the man behind her said, in a deep masculine voice that felt so familiar, like she had known it her whole life.

Tara smiled and began to turn around slowly.

'Don't turn around,' the deep voice said. She obeyed him immediately. He was in control and she loved it. 'Just trust me.' The baritone vibrations of Jack's voice made the hairs on her arms stand up.

For reasons unknown, she did trust him. With her life.

'Close your eyes,' he said. She obeyed him once again, not knowing what to expect. She heard the footsteps again. He was approaching her. She stood still, frozen with desire. Her eyes remained firmly closed as Jack came closer. He had given her an order and she didn't dare disobey him.

That's when she felt his embrace from behind as he turned her around and brought his lips to hers. She began to melt in his arms as she lost herself in sweet consensual surrender. Tara then had the feeling of déjà vu, as if she had lived this moment endlessly in the past and would live it forever in the future. She could feel goosebumps all over her body and a tingle on the back of her neck. The feeling was as familiar as it was fantastic.

It was the most powerful synchronicity Tara had ever experienced.

Even with her eyes closed, Tara could see she was exactly where she was supposed to be.

But she couldn't take it any more, she had to see his face. She began to gently open her eyelids to get a peek at the love of her life.

But what Tara saw gave her the fright of her life instead.

'COLIN!' she screamed.

'TARA!' Colin shouted, opening his eyes.

Tara let out an almighty scream and pushed Colin off her with unyielding force. 'WHAT ARE YOU DOING HERE?'

'What am I doing here? More like what are you doing here? I was supposed to be meeting someone called Claire!' Colin said, utterly dumbfounded.

That's when the penny finally dropped.

'JACK?' Tara screamed.

'CLAIRE?' Colin roared.

'No, no, no, this can't be real,' Tara said, still in pure shock. 'You can't be Jack, that's impossible. Oh my God, Colin, have you been catfishing me this whole time? Was this some kind of game?' she said, desperately trying to understand.

'Me, catfishing? You were catfishing me!' he snapped back, offended.

'I DIDN'T KNOW YOU WERE JACK!' Tara screamed.

'WELL, I DIDN'T KNOW YOU WERE CLAIRE!'

'Hold on, I feel dizzy. Are you saying that for the past few weeks, we've been on Fling talking to *each other*?' she said, the irony hitting her like a ton of bricks.

'No, this doesn't make any sense. Claire and I have been chatting for ages!'

'At 11.11 every night?' Tara asked, knowing the answer.

'Oh my God, while I was on the couch, I was texting you upstairs in bed? No way, Claire sent me these sexy photos of her in lingerie! You don't own anything like that!' Colin said.

'I bought that lingerie to try and look sexy for Jack. But Jack sent me photos of him in the gym. There's no way that was you in those photos!'

'Rory brought me to the gym so my pics would look more attractive.'

'Oh my God, that's why you were on the Luas outside The Vine on Dawson Street! You were coming to meet *me*!' she gasped.

'You were there? I thought Claire stood me up!'

'I saw you and I was afraid of you catching me with Jack so I ran for my life!'

'Wait, that's why you saw me going into the hotel! You were on Harcourt Street to meet Jack!' Colin said, figuring everything out.

'So you were booking a room for you and Claire?' Tara asked.

'YES!'

'So you were cheating on me ... with me? I'M THE TRAMP YOU WERE MEETING?'

Suddenly everything had changed.

Tara had been so deeply hurt by Colin's affair. But he had been telling the truth about not sleeping with another woman.

And the other woman was her! She was the home-wrecking harlot she had cursed!

'Hold on just a minute. You had a fit when you found out I was having an affair. But you were having an affair too! Talk about the pot calling the kettle black,' Colin said, pointing out the hypocrisy.

'I never meant to have an affair! I only downloaded Fling because we were handling their advertising campaign,' Tara explained.

'So you're telling me our countless late-night conversations were just research? Give me a break,' Colin said, not buying her story.

'It started off like that. But when I matched with Jack, I got the same gut feeling that I felt the moment I first met you.'

'Go figure,' Colin said.

'I thought my gut feeling was a sign I was destined to be with Jack.'

'Well ... maybe you are,' Colin said, his heart on his sleeve. 'You dyed your hair.'

'Do you not like it?' Tara asked, trying to tame the flames in the wind.

'No. I love it. You look like yourself again. The Tara I fell for in O'Malley's,' Colin said, his voice warm.

'The O'Malley's in Galway or the one in our shed?' Tara smiled.

'Oh you saw that, did you?' Colin said, smiling back at her.

'How the hell did you pull that off?'

'You'd be surprised what you can find online.'

'And you already had all the pub signs,' Tara said.

'I was hoping you would see the signs as a sign not to sign the papers.'

'Seems like a very over-elaborate plan.'

'Did it work, by any chance?'

Tara bent over and grabbed the separation agreement out of her handbag. 'See for yourself,' she said, handing the papers to him.

Colin flicked through to the final page of the agreement. It was blank. 'You didn't sign,' he said, looking up. 'Is there something wrong with the agreement?'

'No, it's fine . . .' Tara said coyly. 'I just think it's funny how—'

Colin ripped the separation agreement in half and shut Tara up with a kiss. As he pulled her close and held her tight, she felt safe enough to let go.

In that moment, Tara had complete cosmic certainty of her place in the world. As her husband held her in his arms, she knew she was right where she belonged. She felt the sunshine of his love melt the cold ice of winter and bring forth her summer bloom.

Her inexplicable feelings for Jack finally made sense. She had her proof that there was an underlying design to the universe, that there was no such thing as coincidence. When two people are destined to be together, fate will always find a way. The synchronicity wasn't guiding her into another man's arms.

Destiny was guiding her home.

'I love you, Jack,' Tara said, safe in his grasp.

'I love you too, Claire,' Colin replied, gripping her tightly.

'Forever and always?'

'Always and forever.'

'Of all the pubs in all the towns in all of Ireland, you had to walk into mine,' Tara said, smiling, unable to hide the joy emanating from her soul, the love radiating from her heart.

'So tell me,' Colin said. 'Would you get on the back of my bike and do it all again?'

'It depends on your answer to one very important question,' Tara said coyly.

'Yes, babe,' he said with a knowing smile. 'I'd still love you if you were a worm.'

'That's all any girl ever needs to hear, honeybun,' Tara laughed as she leaned in for another kiss.

They both knew they had renewed their vows to each other there and then, without needing to say another word.

But as Tara kissed Colin once again, she suddenly felt the knot in her stomach return. This time, however, the nausea was far worse than before, to the point where she felt like she was about to throw up. She could feel an overwhelming dizziness taking hold of her. She didn't know how to describe what she was feeling but she knew it wasn't normal.

'Colin, I don't feel so good,' Tara said, as her vision started to fade.

'Tara, what's wrong?' Colin said, terrified.

'I . . . I . . . think I'm about to—' Tara said as her eyes rolled to the back of her head. As she faded into unconscious darkness, she could hear Colin desperately shouting for help as he watched the colour fade from his wife's face.

Chapter 40

When Tara woke up in the hospital, she saw something she never thought she would ever see. She saw Colin praying. She had slipped in and out of consciousness several times after fainting, and she vaguely remembered the sound of Colin calling an ambulance and being taken to the hospital. This was the first time she felt lucid enough to realize what was happening.

'Colin,' she said, reaching for him.

'Oh my God, Tara, you're awake!' he said, standing up and kissing her forehead.

'What happened?'

'You fainted on the pier. We don't know why yet. The doctors are running some tests now. You fainted again when they took a blood sample so they brought you here.'

'Oh God, I'm dying,' Tara said, sitting up.

'Don't say that, Tara!'

'I probably have cancer. I need to check WebMD,' she said, reaching for her phone.

'No,' Colin said, putting down her hand. 'You're not looking up your symptoms. The test results will be back any minute. And no matter what it is, we will face it together. Nothing will ever tear us apart ever again.'

Emily and Rory suddenly barged into Tara's room.

'OMG! Tara are you OK?' Emily said, rushing to her side.

'You two didn't need to come!' Tara said. 'I didn't mean to interrupt your date.'

'Don't worry, we've done it three times already,' Rory said, fully serious.

'And you're both still together?' Colin asked, shocked. 'What happened to post-nut clarity?'

'It's the weirdest thing – after we had sex, we still actually liked each other!' Rory said, shocked.

'But Tara, what happened? Did you faint when you found out that Colin was Jack?' Emily asked.

'YOU KNEW?' Tara shouted.

'We literally only figured it out a few minutes before your date,' Rory said, defending her. 'We pieced it all together.'

'You could have called to let me know!' Colin said, unimpressed.

'We thought it would all just work out. We didn't know you'd end up in the hospital!' Emily said.

With that, a doctor entered the room holding a clipboard chart.

'Tara, my name is Dr Boyd. How are you feeling?' he asked.

'Doctor, please give it to me straight,' Tara said starkly. 'How long do I have left?'

'My guess is about eight months,' Dr Boyd said, looking at her chart.

'Oh my God,' Colin said, gripping Tara's hand.

'Let me guess, doctor,' Tara said. 'Cancer?'

'Possibly,' the doctor said without expression.

'Sweet Jesus,' Colin cried.

'But more likely a Gemini,' Dr Boyd said.

'Doctor, I didn't come here for you to read my birth chart. What does my blood chart say? Why did I faint?' Tara said, both confused and furious.

'Well, it seems you had some low blood sugar but it's not that serious. Fainting is very common for women in your condition.'

'WHAT CONDITION?' Tara shouted.

'Wait, you don't know?' Dr Boyd said, confused.

'KNOW WHAT?'

'You're pregnant.'

'PREGNANT?' Tara and Colin said in unison.

Tara was completely taken aback. It was impossible. Surely there was an error.

'No, doctor, there must be some kind of mistake. I'm not able to have children,' she said.

'Well, according to these tests we ran, you most certainly are,' Dr Boyd confirmed.

'I thought I was just late. I didn't think anything of it,' Tara said, completely bewildered. 'But Colin, when did we even last have sex?'

'It must have been the night we watched our wedding video like Dr Burke told us to. My God, she's a genius!' Colin said, realizing that session was the best €300 he ever spent.

'But we've failed IVF three times! Doctor, can you run the tests again to be sure?' Tara said, still positive it was a mistake.

'We ran them three times. Lots of women get pregnant naturally after IVF failing. Just takes the right sperm and the right egg.'

'So you're one hundred per cent sure I'm pregnant?' she asked again.

'Yep, you can expect a little Gemini in June next year. Based on your bloodwork, you're completely healthy. The fainting seems to be a mix of your body adapting to the new hormones and low blood sugar. Make sure you don't skip any meals and get plenty of carbohydrates.'

'This is the happiest day of my life,' Tara said, tears of joy in her eyes.

'I'm happy to discharge you now and we'll see you in a few weeks for your first ultrasound,' Dr Boyd, said before turning and leaving the room.

'Tara, can you believe it?' Colin said, turning to Tara. 'We're gonna have a baby!'

'I can't believe this is real,' Tara said, tears still in her eyes. 'I thought I had cancer!'

'That guy really needs to work on his bedside manner,' Emily said. 'But more importantly, congratulations! Can Rory and I be the godparents?'

'Only if you two are still together in eight months' time,' Tara said.

'Challenge accepted,' Rory said confidently.

'Come on, Rory, we'd better give these two some privacy. Let's see if we can find an empty supply room around here,' Emily said, as Rory followed her out the door in a lustful daze.

'I guess there really is someone for everyone,' Colin said, laughing at them as they left.

'Narcissus and the nymph, together at last,' Tara joked. 'Colin, can you believe it? I think I'm going to cry.'

'We're having a baby!' Colin said, putting his head to Tara's stomach. 'Think of all the dad jokes! What are we going to name them?'

'What do you think about Claire for a girl?' Tara smiled.

'And Jack for a boy?' Colin smiled back. 'It's going to be one funny bedtime story.'

'I can't believe we almost lost each other. If I ever start another fight, just shut me up with a kiss,' Tara said, squeezing his hand.

'And if we ever start to drift apart again, just meet me at O'Malley's,' he said, touching her face gently.

'You're going to have your hands full with two Geminis in the house,' Tara laughed.

'I promise to love all four of you,' Colin joked. 'All that's left to do now is to delete Fling off our phones.'

'Just one last thing,' Tara said, taking hers out of her bag. She began typing something and Colin suddenly felt his phone vibrate. He opened the notification and read the message that appeared on screen.

Claire: Nice to finally meet you, Jack x

Colin smiled and began typing his reply.

Jack: So long, stranger ☺

Tara and Colin both deleted their Fling accounts and removed the app from their phones. They had met their 100 per cent match, and there was no score higher than perfection. They had downloaded the app to escape from their lives but the stars had brought them home.

'You were right, Tara. Everything really does happen for a reason,' Colin said, taking his wife's hand.

'You finally believe me?' she said, drowning in his ocean eyes like the moment she first saw him.

'Yes, Tara . . . because now I know . . . my reason is you.' Colin wrapped his arms around Tara and kissed her the way he would kiss her for the rest of his life. With their eternal flame burning brighter than ever before, reignited by a single match.

All because of an affair that was every bit as fateful as it was faithful.

And all thanks to a little app called Fling.

'Let's go home,' said Tara, feeling as if her life had just begun.

Acknowledgements

First and foremost, I would like to thank my wonderful parents Kathleen and Finian for being the most inspiring, accepting and caring parents anyone could ever ask for. Thank you for giving me the most amazing childhood and for always telling me to pursue my dreams. Without your love and support, this book never would have been possible.

I would also like to thank my sisters Jessica and Lisa for their amazing feedback on *Fling* and their encouragement at every step.

A massive thank you to my powerhouse agent Marianne Gunn O'Connor who believed in *Fling* from the very beginning. Thank you for seeing my potential and literally making my dream come true.

To Vicki Satlow, Patrick Lynch, Dan Bolger and Alison Walsh at MGOC, thank you for all your hard work and for helping to get *Fling* to where it is today.

To Jayne Osborne at Pan Macmillan, thank you for fighting for and championing *Fling* from the moment you read it. Your vision for my debut novel has changed my life forever and it will never be forgotten. And to Francesca Pathak, thank you for your amazing ongoing work on the book.

Thank you also to Samantha Fletcher for being such a joy to work with through the entire editing process. Your attention to detail on every draft means a lot.

And to the rest of the team at Pan Mac, your outstanding work is so truly appreciated and I can't think of a better home for *Fling*.

Many thanks to my closest friends Emmet Mahoney and Tim Graham for pushing me to make *Fling* better and better with every draft. Your friendship means the world to me.

To Matt, Deirdre and Angela Murtagh of Causey Farm, you have given me so many opportunities to channel my creativity and I would not be the person I am today if our paths never crossed. Thank you for everything, including your invaluable feedback on the book.

To my English teachers Eoin Winters and Sinead Feeney at O'Carolan College, thank you for seeing a creative spark in me before I even did. Your belief in me means more than you know.

And to my granny Rita McGarry, who passed before the book was finished, I hope you are proud of your many wonderful sayings that ended up in the book. Miss you every day x

Finally, to everyone who picks up a copy of *Fling*, thank you with all of my heart. The goal of my writing is to uplift my readers and I hope the story of Tara and Colin's faithful affair does exactly that.